"You are so straightforward, it's refreshing," he whispered.

"I thought here that was called brash."

"Not to me." Rhys stepped closer to Ann, his words barely more than a whisper, but growing urgent, demanding. "Curtsy to me, Ann," he insisted.

"You are kind, Rhys, but—"

"I will not stand by and watch you ruin your reputation because you failed to observe the rules. Ann," he pleaded, "why didn't you speak with me on Tuesday in Rotten Row?"

"I couldn't." Her eyes darted over the others, who pretended to return to their fencing practice.

"I went there to see you."

"No," she whispered, struck by his admission.

"Oh, yes. I stood on that corner waiting for you to ride by." Amusement twinkled in his eyes. Self-deprecation swept it away. "I deserved what you did, though, of course, *The Gazetteer*'s reporter could not know that, nor could he possibly take sides with a gorgeous American against a peer of the glorious kingdom of St. Andrew and St. George."

"You need not worry about me." She took a step away.

"But I do," he confessed, and that stopped her. "Don't leave me like this. They're watching. Curtsy to me. Just enough to restore you to acceptance."

Books by Jo-Ann Power

You and No Other
Angel of Midnight
Treasures
Gifts
The Nightingale's Song
Never Before

Published by POCKET BOOKS

JO-ANN POWER

NEVER BEFORE

POCKET BOOKS
New York London Toronto Sydney Tokyo Singapore

This book is a work of fiction. Names, characters, places and incidents are products of the author's imagination or are used fictitiously. Any resemblance to actual events or locales or persons living or dead is entirely coincidental.

An *Original* Publication of POCKET BOOKS

POCKET BOOKS, a division of Simon & Schuster Inc.
1230 Avenue of the Americas, New York, NY 10020

ISBN: 0-671-00898-6

First Pocket Books printing May 1998

10 9 8 7 6 5 4 3 2 1

POCKET and colophon are registered trademarks of
Simon & Schuster Inc.

Cover art by Lina Levy

Printed in the U.S.A.

To Ann,

with my love and thanks for the suggestion of a dark-haired heroine whose beauty could never match that of her real-life inspiration

Acknowledgments

For sharing with me her knowledge of Tennessee walking horses, I am very grateful to fellow writer Victoria Presley.

NEVER BEFORE

Prologue

"The mate for beauty should be a man, not a money chest."

—EDWARD BULWER LYTTON

Alexandria, Virginia
February 1875

"GETTING MARRIED IS GIVING ME COLD FEET." ANN wiggled her numb toes beneath the thin coach blanket.

"Sugar," her cousin Raine crooned, "I just hope you don't get a cold heart living with this man."

Ann avoided Raine's eyes and her latest attempt to dissuade her from marrying someone she did not love. Quinnten Langley possessed other attributes Ann valued. He was calm, resolute—and trustworthy. "He'll come soon." She settled against the squabs of the hired cab as the bells in St. Edward's Church across the street tolled eight. "He's only . . ."—she sneezed—"half an hour late."

Her hat promptly slid from its moorings down over her forehead. She pushed it up and stabbed the lethal hatpin into the felt. "Raine, please don't be angry with me about this elopement."

"How can I stop you from making such a big mistake?"

Ann wiped the window free of frost to peer down

the darkening city street. The snow fell faster than at seven o'clock, when she and Raine had left their friends' carriage to hire this one. "I admire him, Raine." In her adamance, her heavy hat slipped toward her left eye. She uprooted it and plunked it on the seat. "He's orderly, methodical—"

"And stuffy," Raine objected. "Better put your hat back on before he catches you without it."

"Quinn accepts me as I am. He *wants* me to take over his household and farm accounts because he knows my sums are accurate—and his aren't always. *And* he thinks it's delightful that I don't take gladly to pins and whalebones and tight little garters."

Raine sniffed. "Clothes don't constrict you as much as your mother's warnings not to marry for love."

"Don't you think it's best to find a man you respect first and grow to care for as a result?"

"Aunt Elizabeth was as much my mother as yours since your father brought me north to live with you. She's gone only six months, and I miss her dearly, but she had this odd belief that people should wed—"

"For solid reasons, not emotions. Raine, I've known Quinn since I was six. He's reliable and usually punctual—"

"With the affectionate nature of a potato. Sugar, just because your mother and father failed at their marriage, that does not mean that you must take from it a lesson which cannot make you happy."

"You can't predict that, Raine. Besides, I want to have a friend and a helper through life, and I am determined to have a husband I respect, a home that is peaceful, and a farm where I can quietly raise horses."

Raine snorted. "If you join the Langleys, neither

their crumbling house nor that weed patch of a farm will be yours. I don't care how much you contribute to them by balancing their books or adding your much-needed charm to their moldy existence, Langley Oaks belongs to his parents."

A gust of wind buffeted the carriage. Ann shot forward for another big sneeze. "They will see I am generous, Raine. I'll help renovate their house and farm with half of my inheritance from my mother." She patted her reticule which contained eight hundred dollars. "I plan to use the remaining money to buy a new mare to mate with my stallion."

Her cousin looked out her window. "Stubborn."

"A family trait, wouldn't you say?"

Half an hour later, Ann bemoaned the lack of a brazier in the floor of the hired brougham. She frowned out at the street, where huge flakes covered the cobblestones like a lumpy white sheet. Under the lampposts, two pedestrians scuttled toward the White Swan Tavern. Ann shivered, hating winter, wondering where Quinn was. Growing furious. Whenever he had been delayed before, he had always sent a note. Whatever he might lack—such as the ability to be affectionate—he had always been polite.

Nine o'clock came, and Ann called their cabbie down from his perch. "Please buy us two mugs of hot tea from the tavern's barkeep and have him add a jigger of brandy."

Raine chuckled. "You should elope more often."

By the time they'd drained their cups, the church bells were chiming nine-thirty, and Ann had a sweet buzz in her head and tart words on her lips for men who made promises and didn't keep them. "At least I'm not sneezing anymore."

Raine peered at her. "Are we waiting anymore?"

"I never suspected that Quinn would leave me at the church door. I am surprised . . ."

"Wounded?"

Her pride smarted. "But not heartbroken."

Raine murmured a little prayer in French. "And what will you do about your papa's demand you have a grand tour of Europe?"

"He'll only parade me in front of men whom *he* wants me to marry. If I ever wed a man, I'll pick one for my reasons. Not necessarily one with a title or one my dowry had bought."

"He wants to fill the void of your mother's loss."

"It's as if he's rushing you and me to end our mourning. He has to realize that we both need time to recover—instead of whisking us away to Europe to pawn each of us off on some unsuspecting male."

"Well, Uncle Skip can't pair me off, because I have no dowry and I refuse to let him give me one. His wealth goes to you, *only* you. The only way I'll ever have money is if I earn it. Drawing advertisements for *The Washington Star* may not make me wealthy, but it keeps me in pocket money."

"My father won't let you off his hook. He knows how much you'd love to see the museums of Venice and Paris—"

"The trip wouldn't be any fun without you. Besides, I hate taking charity from him."

"He is generous to his family," Ann admitted, "with his money, if not his time." Raine, along with their Aunt Peg and Ann, were the only members of the once large family of Brightons to survive the Civil War. Her father saw to it that all three were housed and clothed in the best of style. There was money to spare, which Ann knew because she had kept the household accounts for three years and often sent a percentage of the surplus, including any unspent portion of her own allowance, to the Mount Vernon Home for War Orphans.

"Blockade running made Uncle Skip value life."

Ann thought he cared more about controlling all the lives of those near to him. "He likes taking risks."

"I wouldn't be here today if he hadn't risked his life to smuggle me out of Baton Rouge. Wily man. Tenacious, too. God knows, he served the South to the bitter end."

"Being exactly what he is," Ann added, "a renegade. A man who ran away from his wife and children to build a fortune." As the church bells told her it was ten o'clock, Ann's thoughts fled from her father to the younger man whose rejection here tonight insulted more than saddened her. Could she have grown to love Quinn if she couldn't even cry now over losing him? She put a hand to her heart and drawled, "Meanwhile, my deeply wounded pride demands some Southern satisfaction."

"You could take your derringer out and fill Quinn with a little lead." Raine eyed Ann's purse.

Ann chuckled. "To be honest, I never did like the idea that my children might inherit the Langley family trait."

"The lantern jaw?"

"The jackrabbit ears." Ann simply didn't want any part of Quinn for her husband now, especially his ears.

She didn't want to go home to her father, either. She and Raine had told him yesterday they were spending the weekend visiting their best friends, Colleen and Augusta VanderHorn, across the river in Washington City. So she and Raine had two days before they were scheduled to return to their town house on King Street. Although Skip Brighton knew nothing of her elopement, he had eyes like an eagle and the nose of a foxhound. Ann need only appear tonight unexpectedly in the Brighton family drawing room, and the most notorious blockade runner of the Confederacy would conclude something was amiss. He knew full well that she never ran to him. Not for comfort, help, or money. She had learned long ago it was a waste of time to seek or even hope for his attention. She had more of it since her mother died, and the novelty made her itch to be free of him. That was another reason she had accepted Quinn's proposal.

The bigger reason was that she wanted a home of her own. Free of her father, old resentments, and conflicts.

Why couldn't she find a way to get one without Quinnten Langley or her father?

She clutched her reticule closer. She could never afford to buy her grandparents' hundred-acre farm in Winchester from the Yankees her grandmother had sold it to. The sixteen hundred dollars from her mother's bequest wasn't enough to buy land, seed, food for herself, and the three animals she needed to begin to breed a new generation of Tennessee walking horses. If she only had eight thousand dollars more, she could make a deposit on the run-down twenty-acre farm she'd seen last month in Leesburg.

Without a doubt, she needed more money. How could she get enough to buy that farm before she went home on Monday?

No bank would loan her funds. She was not twenty till June thirtieth, therefore under legal age to sign any papers. Well known in Washington and New York society because she was millionaire Skip Brighton's debutante daughter, she knew the first act any businessman would take would be to visit her father and inform him of her request.

Unless she asked for a private loan. Certainly, she wouldn't ask Raine for one of her hard-earned pennies. Nor could either of Ann's best friends give it to her. Colleen and Gus VanderHorn were women dependent on their father for their allowances, their status, their futures. In addition, Thurston Vander-Horn was Skip Brighton's friend.

Ann's chin came up. Her eyes scanned the dingy coach.

Why not go to Thurston VanderHorn for a loan?

He had known her for eight years, ever since she and Raine had met his two daughters when they enrolled in Mrs. Drummond's Finishing School for Young Ladies in Manhattan. He had as much money as Skip. Gained it the same way, too, from cotton and gun smuggling during the Civil War, then investing in silver mines and transcontinental railroads.

Thurston VanderHorn was exactly like her father in another way. He'd never turned down any business proposition. She could offer him an outlandish profit in interest or half her crops. God, whatever it took, she'd give, because her father expected her home by Monday, and she wouldn't return defeated. Skip Brighton could smell failure on a person's skin, and she hated it when he won without a contest. She would give him one, as she always had.

"Sugar, I do believe I see a wicked look in your eye."

"You always wanted me to break a few more rules than mere dress codes. Tonight's your chance, Raine."

"I get to come along and watch?"

"I wouldn't deprive you of my debut." Ann knocked her umbrella on the front of the cab. When the driver opened his peephole, she raised her voice. "Please take us to Massachusetts Avenue. Number four-ten."

Four blocks from the Capitol Building, the street was usually a bustling thoroughfare for politicians and lobbyists day or night. As Ann emerged from the carriage, she halted at the odd sight of one thin man marching back and forth, checking his timepiece and snapping it shut. Why would someone loiter about in such a bad storm?

Dismissing the need for an answer, she raced to the front steps of the VanderHorn house with Raine right behind her. When the head butler opened the door, Ann charged inside, thrusting hat, reticule, and coat at him.

"Miss Brighton, Miss Montand! Where are the Misses VanderHorn?"

"Still at Senator Cragmore's lecture." Ann hoped Colleen and Gus would keep to the scheme the four of them had devised to cover Ann's rendezvous with Quinn.

"Are you ill, then?"

"No. I have a problem." She scanned the long hall. "Where is Mr. VanderHorn? I must speak with him. I—"

There was no need to go on. The very man she wanted swung open the drawing room doors. He didn't look at all surprised to see her or Raine. "Ann, you're back early."

"The lecture was boring." She grinned at him and sailed forward. Raine followed. "Mr. VanderHorn, I am so pleased you're at home." He wore his smoking jacket, a sign his evening was relaxed—and, she hoped, so was his attitude. "I must talk with you now. My cousin can hear this."

Ann walked toward him, and the stout fellow who observed the rigid manners of his Dutch patroon ancestors stepped backward to allow her the room. "Ann, I have a gue—"

"I won't detain you, sir." His back was to his marble fireplace. In the mirror above the mantel, she caught a glimpse of cigar smoke spiraling upward. But she charged on. "I need money."

"Ann—" Raine sounded as if she were warning her.

Ann ignored her. "It's not a lot. Ten thousand dollars would do." He scowled. "Please hear me out, sir. I don't want you to give it to me. I wish to borrow it. Legally but secretly. I don't want my father to know."

"Why?"

"I want to buy a farm. Raise walking horses."

"Alone?" His black eyes narrowed.

She balked. Did he suspect what her plan for tonight had been? "Yes. I've always talked about doing it."

When he started to object—and she could predict the argument would run along the lines of how a young woman needed protection and direction—she stopped him.

"I'm a very good planter, Mr. VanderHorn. You did not know me, nor did Colleen or Gus, during the war, but I was a great help to my grandparents and my mother on their farm. Despite the fact that the Yankees traipsed over every acre and the Rebs hid in our barns, the four of us raised corn and lots of apples and peaches. We survived and even managed to share our surplus with a few Southern regiments now and then. Oh, sir, I know you think that women should be seen and not heard, but—"

"They shouldn't be concerned with money!" he growled.

"I mean no offense, sir, but this is important to me."

"How important?" asked a voice she knew better than Thurston VanderHorn's. "Enough to make a deal with *me?"*

Ann stared straight into the mirror at the very man she wished to foil. His hazel eyes, which so like hers deepened from green to brown depending on his mood, drilled into hers with the self-confidence that inspired her to match his own.

"Be independent" was his cardinal rule. The fact that he had lived his philosophy so well was the reason the two of them did not get along. His infidelity had killed her mother. His indifference had estranged her brother. His abandonment had infuriated her.

But she would not allow him to trap her.

He strode forward to stand behind her. At forty-five, Skip Brighton still possessed a full head of wavy mahogany hair, as unlined as his devilish face. Compared to most men his age who began to paunch and hunch, this former Rebel was still eluding daily cares.

Well, she would help him keep his beloved independence while she seized her own. She faced him.

"Yes. I have a few terms I'd like to discuss."

Chapter 1

"The world is his who has money to go over it."
—RALPH WALDO EMERSON

Dublin, Ireland
March 1875

HE HAD LOST HER! HE BEAT HIS HAT AGAINST HIS THIGH AS he emerged from the clubhouse stands. Lost her! For the sake of money! Broad chest. Strong legs. A lustrous mane and gorgeous tail. To have mated her would have brought him the greatest delight he'd had in a decade. And for want of fifty more miserable pounds, she now belonged to another.

Ah, hell. Why was he surprised?

In the last ten years, he had lost his savings. His hope. But not his friends or his determination to lead a respectable existence. He couldn't lose those, too.

He plowed a hand through his hair and plunked his derby back on his head. Such silliness to expect intelligent people to wear stuffy day clothes to horse trials and sales.

In a fit, he yanked the damn hat from his head and sent it sailing across the yard. Missing milling members of the crowd inspecting the next set of horses for sale, the black felt spun toward the nearest trash barrel and dropped in.

Rhys Kendall grinned.

His expression died as he spied the new owner of the horse. She emerged from the other side of the clubhouse, fishing in her reticule, no idea she stood beside him. He bent close, the fragrance of magnolias sweetening the acid of his disappointment.

"Congratulations." His words held more sarcasm than cheer, and she startled. "I hope you enjoy her."

"Thank you." She took a better look at him, while her hand paused inside her purse. Wary, she registered that he had been her opponent in the bidding. "You gave me a hard run for my money. She's beautiful."

She walked off, taking his breath away with her.

"An understatement," he muttered.

She marched over to the bursar and pulled open her reticule. From its abyss, she brought forth two eye-popping items. The first was a pistol that looked like an American derringer. Its partner was a roll of bills so large he would have trouble putting his fist around it.

But she was more arresting. He had suspected she was a woman of consequence when he'd seen her across the show ring. During the ten-minute auction, she had become increasingly animated as their contest over the Irish draught horse dwindled to a battle between the two of them. She'd cast him an evil eye when he'd upped her bids—and doubled his raise. He admired her pluck. Women of class allowed men to do their bidding. Not this one.

He noticed, too, that she was unescorted. Oddly alone. A bright sprig of green amid a somber plain of men, she was attired sensibly for the sale in a riding habit, as if she intended to mount her purchase immediately and ride off into the sunset. Most ladies came to the Dublin Spring Horse Trials and Sale dressed to impress, unless, of course, they were unmarried, and then they came dressed to lure.

He wished this one had not dressed at all. He scanned her lithe body, mentally snipping every stitch she wore. She had without a doubt the noblest conformation he had seen on any track or off. Nor did she walk, but floated.

Her height and leanness gave her presence. Her curves granted elegance. Her legs would match his in length, but he was certain that when he lifted her an inch and pressed her close, she would fit him, tight and moist.

He shifted, his appetite surging at the sight of her firm breasts. Delicacies to fill his hands and mouth . . .

He dragged his eyes to her rosewood hair. The same color as the bright bay she'd bought, her unfashionable fat braid was topped with a pert—but slipping—straw hat. His fingers rubbed together, itching to unwind her hair and wrap it around his wrist. His waist.

His mouth watered. He told himself to walk away, but cool reason was not talking down a hot erection. He muttered rueful words, unable to stop his eyes from nibbling away, feeding a hunger for what was forbidden to him. *And she most certainly is beyond your means, old man.* Because from her purse and her clothes to her independence, she was a woman with money. Buckets of it.

No match for a man of modest means.

His eyes snagged on a movement to his left. From a tight group of people, a short, thin man pushed through to halt at the sight of the same woman Rhys admired. The fellow checked his timepiece and snapped it shut.

Suddenly, the lady clapped at a remark of the bursar. "Oh, wonderful!" she said, and her hat fell over her eyes. She silently swore and ripped the thing off. Her braid unraveled. A few pins scattered. She shook her hair free of more, and Rhys could imagine combing through strands of dark red silk. But she turned, and, amid all those people, she gazed into his eyes.

She paused, bewildered that he had been studying her. But, dismissing the issue, she trudged to her left and deposited her hat in the trash barrel. Though she didn't dust her hands, Rhys noted the little flick of her chin as if to bid the tiny bit of trouble good riddance. Then she peered into the trash. She frowned, turning her face toward him to examine his empty hands and his bare head.

She reached in and retrieved his hat. Nose wrinkling, she held it up by two dainty fingertips. The remains of a watercress sandwich dripped from its brim. "Yours?"

"No longer," he replied, shoulders shaking in laughter.

She opened her fingers and let the hideous thing fall back inside the barrel. This time, she brushed her hands off and tossed him a grin that made him wish he were a rich man.

She retraced her steps, got her chit for her horse, and walked toward the stable block. With every step, her rippling hair tapped against her trim derriere.

Rhys wrestled with the temptation to follow her and introduce himself. They shared an admiration of good horseflesh and a hatred of hats. What's more, he needed to get close to her. Learn her name and the reason she could make him chuckle when no one had in—God help him—years.

Into his reverie darted the little man who had found her so intriguing before. Rhys watched him trail after her.

Rhys felt a stab of fear and began to track the sway of emerald green, followed by the little man's brown coat weaving through the crowd like a garden snake. But, unexpectedly, the man paused, jerked around, and flattened himself against the stable wall. As if he recognized someone he feared, he ran in the opposite direction.

Rhys memorized his needle mustache, his hooked nose. Rhys turned to check on the lady and bumped into someone.

"I apologize—" Rhys offered, but further words died on his lips. He was face-to-face with the one man who was responsible for everything he had become. Angry and poor.

"Brighton."

"Rhys." Skip Brighton's face went white with shock. "Hello. I never thought to see you here in Ireland."

"I will say the same."

"I come to Europe at least once a year."

"I know."

Skip sighed, looking sad and definitely older than his forty-five years. "We arrived last week."

"I will inform my solicitor he is flagging in his duty to inform me well in advance about your travel plans."

"He's not remiss. I came to Dublin unexpectedly."

"All the more reason to be vigilant. I claim the *droit de seigneur* to shoot all wolves invading my territory."

"Or attempting to buy it?"

"That, too." Why in hell a pirate like Brighton would try to purchase Kendall Manor baffled Rhys. In the fourteen years since Skip began to amass his fortune by smuggling cotton and artillery between England and southern ports during the American Civil War, Skip Brighton had never endeavored to buy property in London. When Rhys's solicitor had said Skip approached him to buy Kendall Manor, Rhys had rejected the offer immediately. Yes, he had given word out that he would sell his three-hundred-year-old home on the banks of the Thames for a decent price to the right person. But he'd rather keep Kendall Manor, even if it meant not having enough money to invest in a new venture like Guardian Shipping's new cruise line.

Rhys's pride demanded he keep the rarest jewel of his family from the man who had taken most else from him. He'd never give Skip the satisfaction of possessing the Kendall family London residence. It was irksome enough to Rhys that he was considering joining a group of ten men in a new company to develop a transatlantic cruise line—a group that would include Skip, once his friend, now his nemesis.

Skip shot him a fleeting smile. "It's true, Rhys, that I never stayed anywhere for long, but I grow older and I need stability. I knew you considered investing in our cruise line, and I thought any profit you earned on the sale of Kendall Manor might make that investment a reality."

Rhys balled his hands in frustration. "It is kind of you to be concerned for me, but if I join Guardian

16

Shipping, it will be with money I think I can readily invest. I will not sell my family's assets."

"And certainly not to me?"

"Your money was gained from my people's loss, Brighton. I'll never take a bloody penny from you."

Skip tightened his jaw, his tone melancholy. "Old resentments die as hard as old habits. The bigger tragedy would be to die without making amends." He smiled. "I was pleased to hear from my friends that your factory in Lancashire is producing fabric up to its full capacity."

Rhys's guard went higher. Skip's shift in topic was subtle and intentional. Rhys couldn't resist the need to brag. "We'll earn a profit this year for the first time since your Southern states seceded from your Union. I'm importing Indian cotton now."

Skip's hazel eyes faceted in unreadable shades of gold. "I'm glad to hear it."

Damned if Skip didn't sound sincere. But Rhys would never forget that the ruin of Rhys's textile business after the fire in his largest Liverpool mill had much to do with Skip's greed during the American Civil War. Rhys was already stepping away. "Excuse me."

"I look forward to seeing you again at our next investors' meeting," Skip called after him.

The feeling is not mutual, Rhys told himself. But he noted that his ancient anger against Skip was not as wild as it once was. Wary of that decline, Rhys forced his mind to a finer topic. He focused on the way his blood had heated when he'd admired the woman in green. He had to find her and assure himself that the slimy creature who followed her hadn't decided to do it again.

He'd bet his meager monthly income that he knew

where she'd be. With her new possession. He turned in the direction of the stable block where the animals were housed in preparation for their departure with their new owners.

When he found her, she was at the far end of the stable in a loose-box, crooning to her Irish bay. Rhys strained to hear her voice, low as a June breeze and just as sultry.

The mare liked it, too. Rhys watched in fascination as the animal drew in the woman's scent, whiffling over her hair, nudging her hands in invitation to stroke her.

Rhys felt the fires begin again in his body as the horse nuzzled the woman's breast. The material of her riding jacket hugged her torso like a kid glove. She didn't wear a padded bust improver. Who would ask her to?

Not me. He'd want her free. Hair, breasts, legs.

What was the matter with him? He did not permit himself to want any woman. He could not afford to desire anyone for any time longer than an evening, and certainly not one with any breeding or style . . . or money. He straightened.

At the opposite door, a shadow moved.

Something small glinted in the man's hand. If it was his watch or a gun, Rhys didn't take time to note.

Rhys charged forward. But he was too late. The culprit hurled himself through the door.

In the same second, the woman whirled, astonished.

The horse shied, whinnied. Straining at her tethers, the animal tried to rear and defend her new mistress.

Rhys halted at the threshold. The worm had vanished amid the throng.

Rhys spun with the need to find the woman, comfort her.

Instead, he heard the cock of a hammer. A hard circle of steel bored into his coat.

"Don't move," she ordered him, her voice steely.

"I wouldn't dream of it. Put that away, though. I'm not the one you want to use it on."

"No, no, of course not." He could feel the pistol wavering as she began to breathe—and tremble.

He placed his hand atop hers. "Give it to me."

"I'm sorry. I don't like to be surprised." Her body swayed with terror. It was the most natural act in the world to wrap her in his arms.

His brains became mutton when his loins registered what a prize he held in his embrace. "You're safe. You're unhurt. He's gone, and I've got you." He speculated that were he to keep her, he'd soon put her in a bed for nights and days—or more. "Very wise of you to have your pistol at the ready," he whispered into the thick glory of her hair.

She gulped. "I'm usually a quicker draw."

"No need for that. My liver is already quivering." He smiled when she laughed. "If I were a pickpocket or a highwayman, I'd be impressed and change my profession."

"So you are telling me Ireland is not safe for women?"

"The leprechauns protect them usually." He drew back, brushing soft tendrils from her cheeks. "But the day before yesterday was Saint Patrick's Day, and the little fellows had a pint too much, so they're a wee bit under the weather."

She brought her face up. Their gazes locked, and he discovered her eyes were a mix of brown and green and gold nuggets, bright with fear. "I'm glad to see you took their place. Leprechauns are supposed to be ugly little elves with pointed ears. You're definitely not small." Her hands drifted across his shoulders, building fires in his blood. "You're far from ugly, and you have very symmetrical ears."

"I think yours are passing fair, too." He grinned. "I'm thrilled you're safe," he told her, suddenly serious. "Do you have any idea why that man followed you?"

Her eyes darted toward the paddock door and back up to him. "No. Was he?"

"I saw him watch you at the bursar's post. Then he must have tracked you here. Did you recognize him?"

She frowned, glancing at the door. "I didn't get a good look at him."

"He was short, thin, with a mustache. No? Not familiar? Well, I will tell you that I am very glad you carry a gun in your handbag."

"I learned to keep one with me during the war."

That jarred him. Suddenly, so did the cadence of her speech. She was American, and the conflict she spoke of had to be their War between the States. She would have been so young then, too young to carry a weapon. "How old were you?"

"Nearly six when the Southern states seceded. Almost ten when Lee surrendered to Grant."

Rhys chastised himself heartily for being attracted to this charmer who was therefore no more than twenty years of age. He didn't fall for women. Rich, poor, smart, not pretty or drab, they could not matter to him. He'd sworn himself off involvements to protect his heart from pains, his reputation from stains. Five years ago, he'd removed himself from the endless circuit of balls and dinner parties, as much to declare publicly that he was not husband material as to protect himself from finding a woman whom he might want but could never keep. Not in any style which her hope or his affection might wish he could afford. He wanted to hoot in irony that he'd condemned himself to eternal bachelorhood because he never thought to earn more than a middling income, only to be tempted by this golden-eyed girl who was twelve years his junior.

She stepped backward from his embrace. "Thank you for your help." She put her hand out. He took it and swore it was no compensation for the lack of her in his arms. "I'd like to ensure your safety. Are you with someone? May I escort you back to the clubhouse?"

"Yes, I'd like that. Should I address you as 'my lord' or 'sir' or—"

"Rhys Kendall." He eschewed all formalities. "Just Rhys will do."

She repeated his name, and he longed to hear her say it often in secluded dark rooms. "That's unique."

"It's Welsh. Traditional name for boys among my mother's family. The Kendall is a wee bit of Scots. We hail from the northern borders of England." Instinct told him that he needed to be able to find her, call on her. Common sense shouted that he ask nothing of her. He should, if he were smart, run the other way.

"And I am Ann—"

He laughed. "Well, of course. Full of grace." He was floored by the aptness of her name.

"What?"

"Full of grace. It is what *Ann* means."

"I never knew."

"I did. I saw it in the way you seem to glide."

She did not breathe. "You are very complimentary."

"It's an act I perform with utmost discretion." He grinned at her, marveling at her ability to cheer him and thus unwittingly blot out years of somberness. "Come along. I'll see you out. You've made friends with your mare, and you can send your stable hands to come fetch her."

"Yes, thank you. My party are having tea before the next round of bidding. Perhaps you would like to join us." He readily accepted, wishing to stay longer in her company and view the easiness of her smile, so contagious a condition. She hooked her hand over his arm, and the effects of her frightening experience vanished as they walked into the sunshine and her hair caught the rays like flame.

"Where do you stay in Dublin?" *Who are you with? Your parents? Your husband?*

"We're at the Imperial Hotel."

"A fine place, but it has no stables."

"I'll keep her two streets away at Rooney's."

"Tim Rooney will take great care of her."

"Good, because I intend to keep him busy. You see, I have a long shopping list for Ireland and England."

"So you'll purchase more than one mare? I'm glad you told me. I care not to bid against you a second time. It's humiliating for a man to lose to a lady with so much money," he teased her. "But why do you carry cash? That fellow who followed you probably wanted to relieve you of it. That's a choker of a roll, and bank drafts would be better, you realize." They took the dusty lane toward the two-story clubhouse. He hated to come to the end of the road.

"Maybe. But I like the feel of currency. Makes me

think I'm secure. That's a result of what happened to us during the war, too. When you're tired and hungry, you take what money you have and spend it before it disappears."

That urge Rhys knew too well. He pressed his hand to hers in sympathy. "Did you live in the South?"

"Yes. Virginia."

Skip Brighton hailed from Virginia. Odd to meet two people in one day so far from their home and at the same event. Unless they knew each other. Unless this lovely woman had become Brighton's second wife. Riled by that thought, Rhys patted her hand again, but it was her right hand. If she wore a wedding ring, it would be on her left.

"My grandparents were farmers." She was reminiscing as if she and he had known each other for decades. "They owned one hundred and twenty acres of the finest cornfields and fruit trees you have ever seen, until the Yankees moved in after the declaration of war. Then everything changed. We saw battles almost every day." Her tone went hollow, her body taut as when she'd become frightened and drew her pistol on him. "I'd like to raise my horses on my own farm in peace. I never want to see violence of any kind again."

"A solid goal."

"I think so," she murmured, and then inhaled, suddenly drawing herself up and away from her memories. "I'm here in Ireland to find fresh blood to breed a new type of horse. In Tennessee, they call them walking horses."

"If these horses come from Tennessee, why do you search for stock in Britain?"

"Walkers are a mix of Thoroughbreds, Morgans, Standardbreds, and pacers. Unfortunately, American horse breeders have not kept records of their stud activities and refinement of walkers has become, like so many other breeds, a guessing game. My thought is that many walking horses are too skittish and too fine-boned for the work they must do. The stallion I keep stabled back home at our house in Alexandria is like that, and . . . I am running on. If I'm boring you—"

"Not at all. I know a bit about horses. Tell me more."

She beamed. "Well, he has many wonderful qualities, but he's very nervous. I'd like to put him to stud with a mare who has heavy bones and a gentle disposition."

"Ah, yes. A woman to tame him."

"Precisely. And the Irish bay is tall and strong and beautifully colored. She'll bring out the best in him."

Rhys's eyes swept from her hair to her lips. "What any good partner should do."

"But in case she can't provide the total answer to my needs, I want to take home another mare. A Thoroughbred who's a fast pacer. And if my inheritance money stretches that far, I'll buy another stallion with strong bones to strengthen the line."

"Perhaps then you'd permit me to advise you on where to look for the best selections. Tattersall's in Newmarket is an excellent auction house, but they run a stable in London, too. Their sale every Monday morning is without peer. I also have a number of books I could lend you to read up on lineage in Britain. Two of them were written by my father, who was considered an expert on breeding and equitation. He owned a sizable stud farm and raced more than a dozen Thoroughbreds before he died."

"Thank you. I have limited funds and can't afford

to make any mistakes in the quality of the stock I send home."

Rhys smiled wistfully. "I'll have my books sent to you. How long do you stay in Dublin?"

"Two weeks. Then we go to London."

"Not Paris? Most American ladies begin their grand tour by going to the dressmakers."

She wrinkled her nose. "Yes, but I insisted we come to this sale to begin my purchases. My father and my aunt didn't mind that we waited until June after we're settled in London. My father has business meetings scheduled in London, and he's eager to get there."

Rhys felt a rush of panic. Did Skip Brighton have a daughter? He could remember him mentioning only a son named Taylor. Rhys forced himself to listen to Ann as she talked about her cousin and two friends who had traveled with her father and aunt.

"Raine isn't very interested in gowns but in classical art. But our friend Colleen was disappointed because she wanted to start the London season with new clothes. I promised to make it up to her, which means I owe her big favors. Including introductions to anyone I meet."

Rhys felt relief there seemed to be no husband in the bunch. He cocked a brow. "Meaning me?"

"Do you mind?"

"No."

"I do," she confessed. Then, unlike an English girl who would have lowered her lashes to cover her fluster, Ann grinned up into the sky. "Am I blushing?"

"Wildly."

"Where is a hat when you need it?"

"I'm glad you threw it away."

"I amused you."

"You reminded me that laughter does exist. Only I must look for it."

"Something I should remember myself." She gave him half a smile.

"We both need a little more fun, it seems." They had reached the entrance to the clubhouse.

"We have a box in the second tier," she told him, and they began to climb the steps. She glanced up at him, her gaze drifting to his lips with an appreciation that fired his imagination of how he'd kiss her first. "Would I be too forward to ask if you live in Dublin?"

"I own a home north of here in Dundalk and another in Lancashire, England. I came to the horse show today to buy an animal for a large farm I own in England."

"Do you go to London often?"

"Not unless I have good reason."

"I see," she said as their eyes held and someone called to her.

Rhys sensed people stirring within one box. He looked up, and one buxom young woman with black hair waved at Ann. Beside her stood a silver-haired older lady who squinted at him through a lorgnette. Next to her was an extremely shocked—and suddenly pleased—Skip Brighton.

Rhys felt a gush of sorrow sweep through him. Ann's expensive little derringer, her wealth, her confidence all indicated she belonged to Skip. But in what way?

Ann's gaze trailed Rhys's. "The lady in ivory is Aunt Peggie, our chaperone, and that man is my father. Do you know him? He's smiling at you, but . . . is something wrong?" She became concerned. Almost angry.

"I know him well." *Too damnably well.* Rhys pressed her arm to his torso and picked up their pace.

Rhys watched Skip Brighton work his way past the older lady and the three younger women, each as distinctive as a feather from a different bird. Aunt Peggie seemed like a snowy owl in a ball of white plumes. The well-endowed one looked like a flamingo in rose ruffles, the blonde was an egret in tailored gray, while the last girl resembled a pudgy raven in a froth of peach sateen. Every one was the epitome of fashion and enormous wealth.

"There you are, Ann," Skip greeted her as he came upon them, his attention fastening on Rhys as if they were warm friends. "You two have met. Nice to see you again."

Rhys resisted the urge to grind his teeth. He turned to Ann, unwinding her arm from his. "It was the highlight of my day to have assisted you, Miss Brighton. I will send round to your hotel a list of the best horse sales establishments in Britain and the books I promised. I wish you well in breeding walking horses. Rely on leprechauns from now on," he advised so sweetly she might have missed the sorrow in his last two words. "Good day."

Good-bye was what he'd meant. Ann knew she would never see him again. She was certain the reason was that Rhys and her father did not get along. Or, to be precise, Rhys hated Skip. While part of her was not surprised because so many men distrusted the man who had made millions rapidly and ruthlessly, Ann added this grievance to her resentment for his abandonment of his family in time of war.

"Who was *that?*" Colleen came to Ann's side.

"His name is Rhys Kendall." He was so tall that she

could watch his departure easily. His broad shoulders in the charcoal frockcoat were rigid. His gait was swift, sure.

She felt the urge to run after him and knew she could not bring him back. What had her father done to Rhys? She would not ask him. Her father never spoke to her about his business or his personal conflicts, only about his successes. But Aunt Peg might know. She'd ask her.

Colleen hummed. "Divine-looking man. Is he married?"

"I don't think so." Ann remembered the tenderness of his touch and wondered if he held many women in his arms.

"Fair game, then."

Raine watched Rhys go. "Mam'selle VanderHorn, you had best kill your admiration. I think my cousin has her cap set for him already."

"Raine," Ann admonished, "I've lost my hat, not my—"

"Head?"

"Sense."

"Then do stop watching him, darlin'." She put up her parasol as raindrops began to fall. "Lord, the weather is unpredictable here. Let's go back and sit under the roof."

Gus mused, "I like blond men, and he's got brown hair."

Chestnut, Ann corrected. Which curls abundantly.

"Hmph." Colleen would not be shaken. "Blonds are all right for other women, Gussie, but not you and me. With our dark coloring, we'd get children with dishwater looks."

Skip was chuckling.

Aunt Peggie was *tsk*ing, hands fluttering toward

their seats. "Girls, please! Come back to the box. We mustn't gawk at each handsome brute who walks up. We want lots of invitations here and in London, and we won't get them if we act like we're buying bonbons at the confectioner's."

Raine winked at Ann as she turned away. Gus VanderHorn promptly followed.

But Colleen put a hand up to shade her view of Rhys. "I wonder if he's rich."

Ann pivoted. "I have no idea."

Her father stopped her with his gaze. "I do."

"Ann, wait. Don't you want to hear this?"

I want to know everything about Rhys Kendall—and I fear if I do, I'll be more entranced.

Her father's voice, quiet and even, made her pause. "Rhys Kendall and his father were once friends of mine, Colleen. I met Rhys when he was ten. The family owned cotton mills on the west English coast. I shipped them raw goods until one night eleven years ago, the largest building burned down. Rhys has not recovered from the loss."

"What does he do now?" Colleen persisted, and Ann was silently grateful for her insistence.

"He still runs one cotton mill, and he owns a lot of land, collecting rents from his farmers. He also considers investing in the cruise line I'm opening with nine others."

"So he *is* wealthy," Colleen proclaimed.

"Well, Colleen, I'd say Rhys is careful how he spends his income."

Ann wondered if Rhys were struggling financially through any actions of her father. The possibility riled her, drowning the polite rapport that had developed between them during their ocean voyage the last six weeks.

Skip continued dispassionately, "If Rhys can see his way clear to contribute at least two thousand pounds, he'll become one of the founding directors of Guardian Shipping."

Colleen was stricken. "Is that virile creature *poor?*"

Skip pursed his lips. "Rhys thinks he is. He certainly lives on much less than what his father did."

"A pity. He could have been a great match. But Mother and Daddy wouldn't approve of me liking a poor man. I wouldn't approve of it myself." She laughed lightly.

"Nonetheless, Colleen, he is considered quite a catch."

"Stunning to look at, but if he has no wealth—"

"Ah, but he has *things.* A rare twelfth-century tapestry, a few suits of medieval armor, and a collection of Van Dycks the Queen envies. He keeps them in one drafty castle or one noted London mansion."

"Well, he should sell them and make money."

"But he won't."

"That doesn't make sense."

"The man is part of an ancient but aging society. One that doesn't approve of its sons selling their heritage. You see, my dears, Rhys Westport Kendall is His Grace, the sixteenth Duke of Carlton and Dundalk."

"So if a girl had money," Colleen rhapsodized while Ann stared into her father's calculating eyes, "she might make the perfect wife for him and in the bargain become a duchess, twice over."

"An intriguing prospect, isn't it?" Skip asked, and Colleen agreed.

Ann did not bat an eyelash but headed for the family box. Her father's words rang warning bells in her head, bringing her to her senses, so addled by a charming man.

Skip wanted her married. He'd made that plain the day after her mother's funeral when he'd first proposed the trip to Europe. If he thought Rhys Kendall a viable candidate, good for him. She had her own goals and five months remaining to her stay abroad with him. According to their agreement that night at the VanderHorns', she was here in Europe visiting, earning a monthly income from him in exchange for being a congenial traveling companion and dutiful daughter. On September first, she would leave, taking with her eighteen thousand dollars for six months' services. Until then, much as she would enjoy Rhys Kendall's companionship, she didn't want to see him.

He was too attractive. Too debonair. She'd reveled in his company for less than ten minutes and found him utterly enchanting. Continue to see him, and she could find herself in the same circumstances as her mother once had been. Caring for a man more than he cared for her.

Chapter 2

"Over here husband-hunting?"
—Sir William Gordon-Cumming

London, England
April 1875

"THERE YOU ARE!"

Ann started when her father walked into the library two mornings after they'd moved from their hotel to their newly rented town house in Belgravia. He sidestepped a vase of gladiolas. This arrangement was the latest in a profusion of hothouse gifts from admirers for Ann. It duplicated others for Colleen. Raine received none, a confirmation of her apathy toward the eligible men she met.

Skip shook his head. "Damned place reeks worse than a perfume shop. Men need more imagination."

"What might you suggest they send?" she asked, putting a bookmark in one of the journals Rhys Kendall had sent her three weeks ago.

Humor twitched his mouth. "For Colleen, a nobleman with a fortune. Quickly. For Gus, a dose of Mrs. Filbert's Female Drops to calm her exuberance for men, none of whom she's supposed to attract until she comes out two years from now. For Raine, I haven't found a cure. She's cool as a cucumber. But for you, a strong-boned stallion is what you want, right?"

His double entendre couldn't make her smile. "I prefer to search for him myself." Ever since she'd met Rhys Kendall at the horse sale, she'd felt torn between her sadness that she would not see him again and her knowledge that even if she did, she would enjoy his company too much. She told herself she mustn't endanger her own plan to go home in September with her mare, buy a farm, and live alone.

"My dear, you'd need not beat the bushes. The men are coming to you like cattle on a stampede. I knew they would, and that's *without* seeing you in those trousers."

Dark with frustration, his eyes darted to her gray twill trousers.

Ann had grown accustomed to the ease and usefulness of men's pants when she worked the farm as a child. She had never outgrown her love of their comfort, much to her father's dismay in Washington and New York. There she wore them to ride in comfort. Here in Britain, the chilly spring compelled her to wear them for warmth—and social rules forced her to wear them to escape the censure of riding alone and astride. This she accomplished with the aid of black trousers with matching frockcoat. She didn't think her father knew that she ensured her disguise with her hair stuffed into a net under a men's tophat, complemented by a mustache she made from her own hair clippings.

"They won't see me, either," she assured him, positive that when she had left their hotel these past two weeks they'd been in London, no one had noticed she was a woman. She would keep it that way, too. "I'm here, aren't I, to please you, be your hostess, and, you hope, allow some man to take me off your hands?"

"To earn your three thousand dollars a month from me, you are giving the appearance of cooperating in all those endeavors, yes." He flicked a petal of a gladiola. "Doing a damn good job, too, when you're not reading those books by Bennett Kendall again."

She shut the journal. Rhys had sent them to her hotel in Dublin a few days after they'd met, and she had devoured them over and over. "I'm absorbing more each time I go through them."

"What's that one about?"

"It outlines how to breed for certain traits. Especially what to look for in a dam when so many discount her contribution to the mating." She'd been reluctant to inject anything about Rhys into any conversation with her father. To do that would have given him leverage over her. She had waited for him to bring up Rhys's name so that she might appear nonchalant in gaining information about their conflict. Aunt Peg, unfortunately, claimed no knowledge and referred Ann to her father for an explanation. His tendency to talk about the Kendalls was a golden opportunity she could not miss. "The old Duke was an expert for his time."

"A gambler, too. He piddled away the family fortune. I knew Bennett well. Polite man, good horseman, poor head for business. Rhys has tried to make up for his father's financial losses, and he's courageous and dogged, I'll give him that. But so far, not lucky. If he decides to join us in this cruise line venture, he'll need no luck."

"Two thousand pounds does not seem like a lot to invest." The topic of money would keep her father talking.

"It's not, and I think he can afford to spare it."

"How do you know?"

"Bennett and I were good friends, Ann. I knew what his income was. I expect Rhys's is similar. About three thousand pounds per month from his estate rents. I know Rhys banks most of it and reinvests it in improvements to his farms. New roofs for tenants' homes. New wagons, tools, whatever they need, he sees they have it. Rhys also lives modestly here and in Lancashire. He does not care to lose what he has in savings, and so he is being very cautious about joining us."

"Is the venture that risky?"

"Not at all. Simply put, Rhys debates if he can trust me enough to join in a business with me. Eleven years ago, when that fire occured in his mill, I had just shipped him a major supply of raw cotton. I demanded payment for it because I was in a financial bind myself. I had lost my only other remaining ship coming through the Yankee blockade. Rhys asked to delay paying me. I refused. He put together the money by taking a usurious loan. It hurt him further. Since then, I have apologized to him, but that is poor compensation. So I have decided to make amends by asking the other nine directors to join me and invite Rhys to participate in forming our cruise line company. It will be a lucrative venture with more people traveling from America to Europe." He threw her a sad smile. "Stunned, aren't you, that I could do anything so honorable?"

She was certain the look on her face gave her answer.

"I attempt to make amends to others. You are first."

She had perceived it but felt uncomfortable to be beholden to him. "I want to earn my money from you fairly. Our agreement that night at the Vander-Horns'—"

"Oh, you are being gay and charming to everyone."

"Those were your stipulations. I'm doing my part, acting as if I'm your darling daughter."

"But you are."

She stared at him.

He stepped in front of her. "You don't believe me."

"I won't argue with you. Your temper is too unpredictable." *And I'm not as skilled at debate as you.*

He chewed at the inside of his cheek. "We must *talk,* Ann. We've let this pot simmer too long, and the tension is ruining our trip. Our *lives.* Your mother is gone, unable to do anything about the fact that you and I are together at last. She can't ridicule you for spending time with me and enjoying it."

"Mother has nothing to do with how I feel about you."

"No?"

"You do." Ann took a big breath and let it loose with her recital of his crimes. "You left my mother and Taylor and me in Winchester in the path of the worst fighting of the war. I was almost six years old the morning you rode off on that gray horse. You seemed so sincere when you promised to return and take us away. But you didn't. You let us rot there for four long years while our fields were trampled and burned and men bled to death in our corn rows. Years when Taylor began to scout for Mosby, and Grandpa Jack grew white with worry, Grandma died, and Mother took ill with consumption."

"Ann, I swear I thought I could get back to you, but the blockade was too tight—"

"You expect me to believe that a man who could

run ships through the Yankee lines at sea couldn't get across a picket line on land?"

"I did!"

"Once."

"Four times!"

She froze in her chair. "When?" Was she so young that his visits had gotten lost in her memory? No, she would have recalled the return of the dashing man who had told her sea adventures and taught her how to ride and fish and laugh.

"Your mother didn't tell you about the other times. She didn't want you and Taylor to cry your eyes out that I'd come and gone—or so she told me. I began to wonder if she just didn't use it as a way to blacken my character with both of you."

"That's a terrible accusation to make."

"Yes," he seethed, and spun away. "And how can I possibly speak so poorly of the dead?" He removed a handkerchief from his trouser pocket and coughed into it. This was a recurring affliction lately. He hated the English chill as much as Ann, and he had had a bronchial problem since they'd sailed from New York. He'd finally seen a doctor in Dublin, and his condition had cleared with the aid of a syrup. But the cough was back again—and it reminded her of her mother's. Rough and deep. "I can't let this antagonism continue between us, Ann. Life is too short, and I grow older and, I hope, wiser."

Her concern about his health made her resist the urge to declare it was too late for them to enjoy any normal relationship. That would be as cruel as what he'd just said about her mother.

"I have avoided arguments with you since your mother died because I wanted to spare you unnecessary anguish. But there are things your mother may have said about me that are not true. I must correct any false impressions you have—"

"That you left us in Winchester to make a fortune running contraband through Yankee shipping lines?"

"That was a business decision. I owned two ships out of Baltimore, and if I didn't use them, the Union was going to commandeer them and give me half what they were worth. I would've lost my only assets. I had a family to support. I knew the Confederacy would need imports and pay dearly for them, so I sided with the South to make money, lots of it."

"Smart man. Then you took us to Winchester—"

"I asked your mother to stay in Baltimore at our house on Charles Street. She wanted to be near family. I begged her to go live with Aunt Peg over on St. Paul Street, but she insisted on returning to her parents in Winchester."

"She didn't know how dangerous it would be."

Her father gazed at the ceiling. "Elizabeth thought her girlhood home was a sacred place only love could touch."

Ann felt the same about Virginia. That was one reason she wanted to return. "None of this does us any good. It only makes us sadder. I'm here with you, being kind to the gentlemen who come to conduct business with you."

"Your heart isn't in it. You just want to take the money you earn from me here, buy your horses, and go home alone as fast as you can."

She crossed her arms. "What more do you want from me?"

"A chance, dammit! A chance to show you that I am not an ogre. That men have their desires and their faults just like women. That you don't have to love me as you once did, but you can at least recognize that I am human."

"I might have, if you had let me get to know you. If you had stayed in Alexandria once you took us back to live there in 'sixty-five. But since the war, you've acted the same way as during it. You've sailed away to Shanghai or Yokohama, any port at any time. You left Mother and Raine and me in Alexandria and sent home gifts of silk and porcelain and diamonds as substitutes for your company. Only once in the eight years Raine and I attended school in New York did you come to visit, and you had an office less than five blocks from us. Why did you stay away? And why do you come to me now with your time and your presents and your attempts to make amends to me?"

He slowly turned and locked his eyes on hers. "Because your mother wouldn't let me."

That sucked the breath from her. "That's—"

"Despicable, but it is also the truth."

She didn't think he was lying. "Why would she do that?"

"Revenge."

Ann felt her stomach clench with pain. "Because—?"

"I had an affair."

Ann closed her eyes. Her fondest memories of her mother were of a laughing woman, singing to her, combing her hair, and telling her the tale of how she'd met a charming man who had said he loved her the first time he saw her. But the memory became one of a tight-lipped lady who frowned and muttered of men's intemperate appetites. "Be independent," Elizabeth echoed her husband's motto. "Love is no more than lust. A dangerous delusion."

"Your mother could not forget or forgive my mistake. I should never have bared my soul to her. Then I might have been able to make it up to her, with her none the wiser."

"When did it happen?"

"Just before Virginia seceded. I think if I'd never told her, she would not have insisted on going to Winchester. She needed to go home to lick her wounds. I was the bigger fool because I let her leave."

Ann whispered, "She loved you."

"Yes, madly, once upon a time. I loved her, too."

"Then why did you go to another woman?"

"Hell, who knows? Because I thought I could enjoy her body and it wouldn't affect how I loved your mother. I hadn't counted on feeling guilty—or needing to confess it to her and be forgiven. Lust is a powerful lure."

Ann raised her gaze to his. "I think it is."

"Your mother felt betrayed," he said, his tone hoarse. "I understood. I let her go to her parents to get over it. She didn't. She grew bitter, maybe because of the hardships of the war or maybe because I wasn't there to speak for myself. Anyway, her unforgiving attitude drove me farther away. There were"—he looked at the floor—"more women. I didn't tell her about those." He inhaled. "I think she had a sixth sense and knew. She grew colder toward me. Then she grew mean. She told me I had to go away and stay away."

"No." Ann recoiled from the awful knowledge that both her parents had been at fault for the death of their union.

"I refused. She told me that if I didn't, she would tell you and Raine about my lurid past."

"She blackmailed you?"

He jammed his hands in his trouser pockets. "I couldn't let her tell you."

"So you didn't come home or come to see us in school."

"Only last June, when I knew her illness was terminal, did I return to Alexandria, and this time she didn't send me away. I think at the end of her life, she may have had second thoughts about what she'd done to our marriage. The night she died, she took my hand and told me she had loved me." He blinked away tears. "I told her I had known that, always. But her kind of love was one that controlled."

Ann shivered. "And what is yours?"

He frowned. "I don't pretend to be a saint. One reason I wanted you to come to Europe with me was to show you that I've got some good in me."

"And to marry me off."

"To make you secure. What's wrong with that? There are wonderful men here who are educated and refined—"

"There were men in America like that." Quinn sprang to her mind but quickly paled beside the memory of Rhys.

"Yes, but not as many. Here men have a sense of pride, heritage, and family."

"With titles, estate debts, and a need to fill their purses with American heiresses' money. I've met them, ready to put a ring on my finger and their hand in your wallet."

"Yes, Ann, men here marry for those reasons. But I'd never let you get married for that alone."

"Let me?"

He set his jaw. "Approve of, then. Men here tend to marry for life, and that's what you want and need."

"How would you know?"

He sighed. "Because you are your mother's daughter, as well as mine. We believe in marriage for life, enduring through all kinds of problems. But I'd bet my last dollar Elizabeth fed you ideas that rule your thinking about men and marriage."

"Of course she did. Just as you do."

He hitched up one corner of his mouth. "Giving me a run for my life, aren't you? All right. I'm telling you I wanted you to come here to have your pick of the litter. To find the best man for you."

"I was doing fine by myself in Alexandria."

"Were you?" He went very still. "Quinnten Langley rode up to your grandpa's farm when you were six years old. He may have been impressive because he was a war hero, but he was no prize as a man."

Ann searched his face to see if he knew about her plans to marry Quinn. She saw no hint of it as he raved on.

"You spent the past two years nursing your mother. When most young women in Alexandria and Washington were going to afternoon teas and dinner parties, you sat in a sickroom with death at the door. But you did your duty by Elizabeth. Now it's time for you to see the world. Time to enjoy the fruits of my labors."

"I don't want more than what we agreed to. A monthly allowance in exchange for me coming to Europe with you, acting politely to your friends, and allowing you to show Raine, Colleen and Gus, and me the sights. The eighteen thousand—coupled with my sixteen hundred of Mama's inheritance—will buy a suitable plot, perhaps two more horses, and I'll even have a little money left for feed. Don't expect me to marry any of these men who come to call on you. Just keep to our agreement."

"What is wrong with getting married? Your mother is gone, Taylor has disappeared into the West, and only God knows if he'll return. Your friends and Raine will marry someday soon, and you, my dear, will be alone."

Ann noticed he hadn't included himself in his list of those available to her. "Are you going somewhere?" Despite what he'd revealed a few minutes ago, she wouldn't be surprised if business took him off again at any time.

"Not that I plan, no." He tried to smile and failed. "I worry about you."

As reassurance, it was small. She rose from her chair, the ebony leather book clutched to her chest as if to shield her heart from him. "Don't." She lifted her chin in defiance. She knew it was a gesture which imitated his.

"God help me, why are you so stubborn? I know, I know. You inherited it from me, damn my soul. Well, what a comeuppance. And I can't cure it in a minute, so I guess I'll do the next best thing and leave. Satisfied?" he asked with bluster. "Here. Look these over." He took two folded papers from his vest pocket. "This is your copy of the guest list for our first dinner party here. Five of them are bachelors, two have joined the cruise line company, and one considers it. If you like any of them, or they like you, tell them to send jewelry or chocolates. We have enough flowers. No sense to break too many hearts while you're here." He walked toward the door. "I do have to work with these fellows after you've gone home to breed horses. Meanwhile, if you won't husband-hunt in earnest for yourself, help Colleen trap a proper man to take home to her mama. Then go to the dressmaker's, will you? Spend my money on something foolish."

"I will *after* I go to Tattersall's to look over the

stallions for sale this morning to spend *my* money."
She relented a little. "Then I'm on to the milliner's."

"Good. The English like their women crowned in
huge, ugly hats. I hope this fellow has a new remedy
for keeping one on your head of silk. Glue, perhaps?"

She couldn't help but chuckle. *"Go* to your
meeting."

"I'm leaving. I think Aunt Peggie has visitors for tea
today, so take O'Leary with you."

"Well, of course. Our Irish chaperone," she murmured, eager to move onto a lighter subject. "Or, as
Gus calls him, our gargoyle. Does he need to go
everywhere with us?"

"This is London, Ann. Portions of it are notori-
ously depraved. I don't want any of you girls wandering into a bad neighborhood accidentally and being
unprotected." Ann suddenly recalled Rhys's protection from a short, thin man with a mustache who had
followed her in Dublin. A picture of a snowy night
flashed in her head. The skinny man had loitered
outside the VanderHorns' in Washington. Had he
been short? She couldn't remember. Had he sported a
mustache? She had not seen his face clearly in the
whirl of snow. She had to dismiss the two incidents as
unrelated. Why would a man who had stood outside a
Capitol Hill house in a snowstorm track a woman at a
horse sale thousands of miles away? He couldn't be
the same man. But she felt wary nonetheless.

"You look concerned. What's the matter?"

She lifted a shoulder. "I suppose you are right. I
won't go out unprotected. Besides, I still carry my
derringer with me everywhere." *I'll be more obser-
vant, too.*

"Even so, you don't know this city the way you
knew Washington and New York. Your little escapes

in trousers to ride are innocent enough, but O'Leary accompanies all of you everywhere else. That's my rule."

"O'Leary could scare off a lot of men," she teased. "If he could smile—"

"I don't pay John O'Leary to look happy. I hired him during the war to supervise my ship in dock, and I count on him to protect you four girls now."

"What is there to protect us from?" Would her father know a thin man with a mustache? Hundreds, probably. But one who might follow her in Dublin? *Why?* That made no sense. She had nothing . . . except her small amount of money. Rhys had been right when he said the little man followed her to rob her of her cash. "Is there anyone in particular I should fear?" *Or you?*

"Not that I know of, but it's best to be prepared." Then he grinned. "Go talk with Aunt Peg, and prepare yourself for our first dinner party in our new home."

"And for the men you're inviting." She waved his list.

"Most especially them, princess," he said as he shut the door behind him and, with his endearment, ruined the rapport they'd begun to build in the last few minutes.

Long ago, before the war, he had dubbed her his princess. When he had returned from his four years on the high seas in pursuit of riches, he had called her that again, and she had yelled at him never to do it. She had run away to hide in her hayloft, unable at the age of ten to put into words what she understood now. The name implied he cared for her far more than his attention had shown.

Today, his use of his little name for her made her

angry. At him for his affair. At her mother for her inability to work with her husband to overcome the challenge to their marriage. At herself for never seeking the cause of her parents' rift.

Ann whirled toward the reading table and plunked the journal down, her father's papers fluttering to the carpet.

Her father had suffered as much as her mother during their estrangement. He was trying to build a life with Ann now. Over the eight weeks since that night in Thurston VanderHorn's town house and the inception of their agreement, Skip Brighton had occupied his daughter in numerous conversations. From her desire to breed walking horses in Virginia to her dislike of the constant chill of European weather and her advice in his choice of furnishings for their London residence, Forsythe House, her father tried to bridge the gap in their relationship.

His attempts began soon after her mother died and was buried. In mourning herself, Ann had not noted the change until that night they made their business deal. He'd been so accommodating to her needs, even Thurston gaped.

"You want money?" Skip had asked her. "I'll see you get it. Regularly. Payment for services rendered as my loving daughter, a sweet traveling companion, an American girl on her grand tour. Does that suit you? Say, two thousand per month. Is that enough?"

"Three," Ann countered, bold enough to lead him higher.

"Done."

"That simple?" Ann couldn't believe it. "Why?" she'd asked then, but knew the full answer now. He felt guilty still, wanting to make up to her for any grief he may have caused during his absence from her life.

Skip had spun away from her. His hand to the mantel, his head down to view the fire, he coughed.

Ann shut her eyes now, remembering the symptom manifested for the first time that night. Not on shipboard.

Even when he had spoken, his voice sounded like gravel. "I know how you feel about me. Your resentment has been plain for years. I left all of you. It was a mistake, but I had justifiable reasons. You don't want me in your life. So I'll help make it possible that you live without me."

He had offered her a business deal to set her free. In reality, he had bought himself time to try to become a true and affectionate father to her. She had refused his efforts. This morning, when he could take no more rejection, he had taken the only route left to him and revealed the worst there was about him and her mother.

Yes, his money had bought him her company. Her wish not to travel alone with this stranger who was her father had won her the companionship of her cousin Raine and their two best friends, Colleen and Augusta VanderHorn. The party of six had already enjoyed many an evening of cards, charades, and laughter together.

Ann now admitted she enjoyed the harmony. But years of listening to her mother's warnings about him had taken their toll—and she could not quite let down her guard against him. Her father got what he wanted. She had no doubt that he would use any means to obtain his goals. Her affection. Her forgiveness. Maybe even a husband. A man not only personally approved by him but perhaps even chosen by him.

Vowing to ignore her father's sweetness, she picked

up his papers from the floor. Among the list of those he wanted invited to his dinner party, she found a new cause to be wary. He had written a name there that endangered her own peace of mind.

Rhys Kendall.

Her father wanted Rhys to come here for business reasons, but also personal ones. His last words to Colleen that afternoon in Dublin had reminded Ann all too clearly that he intended to marry her off. Rhys might be one of her father's prime candidates. A duke, a man who had little money, and one who wished to earn it. That last made her smile because she doubted that Rhys Kendall was the sort of person who would stoop to mix money with marriage. Especially Skip Brighton's money—with marriage to Skip Brighton's daughter.

But her father continued his plotting. Inviting Rhys to dinner was the evidence.

Interesting that Rhys Kendall's lack of money did not seem to deter her father from his matchmaking. The same way their past enmity seemed not to deter Rhys from considering investing in the same venture with her father.

An ugly idea crossed her mind. Did her father need Rhys for a specific reason? Was she the lure to ensure that Rhys would come to the group with his name, his prestige, his influence?

The thought that Rhys and she could be used in such a way appalled her. But she could not quite dismiss the possibility that her father might do it.

This meant, of course, that she needed to be very strong. Stick to her own objectives, and, as her mother often warned, she must never let her heart rule her head.

"Hello, sugar." Raine beckoned when Ann entered

the dining room for the girls' morning meeting with Aunt Peg. "Aunt Peg is telling us the life history of the available men on Uncle Skip's guest list." She winked. "Intriguing names."

"Aren't they?" Ann muttered, sitting beside her cousin.

Gus popped another gumdrop in her mouth and flipped a page. "I count five unattached men. You three are so lucky you get to do this."

Aunt Peg gave Gus a consoling smile. "Now, dear, buck up. There's much to do here. You will study painting from an Italian instructor and fencing from a renowned master. Your parents have provided well for you, Augusta."

"In New York, at least we had Sunday at-homes I could go to." Gus pouted, and Ann suppressed a smile. Gus was sulking to get Aunt Peg to relent and allow the sixteen-year-old out with the rest of them.

Raine patted her hand. "Sugar, imagine how well you'll know these things long after we've returned to America."

Colleen shot Raine a reproving look. "Speak for yourself. I like it here. Please, Mrs. Gallagher, let's go on with your little histories."

Colleen had found the three weeks in Ireland boring and often made her feelings known to Ann as well as her father and her aunt. When Raine had taken her to task and reminded her that they would not even be in Europe were it not for Ann's request for their company, Colleen had sulked at the reprimand. Ever since they had settled into Forsythe House last Friday, she cast off her pout and became the fun-loving girl the three of them valued.

Aunt Peggie smiled and donned her glasses, then reached for her morning tea, which Ann knew always contained a fortifying dollop of apple brandy. Her gray eyes twinkled as she gazed down the dining room table at Raine, Colleen, Gus, and finally Ann. "I was relating the background of the first gentleman your father wants us to invite." She ran an index finger down the first page.

"Please take notes if you like. To be thought smart and proper, you must recall as much as possible. Committing a *faux pas* can ruin you in one evening without recourse. Believe you me, I learned the hard way the first time I came abroad with my parents thirty years ago. And with or without our dowries to commend us, we have more than an ocean of differences that separate us.

"Now, the first man," Peggie continued, "is Adam Litchfield. The tenth Earl Litchfield. A charming man. Tall, black hair, sharp features. Very appealing to many ladies. He is a widower, twice over."

"Rich?" Raine asked.

"Well off. Adds to his estate earnings by dabbling in textile manufacturing. A friend of your father's, Ann, but, I am sorry to say, not a possibility to come to dinner."

"Why not?" Gus asked.

"I haven't had a chance to tell Skip yet, but I learned yesterday at luncheon with Adam's aunt that he has gone up to his mill in Liverpool. Some unrest among his workers."

Raine mused, "What is it they want? More wages or fewer hours?"

Colleen chuckled. "Raine, sweetie, the man is not coming. You don't have to understand his business. Or the politics involved."

Aunt Peggie was enduring Colleen's outburst. "It's a good idea for Raine to know current political trends, if she's interested. Makes for better drawing room conversation. Although, I must say, you don't want to look too eager. Women do not concern themselves with such issues here. It's best to look informed, never avid."

"Let's talk about the next man," Colleen urged. Rhys.

"Ann's duke," Gus put in.

Aunt Peg ignored the exchange of smiles among all but Ann. "The sixteenth Duke of Carlton and Dundalk. Viscount Neville. Baron Chelmsford and Roulard. I think I've remembered it all. Did you write that down?"

The other three scribbled and glanced at Ann.

"I can remember it," she provided. She had failed to forget Rhys Kendall. Their brief encounter fascinated her. His interest to follow her, protect her from an attacker, embrace her, and joke with her about leprechauns pulsed in her reverie like a bright light she couldn't block out. She knew the reason. No man had ever paid so much attention to her. Even Quinn had been formal and detached, though she'd known him most of her life. She knew the cure. Permit Rhys's absence to help her forget him.

Yet how could she, if he came to dinner?

Raine turned to Peggie. "What else should we know about him?"

"He's thirty-two, the only son and heir of the Kendall family. A line that stretches back, say British folk tales, to Welsh warlocks, Scots outlanders, and Norman invaders."

"And where did they get the Irish title?" Gus prompted, agog, her chin in her hands.

"Dundalk?" Peg loved to weave yarns. "Well! Folklore says a leprechaun gave it to them." Peg didn't

51

pause when Ann's eyes widened. "But, if I recall the true story correctly, Rhys's ancestor bought the estate in Queen Elizabeth's reign after the last owner died impoverished."

"So once upon a time," Colleen concluded, "the Kendalls had money. How did they lose it?"

"Rhys's father preferred racing horses to tending the family estate. Tragically, his mind was often muddled, especially after his wife died. Rhys, even as a lad of twelve, would come down from school to help Bennett manage the farms and mills. What did a child know about growing wheat or making yard goods? But Rhys tried. He succeeded for a while, and then his major supply of cotton from our Southern states was cut by the outbreak of our Civil War. They called it the Cotton Famine here. In 'sixty-four or five, Rhys suffered a catastrophe when his main factory burned to the ground. He and your father, Ann, have not been friendly since. Skip does not tell me why. Rhys tries to keep his businesses and farms profitable, but it is a struggle. He lives frugally. Worse, he cuts himself off from the very society who could help him."

"So then you doubt he'll come?" Ann concluded, torn between elation and regret. Ann felt Raine's glance on her but did not meet it. When Ann had received the two books in the mail from Rhys, she had not mentioned it to Raine. But her cousin spied Ann reading them the next day and asked why she had not told her. Ann replied she did not think their arrival was that important, but Raine had stared at her and said, "You mean you wish they weren't."

Raine was so right. In the past three weeks, Ann had not seen Rhys at any of the horse sales in Ireland. He had disappeared from the earth, except for the package that had arrived at their hotel from Liverpool days after the Dublin trials. Rhys's loan of his father's two books about horse breeding in England thrilled her. Her joy at receiving them and reading them never equalled her disappointment of not finding him at any of the events he recommended in his accompanying note. Logic told her that she was just someone he had met by chance, a horse lover worthy of speaking to, lending books to, but not impressive enough to seek out.

She understood his reasoning. She distrusted her father, too, for reasons as old and painful. Yet this morning she knew her father wished to mend those rifts. Commendable of him as that was, her father might also have other less noble goals in mind when he added Rhys to the dinner list. She would be vigilant of that, too.

"Rhys might come." Aunt Peg nodded. "God knows he should. He wants to invest in the cruise line that your father wishes to begin. We shall see."

Skip's dinner party went extremely well. So well that three newspapers noted the event hosted by the millionaire American shipping magnate. *The Gazetteer* had somehow obtained the complete guest list and printed it. *The Illustrated Two Penny* ran a cartoon of two Lords A-Leaping arriving at the front door to Forsythe House with their wives, rendered as diamond-laden Calling Birds. Most surprising to Ann and her friends was *The Tatler,* which described the three American debutantes who accompanied Mr. Brighton to Europe. The paper dubbed them "The American Beauties. Each a cultivated rose of grace, wit, and drama."

Colleen gushed at their newfound fame. "You are grace, Ann. Raine is wit, while I"—she draped herself over a divan like a music hall queen—"must be drama."

Ann buried her nose back in Bennett's tomes about English horse breeding. Of the bachelors who came to inspect the new American wares, one found Ann the highlight of the evening. He was Adam Litchfield, down earlier than expected from Liverpool because of the resolution of his labor dispute. As he bid her good night, he told her he was thrilled he'd come "for the pleasure of becoming acquainted with you." Though Adam was wolfishly attractive, Ann wondered if his attentions to her had any effect on his stoic friend who stood beside him.

Rhys Kendall did not even blink. In fact, he had been businesslike to her father, sweet to her aunt, and polite to Ann. His behavior, she told herself, was exactly what she expected from him. But it was not what she wanted.

Chapter 3

"Every American girl is entitled to have twelve young men devoted to her. They remain her slaves and she rules them with charming nonchalance."

—OSCAR WILDE

"OH, YOU DO REMEMBER ME FROM THIS MORNING," ANN crooned to the black stallion.

She had ridden him at dawn. Tattersall's stable boy had opened up for the sour-faced slim gentleman in the mustache who insisted on seeing—and riding—the black stallion in the loose-box at the rear. Ann had walked him along the empty street of Rotten Row and quickly broken him into a trot and a canter. The animal, more than sixteen hands high and with the strongest, longest legs she'd ever seen, had carried her away like the wind. She had known instantly he was the one she needed to improve her breeding efforts. What's more, she liked the animal's temperament—and he liked hers.

She had returned this afternoon in a skirt to examine him more closely and perhaps buy him. She patted him. "Or maybe you just like women in general, hmmm?"

She chuckled as the horse nuzzled her hair and knocked her hat askew. "I hate the contraption, too," she reassured him, whisking it off and tossing it so it whirled atop one of the stall's iron posts. "You could eat it. I wouldn't mind. You'd get indigestion. I did see a bucket of carrots when I came in, though. How about that instead?"

She left the box and headed back to the front of Tattersall's where the attendant sat. A scuffling in the hayloft above made her crane her neck, but she saw no one.

Odd, she thought as she fetched the carrots. She had heard someone up there at dawn when she'd finished her trial ride of the stallion and returned him to his box. Maybe a stable boy slept up there. *Or maybe I'm too jumpy, looking for mustached thin men who don't exist.*

She returned to the stallion, her reticule draped over her arm, her hands brimming with his treat. "These are the most I could carry," she reassured him as he nibbled, tickling her palms. "You are impeccable. Broad-breasted and straight-backed. I wonder"— she leaned close to whisper in his ear—"do you respond to mares the way you do to me?"

As if he understood, the horse nodded his head up and down, making soft nickering noises. She flung one arm over his neck and hugged him.

But a quick intake of breath had her spinning. Spilling carrots. Reaching for her reticule and her gun.

"Don't shoot!" Rhys Kendall emerged from the shadows, hands up like the soldiers she used to find in her grandfather's barn.

"You surprised me!" Frightened, elated, she aimed her pistol for his heart.

"I must learn not to do that."

She dropped the gun in her bag. "What are you doing here?"

"The same as you. Looking for a good horse."

"I hope it's not this one you're interested in buying."

"No. He's yours, if you like him. I'm looking for a mare."

The head stable man charged around the stall door and peered at her. "Miss Brighton?" Then he took in Rhys Kendall. "Oh, Your Grace, I did not know you'd arrived. Are you"—he turned to Ann—"all right, or shall I call your Mr. O'Leary for you?"

"No, thank you. I'm fine. I know the Duke."

"Very good, miss. If you need assistance—"

"She'll be safe from me, Howard." Rhys leaned back against the timber wall and crossed his arms.

"Yes, Your Grace," the man muttered, but shot Rhys a warning glance before he left them alone.

Rhys smiled slowly, running his eyes over her face and hair so fast she stopped breathing. "I am sorry I frightened you. I'll be sure to clomp loudly when I approach you from now on. You look wonderfully fresh," he said so softly she could barely hear him. "The weather in England agrees with you. Makes your skin a deeper rose."

She suspected her color came from a blush at his compliment. She knew he was making small talk, but he didn't have to. The way he had ignored her at their dinner party told her what he thought about her, which was very little. Distance from him was what she needed, and so she gave him a curter reply than he might have expected. "I think the British Isles should be inhabited by penguins. It's nearly May"—she tugged at the collar of her amethyst cape—"and I'm still wearing wool."

Two men ambled along the length of the stable. One with rimless spectacles examined them with leisure on their way to the next stall. But it was the other man who didn't look at her who gave her a moment's doubt. He was short, thin, but without a mustache. She squinted at him, not recognizing anything else familiar.

"Did you come here alone?" Rhys asked when the two had passed—and he had not done more than blink at the thin man.

"My father's man escorts us almost everywhere. My Aunt Peg says Tattersall's is one of the few places it's acceptable for a woman to go without a chaperone."

Rhys moved a fraction so that the sunlight streaming in the window bronzed his thick hair. He hadn't gotten it cut in far too long, and the curls were now so unruly that his locks reminded her of those on statues of Greek gods. The rest of him matched that image, too. Dressed in chocolate tweed riding jacket and fawn jodhpurs that clung to a powerful body, he seemed taller, broader, sweeter than her memory had allowed.

"Howard likes to make certain it remains that way." Rhys was talking about the stable man, and she forced her mind from measuring Rhys's exciting dimensions to addressing his topic. "The owners hope they'll make more sales if ladies feel free to inspect the wares unencumbered."

"Women prefer to shop by themselves," she replied. "I do. Especially for horses. You never know what kind of animal you're getting until you put him through his paces. Bareback, preferably."

The oddest look spread over Rhys's face. "Are you

telling me that you have ridden this stallion? Bare-back?"

She lowered her voice. "Don't say anything to anyone, will you? They all think that a Mister Bridgeton came to look over the animal this morning. He rode him, but alas"—she feigned displeasure—"this is London, after all, and bareback is not done. The gentleman regretfully rode the beast in a regular English saddle."

"I see." Rhys pursed his mouth in glee. "What does this gentleman look like? Might I have met him?"

"Oh." She shook her head adamantly. "Absolutely not. He's very reclusive. Keeps to his house."

"But he is . . . ?" Rhys put a hand up as if he were measuring someone.

She nodded, loving this banter. "About my height."

"Hmm. Your weight?"

"You might say. He has a mustache, though."

"Thin, is it?"

"Tough to keep groomed, too." She twitched her nose, then sawed a forefinger under it. "Glue is hard to remove."

Rhys guffawed. "A tall, thin, stuck-up fellow. Sorry I missed him. I wonder about his taste in tailors." His gaze swept from her throat to her hem, and as it meandered back, her knees knocked, her thighs pressed together, and her breasts burned. Her ability to think ceased as he vowed, "I'd love to see the cut of his clothes. Especially what he likes in hats."

She snorted. "He *loathes* them."

"How did I know?" he murmured, licking his lower lip in a lazy way while he considered her curls. "What does he do with all his hair?"

"Wears a net," she whispered. "Like ladies do

under wigs and hairpieces. It keeps his hat on fairly well."

His shoulders shook in laughter. "Extraordinary. Does he come out only at dawn?"

"Yes, he's shy, but he needs to train an Irish bay mare he recently bought in Dublin. He becomes more adventurous, though, and so you never know where he might appear."

"Forewarned is forearmed. Well, tell me, does he travel with a lot of money?" She could have sworn he forced a grin as he indicated her reticule. "How much cash do you have in there today?"

"None," she replied, enjoying his look of amazement. "I have deposited my money in my own account in a bank, you'll be happy to hear."

"And you've seen no one following you?"

Though she had looked, she hadn't seen anyone. "Not anywhere in weeks. I find only you. Again."

"Should I flatter myself to think you now take my advice and write only bank drafts?"

"When I do buy something, which is rare, yes, I write a check. I've been coming here for three weeks regularly, and I began to doubt there'd be anything I wanted." *But now I see more than I hoped for.*

His gaze went to her mouth.

Her mind went to mush. "The only other horse I've admired in London was one I saw last week on Rotten Row. A stallion ridden by a young man. But he was not for sale."

"The young man?" Rhys arched a wicked brow.

She rolled her eyes. "I didn't ask."

"You were with your friends. You didn't have to ask."

She chastised him with a sidelong glance. "Your newspapers say my cousin and friends and I are here to buy husbands the way the Jerome sisters seem to have done. But that's not entirely true. I'm not," she amended, leaving Colleen to explain her own motivation.

"I know what you want. Horses. But that doesn't stop people from gossiping, Ann. They'll take what they see and draw conclusions. The word is that the American Beauties—especially the tall, graceful one with rosewood hair—have sent a few London bachelors to their knees."

"Good heavens," she murmured. "How undignified."

"It's a useful pose, if one is looking for a wife."

"American women like men who stand up. These fellows are just getting their trousers dirty."

He chuckled. "Grace, wit, and drama. Perhaps *The Tatler* should have changed the 'grace' to read 'pluck.'"

"That would certainly scare most men away from me." She turned away to stroke the neck of the stallion.

"I thought it from the start"—he moved closer—"and I'm not frightened."

"Really?" She could smell his soap. The balsam aroma reminded her of warm fires and winter. The first she loved, the latter she could do without. In the same way, she felt caught between the extremes of what he said to her now and how he had acted at their party. "At dinner, you assumed I had the plague, I guess."

"No. I hurt you. God, I didn't mean to. My manners must be rustier than I thought, and . . . well, the damn truth is I thought I could be polite to you and you'd never notice me, especially since Adam Litchfield was doing such a good job of occupying your time." He sounded hoarse. "I have made it a rule to avoid social gatherings. When I first received your invitation, I was ready to refuse it, but I came because I had to. Because I wanted—" He touched her arm, and she eluded him.

"How long do you stay in town?" She changed the subject, praying for composure and a quick escape.

His hand fell to his side. He balled his fist. "Only until next Wednesday. Perhaps longer if I decide to buy into a new venture—"

"The cruise line."

"Yes. I must come up with the two thousand pounds for the initial investment next Monday."

"Their first stockholders' meeting."

He nodded. "I must work quickly if I'm to raise enough capital. I refuse to speculate with any regular income I receive from my estates. I never gamble, you see. So I have decided that I must sell a few small assets."

She was surprised at this when her father had said Rhys was not the type to part with any valuable goods. "Nothing irreplaceable, I hope."

"Everything we love is irreplaceable." The desolation on his face reminded her of a captain in the First Virginia Cavalry who had shot his injured mount through the head to end the animal's misery. "Necessity forces us to be bold."

Her finely knit composure unraveled. Compassion for Rhys rushed through her like a swollen river. His eyes went blank as they drifted from her to the stallion. Insight flashed through her. "Oh, Rhys, he's yours, isn't he?"

"He is precisely what you've been looking for, Ann. His sire earned more than a hundred blue rosettes for my father. One Derby. One St. Leger. His dam almost as many. They have other get as beautiful but not as serene. Buy him, Ann. He'll do you proud."

In the set of Rhys's broad mouth, she could see his anguish. She had the mad desire to smooth it away. With her fingers or, better, her lips. "Don't sell him."

"I must."

"But—"

"I found a mare here I want to buy for my tenants on one of my farms in the north. They made me promise I'd spend no more than their rent money, but the price of the mare I want to buy here is higher than the rent, and I need the extra cash."

"If I hadn't outbid you in Dublin, you—"

"Ann, I would have had to sell Raider sooner or later. I do not have the time, money, or interest to race him or put him to stud. He can breed new racers for other men or walking horses for you. If you don't buy him, believe me, he's got such superb lineage that someone else will."

"I hate to take your horse from you."

"I inherited Raider when my father died five years ago. I have kept him, but I'm not the expert horseman my father was. I have too many other occupations. I have mills to run. Farms to administer. The largest one is this one near Blackburn." His glistening brown eyes admired her features. "I'm glad it will be you Raider goes to. You'll take great care of him." He stroked the horse's mane, an intimate good-bye that made the animal whinny and brought a lump to Ann's throat. "Be good, old man. You have a fine life ahead of you in America with a lot of willing mares. What more could a man ask for?" He turned, his smile no mask for his loss. "You pay the bursar here as in Dublin. They send the money round to me." He put his hand out, but she did not take it. "Say good-bye to me, Grace."

She couldn't let him go this time without knowing the full story of what had happened between him and her father. "What did my father do to you?"

Rhys looked at her squarely. "I find it difficult to be with your father in public or private. I debate if I want to be associated with him in any way. But I was encouraged to participate in this company by Adam and another old friend, and I am attracted by the potentially high profits of the cruise line. Still, I am wary of your father."

"You and so very many others."

"Do you mean"—he searched her face—"that you, too, distrust him?"

"I wish I didn't."

"He is a ruthless man. Or, at least until I saw him in Dublin I always thought so. Now there is some aspect to his behavior that begins to change my view of him."

"He is different," Ann agreed, thinking that if she told Rhys about her father's hope to make amends to him, Rhys might scoff.

"Yet I question your father's motives. I have great reason to.

"More than fifteen years ago, I took over the running of my father's textile mills. I was young but eager—and my father preferred horse racing and stud farming to mundane matters of import and manufacture. I was nearly eighteen, but youth and arrogance are often brothers in self-delusion. I began to import raw cotton from ports out of the Carolinas and Georgia. Your father delivered most of my supply regularly throughout your Civil War. One night, as the bales were being delivered by your father and his men to my docks, my mill caught fire. Everyone pointed to your father's best friend and partner, Owen MacIntyre, as the culprit. According to all accounts, he lit a bale in revenge over a fistfight he lost to my foreman. Thirty-two people died in the blaze. Twenty-one survived, hideously burned and maimed. MacIntyre disappeared. Your father claimed no responsibility and demanded his payment for the shipment. Either that, or he threatened to sell it to a competitor of mine. I needed the bales that were untouched. I had to provide what work I could for my people. I got a loan and paid your father, but it put me in such straits that I have not recovered. I have resented Skip Brighton for more than a decade."

Unsurprised, knowing the bitterness of her own feelings against a man for whom money justified every act, Ann narrowed her eyes at the crossbeams. "I understand."

"No, you don't." He caught her chin with two fingers and brought her gaze to his. His thumb brushed the edge of her lower lip, a tantalizing caress of man to woman the likes of which she'd never experienced. He caught her around the waist and pressed her flush to him. He moved, molding their bodies into a landscape that fired her imagination and made her yearn for a different time and place without this conflict between them.

His breath was warm against her temple, his voice rough with regret when he explained, "Graceful Ann, you are the most intriguing woman I have met since I was nine and proposed to our milkmaid in Dundalk. My father told me then that one does not court disaster, especially where women are concerned. Absence, he said, does not make the heart grow fonder, it makes the heart forget. My father was right"—he glanced down to adore her eyes—"until I saw you. In the past few weeks, I could not roust you from my mind. I could not do more than be polite to your father and civil to you, because if I did, I'd break my own code of ethics."

Rejection by a man was not new to her. She had felt its sting from her father. She knew its punch from Quinn. What she had not predicted was the way Rhys's gutted her.

She stood her ground. "I'm so glad you told me."

"Are you?" He dropped his hands, his expression bleak. "Perhaps then you can walk away."

She never knew how, but she turned.

Before she took two steps, he caught her around the waist. "To hell with ethics, when this is what I want." He crushed her close, seizing her mouth in a tender assault. The force of his need drove her head back, and, to steady her, he braced her neck with hands plunging beneath her chignon. She felt her hair spill around them. He made a strangled sound while he taught her how to kiss in endless new ways.

"Ann," he muttered while he fought for air and she for sanity, "you taste better than I dreamed."

He kissed her again, softer, sweeter, but no less insane than before. This time, his tongue slid along the seam of her lips and delved inside to savor her in a shocking delight.

Ann wrapped her arms around him. Solid, warm,

wonderful, Rhys anointed her with fire and the desire for more kisses than she knew they should share.

Hopeless with that thought, she pushed away. He stood, brown eyes wide with shock.

This time, when she walked away, he did not stop her.

Chapter 4

"Girls may be divided into two classes—the Visible and the Invisible. . . . To be beautiful implies to be seen, and it follows that one of woman's first duties is to be visible."

—MRS. HAWEIS, *The Art of Beauty*

THE NEXT AFTERNOON, ANN NUDGED RAIDER INTO ROTten Row.

Beside her, John O'Leary drove the black victoria her father had recently purchased to display "his girls," as he termed the four of them. Aunt Peggie propped herself amid the voluminous scarlet needlepoint and cut brocade cushions, nodding to this one and that, stopping the carriage occasionally to speak politely to another. Next to her perched Gus, who was young enough to view the spectacle but not considered old enough to ride independently and thus show off her horsemanship or her figure. Behind the open carriage, Colleen and Raine rode two matching blue roan geldings from the Forsythe House stables. The throngs of proper London set out today in their finery to enjoy the warmest sunshine yet of the spring season. Men, married and unattached, and women, young and old with their husbands or, barring that, their chaperones or mamas—came to preen, see, and be seen.

"Ann," Raine called, "look over at that corner. It's Rhys Kendall."

In black riding jacket and bisque jodhpurs, one hand to the reins and one to his thigh, he sat his mount like a king reviewing a personal procession. He'd acquired a horse almost as impressive as Raider, but it was he who looked formidable and dashing. He who made her spine tingle and her eyes blind to any other man.

Ann was not the only one bedazzled. Ladies paused their tidy tilburies and topless barouches before him. Words idled among them; laughter tinkled the air like crystal chimes. He nodded; they inclined their heads as was the proper way to exit the presence of a duke of the realm.

There was no way to avoid him. Ann's hands fisted on her reins. Her insides rolled like a butterchurn. Didn't he say he did not attend public gatherings? Why had he changed his mind? They would pass by him, have to speak, and she would have to thank him publicly for the gift he'd sent her this morning. One white rose.

"Good afternoon, Mrs. Gallagher," he greeted Aunt Peggie with a grin that could have melted polar ice. He doffed his hat, the wind ruffling his mane so badly Ann clenched her fingers with the wish to comb it. "I'm delighted to see you again."

"As am I, Your Grace. I hope you remember Miss Augusta VanderHorn." Gus lowered her head.

"Her sister, Miss Colleen VanderHorn." Colleen murmured her delight to see him again and dropped her chin in recognition of his status.

"My niece, Miss Raine Montand." Raine smiled and nodded.

"And our darling Ann, you know so well." After his

lavish rose had arrived this morning at Forsythe House, everyone buzzed with conjecture about precisely how well the Duke of Carlton and Dundalk wished to know Ann Brighton.

"I do, indeed," he said in a voice deep with concern.

Ann felt her blood pulse with frustration that she couldn't find the right words to convey her joy over his elegant rose—and her anger that he'd sent it when, for so many reasons, their relationship could never blossom.

Her gaze met his. *Why did you send that rose? Your card? Why write the rose was "no beauty to your grace"?*

Edging forward, Raider whickered softly, nudging Rhys's knee. The move was so poignant Ann understood how the animal must have remembered his former master's sweetness. How could anyone forget it?

Or his kisses?

She'd recalled them too often yesterday and far into the night. Then she'd relived them after breakfast when their butler presented her with a small box. She'd lifted the lid and torn open the vellum envelope to view the heraldic emblem of the Duke of Carlton and Dundalk. Embossed in gold, two arrows crossed with one lush rose upon an oblong shield. To push aside the golden tissue and find a freshly cut fullblown flower stunned her. But not as much as when she'd touched the petals and recalled the texture of Rhys's lips the more. Velvet. Sleek and moist . . .

Fear clogged her throat. She tried to speak and couldn't.

She liked him. She cared for him with an ache of longing she had never felt for Quinn. That she could desire Rhys—his laughter, his kisses—frightened her. Her father had been right to conclude that her mother and he had influenced her thinking about men and marriage. She'd learned that opening her heart to someone meant she could be hurt by him.

Aunt Peg cleared her throat. Raine spoke her name.

Rhys tilted his head. "Ann, I hope you liked—"

She drew back on her reins to pull Raider from him.

Adam Litchfield rode up, stopping next to Rhys. Urbane and sleek with piercing delft blue eyes that wandered over Ann with appreciation, he greeted the others first.

"Good afternoon, Miss Brighton." Adam examined Ann and Rhys in one sweep. "Wonderfully sunny day." When Ann gave him a halfhearted smile for an answer, he turned to Rhys. "You're looking pale. Perhaps you need a ride in the sun, oh Duke of Tweedledum and Tweedledee," Adam jested.

"Perhaps I should give you a run for your money, Lord Rich Fields," Rhys retorted with a friendly smile.

"Never known you to bet, old man. What's the occasion?"

Aunt Peg put a hand to her throat, dismayed at this thinly veiled hostility among friends in public.

Adam spied her reaction and chuckled. "Not to worry, Mrs. Gallagher. His Grace and I are only sparring as we have for decades. We met when our mothers exchanged visits—when was it, Rhys?— when we were first in knee pants?"

"Before we were breeched, Lord Rich Fields."

Ann couldn't bear the tension anymore. "Perhaps you could ride with me, Lord Litchfield, and inform me."

Adam glanced at Rhys, playfully triumphant. To her, he was serene. "I'd be delighted. Shall we, Miss Brighton?"

They rode together for a few blocks along the crowded lane, with Ann attempting to put on a show of interest and succeeding when Adam asked if he might call on the morrow. Ann's first thought was to refuse him. But as she scanned the throng, looking for a genteel way to do the dastardly deed after she had led him on, she found Rhys Kendall close behind, staring back at her. Alone, he sat his horse with a solemnity that made her eyes sore from the glow of his perfection. But when he turned his horse back the way they'd come, Ann decided she would need amusing company to rid her of a rampaging desire for this man.

"We'd like very much, Adam, if you'd come to tea."

He flashed a roguish grin. "Thank you. I remember fondly the dinner party of a few weeks ago. I look forward to developing our acquaintance."

"You'll enjoy all of us, I hope," she said vacantly, trying to keep track of Rhys's newest female admirer, a blond beauty in scarlet who sat her sidesaddle like a queen, damn her rich blue blood. "At five, then."

"When?"

"What?"

"Tea. Today?"

"No." She didn't want Adam so soon, preferably not at all. "Next week. Tuesday."

"Tuesday it is."

Ann wished it would never come and took the next few minutes to distance herself in word and politesse from a man she'd led on unfairly. When she saw her family's entourage came abreast of her on the Row,

Ann eagerly rejoined them and left Adam with a serviceable smile.

God, what had she done? Encouraged a man she cared little about to enter her home and try to charm her, her cousin, and her friends. Her father would welcome him because Adam had already invested in the cruise line. He would also be thrilled that she had invited an eligible man to call on her. She dreaded it.

"My God," Aunt Peg moaned two mornings later, crushing a newspaper in her lap. "The *Gazetteer*'s reporter saw what happened with the Duke of Carlton in Rotten Row, and they've printed a story in this horrid gossip sheet!" She reached for her tea and, thus fortified, plopped her glasses on her nose for another look. The other three girls huddled over her shoulder to read while Ann marveled at the words.

" 'What Grace-ful American debutante delivered the cut direct to the Scion of one of the oldest dukedoms of Our Fair Land? And, Dear Reader, you may inquire, why? To favor his friend. How did the gentleman recover from the affront? He smiled as if it never happened. *That* is the stuff of good breeding.' "

That sent Ann from her chair. "That's not true! I was polite."

"You rode off with Earl Litchfield before you said one word to the Duke." Aunt Peg was shaking her head. "These breaches of etiquette are not overlooked here, my dear. And now to have Lord Litchfield for tea."

"What's wrong with him coming?"

"A young lady does not invite a single man for such an intimate at-home event unless he is a candidate to become a formal member of the group."

"Well, he's not. He's just—" Not a friend. Or a suitor. "An acquaintance."

"We'll simply rally around." Aunt Peg tried to look valiant. "We'll show him a miscalculation has been made, that's all."

With the need to escape them and her own self-criticism, Ann decided she needed some exercise to keep her embarrassment at bay, and she turned to Gus. "I think we need to leave for our fencing lesson now. Heaven forbid we'd offend anyone by being late."

The Frenchman whom her father had found to perfect Gus's and Ann's thrust and parry operated his academy on the edge of Leicester Square. Monsieur de la Roche, who had fled his native Paris when Germans marched in five years ago, came to England to make his mark teaching young men and women the refinements of wielding foil, saber, and epee. He was succeeding in polishing Gus's skill faster than Ann's and for the past two sessions had sent Gus upstairs to individual instruction with one of his best swordsmen.

This afternoon, as the sun blazed through the two-story Palladian windows, Ann ignored the stares she got from his other patrons who had obviously read *The Gazetteer* or heard about its contents. Luckily, she knew none of them personally, save for one. Adam Litchfield.

Determined to be kind but brief with him, she was relieved when he said he awaited his usual partner, a childhood friend. "We have a standing engagement when both of us are in town." He nodded toward the balcony along which private jousting rooms awaited patrons with a fine skill and great taste for the sport.

If Adam examined her too long for her comfort,

Ann put it down to his interest in her severely cut fencing outfit. Unlike the other women here who thought pantaloons might do, Ann had tried that ridiculous fashion in New York and found it wanting. When she and Gus had first enrolled in the class at Mrs. Drummond's, their teacher had recommended the sparer cut of a soft gray cotton suit tailored to the needs of the sport. The material not only breathed, it moved. Ann's strokes became quicker and surer, more supple in the suit. If Adam did not like the outfit, so be it. She had come to enjoy this lesson, and, by heaven, despite Adam Litchfield, cursed newspapers, and English propriety, she would wear what she wished, speak to whom she wished—or not.

She smiled and excused herself politely from Adam. Disappointment fled across his features, but Ann dismissed his reaction. He was coming to tea next Tuesday. That was enough, or rather too much attention to give him.

With a flourish of her sword, she became accustomed to its weight and began to practice her positions before the floor-length mirror with a fury that had Monsieur appearing at her side, circling her and clucking.

"Mademoiselle Brighton, non. The foil, it requires a diplomacy. It is sharp. So, we must be cool to deliver the worst cut."

Hand on her hip, she blew strands of hair from her brow and ruefully considered her blade. "Monsieur, by all accounts, I know how to do that too well."

"But I understood why," a consoling baritone explained.

She spun.

Rhys Kendall, dressed in a stunning white jousting

suit, raised his mesh mask, then saluted her with his epee and the flourish of a worthy opponent. "At your service, *Mademoiselle.*"

She could feel the other patrons in the room pause. Adam headed for the stairs. Monsieur drifted away.

"The one time I don't have my derringer, and I could aim it well," she complained to hide her thrill that Rhys was here and so damned courteous. Yet she had insulted him badly Tuesday in the Row.

"On me, of course." His verbal parry held a rogue's dégagé.

"No. On me."

His eyes darkened to a delicious fudge. "You are so straightforward, it's refreshing."

"I thought here that was called brash."

"Not to me." He stepped closer, his words barely more than a whisper, but growing urgent, demanding. "Curtsy to me, Grace. If you don't do it, I shall have to pursue you until you surrender."

"Is this a show of ducal power?" she challenged when she wished to hug him for this act of graciousness.

"This is one man's concern."

She relented a bit. "You are kind, but—"

"Don't try to dismiss me. You can't drive me away. The truth of the matter is that I will not stand by and see you ruin your reputation because you failed to observe the formalities. Ann"—his voice was husky with need—"why didn't you speak with me on Tuesday?"

"I couldn't." She would tell him some of the truth. Her eyes darted over the others, who pretended to return to their practice but seemed to be listening to the echoes in the cavernous room. "I saw how Raider missed you, and it broke me in two. I should never have bought him."

"Yes, you should. He deserves to go to someone who will love him and develop his potential. You are that person. I would not feel half so good at losing him were he to have been bought by anyone else. But I am desolate, sweet Grace, that you suffered in the meeting. I went there to see you, and I—"

"No," she whispered, struck by his admission.

"Oh, yes. I stood on that corner on that miserable nag waiting for you to ride by." Amusement twinkled in his eyes. Self-deprecation swept it away. "I deserved what you did, though, of course, *The Gazetteer*'s reporter could not know that, nor could he possibly take sides with a gorgeous American against a peer of the glorious kingdom of St. Andrew and St. George."

"You need not worry about me." She took a step away.

"But I do," he confessed, and that stopped her. "Don't leave me like this. They're watching, Grace."

The endearment sliced her heart open as surely as if he'd used his weapon. "Don't call me that."

"Grace? You live and breathe the word. I saw it from the start, remember. I am not alone, either. Others recognize it. Friends of mine. Adam especially appreciates you, and I am jealous. To be precise, I am bitter. Galled because other men might have your company, and I tell myself I cannot."

"Oh, Rhys, please stop. This gets us nowhere."

"I—am—here," he pronounced with a precision that skewered her and made her face him, "because I wish to offer you the opportunity to redeem yourself."

She swallowed, fearing to look left or right and find her surprise reflected in the others' expressions. "You mean to say you sought me out here as well?" Since Adam said he was here to meet a friend, she had concluded Rhys was that person.

"After I saw that entry about us in the paper, what else could I do? I knew I would go anywhere to save you from yourself. I asked about. I may possess little money, but I have friends and those who wish to think they are. Many people know you come here for lessons. It served my purpose to meet you in a public place."

That left her speechless.

"Close your mouth, darling. Curtsy to me. Just a little to salve their need for order. Just enough to restore you to their acceptance. Do it, and I will smile politely and show them that we are—I hope—still friends."

"Is that what you call our relationship?" She was piqued at how impossible—and how sweet—friendship with him could be. "How can we be while you and my father remain enemies?"

"Your father has absolutely nothing to do with what I feel for you. The minute I first saw you, I was attracted to you. Yes, I was shocked when I learned who you were, and I had to walk away. I pondered what I did think about you for weeks between the Dublin sale and your dinner party. I realized Monday at Tattersall's how much my behavior hurt you. But Ann, our kisses showed me I never want to cause you pain. Do *not* go yet." He stepped to one side to block her from leaving him. "Against my will and my better judgment, I began to care for you enough to want to see you on Rotten Row Tuesday, and I sent the rose in an attempt to apologize." His voice dropped to a whisper. "Let me, Ann."

She delighted in his revelation. "I was terrible to

you. I owe you the apology. Your rose"—she found only poor words to match her gratitude—"was lovely."

"It was the most perfect one I could find in Kendall Manor's garden. Still, it was not worthy for you."

Tears sprang up. She couldn't cry here. Not for this wild joy she felt. Someone might see. Did the reporter for the *Gazetteer* fence?

Rhys smiled compassionately. "My family has grown alba roses on our estates since one of my ancestors brought them from a Crusade in Damascus. We give them as a sign of support for an ally or admiration for a lady."

For an eternity, she stood, absorbing the meaning of his words. "I am"—*thrilled*—"honored."

He inhaled sharply. "Please gaze at me with dispassion, can you, Grace? They're recording it for repetition at teatime, and I want them to say how the lovely American recovered her reputation this afternoon, not"—he looked desolate—"how she looked at the Duke of Carlton and slayed him with the appreciation in her eyes. Darling, listen to me now and understand this." His throat contracted with an emotion that made him fierce. "I care about you, what happens to you. I fear nothing can change that. So, in recompense for a duke's broad-mindedness to overlook a public slight, do me this service, will you, Grace, curtsy to me now?"

She sank as Aunt Peg had taught her, soliciting one of Rhys Kendall's broadest grins. He took her hand to help her rise, and his happiness faded. "Say good-bye to me now and walk away."

The last time he'd told her to walk away and she'd done it, he had captured her. Kissed her. Tested her belief that it was best to appraise a man objectively, never desire him physically or need him emotionally. Panic that she would leave now and never see him again swept through her like a brushfire.

"Please don't look so bereft, darling. It's proper etiquette for the lady to leave a duke's presence once she's done her duties by him."

"I suddenly fear the word *good-bye* is not in my American vocabulary."

"*Au revoir?* Or perhaps *auf Wiedersehen?*" he asked, his forlorn look adding fuel to the blaze of her despair.

"Languages," she replied with a dwindling hope he would seek her out in other places for new and stirring reasons, "were not my best subjects in school."

"I can interpret," he ground out, and against every rule, each propriety, he lifted her hand to his lips and dropped a hot, hard kiss to her knuckles. "Until we see each other again," he said against her tingling skin. "Go quickly," he commanded, his head bent so that her last glimpse of him was of his dark wild curls.

" 'Grace curtsies!' " Aunt Peggie read at teatime the next afternoon, and then crushed her paper in her lap. "Oh, my God, Ann, *The Gazetteer* has another piece in here about you and Rhys Kendall."

Raine emerged from her copy of *The Times.* "Sugar, you saw him again?" Her cousin had reason to frown because Ann confided in her about most things. Telling Raine about Rhys's encounter was an exception. Ann wanted to savor what he had said and done to redeem her. With the *Gazetteer*'s newest report, Rhys's efforts might still be for nothing. "Please read us the whole piece, Aunt Peg."

Colleen and Gus echoed her instructions, their needlework gone idle in their hands.

Her father peered at her from his desk, where he stopped reading his pile of private correspondence. "What have you done, Ann?" Rising anger stained his pale cheeks.

"What I should have the other day in Rotten Row. I remembered my manners. Read it, please, Aunt Peg. It should—it had better say that."

Peg cleared her throat and shook out the tabloid. "'Our American visitor seems to have learned that to rise to one's duty often means sinking prettily out of respect. Our Scion has restored her to Society. Meanwhile, Your Observer wonders what His Grace intends for the young lady whose hand he kissed so madly that the two of them parted with such sweet sorrow. And how does this affect His Grace's best friend who comes to call on Grace at teatime Tuesday?'"

"Who can this observer be?" Ann was out of her chair, to the bay window of their drawing room to glance out on the street. The elderly woman with her flower cart was finishing her daily turn into Belgrave Square. Lord Ravensby was arriving home from his afternoon wherever he'd spent it. No one else walked the street. Ann found no one loitering or following her about. Not even any short, thin man with a mustache. She hadn't seen a soul like that, not in weeks of rabid searching. So just who was this reporter who seemed to go everywhere she did? "How can he learn these things?"

"Let's hear the rest of it, Aunt Peg," her father requested.

"That's about all, Skip. Just 'We shall endeavor to discover this for you, Dear Reader.'"

"What went on between you and Rhys?" her father probed, his voice at a dangerous low.

Ann faced him as he removed a handkerchief from his pocket and wiped his brow. "Nothing as auspicious as it recounts, I'm afraid." That bit of fabrication concealed her own need to keep Rhys's words as a treasure to be savored personally. Especially since she was positive she would not see him again. "Rhys sought me out to give me the opportunity to curtsy. I did. That is all."

Her father examined her thoroughly. "He kissed your hand?" She nodded. "You made cow eyes at each other?"

"Good heavens." She gave a sharp laugh and dragged a hand through her hair. "How would I know?"

He cut her a look from the corner of his eye. "How, indeed. Some way this *Gazetteer* fellow learns a lot. Who would tell him that Adam is coming to tea on Tuesday?"

Ann strode forward to deposit her cup and saucer on the tea tray. "I'd bet none of *us* has talked with our friendly observer."

Her father ignored her sarcasm. "I worry that these gossip sheets may decide to capitalize on your actions."

Aunt Peg agreed. "The English have a haughty attitude toward jolly American girls with money. They think we've come to show them up, buy their castles and their pride—"

"When all we're doing is visiting," Colleen added and the others gave her a glance that said, *Oh, really, from you of all people!* "Well, we *are*."

Gussie reached for another cake from the silver tier. "*We* are. You lie in ambush for a prince of the realm, Coll. Don't fuss now, we love you for your honesty."

"The fact remains," Skip insisted, "that you three

82

are intriguing subjects for newspapers." He focused on Ann. "Scandal is no way to endear the English to us."

Nor to finalize your negotiations on the cruise line. "I realize, Father, that you wouldn't want one investor pitted against a potential one."

"Especially not days away from the first meeting of the board of directors. If Adam pulls out, Ann, I know at least two friends of his who may go with him. I'll have to replace them. I cannot do that by Monday. They are men with ties to the government. Men whose influence with trade and foreign issues is vital. And if Rhys refuses to sign"—her father stepped closer, a white edge of fury around his mouth—"he'll throw over his best chance to earn a fortune. My only chance to . . ." He stopped, stared at her. His nostrils flared. "You could *ruin* us all."

"I assure you, Father, I have no intentions of creating problems for you."

"Tonight is the perfect opportunity to show me that." He meant the Rothschilds' masquerade ball. "Adam will be there, and Rhys won't. Or I should say, he never used to attend these events. But if Rhys comes or not, you must treat Adam courteously. He probably assumes that since he is to come to tea Tuesday, he has your favor. You must clarify what you feel for him because—"

"I will not jeopardize your company, Father. Nor my own agreement to act as your devoted daughter." *That would dash my own hopes to return home with enough money to be independent of any man.*

Only four and half more months, and she'd be free.

She swept up her skirts. "If you'll excuse me, I think I'll take a nap before we dress." Her smile wobbled.

Her feet served her better. Walking evenly out of the drawing room, she closed the double doors and hurried up the circular stairs. She reached for the knob and noted her door stood ajar. She had not left it that way less than half an hour ago. She knew, she remembered, because she was so methodical and always put things in their proper places.

Like her reticule. A firm leather bag, which she used every day and stood upon her tiny French desk, closed. Never open, as it was at this moment, on her dressing table.

She stood for a minute, trying to reason how this might have happened.

The only solution was that someone had moved it. Her maid, perhaps. But why? To clean? No, the day for dusting was not Fridays but Tuesdays.

She checked the contents. Her gloves were there, ones she'd worn this morning to the bank to make a deposit of her father's monthly check. They were folded, thumbs tucked inside precisely the way she left them. Her palm-sized mirror and a small rouge pot were there, too. She extracted her small crocheted purse and drew open the strings. Her money remained. All of it. Five pounds, ten pence. So, too, did her bank book in which all her assets were listed, including her sixteen hundred dollars of inheritance money and the monthly deposits from her father. Now a total of seven thousand and six hundred dollars, converted and listed in the British pounds in which he paid her.

Why would anyone examine the contents of her purse?

She scanned her bedroom. Nothing else seemed misplaced. She checked her drawers, her lingerie chest, her writing desk. Not until she opened her wardrobe, however, did she have reason to pause. Her black serge trousers and coat in which she rode each morning hung at the back of the rack. Askew on their hangers.

Whoever had invaded her room had botched the job.

Chapter 5

"There is only one thing in the world worse than being talked about, and this is not being talked about."

—Oscar Wilde

"I MUST TALK WITH YOU BEFORE WE LEAVE FOR THE ball," Ann began when her father responded to her knock at his study door three hours later. She had dressed and come downstairs earlier than the others going to the Rothschilds' masquerade ball. She had predicted he would be there working, attired in his tails and not any costume like all others would wear. She would never have predicted that he would look so harried—or unkempt. His hair was ruffled, his cravat, once tied, now undone. "I have a few questions, but is there something wrong? You look—"

"I'm busy." He remained seated, carefully folded a paper in his hand, but stuffed it underneath a pile of others on his desk.

"I won't take more than a few minutes," she told him after a few seconds of examining him.

"What is it?" he asked sharply, eyes on the stack of papers. When she didn't answer, he said in a kinder tone, "Sit down."

His office bespoke Skip Brighton's wealth and de-

termination. He had furnished the manly burled-ash
room in caramel leather sofas and chairs and created
a golden cast over a room fit for the man with the
Midas touch. The reading table held one book only, a
testament to his neatness. So, too, was his desk. Ann
knew from whom she inherited her tendency to put
each thing in its own place.

"I will stand, thank you." *The better to keep my
advantage.*

His eyes fell over her medieval costume of gold-shot
teal. "The gown is too lovely to crush. But the hat"—
he indicated the huge conelike contraption she held in
one hand—"is superb, if you can keep it on."

He was being polite, avoiding more conflict between them. "I will try," she gave him, and plunged
on. "When you and Aunt Peg reviewed the references
of our servants, were there any who had questionable
reputations?"

"If there were, we did not employ them. Why?"

"I think someone went through my belongings in
my bedroom this afternoon. Nothing is missing."

His eyes popped wide. "How do you know, and
what exactly did they disturb?" When she told him,
he frowned. "Is this the first time it's happened?"

"As far as I can tell, yes." When his expression
deepened to a scowl, she asked, "Why?"

"Well, that does it," he said, coming to a conclusion. "You must stop going out to ride in that man's
suit."

She balked. "Someone invades my privacy and you
punish me? That doesn't make sense."

He drummed his fingers on the pile of papers. "I
will speak with the housekeeper and the head butler.
Whoever has gone through your room must be found
and their services terminated. But in the meantime,

you must cooperate. Clearly, there is a spy in the house, and that person is working for the *Gazetteer*'s reporter."

"I concede there is that possibility, but to coop me up as a result is not—"

"You will do this, I tell you." He surged to his feet.

"Do not treat me like some nitwit, Father. I am old enough to ride astride or bareback if I want. You cannot control me all your life."

"Is that what I'm doing? I thought I was protecting you. Isn't *that* what you accuse me of failing to do during the war? Aren't you the one who is in control now? Earning money to leave *me?*" He took his ever-present handkerchief from his pocket and wiped his brow. Perspiring was a new symptom to add to the ever-present cough.

Concern for his health had her stepping forward.

His bout had him sinking to his chair.

"You are not well," she said with a compassion she knew derived from their recent months of companionship. "You haven't been since February. The cough grows more liquid, you become more pale, and now you break out in a sweat when you are angry. Have you seen a doctor lately?" When he nodded, she put a hand to his desk and leaned over. "What does he say?"

"If I go to the Riviera, I might get enough sun to burn it out of me."

"But finalizing the cruise line is more important. What good is a fortune if you're *ill?*" *Or dead.* She snapped away, shocked at the possibility—and her fear he might die.

"This company will make *millions* of dollars. The first liner will be unique. A traveling paradise. People will clamor to sail on it. Soon we'll have to build two, then ten and twenty of them. All floating palaces. Do you think I can pull out now?" He was ranting, snatching at breaths so hard that his face purpled. "Never!"

"Why is *money* more important to you than your life?"

He shot up, his chair banging against the wall. "Because it *is* my life! Because I don't have *anything* else *anyone* values me for! I failed you. I failed your mother. I failed your brother. If I could buy my way out of this illness, I would."

The desolation of his words rocked her. She'd never known him even to consider defeat. That he would surrender his health for the sake of wealth didn't surprise her as much as the fact that he'd do it without a fight. He was, always had been, more than a survivor. He'd been a fighter.

She had never pleaded with him for anything, but she would now, for his own sake. "Don't do this to yourself. You have enough money to live well for the next century." Her attempt at levity had him glaring at her. "Finish this organizational meeting on Monday, then let's go to the south of France."

"You'd go with me?"

"Of course. If you want me," she added, realizing she had just shown him how much she cared about him.

"It's no escape from the marriage market. Scores of French and Italian noblemen seek lovely brides."

"And fortunes."

"I'd prefer you to marry an Englishman."

"I'd prefer you to mind your own business. Now, do we go south and get toasty or stay here for the

spring chill?" Noises from the hallway meant Aunt Peg, Raine, and Colleen were assembling for their departure.

"I'll consider it." He stood and buttoned his cutaway.

She detected his note of dismissal. "What would make you *do* it?"

He grinned broadly, and she wondered if she had just fallen into a carefully laid trap. "If you charm the pants off Adam Litchfield tonight—"

"Hmmm. There's a charming scene to have printed in the *Gazetteer.*"

He chuckled. "That reporter doesn't have a chance in hell of getting into One forty-eight Piccadilly. Help me, Ann."

"Then you'll show me Monte Carlo."

Aunt Peg was knocking. "Skip, are you ready, dear? The coachman is waiting."

As the party of five got into the brougham for the short ride to the Rothschild mansion, Ann knew she had let the subject of Skip's health take precedence over the intrusion into her room. At breakfast tomorrow morning, she would ask her father to sit in on the questioning of the staff. Only her personal maid, a little girl named Nora, and the upstairs maid, an older woman of thirty or more, had regular access to her room. But any one of the others may have entered when she'd been out. For tonight, she would put the issue aside while she dealt with the rest of London and Adam Litchfield, in particular.

That became easier than she expected.

With Raine and Colleen flanking her, Aunt Peg and her father close behind, Ann climbed out of their brougham. She felt protected if perchance someone would snub her for past meetings with Rhys Kendall and the flurry of newspaper articles about them. She glided up the marble staircase past the footmen liveried in the family's blue and yellow and made her way toward their hosts, Lionel Rothschild and his wife, Charlotte—and not one jaundiced eye perused her.

Inside the gilt and scarlet ballroom, she waltzed and she polkaed. She performed endless quadrilles. She also perspired in the two layers of spun silk with daggered sleeves that weighed her down. As for the whalebones that pinched her ribs, she had mixed reviews. If they crushed her lungs, they also pushed her breasts up to do justice to the daring square décolletage. Anyone who knew her would note that this gown set up greater expectations than the naked truth would tell.

But few people detected who she was. Her medieval costume of teal tunic with golden girdle disguised her identity well. The corset may have exaggerated her measurements, but her mask hid more. Nor did she remove it as some women did. She had enough to contend with whenever her tall horned hat with its froth of a veil slipped from her head.

"Why not just leave it off?" an amused male asked.

She turned to find an elegant Don Juan with two bright blue eyes twinkling at her from beneath a silver half-domino. Only Adam Litchfield possessed eyes that lightning blue. She smiled, politely, careful to lead him on to friendship and nothing more. "I'd like to burn it."

"Ah." He offered his arm to lead her to the dance floor. "After our waltz, we can take a stroll in the garden and I'll help you torch it."

She laughed. "Lovely idea. I'm afraid of who may lurk in the bushes, however."

He looked bewildered. "Who?"

She rued her own honesty. "Reporters."

"Not here, surely." He took her in his embrace.

"Anything is possible," she told him, and they began to waltz. "You're very good at this."

"You sound surprised. Am I to take it that you didn't think I could dance or that most men in America can't?"

"Most American men do a two-step imitation, and those who think they have some grace have forgotten what they learned at age twelve in their Saturday etiquette classes."

"In that case, I am glad you've come to Europe, where it is a mark of a true gentleman to waltz and do it so that his partner is shown to best advantage."

"Interesting."

"What?"

"I think that is another difference between American and European men. Americans would not want to have another man admiring a woman they valued. But here, you consider it your duty to show her off."

"If she is yours"—he smiled down and brought her closer in the turn—"you wish the world to know."

"As a declaration that you value her."

His grin was salacious. "That you possess her." His turn was so swift that she felt crushed to him. She did not like the feeling, his words, or his adamance.

She purposely faltered. "Oh, I am sorry. I . . . think I should stop."

"Are you hurt?" He was solicitous, as he held her arm and she feigned needing his assistance.

"I don't think so. If you could help me to a chair."

He did, and offered some punch. "I'll be right back."

For the sake of show, she lifted the hem of her tunic and twisted her foot this way and that.

"Are you injured?"

She glanced up to find a cavalier with a caring voice and all the other characteristics she had longed to find here but told herself she shouldn't—and most likely wouldn't. He was the right height, the exact breadth for the only man she desired. His thick brown curls gave away his true identity. "Rhys."

"I do not know this man, *mademoiselle.*" He bent from the waist, brushing his ostrich plumed hat against his thigh-high boots in his bow of chivalry. "I am another who seeks your company."

"Yes, well." She glanced around him at the ballroom where many of the guests had just finished the waltz, and Adam had halted in his tracks, each hand holding a punch cup, to watch her. "You'd better hightail it, as they say in my country, sir, because I am notorious—"

"I know that characteristic, my dear, from a brief incident in my otherwise all-too-boring youth, and you do not qualify for that description."

"Ah, but I'm getting close," she insisted. "I am not interested in appearing in the papers again, and no matter who you think you are—"

"Bonnie Prince Charlie. A rebel and a rake."

"Well, you'll need more than a costume to assume those qualities. Pardon me if I'm too curt, your highness"—she worried the inside of her cheek—"but I should not be seen with you."

He came even nearer, his gaze radiating heat and joy behind his stark black satin mask. In the terracotta velvet doublet, molded black hose, and boots, he cut a gallant figure. "Nor I with you, Rapunzel."

"She had golden hair, if you remember, sir. While I am Sleeping Beauty."

His dark eyes dropped to her lips. "Of course you are."

The compliment stole her breath.

His gaze ran to her unbound hair. "Your hat is slipping."

"You haven't thrown yours away yet."

"That's because you soothe the savage in me."

She considered him with equal parts of mirth and objectivity. "I doubt you're ever irrational."

He hooted in laughter. "You're wrong there. For the past two hours, I have mentally taken all the men who've danced with you down to the coal bin, tied them up, and left them there to rot."

Warmed by his sentiment, she focused on the nearby crowd, none of whom seemed particularly interested in this encounter in this obscure corner. Except Adam, who threaded his way through the throng with dexterity. Keeping track of his progress, she asked Rhys, "Why are you here? I haven't seen you before this."

"But I've seen you," he crooned. "I came because I knew you'd be here."

"You shouldn't have."

"I quite agree. I told myself I'd come to practice being indifferent to you."

She cut him a look.

"But I could barely do it weeks ago at your dinner party. Why could I do it better now that I've laughed with you and kissed you?"

"Rhys." She said his name as a warning not to continue.

"Now I know I cannot leave here, Ann, until I waltz with you."

"I can't dance with you. People would recognize us, and . . ."

Here was Adam, mouth thinning with sly humor at Rhys.

"I brought punch for Ann and me. Had I known you'd come, Tweedledum, I could have brought two more glasses."

Rhys ignored Adam's sarcasm in favor of a smile. "Well, Rich Fields, it's good to see you out. You've needed to get back in the whirl for four long years."

"No less than you, old man," Adam replied after a quick assessment. "If you are changing your interests from farming to waltzing, you must warn the rest of us so that we can brush up on our technique."

Though Adam's words seemed innocent enough, his tone was feral. It angered Ann. She rose, unwilling to tread the fine line of courtesy to him in such a situation. "If you'll excuse me, Your Grace"—she inclined her head—"my lord." She made sure her coned hat was firmly in place and left them for the ladies' retiring room. With each step, she worried that someone had seen something, anything she might not have intended.

Whimsy struck her as she passed through the dining room and a footman from the kitchens emerged with a tray of champagne flutes. So she took one. With a sip of the popping bubbles, she felt someone take her arm. Scowling up, she feared it was Adam.

It was Rhys. "What are you doing now?" she asked.

Four ladies whose masks were firmly in place had wide eyes which asked the same question of him.

He scanned the narrow hallway which led only to the ladies' room. "Actually"—he stopped and pivoted, his hand never leaving her elbow—"I came here to steal."

With a winsome smile, Ann surveyed the women walking around them. "Sapphires? Diamonds?"

"You." He drew her with him, clutching her arm, robbing her of reason as he explained, "Sweetheart, do not stop. Come in here." He took a turn at the end of a hall, thrust open a door, drew her in, and shut it.

"I think this costume is going to your head," she countered when he turned to her, his long, hard strength lining her flesh in one scalding temptation.

"Wanting you is becoming a curse," he told her. She could not see his face in the darkness except for a slant of light from a narrow window. In the spill of moonlight, his mouth was grim, rueful.

"Rhys, we can't do this." She lurched backward and bumped into a cupboard which rattled and shook. She managed to spin around, put down her flute, and feel a teapot, empty and cool, and then a sugar bowl with similar qualities. They had found the family silver in the butler's pantry. Wonderful. Thank heavens they had not discovered the family jewels. Or the butler. Getting lost was possible in a house this size, but looking as if you were about to steal your host blind did not endear you to him. And she had promised her father to be more than proper tonight. "Rhys"—she appealed to his logic—"please, don't."

"Don't." He groaned the word, but his hands captured her shoulders in one long caress down to her hands. And then he pressed her back against him, wrapping his arms and hers about her waist. Hard and sensuous, his body felt like breathing marble. "God, Ann, I've lived with that word all my life. It's brought me little I've wanted. Nothing I've needed. I'm here tonight because where you are concerned, I am no longer listening to the warnings. Not interested in the rules." He turned her to him, caught handfuls of her unbound hair and wound them around his wrists. "Have you lived the same way, sweet Grace? Something whispers that you'd like to break the rules. With me."

"If someone finds us"—she licked her lips, wild to savor what he was offering and mad to be gone from here and him—"our adventures will be served with tomorrow morning's kippers."

His fingers framed her face. "You're too prudent, darling. But I'm not. Can't be. Not with you." He trailed his lips along her throat.

That tore her self-control in two. She could not free herself, and she pushed against him, tears not far off. "What do you want?"

His arms bound her like silken ropes, forcing the air from her as his mouth whispered against her ear. "I don't want to hurt you. I don't want to hurt myself. But I am changing, and it is frightening just how much, how quickly. I couldn't stay away tonight. Couldn't refuse this invitation to this ridiculous affair because I learned you'd accepted. So then you wonder what do I want?" He asked as if he searched for the answer with her.

"Well, I now know this. I *do not* want to be merely your acquaintance. I have tried that repeatedly and failed. I want to make you laugh and do it with you. I want to protect you from others as I did the first day in Dublin, and from yourself as I did that day in the Row and at de la Roche's. I want to be with you. Enjoy your company. I have to find a way to do that."

She could find no solutions.

Frustration had her reaching up a hand to wind her fingers in those unruly curls she'd yearned to touch.

He brought his head down, and his kiss to her cheek set her skin on fire. He cradled her closer in his arms. With tear-inspiring tenderness, he sank his fingers into her hair. Her hat fell. And then, if her instinct predicted correctly, she knew his lips would have taken hers.

But he'd been so right—prudence had always been her watchword. If she kissed this man, she knew with absolute clarity that afterward she could never be reasonable about wanting him. Never sensible about needing him. The possibility that she could feel desire for a man went against every rule she had set for herself. If she cared for him too much, she might wind up the same way as her mother, living and dying alone with love unrequited. Wasn't it safer to live without love than to risk losing it? She'd always thought so.

Until she met this man. Until she knew his concern, his protection, his desire. She felt the heat of him enfold her. She perceived how cold she'd be for decades to come when he remained here in England while she sat in her house in Virginia, watching the years drift over the blue ridge of her land and dim the horizon of her loneliness.

"What's the matter, Ann?" he asked raggedly, his mouth an angel's temptation. "Was I wrong to think you wanted me as much as I did you?"

"I want to kiss you. But I want to do more, and I'm afraid."

"Surely not of me?"

"I refused to allow my life to be ruled by what I feel for a man."

In the dim light, she saw him pause to ponder that, but only for a moment. "Don't feel, then. Think." He took her lips and leisurely explored the dark recesses of her mind. "Think what we might find, together." And then he demonstrated how two lovers could discover passion. With brief, hot kisses. With sighs and urgent cries for more.

She felt herself slipping into mindless ecstasy, and, terrified by her lack of control, she clung to what little she had left. She forced herself backward from his embrace. "I can't do this." This time, she said to him what she could not before. "Good-bye."

When she yanked open the door, a solicitous Adam stood in the blinding light. She knew him only from his rigid stance when he asked, "Are you all right? Where's your hat, Ann? Get it. Good. Come with me. Quickly."

Hating that Adam was gloating over Rhys, Ann walked from the pantry beside him. To her surprise, Raine stood just behind him and had witnessed the scene. Grateful to her cousin, Ann disappeared with her into the ladies' retiring room and left Adam to cool his heels in the hall. She began to brush her hair and straighten her clothes, looking at herself in the mirror for long minutes, glad no one else was there and no one came in.

Her cousin examined her for a minute, then sank into the slipper chair beside Ann. "Do you want to talk to me, or shall I go?"

"Please stay, although there's nothing you can do except listen to me."

Raine tilted her head. "I know you have not wished to share your thoughts lately. I wondered why. I hoped I had not disappointed you in some way, but I decided not to push you to talk to me."

"You haven't done anything, Raine. I am confused about my feelings for Rhys Kendall and didn't want to discuss them. If I did, I knew I'd look indecisive at best or foolish at worst. Now, to make matters worse, there's been a huge scene here with Adam and Rhys. I promised my father I would treat Adam politely, I do, and then Rhys appears."

Raine's sapphire eyes softened in sympathy. "He's been watching you all evening. I wondered when he would come forward, and I am afraid many saw you depart with him."

Ann winced. "My father? Any reporters?"

"Half of London."

"What good is a mask when people may know you by your deeds?" Ann combed her hair and plopped her hat on her head.

"Or your suitors?"

Ann stuck her tongue out at herself in the mirror. *"Oui, mademoiselle.* Now I ask myself what will I do with our Lord Rich Fields?"

"What do you want to do?"

"Appease him with a dance and escape!"

"Good. I will find you, claim a crashing headache, and ask you to accompany me home."

"Aren't you having fun?" Ann should never have asked. She knew the answer to that.

"Ma cherie, there is no man here from whom I wish to flee. I want only to go home to my own pursuits." Raine paused to study Ann's befuddlement. "What did I say?"

"I thought my own goal was to go home to my own pursuits . . . and now I wonder if that was a goal or a substitute for what I really wanted and never thought I should."

"Which is what?"

"A home with someone I cared for."

"Ah, at last, you can say it." Raine looked relieved. "Now can you find the courage to discover if there is such a person with whom you can love and live for many years?"

"You make it sound so simple, Raine. Why did I think that talking with you would make me more confused?"

"I suppose I could be insulted by that last, but I will decide not to be. Instead, I will say what you must know. You were not ready to look yourself in the eye and be honest. Now you have met a man who interests you enough to question your plan. That is no tragedy, *ma cherie*. That is romance."

But was it love? And even if she dared to name it that, was it an emotion that could sustain people through years of tears and laughter?

Ann stood. Why ask herself those questions when the chances of developing a rewarding relationship with Rhys Kendall were so small? Too many problems barred the way. All of them took time and patience to tear down. All of them took two people's devotion to each other. Hadn't she learned that, too, from her parents' example?

Infatuation or love, her feelings for Rhys Kendall could progress no further—and shouldn't tonight, lest she become London's most talked-about American girl.

"I'll waltz with Adam. You sit here and develop a headache." She winked. "Thanks."

"It is I who should thank you, *mademoiselle*, fo rescuing me from boredom."

At the door, Ann smiled at Adam pleasantly and took his arm. He looked triumphant when she suggested they return to the dancing. Her injury, she assured him, was minor, and she'd love to take the next waltz with him. Their conversation continued to be stilted, and Ann marveled at the meaningless things one could find to piddle away time. When the orchestra took up instruments for the next dance, she felt relief not to talk to Adam but a definite distaste to endure his arms around her. Raine came none too soon.

Within minutes, the two of them said the proper good-byes and waited in the foyer for their coachman to come around with their brougham. With the head butler hovering over them, Ann encouraged Raine to come stand outside with her along the drive. "My cousin needs the night air," Ann fabricated for the doddering servant, and headed for the door. The breeze through the ashes and oaks whispered of a coming storm.

"The servants' party belowstairs must be a good one," Raine conjectured when they'd waited for ten minutes or more for their lagging coachman.

Ann wished she'd worn a cape. "He must like his whiskey. I think tonight I'll have one to warm up."

Five minutes more passed, and Raine shivered, too. Two figures appeared in the lamplight across the street. One of them was thin, the other short and fat. Ann squinted into the bleakness but could see nothing more about him, as he sank into the blackest of the shadows.

"Ah, here at last," Raine exulted. "Ann? What . . . ?"

"Let's get in. Quickly. I'm cold."

"You're petrified." Raine squeezed Ann's hand once they settled into the squabs. "What frightens you, *ma cherie?*"

Ann debated for half a minute what to tell Raine. She didn't want to scare her cousin, but Raine would not let Ann cry this off without explanation. "I saw a man across the street who appeared to be watching us."

Now Raine did look pained. "The reporter."

"Of course," Ann murmured, realizing that the *Gazetteer*'s reporter in no way resembled the thin man with a mustache.

"We must tell Uncle Skip we know what he looks like."

"Tonight."

Rhys Kendall careened to a stop. One hand to a lamppost, he stood panting, cursing silently that the two men who'd watched the Rothschilds' house—and Ann—had dissolved into the murky night. He scanned the stately stucco town homes, serene, windows blank, unseeing. The tree limbs, lush from spring rains, bent to the sidewalks, their new leaves laden with the mist which grew heavier by the minute. He listened and heard no footsteps, only the patter of the rain as it now began to pour upon the pavement.

Wiping water from his eyes, he reconsidered the plan he'd formulated after Ann had left him in the pantry. There, their words and kisses had proven to him that he had to see her again. Court her. Discover if this passion he felt for her were lust or love.

He'd have to make enormous changes in his life to do it, too. But he was determined to find the means. He was on his way home to plan it and had left the mansion by a side door to hail a hackney when he saw Ann and her cousin. A movement across the street caught his eye. In the shadows, he had spied two men, loitering. When Rhys drifted back into the boxwoods to observe their actions, only one emerged into the light. A burly one.

Rhys felt as if he'd been socked in the stomach. The man he saw illuminated was one he knew well and wished he never did. He was Owen MacIntyre, Skip's former partner and agent in Liverpool. The man who had disappeared after the fire in Blackburn mill.

Why was MacIntyre here in London? Why was he loitering outside the Rothschilds'? To meet someone or observe someone?

Would Skip Brighton know?

Rhys considered going back to the ball to ask him, then thought better of it. He'd not ask. He'd wait outside the house—if he could stand to remain sopping wet that long—and see if MacIntyre returned . . . and met anyone . . . such as Skip.

Rhys didn't have long to wait. Skip Brighton left the ball approximately half an hour later, alone in a hack the Rothschilds' footman had hailed from the corner where many waited for just such a summons from this imperious crowd.

Rhys went home to plan his actions.

At seven the following Monday morning, Rhys dressed for three business meetings. The first was an unscheduled call upon one of his two best friends, Bryce Falconer. Bryce, poor chap, would not appreciate that Rhys had changed his mind about investing with him in the Guardian Shipping Company. But Bryce, once acquainted with Rhys's novel reason to withdraw, would forgive his change of heart. Bryce was a romantic, a man who fell in love with a different woman each new dawn. He could understand, as few others, how urgently Rhys needed to rearrange his finances, his business, and his immediate schedule.

"It is with regret, then," Bryce told him, "that I hand these over." He gave Rhys three daily tabloids. "What they've printed about you and Ann at the Rothschilds' will only make you more angry—and more dedicated to your goals."

Bryce was right.

The Period ran a caricature of a fork running away from a knife with another one. *The Illustrated Two-Penny* ran a cartoon of a medieval Cinderella escaping a ball and the attentions of one bereft cavalier on the arm of another sterner one, her hat in her hand. *The Gazetteer* ran the piece that clarified both illustrations for those who had no idea what the meaning was.

The gossip columnist had noted how Grace had created a stir at a masquerade Friday before midnight, "seeking her carriage earlier than her family and friends, minus her hat. Has she lost her head and heart in the chase? And who, Dear Reader, do you think she ran from? Our Scion, of course, who appeared at the ball, a prince of the Realm."

Rhys balled it up and threw it into Bryce's fire.

"What a lie." He seethed against the distortions that could ruin Ann. "I'll make it up to her."

He left quickly for his second visit, which took h to Threadneedle Street. When Rhys was in Lond. this meeting was a regular occurrence each Monday a ten sharp with his solicitor, Edward Whittier. Far from applauding Rhys's decisions this morning, Edward would gape, then politely argue. Rhys was ready for him. After all, when had Rhys invested in any scheme over the past decade that made him any profit of note? Not once. Why start now? Rhys simply wanted to notify Edward of his decision to refuse joining the cruise line and implement his other strategy to earn him a sizable bit of cash immediately. Money was definitely what he needed to court Ann Brighton.

That made Rhys pause on the sidewalk. Next he must see Adam and find subtle words to break the news that he would pursue Ann. Openly. Adam's interest in her was apparent, and Rhys would not have Adam hear of his own pursuit of Ann from rumors. Rhys wanted Adam to know precisely when Rhys had decided to test his feelings for her. He and Adam had counted too many years together, endured too much laughter and sorrow for Rhys to ignore his friend's regard for Ann.

So satisfied was he at his decision that he decided to walk the six long blocks to Watling Street. On the doorstep to the building where most of the major investors in the cruise line had offices and where today they planned to sign contracts inaugurating the Anglo-American Guardian Shipping Line, Rhys paused long enough to realize he'd done something he hadn't in years. He had whistled his way along the street. He liked the feeling. He loved the freedom. Ann Brighton was most definitely responsible.

Inside, he climbed to the third floor and asked for Adam, only to be told by his assistant that Lord Litchfield was out and would not arrive until one o'clock.

Rhys told the man he would return then.

He took the stairs down to the first floor and announced himself to the dapper little mongoose who served as secretary to Mr. Skip Brighton.

Chapter 6

"Her dollars were her only recommendation, and all were credited with possession of them, otherwise what was her raison d'etre?"

—JENNIE JEROME CHURCHILL, LADY RANDOLPH CHURCHILL

"YOU ARE EARLY, YOUR GRACE." MR. TIDWELL SCRAM-bled around his desk to squint up at Rhys through thick spectacles. "You are not to be here for the signing until—"

"Two. I know. Please inform Mr. Brighton that I have come now for a very good reason and my need to see him is urgent." When the wiry fellow did not budge, Rhys smiled vacantly. "Do take my suggestion, Mr. Tidwell. You'll be happy you did."

Less than a minute after Tidwell huffed off, Skip Brighton opened his own office door to Rhys—a sure sign of his burning curiosity. "Good morning."

"Yes, it is." Rhys understood Skip's surprise—and his wariness as he indicated a chair.

"May I have Mr. Tidwell bring you coffee or—?"

"Nothing, thank you." Rhys settled in the leather chair before Skip's desk and noted how the place had not changed since he'd last seen it at age—what?—ten?

The imposing room resembled the other seven

offices in the two-hundred-year-old four-story building. Each possessed linenfold oak walls, its panels carved and gilded in French boiserie and capped by plaster ceilings sculpted by Italian *scuttadori* whom his great-grandfather had imported to do the work. Skip Brighton had bought the red brick building in 'sixty-two from Rhys's father, making it his headquarters for the European branch of his shipping company. He leased out the other offices, and at present each of the tenants was a principal investor in the nascent Guardian Shipping Line.

"Well, then." Skip took his own chair, folding his hands in his lap. He faced Rhys with not a trace of emotion in his face.

Knowing Skip's lack could only be myth, Rhys took his time. Today, he felt powerful. Totally in command of this meeting and his immediate future. That was more than enough to make him smile broadly.

"You seem very happy," Skip snapped. "I can tell you I'm not. I saw the papers. Good God, that kind of scandal does us no good. The other investors we have in this company do not take lightly to such shenanigans."

"No need to tell me that, Skip. I live here. I will tell you that I bemoan what appeared, not for the company but for Ann." Rhys did not agree that what had been printed could be defined as scandal, though he knew it would become that if the lies continued to burgeon. He meant to use his influence to end them. Meanwhile, if Skip had acquired a puritan set of American standards which he applied to his daughter, Rhys hoped Skip might even apply them to himself now. He should. The man had an old and impressive collection of peccadillos to live down in London. "I came here early because I wanted to talk about the company—"

That broke Skip. He shot forward, his face flushed, his finger jabbing his desktop. "I will not have her seduced and her spirit broken."

"Neither will I. In fact"—Rhys leisurely considered the pastoral oil behind Skip's desk—"what I propose ensures those things won't happen. You really ought to hear me out."

The man fumed, coughed, recovered, then sat back, glaring, waiting.

Rhys unbuttoned his coat and took his sweet time. "I want to talk about the company first. And primary on my list is to tell you that I will not attend the meeting of the principal investors today."

In tribute to his flagging control, Skip sat impassive. *What a man,* Rhys thought with an admiration that had ceased to amaze him. *Were this my daughter, I'd have skinned the fellow alive by now.* The novel contemplation of progeny did not give Rhys pause as much as the coupling of that prospect in the same breath with Ann Brighton. He tried not to grin as he forced himself to speak of his purpose.

"I have decided not to participate. You knew I was vacillating, but now I am firm in my decision."

"Why, for God's sake?" Skip was flabbergasted.

Rhys gloried in his answer. It told of so many differences between them. "I cannot afford to involve myself."

Skip frowned, shelving his anger and bringing out the logic. "That's not what my sources say. You have at least two thousand pounds you could take from your savings—and not miss it. The profit on your mill in Liverpool totals at least one hundred pounds a month, and your farm in Blackburn turns a tidy sum to give you about five hundred clear a year. That is, if you would take it, spend it on you, and not reinvest it in them."

"Your sources are accurate. Disturbingly so. I will discover who revealed my private business and terminate their services."

"You could spend your money with me if you wanted."

Rhys nodded slowly. "I want something else more."

Skip cursed. "I hope it's not that damn omnibus line for Liverpool." He leaned across his desk, noting Rhys's surprise. "Yes, I know you inquired about that venture, too, but listen to me, Rhys. Investing in manufacturing double-decker buses may sound like a socially beneficial idea, but it is not as lucrative as an ocean liner company. Just think how rapidly it'll grow. The rich will—"

"Make you richer, Skip. Not me. *If* I ever see my way clear to use my savings to invest in a long-term project, I would rather put my money in something to help people ride to work than assist others to dine and dance their way across an ocean."

"But the profits here will be immense. How can you turn your back on this?"

"Amassing a fortune interests me," Rhys told him nonchalantly, then dropped the facade. "But it does not possess me."

"How can I persuade you?"

"You can't," Rhys replied, marveling that Skip Brighton would stoop to ask such a thing. Rhys knew Skip wanted him to become one of the company's founding directors because his name would add a certain luster to the group. None of the other potential directors, including Adam and Bryce, had titles as old, as illustrious, or as revered among the upper classes in Britain. A company that catered to wealthy Americans would benefit from that kind of entré and those connections to ensure the success of the business. "If the idea of fortune attracted me, I would have been a rich man before now. But evidently I am not made that way. I like my comforts, but I don't need an abundance of them. More than all else, I need to be able to look in the mirror each morning and like what I see. Hence, if I do decide to spend two thousand pounds from my savings account, I will back omnibuses instead of luxury liners."

"Why did you wait until this morning to decide this?" Skip was now beginning to seethe.

"If you think I planned to put you in a bind for your meeting today, you are wrong. I dislike your business methods and ethics—but I would not wait and purposely sabotage you. Then my practices would match your own."

"Ah, yes," Skip agreed. "I should have predicted you'd act like this . . ."

Skip's acknowledgment shocked him and pleased him immensely. "I had no idea you judged me so fairly."

"I have known who you are and what makes you run for more than fourteen years. You are bound by family and honor." Skip rose from his chair to peer out his window. Hands jammed into his trouser pockets, he rocked on his heels with the force of mounting frustration. "You are forthright in your businesses. Your private life is just as spotless. You have no traces of any indiscretions with women of your set, no hints of affairs."

Rhys sat very still. Five years ago, he had made one miscalculation, giving a tender kiss to a young woman that to him was nothing more than a bit of exploration but to the lady inspired an unrequited devotion. The results had been sorrowful for Rhys, the lady, and her beau, Adam Litchfield.

Rhys had never kissed a woman since unless he planned to possess her completely, free of competition. That he had kissed Ann and he could not quell his need for more illustrated how much she meant to him—and proved to him how far he'd go to move heaven and earth not only to kiss her but to test the depths of his desire to claim her. Especially before Adam became enamored with her. Because if and when Adam wished to do more than save her from a butler's pantry, Rhys would retire from the field, regardless of what it cost him in heartache to part from Ann. "Thank you, Skip. That's good to know. One always wonders if one has committed some error of judgment, left some trace."

"None. You have such a clean reputation, many claim you must be a member of a secret cult that cavorts in the dingy alleys of Seven Dials."

Rhys snorted. "So I am a satyr, eh? I suppose I should be grateful no one thinks I'm a monk."

"No one questions your desires, Rhys." Skip turned to meet his gaze. "But people do wonder how you deal with them."

"Discreetly."

"It's been five years since the incident with Adam's fiancée—"

"That was no affair." Rhys was adamant.

"Everyone knew that. Even Adam."

The woman was a Scottish laird's only child and daughter in London for her first season. Her father wanted her to marry for pedigree and fortune. She wanted to marry for love. The match her father found her gave her those assets her sire required. Adam. Twenty-seven and grief-stricken by his first wife's death less than two years previously. At their engagement party, she wandered from the ballroom to the gardens and met a young man whom she did not know, but flirted and persuaded him to kiss her.

To this day, Rhys could not say what inspired him to do it. Curiosity. Mischief. Probably more appreciation for her gumption to ask than her shimmering pale beauty. Adam had come upon them, and they parted. Rhys had promptly forgotten her. Somehow she had not. She began to write Rhys letters. He returned them, unopened. She tried to break her engagement, openly rejecting Adam in public. Her father sent her to the country, and months later she married Adam. Within a year, one snowy night, she ran from him. To Rhys. Her husband trailed her easily to his friend's home four miles away. He had known where she went and to whom.

Adam appeared in Rhys's courtyard at High Keep Castle. He asked his friend no questions. Mary, however, told lies. Goading her husband with tales of Rhys's kisses and embraces, she stood at the door to the great hall and shouted such love for Rhys that she succeeded in killing poor Adam's tolerance. In the year of their marriage, Adam had become such a somber man, so opposite the carefree youth who had grown up four miles from High Keep. He took his wife home without a word, just a hand to her wrist. Not until last year, which was the second anniversary of Mary's death in a riding accident, did Rhys witness his old friend Adam laugh again. Adam and Rhys's friendship abided. Not as it once was, naive and raucous, but tempered by sorrows of which Adam would not speak.

Rhys had learned the lesson well not to allow himself to be attracted to any young woman in any way. Not to smile, not to flirt, never even to appear delighted with her company. He had engaged in a few liaisons, which for their brevity could hardly be called affairs. All were with educated, witty women who expected nothing more from him but his physical attentions and small favors of his presence, his humor, and occasionally his social influence. His money, they must have known, he did not part with but for the most prudent reasons. Therefore, they dared not ask.

After his father died and he paid off the racing debts, Rhys took on the task of resurrecting his estate from bankruptcy. His dedication to seeing his farm community outside Blackburn prosper for the injured people who lived there remained as constant as before. His need to see his mill make a profit was also a matter of honor. Dalliances with women were a vacuous pastime for an impoverished duke who had no time for fun. The Dour Duke, they called him, with good reason. Now his hopes had changed with the introduction of one appealing lady to his midst.

"Skip, if you are inquiring whether I currently have a mistress, the answer is no." God help him, Rhys hadn't taken a woman to bed in so long, he may have forgotten how. He chuckled to himself, aware that his fantasies of educating Ann Brighton in the delights of love on any one of his numerous beds proved he had a good memory—and a driving ambition.

"For my daughter's sake, I'm pleased to hear it. She cares for you. I see it. You must, too."

"I do. That's why I am here. I care for her as well. I wonder how much, and I can only discover it if I am free."

"Then join us. Money gives you a freedom—"

"Absolutely not. What stands between Ann and me has not so much to do with my lack of money as with our individual resentments of you. I cannot show Ann the way to rid herself of hers, but I have found the way to start to free myself. I'll sever all business relationships with you. I should never have considered them in the beginning. But I was more interested in reaping the rewards than in examining the process. I should have known I could never live with myself if I sold my principles for the chance to live in splendor. But I become a wiser man—I hope a shrewder one—as years go on."

Skip inclined his head. "You do. But let me tell you, Rhys, if you wish to court Ann, you must do it quickly."

"Why?" Would she go home to America? It would take him a while—weeks, perhaps—to sell one Van Dyck or more and be able to afford to court her. Skip was frowning, working at words. That fired Rhys's fear she'd leave.

Skip turned his face away, and Rhys wondered what he hid. "She is startled by the ferocity of the tabloids' attack. She is not used to that, you see. She lived so long in the country, where people are kinder. These people here may wound me all they want, but I will draw and quarter anyone on London Bridge before I allow them to hurt Ann."

"Skip, I want to prevent her being hurt any more." *Nor will I see Adam inadvertently hurt again. If Ann cares for me more than she could for him, we three must learn that quickly, before his heart is wounded one more time.* "Ann has walked through war, disease, death, and abandonment. That's more disaster than a woman should bear in one lifetime, let alone her first twenty years. Her charm and humor are her calling cards. She is a credit to you."

"She must hold her head up."

"I'll see she can, I promise you that. I have always used my influence sparingly, but I will employ it now full force. I'll do more than clear her name, Skip. I hope I'll make her laugh. Amazing as it is to me, I can do that for her, and that appeals to me."

Skip sighed, looking old and tired. "I want her very happy, Rhys."

"Yes, I see that. Why you should have waited all these years to do it puzzles me. But that is your problem to solve. I must act for myself in my own best interests—and in hers. So let me finish with the business aspects and say what I should have long ago. I never wanted to do business with you again. I could never trust you after the fire."

"And I told you I do not know who set the blaze."

"The evidence pointed to Owen MacIntyre."

"MacIntyre." Skip breathed the name. "I paid him his salary, and then he disappeared. I could never learn what happened the night of the fire, other than your part of the story."

"That puzzles me." Rhys allowed amazement to creep into his voice. "You seem capable of so much else."

"I can fail like anyone else."

"Yes, I see now that you have in so many ways." Rhys stared at him. "With many people."

"I'm trying to make it up to Ann," Skip murmured.

"As you said in Dublin, better to make amends now than never. I agree. Have at it. She deserves everything you try to do for her."

Skip's gaze clouded. "I will, too."

"We are of like minds, then, for once in our

checkered relationship." Rhys gave him a consoling look. "But our connection is precisely what I wish to cut."

"I wish you were in this venture with us."

"I know I've left you with a kettle of fish to sort out on such short notice. But my withdrawal is only a temporary inconvenience to all of you. I am certain other prospects will come forward with more money than I ever could have contributed. Two thousand pounds was a small sum to have as the floor, anyway. I often wondered why it was so little."

"It was the way I wrote the articles of incorporation."

"Yes, you alone. Interesting. I do wish you well, simply because Bryce and Adam deserve prosperity. They have both been enthusiastic about this company from its inception, especially Adam, who encouraged me to join you. I don't want what appeared in the newspapers about Ann and me and Adam to hurt anyone, including him. Adam has suffered enough."

"Yes." Skip lowered his gaze. "Too much. At least everyone knows it was Mary who saw more substance to your friendship with her than there was."

"Not a flattering fact for a husband to deal with."

"Adam seemed well matched with Mary. She was the only woman who caught his eye after his first wife's death." Skip narrowed his gaze out the window. "That was a horrible event for Adam, too. Georgianna's neck broken by a fall from that parapet."

"God knows what she was doing up there." Rhys reflected on Adam's adoration of his first spouse. "She'd lived in that old castle for more than a year and should have known those beams in that part of the building were rotting and needed to be replaced."

Rhys shook his head. "Adam took forever to recover from her loss."

"Georgianna was lovely but headstrong," Skip murmured.

Rhys noted how Skip's hands clenched. "I had no idea you knew her."

"Briefly." Skip faced Rhys. "And far too well."

Rhys froze with shock. *My God.* "Does Adam know?"

"No."

Rhys suddenly saw a method to Skip's plans. "Adam told me you invited him to join the company."

"That's true."

Rhys delved further. "Are you making amends to more people than just Ann, Skip?"

The man who smiled at him was older, sadder, thinner than Rhys had ever noticed. "I wish I could change the past."

"I suspected."

"See a different me, do you?"

Yes. You are ill. How ill? "Care to tell me why?"

"A man changes when he contemplates eternity."

Rhys considered that. What was Skip saying? Wisdom came late to him? Or death was coming early? The few times he had seen Skip, his coughing was pervasive. "Are you in good health?"

"Only my enemies"—Skip flashed a grin reminiscent of his years as a renegade—"plan my demise."

He meant it as a barb. Rhys felt the prick of truth. But self-contained as this man was, Skip Brighton would never reveal more or ask for help. Rhys would have to trick him into any revelations of who might harm him. "It would take quite a bit to do away with an old shark like you."

"A lot of people carry harpoons."

"I'm certain." Rhys tried for a facetiousness he didn't feel. "Anyone in particular?"

"Like to join them?" Skip teased.

"I would have at one time, but today I have a more worthy goal. I could offer encouragement to them, though. Tell me whom I should go to."

Skip inhaled deeply. "No one I can put my finger on."

But you're trying. Concern for Skip Brighton blossomed into alarm. Rhys stiffened in his chair. Memories of Owen MacIntyre outside the Rothschilds' house the other evening and a thin man with a mustache scurrying after Ann in Dublin filled his mind. "Is anyone threatening you?"

Shock—and fear—leaped to Skip's eyes. "Why do you ask?"

Rhys told him about the little man after Ann in Dublin.

Skip was stunned. "She never said a word to me."

"That's because she didn't think much of it, especially since she saw no one after that. I scared him off that day, thinking he was a thief bent on relieving her of her bankroll. But now I am more concerned and more puzzled." Rhys noted how Skip's mouth whitened with tension. "Owen MacIntyre stood outside the Rothschilds' Friday night. He was on the corner, watching as Ann and Raine left the house."

"You saw him?" Skip turned away. "I did not know he was there, either."

Rhys sat forward. "You *knew* he was in London?"

Skip's answer came after a minute. "Yes." He shook his head. "Oh, God, that's who she and Raine thought was the *Gazetteer*'s reporter!"

Rhys fumed. "Explain that to me."

"They saw a short, fat man across the street as they left the ball and told me when I came home. We thought it was whoever this snake in the grass is—"

"Why was Owen there? Do you know? Have you any idea? By God, Skip, if he hurts Ann—"

"He won't. He's not after Ann. He wants to ruin *me*. He has tried, Rhys, but I tell you, I've won."

"What? How?" Rhys was very confused now. "What in hell are you talking about?"

"He blackmailed me."

Rhys cursed to himself. He knew he could round the desk and easily lift a very sick man out of his chair and shake him into confessing every secret he ever had. But he fisted his hands and probed. "Why?"

"For money, of course. Why do men hold another hostage?"

"Are you paying it?"

"Yes, last night."

"Why?"

"Because I will have this company." Skip pounded his desktop.

"Of course. At what cost?"

"He wanted me to pay him one hundred and fifty thousand pounds last night or not sign the papers today at two! He says he will not stand by and see me make more money while he suffers poverty."

"What was MacIntyre threatening you with?"

Skip laughed at himself. "Telling the tabloids about my affair with Georgianna Litchfield. Ironic, isn't it? I come this far, look respectable after years of seeming like a bastard to one and all, I want to create a clean slate, and up pops my past to haunt me. This affair with Georgianna was only one of many. Ann just recently found out about one that destroyed my marriage to her mother, Rhys. I couldn't let her learn

about this now, when I need her to think well of me."
He inhaled and drew himself up. "So there you have
it. A man with too much ambition at the end of his
rope. Sad case, but no more than I deserve."

"Owen knew about your affair with Georgianna
years ago?"

Skip snorted. "He used to help me set up our
rendezvous."

Rhys pushed aside his disgust when he saw how
much more repulsed Skip was with himself. "How
long has Owen been blackmailing you?"

"Friday I got the first note."

"This Friday?"

"Yes. A letter delivered to the house in the afternoon post. I know what you're going to ask, and no,
Owen gave no address to reply to. My answer was to
be given by what time I left the house Saturday
morning to come here to work. Eight for yes, the
money would be delivered. Nine for no, he could
proceed to tell the newspapers about my past."

"So you delivered the money yesterday to him?"

"Yes, half in British currency, half in a check made
out to him and drawn from a French bank."

"He met you, and there were no problems?"

"Yes. He looks surprisingly well for a man who says
he has suffered poverty these past ten years. He is well
clothed and healthy enough."

"Do you think he's satisfied and won't reveal anything to the newspapers anyway?"

Skip shrugged. "I have to believe that, don't I?"

Rhys continued to be baffled by the timing of
Owen's crime. "What caused him to blackmail you
now? Why has he waited all these years? You have had
money and power which he could have challenged
before this."

Skip sighed. "I asked him that. He said the time was never so ripe. That this cruise line will be the most profitable venture I've ever undertaken. He's right."

Rhys sat, skeptical of Skip's hope that the likes of Owen MacIntyre could be satisfied with easy, ill-gotten gain. "Did he carry a weapon? Say he'd see you again? Come alone?"

"No gun, no knife, no friends. He just climbed into my brougham at Leicester Square, counted his cash, and left with a little wave of his hand. Bastard."

Leicester Square brought to Rhys the memory of meeting Ann at de la Roche's studio there last Thursday. The whole week had seen a catastrophic series of incidents linking the defamation of her name to his and Adam's. To have it end with the blackmailing of Ann's father created a puzzle with enormous pieces missing. Still, it gave the appearance that someone— Owen—wished to ruin them all.

"I never thought Owen was that crafty." Rhys voiced his assessment of Skip's man with whom he had often negotiated for the best cotton prices. "He was efficient, organized, but not creative. Do you think he is working alone in this?"

"A question I have asked myself. I have no answer for you. I can only say I have made a lot of enemies."

An understatement. "Is there anything I can do to help you?"

Skip blinked, grateful and leery. "Would you?" The devil in him made him smile.

"If I'm granted my request, it will be easier."

"Damn, Rhys. You come here, withdraw from a profitable venture, upset my plans, say you're not sorry because you distrust me still, then ask me a favor. Let me hear the words, Kendall, so that I can try desperately to deny it to you."

Rhys grinned. "You won't refuse me."

"Ask me and see."

"I would like your permission to call on your daughter."

Time ticked by with no clue to Skip Brighton's decision, until finally his eyes darkened. "In public. With a chaperone. No pantries. No absconding from balls."

"I will do it in the proper way, but I must also do it in my own time."

"Agreed. But I want one thing more."

"Name it."

"I doubt it will be easy," Skip suggested with a challenge in his eyes.

"You never do anything the easy way. What is it?"

"Find out who the hell that reporter is and tell me."

Rhys grinned. "My thoughts precisely. But I am in a better position to squash his efforts politely."

"So you do realize that if I ever put my hands on him, I'd kill him."

Rhys got to his feet. "To hell with your methods. I'll do this my way. I don't want Ann hurt by anyone, you especially." He paused at the door. "Even though you've paid MacIntyre, you will have O'Leary watch over Ann, I trust."

"Night and day."

"I won't leave London, though it may take me a while before I will be able to come to Belgrave Square to call."

Skip nodded.

"Promise me you will come to me if there is anything I can do to help you keep Ann safe."

"Of course, Rhys. I want her to have a long and happy life."

"And you, too."

Skip didn't smile. "Haven't you ever heard the Irish saying to be careful what you wish for?"

Upstairs, Rhys found Adam in and eager to see him. Rhys sat, shared a port, and told Adam in the most diplomatic words possible that he would officially court Ann Brighton.

Minutes later, with Adam smiling congenially, they shook hands, and Rhys left. Walking down Watling Street, Rhys replayed how Adam had greeted his announcement. "May the best man win, eh, Tweedle?"

Rhys had gotten what he wished for—Adam's acceptance of his pursuit of Ann—and Rhys was not happy. Adam's anger had glittered in his eyes, though the words on his lips were so friendly, too friendly.

Rhys felt Adam's challenge, and in it he sensed danger.

Chapter 7

"England is all right for splendor, but dead slow for fun."

—CONSUELO YZNAGA, DUCHESS OF MANCHESTER

"AUNT PEG MAY INSIST THAT ENGLISH HUNTING SEASON is over in the country, but I say it is definitely on in London," Ann observed with a deadpan expression as she leaned into the mirror in the ladies' retiring room of Houghton Hall.

Raine caught her cousin's gaze and glanced around to see that the maid who'd accompanied them from Forsythe House and the two English girls who were guests at this dinner party had gone back downstairs. Satisfied, she widened her sapphire eyes in feigned horror. "Feeling driven to ground, like we're the foxes?"

"Thinking I should have put my pistol in my purse," Ann jested. She had discontinued her usual practice at her aunt's request. At least at night, Ann left her gun at home. No need, Aunt Peg had insisted, to appear rustic. God forbid that one of the newspapers draw another caricature of her, this time perhaps as a gun-toting American in crinolines. The *Gazetteer*'s articles had stopped, but that was no guarantee they wouldn't start again. Meanwhile, O'Leary accompanied any of them when they went out with or without Aunt Peg.

Raine chuckled. "To carry it to a dinner party would make Aunt Peg froth at the mouth."

"That would drive off this elderly baron, wouldn't it?"

"Lord Worminster is terribly attractive," Raine conceded, "even if he is a few years older than Methuselah."

"His age doesn't seem to matter to Aunt Peg as much as his eyes."

"Mmm, I'd say they ate *her* up for dinner."

"I have never seen her so taken by a man."

Raine nodded. "Or so disinterested in the wine."

Ever since Ann could remember, her aunt had tippled. In the past few years, when she would come to visit the Brightons in Alexandria, she had begun her marathon tasting during breakfast which would send her to her room soon after dinner. Tonight, one look at this baron with the shock of white hair and electric blue eyes, and Aunt Peg grew younger by the minute and kept herself charmingly sober.

Ann knew that look of enchantment. She also knew its lack. She'd taken to long walks to rid herself of her preoccupation with Rhys Kendall. In the four weeks since the Rothschilds' ball, she had not seen him. However, each morning since then, one white rose arrived at their front door, delivered by Rhys Kendall's housekeeper.

Full blown, the dew of dawn dripping from its velvet petals, the flower would fill her hands, her mind with memories of kisses as lavish, lips as lush. He sent no note. He did not appear at any dinner, ball, or theater. Neither his name nor any reference to him appeared in the *Gazetteer* or any other paper.

Nor did Ann's. Thank God.

Yet she suffered for what had been printed that terrible Monday when most of London read that Cinderella had left the ball hurriedly. Oh, no one snubbed her. The invitations came to Forsythe House in greater numbers, a tribute, she assumed, to her father's rising prominence with his company.

Her punishment was of her own making. She ridiculed herself for succumbing to Rhys's charms. Not for reveling in his kisses. Those were treasures she admitted to herself she valued. But for caring for a man who did not appear to her in the flesh, sent only his roses as indication that he might surface—and had cut his ties to her father by rejecting the invitation to join the cruise line company.

While her bedroom grew fragrant with roses, her anxieties multiplied. She became cool as a cat mousing while she constantly watched to see if her maid, Nora, or another rummaged through her room. No servant had admitted to going through her belongings. Ann didn't expect anyone to have confessed to that, but she had hoped for some sign—some twitch of a facial muscle, some clench of fingers as the staff assembled before her father, Aunt Peg, and her the day after the ball. The three of them agreed afterward that they couldn't sack anyone without more evidence or a confession. In any case, whoever had done it hadn't again. That was sufficient for Ann to conclude it was an incident for which she'd never learn the cause or the perpetrator. If indeed it meant anything at all. She decided not to worry about its meaning or the extent of its malice. She had bigger worries.

Her father's health declined. He neither slept nor

ate well. His face took on lines of worry. His hair had new streaks of gray. She begged him to leave with her for Cannes, Monte Carlo, Naples—anyplace sunny and far from cares. He refused. She argued. He yelled that he had problems to solve. She left him alone in his downstairs study to brood.

To add more tension to her already strained existence, she was cooped up with English manners and English rules, and she could not escape in her male attire to ride. She had complied with her father's wishes and kept the peace between them.

To eat up her nervous energy, she asked her father if she could take on the task of paying the household bills and balancing the account, as she had in Alexandria. Then she went for endless walks along the fashionable sidewalks of Belgravia. She would wave to her neighbors in the square or to the ever-present flower lady. No one followed her, except O'Leary. He went with her to Rotten Row each morning at eight, where she rode sidesaddle before others came to clog the lane. At that hour, she saw few people, except Adam Litchfield, twice. She hoped their meetings were accidental.

She did not care to see him at all. He knew it, too. The Tuesday he had come to tea, he had been forward. When Aunt Peg had left them alone for a few minutes, Ann had thanked him for his help the previous Friday at the ball.

"I would like to perform more services for you, if you'll let me, Ann."

She had purposely ignored his implication that he'd like to get to know her better. "Thank you, Lord Litchfield, I don't think that will be necessary."

He'd gone quite still. "I fear for your reputation."

"That's kind of you, my lord."

"I'd like to help you restore it." He left his chair and sat beside her on the sofa.

She did not shrink from him, but when he put down his tea and caught one of her hands, she snatched it away and rose. "I did not know I had been ruined. If I have, I assure you that I can take care of myself, my lord. Let me tell you how well. Do not touch me, do you understand?"

He looked offended.

For some reason, Ann thought it was an act.

Since then, Ann had not done more than nod and greet him. Twice more, he had asked to call on her again and she had demurred. He did not seem to realize that she cared for him less each time she saw him.

Tonight was no exception. Unfortunately, Lady Houghton had made him Ann's dinner partner. Adam had been charming. When a footman served the courses or the tables turned so that she conversed with the person on her other side, however, Adam's flaming blue gaze had branded her hair, her mouth, her cleavage. She prayed she acted as if she hadn't noticed. But her skin crawled wherever his eyes touched.

Ann hoped the entertainment Lord and Lady Houghton planned was short and sweet. She yearned to go home.

Ann smiled as she forced her attention to her cousin, who once more derided the array of single males constantly paraded before them at such social functions.

"I tell you, sugar, neither snow nor sleet nor bullets will run off these fellows. They're on the scent of money. My gosh, they're sweating so by the prospect that they've melted the starch in their cravats. They think we've all got piles of gold. Even me."

Ann took a comb from her evening bag. "Poor dears."

"If you ask me, these men need more than American girls to fill their beds and their bank accounts. They need fortitude. Most of them look as if they'll fall over in the slightest wind. I'd love to make my nana's étouffée and pecan pie for them. Put some excitement in their lives—and flesh on their bones." She fished in her tiny purse for a minute, then extracted a pot of rouge. "Speaking of which, what *was* that second course we had?"

Ann recalled it with a grimace. "Brains, I thought."

"Any idea whose? My guess is they belong to the little viscount. The color was definitely gray."

"Tasted like India rubber."

Raine daubed a bit of color on her face with a small brush. "These English need to learn how to cook as well as eat. Meat and potatoes are so borin'. Bilious, too." She puffed out her cheeks to illustrate.

Colleen grinned at them from the doorway of the inner lavatory. "Well, my dears, if you thought the menu needed a little spice, I do believe we'll get a good dose of it from the after-dinner entertainment." Sweeping forward in her aubergine watered satin, she came to check her appearance for any repairs before they descended the stairs.

"Madame Fontaine?" Raine queried. "Moves like an alligator through the swamp. Slow and hefty."

Colleen sat in the boudoir chair before the mirror, repositioning her ruby necklace. "She needs a few lessons in proper English custom not to talk too much at the table."

"Did she bill and coo enough during dinner?" Raine drew up her bosom in imitation of the pompous actress currently appearing in Drury Lane.

Colleen complained, "Like a magpie."

"Maybe," Ann said, "because she's an actress, she thinks it's permissible to flaunt the rules and gush over the food, inhale the flowers and—"

Colleen nodded. *"And* her dinner partner."

"Freddy the frumpy Earl of Fiddlesticks? Hmph. She can have him." Raine snapped her purse shut.

Ann chuckled. "Madame appears to be enchanting him."

Raine snorted. "Why doesn't she lean over and enthrall Adam Litchfield? She'd save one of us some worries."

Ann scoffed. "The good Earl is not interested."

"The man needs to take his blinders off."

Ann fluffed the jade silk across her bodice. "You can say that again." Raine and she had talked often about why Adam refused to see how Ann rebuffed him. They had no answers for his stubbornness. "How long do you think Fontaine will honor us? I need to go home. My shoes are too tight."

Colleen balked. "You promised to look as if you were enjoying yourself."

"Oh, come, *ma chaton.*" Raine was seriously aghast at Colleen. "I know you want to impress these people, but—"

"I *like* the Houghtons," Colleen insisted. "I like them much better than the de Villiers on Monday—"

"Ah, the slim Countess," Ann recollected, "and her slimmer Count."

"Who looked like," Raine added, "they were *count*ing their pennies from the way they scrimped on dinner portions."

"My father says they are émigrés from the last French revolution. They have only their son to sell." Ann glanced about, asking silently if anyone would buy him.

Colleen snickered. "They can keep him. *He* looked like a stuffed partridge."

"Mmm, let's give them credit." Raine licked her lips. "At least they served him instead of brains."

Colleen was trying to scowl at them and not succeeding because of her giggles. "If you two would stop criticizing for a few minutes, you would admit that tonight has been our best event so far. The Houghtons are charming people."

Raine tilted her head. *"Comme ci, comme ça.* They have a few important topics of conversation."

"For you," Ann concluded, "they had just one that mattered. Politics."

"Only you, Raine," Colleen murmured, "would find any delight in a discussion of the differences between the British Parliament and the American Congress. You lived too long in Washington working for that newspaper."

"Can I help it, *ma chaton,* if I wished to know something more than the newest slogan for the next soap advertisement I should draw? *Non!"*

"Oh, for heaven's sake, Lord and Lady Houghton are the most fun-filled hosts we've met since the Rothschilds' ball a few weeks ago," Colleen pointed out with a consoling smile. "Let's rise to the occasion, shall we?"

The three of them nodded in the mirror at each other. This was their only acknowledgment of the embarrassment Ann had endured after the Rothschilds' ball. Colleen's ability to overlook any negative event and carry on beautifully was her hallmark. It helped her recover from her own mishaps—and encouraged the others to do the same.

"Come on now," Colleen urged. "They've invited these young men to look us over, spread the word that we might be Americans but we don't have three heads and horns."

"We have been superb tonight," Raine confirmed with flourish. "The Houghtons will spread the word that we are rehearsed, respectable, and *resplendent* in our diamonds and pearls—except for me, who is draped in Ann's, which they can't know."

"But I am certain," Ann mused, "that you'll tell anyone, first chance you get."

"No use raising their expectations, sugar."

"Oh, really," Colleen fumed gaily, "you two outnumber me. If Gussie were only able to come to these events, she would find lots of wonderful things to say about them. I wish we could have persuaded Aunt Peg to say Gussie was old enough for the evening parties. *She* would adore the men."

"Hmmm," Ann considered, "how about the one with the lorgnette?" She squeezed one eye shut, bowed her spine, then let her mouth hang open.

"Sugar, to complete that picture, you need to drool."

Colleen laughed. "Both of you are not being fair."

"Oh, Coll." Ann brandished her hand. "I've never seen such an assortment of oddities in one room."

"First"—Raine stuck up one finger—"we have Mister Pasty. Complexion whiter than my muslin drawers."

"And the Chinless Viscount," Ann added, pulling her jaw back into her neck.

"Well," Colleen said, "I *adore* his friend, Jason Rutledge."

Raine held up three fingers. "Third one's a charm. At least he's got two good eyes."

"Plus a square chin—*and* no spittle," Ann reflected.

Raine lifted both palms. "Jason Rutledge wins tonight's contest. Hands down."

"Jason Rutledge," Colleen informed them with censure, "told me he got tanned like that riding on his plantation in Cuba. He grows sugar cane. Works in the fields himself. *And* have you ever seen shoulders so broad?"

I have, Ann thought. "I'll give you your due, Colleen. He's the handsomest of tonight's lot."

Raine *tsk*ed. "But Aunt Peg says there's something not quite appropriate about Jason's background."

"His family made their fortune and got their barony by brewing beer," Colleen told them, merry eyes running from one to the other, ready for their attack.

"Ah, yes, I remember now." Ann nodded solemnly. "The Rutledges are the first members of the Beerage."

"I don't care, you two. Jason is more exciting than the baking powder king we met at that reception yesterday." Colleen was putting the finishing touch to the repair of her perfect coif. "Jason likes me. He spoke more than twice to me before we went in to dinner. He even asked to refill my punch cup. He's handsome, funny, *rich,* and he told me in so many words that he's looking for a wife."

"Got all that from him during eight endless courses, did you, *cherie?*" Raine bent beside her to check the clasps of her earbobs. "You're efficient, I give you that."

"You," Colleen replied to Raine, "are too flippant."

"You are too eager," Raine insisted, and turned her

friend toward the mirror. "You are one beautiful woman, Miss VanderHorn."

"No, I'm not as—"

"Don't say it, Colleen," Ann warned. "Please. We have been through this too many times in the past eight years. You are lovely." Ann considered Colleen's round face and well-endowed figure. "You have all the attributes of a beauty. A flawless complexion."

"Ruddy," Colleen corrected.

"The pink in your skin brings out your large eyes."

"*Black* eyes. Not bright blue like Raine's or green and gold and brown like yours. I have this frizzy black cherry hair I have to pomade to straighten," she mourned, "and heavy eyes and lips, and I look like a gypsy. Why couldn't I look like Mama? With her golden hair and green eyes, I'd get—"

"*Mon dieu,* here we are again. Why look like someone else when you can be you? Delightful you? Colleen, you have seductive eyes and lips any man would want to kiss."

Ann put her hands on Colleen's shoulders. "You look like what you are—intelligent and fun-loving. Those are assets I wish you'd remember for more than ten minutes. You will find a husband, if that is what you truly want, and God knows, we'll help you, but take your time. Be selective. Be discreet," she offered ruefully, "just like me."

"Ah," Colleen crooned. "You are without trying."

"Colleen's right, Ann. You couldn't be indiscreet if you ran outside in the rain in your shimmy."

"There's a chilly thought." Ann shuddered. "Maybe back home that was true. Here I've rather botched it, as they say. In any case, I will live that down, I promise you. For your sakes and mine."

Colleen gave her a little hug. "We know you're chomping at the bit, sweetie. Not like home, is it? I'm the one people usually talk about, and I know how difficult it is to cover up your urges."

"Honey." Raine put a hand to Colleen's arm. "You've been wonderful here. Pure as the driven snow."

"Sure. I'm scared to death to be anything other," she admitted. "In New York, I lived as I wanted because Daddy's friends would never say a word against me. Here, they can be ruthless—for no reason. You didn't do anything awful, Ann. Imagine what they'd do if they saw one of us at a burlesque."

Ann laughed with Raine over Colleen's most famous escapade, cutting class with the French instructor to go to a musical. "He *was* irresistible. If he'd invited Raine or me, we might have gone with him ourselves."

"Raine maybe," Colleen said, "but you? Never."

"Please," Ann objected. "Let's not rub salt in my wound." Attracted to a man, Ann knew she would not meet him for a rendezvous. She'd tried that once with Quinn in February, and obviously she wasn't the sort of person who did well breaking the rules. Things exploded in her face. Even when she didn't intend to be noticed and tried to escape an outlandish situation—like Rhys at the Rothschilds'—she got caught in the act.

"I am trying to make a new start here," Colleen was bemoaning, "but you know I must not go home without a husband. My mother can be very demanding."

Veronica VanderHorn could be a witch. Requiring an accounting from each daughter of how she spent her personal allowance. Screening which parties they accepted invitations to. Forcing them to wear "posture improvers" since the time each became ten years old. Gus had submitted to the torture without a word because she had witnessed her older sister's useless objections to the tight bands that bound her shoulders back in a painful arch. To gain compliance from Colleen, Mrs. VanderHorn had used the lash of her tongue, her hand, and—Raine and Ann suspected—a whip.

"Your mama," Raine said, "wants you to bring home a title. Well, we're going to see that you take her one, honey. But do us all a favor and yourself a justice, will you? Find a husband you can love and respect. Not just one who's got his hand in your daddy's wallet."

"It's not easy, oh wise one."

"Find one," Ann elaborated, "who doesn't *need* Daddy's money."

"Difficult to do, when the English get such delight from saying, 'All the best people spend money but do not earn it.'"

"Yes, well, they've got to have some sort of code so a body could *know* who's eligible," Raine conjectured.

"The best thing to know," Ann concluded, "is who appeals to you the same way the French instructor did."

Colleen rustled up a hint of her brand of mischief with a smirk. "Anyone who offers cigarettes and blended scotch?"

Ann waved a hand. "It's a start."

Raine zeroed in. "Honey, just don't sell the rest of your life short because your mother wants a nobleman to call her son-in-law. If you find a man here in England whom you love, your mother will be far away—and irrelevant to your daily life."

"She can be ferocious."

"Cherie, she is not going to live with the man. Forget her."

Ann agreed. "The next man you see whom you like, give us the ear pinch, and Raine and I will circle the wagons."

"Oui. To hell with his bank accounts."

Colleen grinned. "The last time you helped me with a man, we all got into big trouble. Raine got caught with the key in the dormitory lock and had to do scullery duty."

"And Ann," Raine recalled, "couldn't go out to ride for a month because she filched the key."

Ann huffed. "I hope we're wiser now."

Raine laughed. "Sugar, we're more polished."

Colleen tilted her head at the door. "Are we ready? Let's go down. Your father should be here by now, Ann, and Lady Houghton wants to launch Fontaine."

They hooked their arms together as they walked along the landing, and Colleen said, "I love these parties. If I can just stop fretting about remembering the thousand and one rules of etiquette. Don't address this one before that one because he has the bigger title or his is older than the other man's. These nits could give you hives."

Raine threw her a wicked look. "Honey, relax. Let yourself live a little."

"The pot calling the kettle black." Ann chuckled. "All right, remember now," she admonished, "not every man we'll meet can be penniless."

"Darlin'," Raine crooned, "as long as they're all

not chinless, I might find myself one who isn't brain-less."

They reached the top of the circular marble stairs.

"You first," Colleen urged Ann.

"I'm last," Raine declared. "Go. *Shoo,*" she insisted to Colleen, who gave her a shriveling glance.

Ann arranged her satin train behind her and took hold of the carved marble banister, beginning her descent. Her attention quickly fastened on the commotion at the front door. The butler was opening it to a few new arrivals. Three men. Ann's father. Another tall gentleman who swept off his tophat to reveal blond hair, generous mouth, and an ebony eye patch. Behind him stood Rhys Kendall.

Colleen sucked in her breath. "Good God," she whispered. "Rhys and *who* else?"

Ann kept walking. Rhys Kendall, who had removed his own black silk tophat and white evening gloves, was surrendering his cape. He looked every bit a duke tonight. The superbly cut swallowtail coat and the ivory complement of his shirt with diamond and emerald stickpin in his cravat added up to a sleek elegance that threatened and appealed. Even his actions seemed more courtly, as if he had grown into his title, assumed his heritage with the wave of his hand. His words were low, his smile serene, until his eyes drifted up the stairs to Ann and took flame.

She had forgotten the power of his gaze. Before it had soothed her. Tonight it consumed her.

As always, his sudden appearance in her life surprised her. But on no occasion had his attention thrilled her to her bones, as he did now.

Why was he here? Why was he with her father? Skip had gone to a dinner party at a gentlemen's club with one of his investors in the cruise line. He had told her nothing more, other than that he had notified Lady Houghton that he would join them in time for the musical entertainment. The three girls had gone on to the Houghtons' with Aunt Peg.

The Houghtons' butler made short work of collecting and disposing of the men's accoutrements, announcing he would notify Lady Houghton that they had finally arrived. Skip thanked him, then stepped forward and kissed Ann's cheek.

"Hello, my dears." He took in Colleen and Raine. "I told you I'd be here as soon as I could get away. Business knows no social rules. I'm sure you did us proud, though." He put out a hand to the elegant gentleman with the dashing eye patch. "I'd like to present Lord Falconer." Skip did the honors with each girl, as Ann's focus went to Rhys.

His warm eyes were flowing down her body like syrup over flapjacks. She felt devoured and shivered. His gaze languidly journeyed up to hers.

"You remember His Grace," Skip was saying to her. *No. Not as well as I thought. This way—sophisticated and every inch a duke of the realm—he is another man to me. Deliberate. Assertive.* "Yes, I could not forget." She told him the unvarnished truth and mentally kicked herself.

"Good evening, Miss Brighton," Rhys offered, and it struck her that she had also forgotten how his baritone voice could brush her jumping nerves like the caress of aged chamois. "I have spent many days remembering you. I fear my mind is not as sound as I suspected, because I had forgotten so many details I should have engraved there." His words were soft, but when he raised her hand to his mouth, his lips were hot.

Blistered by his touch, she pulled her hand away, and he let it go, inch by inch.

She noticed vaguely that the others had paused, shocked that Rhys had kissed her hand in the continental manner and remained reluctant to relinquish it. His boldness eased the ache he'd caused by his absence.

Ann turned and busied herself with introductions. Colleen was enchanted by the nobleman with the patch. He was obviously very taken with Raine, who found him appealing until Colleen reached up and flicked her earbob with her finger. Their sign, created some six years ago, had Raine backing away from the man to whom her friend now laid claim.

Lady Houghton swept toward them in a cloud of blue faille and restiveness. "Oh, my dears, I am so pleased you have arrived before the entertainment. Hello, Skip. I despaired that you might not get here in time." She allowed him to buss her on the cheek. "Bryce, you devil. I was delighted when your footman brought round that note this morning that you were down from the country and able to come tonight after your little dinner meeting. Recovering quickly, are you?" She touched a fingertip to his patch.

"Yes, Aunt Lettie. The doctors say it should be another month before it can come off. Then I shall be good as new."

"Dear boy, you must give us all a present by reforming your ways. Instead, do say, 'I shall be good.'"

Bryce Falconer gave a wry quirk to his mouth. "I try never to promise what is not in my heart, Auntie."

"It is your heart we fear is the next target, you wretch. No more duels, darling. You frighten us. What do you think, Your Grace?" She went from her nephew's arms to Rhys's. "You are such a controlled creature yourself, dear Rhys, why can't you influence Bryce to reform?"

Rhys shook his head. "My dear, since Bryce and I met at school when we were a tender six, I have given him much advice to no avail. Experience is his only teacher."

"While you, Your Grace, need more social life. I am so pleased you've come. I knew you wrote you might not be able to, but Skip promised he'd ask."

"I came tonight not because Skip urged me but because I have settled a few matters just today that preoccupied me."

"Well, then, I hope now you will come out more often."

"I plan on it," he vowed, making Ann wonder why he would change the pattern of his social life. Not only was he emerging from his self-imposed cocoon, but he had withdrawn from the cruise line venture. Hadn't lack of money been the reason he lived a frugal, quiet existence? What brought him out now?

"Good," Lettie Houghton was saying. "Let me offer incentive for that. You take in Miss Brighton, will you? Bryce, do the honors with Miss VanderHorn and Miss Montand." She looped her arm through Skip's. "Come, come. We must join the others, lest they think we've abandoned ship."

Bryce grinned at Raine first and then at Colleen. "Allow me." He offered an arm to each, leaving Rhys and Ann alone and facing each other.

"How are you?" Rhys asked, as if he had eternities to gaze at her.

"Wonderful." *Liar.*

His expression became sultry, as if he perceived her thoughts. "I worried about you."

"You needn't." She applauded herself that she sounded so objective when she felt utterly breathless.

"But I was responsible for what happened at the Rothschilds'." He seemed to memorize her hair and mouth.

"On the contrary." She moved fractionally away, her excitement that he was here and apologizing filling her with joy. "I take full responsibility for my own actions."

"Oh, sweetheart, why do you think I've stayed away?"

His endearment trilled along her spine. She examined him, the drawing room seconds away with no time to ask why he thought he could use endearments. "An ague?"

He pressed her arm to his hard ribs and told her, "It was an affliction not to come near you. But I have seen you riding in the Row and walking in the square." She stared at him. "Yes, I have. You didn't see me, but I noticed you, Grace, and you looked like a bundle of nerves. Can't slip away to ride astride or bareback, can you?"

"You followed me?" She was pleased, but wary that he'd done that and that she'd never observed him. If she had not seen him, had she not seen others? Were her abilities to detect people simply poor, or were her observers superbly skilled at obscuring themselves? "Why would you do that? Why not speak to me?"

"I promised myself not to reappear in your life until my business was accomplished first."

"Business." Her old nemesis. Men's justification for their priorities.

"I had to take care of a few vital matters before I saw you again in public. I watched you only when I couldn't live without the sight of you. Six mornings, in a very lonely month, Grace. A paltry diet for a man who wants a feast." His words ignited her senses, sparking memories of moments in his arms. Her gaze drifted to his. If eyes could kiss, his now mastered the art. "I heard news of you, too."

Her heart opened like one of his roses in spring air. "From whom?"

"Will you shoot him for talking with me?"

"Immediately."

"Good. He was not happy when I told him I cared for you." Rhys *tsk*ed. "Darling, your mouth is open again. He'll still court you if you encourage him. Have you?"

"His name?"

"Adam." Rhys's expression grew desperate. "Do you like him?"

"He is pleasant."

"Has he called on you?"

"Only once." They approached the double doors to the saloon, where Adam Litchfield waited, no doubt ready to maneuver himself next to her or behind her, always somewhere too close. His presence was becoming suffocating. "Why would you care?"

"Because I want you for myself. All to myself."

"You have an odd way of showing it," she retorted, and faced him. "Absence makes the heart forget, remember?"

"Have you forgotten me?" He sounded inconsolable.

She couldn't answer, couldn't move.

Something happened to her expression, though, because he murmured, "You are engraved upon my heart."

She bit her lip to stop her mouth trembling.

"God, darling, can't you see it with the roses?"

"Why do you send them?"

Like a little boy who'd given a present of his dearest possession and had it rejected, Rhys looked forlorn. "Don't you like them?"

"Oh, yes," she whispered, betraying how much she adored them. "They are incomparable."

"To you. Yes."

"Why send me roses when there is no hope of . . . ?" Where were the diplomatic words to say how much she valued his flowers and had yearned for his presence?

"There is now."

She paused at the door to the main saloon. She wanted desperately to come first with a man. This man. Ahead of his business, his money, his friends. The realization that she cared for Rhys against her own inclinations struck her like a blow to the head. She knew it was forward as hell of her, but she had to ask, "How can that be?"

"Come to tea tomorrow. At four at Kendall Great House." Rhys scanned the crowd of twenty-two people, impatient for the two of them to take their seats for the singing. "Then I'll show you my home"—he smiled at the assembly, looking every inch the premier nobleman in command of all he surveyed— "and tell you what I've done."

Chapter 8

"There are uses for American heiresses and their money after all."

— An anonymous lord, on seeing renovations of
Blenheim Palace

Rhys was tired of tea and his multitude of guests long before Ann poured the first cup for the group.

Still he sat, convivial as his years in society trained him to become, masking the need to fling her over his shoulder and escape with her to one of his eighty-four rooms. As Peg Gallagher enthused about his ancestral home, he fantasized that the place he should take Ann to end his suffering was one of his large and much underused twenty-two bedrooms.

"Kendall Great House *is* magnificent," Ann's aunt was gushing, and the lady had not yet seen more than the Italian marbled foyer and this grand salon. "I can't get over that I am truly inside one of the oldest homes in London."

Neither could Rhys submerge his own delight that he was here. He had cast the Tudor mansion from his mind since he'd decided to shut it up four years ago. "I miss it, too," he confessed.

Ann paused as she handed him his tea. "You don't live here?"

146

"No. I live in a suite of rooms in Marylebone. This house is much too big for a bachelor."

Ann's startled gaze returned to the far wall, where the portraits of his mother and father hung—and Rhys smiled. This woman knew his thoughts, his feelings. By her merest glance at his parents, he saw she perceived his heartache. He had missed his home, as one always does the place where one laughed and cried as a youth. Deep in his soul, he'd known he would revel in showing off the mansion to Ann Brighton—and now he understood why. He wanted not only to impress her but also to show her what kind of family he came from and how he wanted to duplicate one as richly satisfying for himself. "I ordered my housekeeper to open this wing for today."

"Divest the hall and east wing of its sheets and dust and cobwebs!" he had ordered three days ago when he'd sold the Van Dyck and his plan to go courting could proceed because he had in hand hard, cold cash. The elderly servant had done a spectacular job, too. The place sparkled in the late afternoon sun streaming through the aged creamy Brussels lace at the windows. He was proud of it today, its scrolled wrought-iron gates, its four colossal stories towering between the main thoroughfare of the Strand and the river, its splendors from the Tudors, Stuarts, and Hanoverians. Imperial in its colonnaded beauty, the residence of the dukes of Carlton and Dundalk was a landmark Rhys had cut from his conscience—and paid for in sorrow. But today, he would show this lovely young American woman his home's reputed glories and try to find a way to break down the barriers that kept her from him.

He searched her face. Elegant Grace. Sweet enough to eat in the apple-green tea gown and matching little hat with citron ribbons round her chin. Did she have any idea when she got into her brougham this afternoon how he meant to sweep her off her feet?

Damn. Why had he invited all these people last night? Propriety, curse it, demanded Ann not come alone to his house. Torture was what it was, to have her here—and not touch her.

Peg chattered on, apologizing for Skip, something about how she wished he had been well enough to come, too. But he'd been out late working last night. "Can you imagine? He came in at two."

Ann considered her tea. "He was soaked to the skin from the rainstorm."

"But he went home with all of you," Rhys said, worried not only about Skip's health but about why he had been out at an odd hour. For what reason?

Ann's eyes locked on Rhys's. "He received some sort of message to go to his office soon after we got home."

"He must stop pushing himself so hard," Rhys stated.

Ann nodded. Worry had her biting her lip.

Peg filled the lull in the conversation with a discussion of the superb quality of the tea cakes. Rhys told her his housekeeper bought them from a local baker. Someone—Raine, Rhys supposed—asked Gordon Worminster about how many people his double-decker bus transported. Rhys did not care but promised to look at it next week. Meanwhile, Colleen and Bryce seemed to concentrate only on each other. Rhys found himself commenting on innocuous topics. The weather, which was growing more humid after last night's downpour. The newest performance of Wagner's *Tannhauser,* which he invited them to join him in seeing next Thursday night. The providence of the Bruges tapestry on the far wall.

Finally, he could stand it no longer. He put down his cup and saucer on the tea table and said, "I will show you the rest of the house, if you like."

Gordon wanted to finish his tea and asked Peg to remain with him. She complied. Rhys learned from Gordon only this afternoon that thirty years ago, his friend had courted Margaret Brighton, wanted to marry her, but had been denied the blessing of his parents. "The little American," as they called her, was simply unacceptable. Gordon had remained a bachelor lo these many years. Peg had married for companionship. Today, she would rather sit and talk with her old beau than see the rest of the house. Odd, but then Rhys would not argue. It meant fewer people he had to rid himself of to get Ann Brighton alone.

When the others got up and preceded him to the hall, Rhys twined Ann's arm over his. "What would you like to see first?" he asked her, fully intending to show her the gallery. But her eyes laughed up at him, and he could not ignore the thrill it brought him.

Today, except for her worries over her father's health, she seemed so natural, so spontaneous in her enjoyment of his attentions. It was as if, since he had reappeared in her life last night, she blossomed like a rosebud into ever fuller flower. He would encourage that.

"Tell me what you want to see," he urged so that his other guests might not hear. "I promise you I will lose them all as soon as possible."

"Do you have roses here, Your Grace?"

"Not very many since I have sent one a day to the most beautiful woman I know."

He could feel her knees give on that. He imagined

pushing the others into the conservatory and locking the doors so that he could savor Ann alone for five uninterrupted minutes.

It took him at least twice that time to wend his way toward a billiard room for Colleen and Bryce to play in and a library to which Raine retired with a wave of her hand and a wink. "Go. *Shoo,*" she prodded. "Come to get me soon, *mon cher*. Afterward, I will exclaim glowingly about all your treasures you have shown me."

Rhys closed the door on Raine and led Ann along the two-hundred-foot-long, scarlet-walled gallery.

Ann paused before a full-length portrait of a pale lady in huge white ruff and yards of black velvet and pearls. "Who is she?"

"The third Duchess of Carlton and Dundalk, Bella. She was said to be adored by Charles the Second, who was fifteen years her junior. What do you think?"

Ann arched her neck, the column of her throat sparking a desire to trace its arc with his lips. "I recognize the family resemblance."

He chuckled, telling himself not to back Ann to the wall and kiss her. He had to treat her like the innocent she was, though he wished to teach her everything he had learned about wickedness. "Good God. In what way?"

"Her hair."

Rhys looked aghast at the woman whose mane was crimped and coiled and teased into a halo of brown curls. "I am glad I got mine cut. If I hadn't soon, I *would* look like Bella."

Ann laughed, her gaze on his locks. "I noticed last night you'd done it. Why?"

He bit his lower lip, temptation to put her hands in his hair a living torment. "It was either that or take up the violin." She got a bigger laugh from that one. "Honestly, though, I cut it for you."

"You needn't have," she whispered, and confessed, "I liked it the way it was."

"I'll grow it back quickly, then. I've done quite a few other things for you."

She stopped breathing as her eyes searched his. "I saw you wore your signet ring last night—and the diamond and emerald stickpin in your cravat."

"I have exhumed the family artillery," he joked. "I also saw my tailor."

She mentally measured his shoulders and memorized his mouth. "Your attitude is very different, too."

Gratified that she noted his new sense of power, he grinned. "How so?"

"You are dashing. Confident."

He took her hands. "There is no motivation greater than knowing what you want and implementing a plan to get it." He pressed her palms to his chest. "I want to know you better, Ann. I want us to have time together and laugh, free of my resentment of your father. I could not deny myself the pleasure of seeing you, and I thought you would want an opportunity to get to know me, too."

She swallowed hard. "You are right."

"But it disturbs you?"

She stepped backward, rolling her eyes at Bella in such a way that her tiny straw hat teetered on her head. "I doubt I can hear more without blushing."

"Ah, so you are complimented I would pursue you?"

"Charmed," she corrected, and suddenly she was not smiling any longer.

So, here we arrive at the challenge which is mine to eliminate.

Rhys collected every ounce of self-control he had learned during the last few bitter years. He had understood the night of the Rothschilds' ball that Ann Brighton rejected the idea of being enamored with a man. What had she said? "I refuse to allow my life to be ruled by what I feel for a man." It had stunned him. He, who came from a loving home where his parents adored each other. He, who believed love far better than friendship between marital partners.

"Permit me, then," he said with equanimity, "to explain my motives as well as my actions." He took her arm again. "Walk with me. No need to talk or even look at me. Just listen to me."

He changed the subject. "Let me tell you more about the house. Kendall Great House reflects a style of life centered around entertaining and impressing others. It was begun in fifteen-thirty on land granted by Henry the Eighth to a gentleman who was the ninth Earl of Carlton. Harry made him a duke when the fellow took an arrow intended for his king. To this day, the rent on this land is the grand sum of three barbed arrows paid to the monarch each January first."

"Wonderful," she mused, the tension in her body easing. "Saves a lot of money for you, doesn't it?"

"I would be paupered to pay the rent or the taxes."

"But the building, its plan and furnishings"—Ann waved a hand at the pastorals and portraits—"are worth more, some say, than the Queen's own possessions. How did that happen?"

"The items which fill the manor," Rhys explained, "came to us in various ways. The art is a good example. The pieces came by default, which is the case with a number of Van Dyck portraits of Charles the First, his family, and his cavaliers when the

Dutchman was appointed the monarch's court paint-er. Also by gift, from a grateful Joshua Reynolds and Gainsborough to their patroness, my great-grandmother. Or by purchase, which is the case for most of the paintings and sculpture. There are so many pieces that I have a devilish time bringing down enough servants each fall from High Keep—my home in Lancashire—to dust and clean them all. But I have taken a step to end that practice. Four days ago," Rhys said, his attention riveting on Ann, "I sold one piece which no one—including me—has looked at for decades. It hung here." He indicated a vacant spot on the red silk wall.

"First you sold your horse." Ann was bereft for him. "Now this."

"Don't be stricken, please. It was Van Dyck's first attempt at a portrait of Charles. To the artist and his subject, the rendering was not superb. Charles got angry at how ordinary it made him appear, and he gave it away in pique to his best friend, a Kendall. But the work is, in fact, so utterly lovely that I criticized myself I had kept it here away from people's view all these years. I intend to use the proceeds in a new enterprise"—his gaze defined her hair and mouth and, fleetingly, the rise of her breasts in the lavish satin—"to court you." His eyes locked on Ann's.

"Exciting," Ann managed, breath lodged in her chest.

"I thought so."

"But I don't think you need a lot of money to see me. I like . . ." She scanned his features with heart-stopping delicacy. ". . . Simple pleasures. Riding, reading, roses."

"I know." He reveled in her acceptance of his news. "Already, I see handsome returns, and it's only been a day or so. I am heartily encouraged to pursue the matter more."

"More?" Ann led him on, loving his banter. "How?"

"Rumor has taken news of my sale of the Van Dyck around to others. Just this morning, I received an offer from the mother of the man who bought the first portrait. She wishes to buy another of Charles's family which I have up at High Keep in my private collection there. This purchaser would like to put it up in her own gallery so that she and her visitors may enjoy it. She has offered a handsome amount, too. Twice what her son paid for the inferior painting. Twelve thousand pounds. Enough to keep me in this house, fed and clothed, with two servants and four thousand to spare for fun for a full year."

"That's absolutely wonderful. Who wanted it that much?"

"The Queen."

Ann's mouth formed a perfect O.

Satisfaction flowed through his bloodstream like a tonic. "I am tremendously flushed with joy over the black ink of my ledger book. I'm so impressed, in fact, that I consider selling the block of town houses I own in Marylebone."

"Where you have your rooms?"

"Yes. A nearby hospital seeks to expand its consulting clinic. They'd like the block I own."

"Why sell it to them?"

Because I begin to want you badly enough that I think I'd sell my name. "They're offering a goodly amount."

"But why do it, if you might earn more in the long run by renting it to them? In perpetuity would be best so that they'd feel as if they had a long-term stake in

154

their own investment. Is it possible here in England to rent in perpetuity?"

"Yes. I like your logic, but my time is already consumed by too many details. I don't have anyone to assist me with money matters, except my housekeeper at High Keep who does the estate books there. Renting requires a great deal of bookkeeping."

"Ah, but the salary you'd pay a good accountant would be negligible compared to what you might earn—especially as prices rise and you increase your rent proportionately and fairly, of course."

She was, after all, her father's daughter, with a good head for business. He paused to stare at her. "I am amazed at you and me."

"But why?"

"I sold one mediocre painting to afford to open this house, take a box at the opera, buy a new wardrobe, and discover if this joy I felt when I'm with you is a permanent one. I told myself the proceeds of the sale of one painting was a small price to pay to discover if infatuation might be more." If it were not, afterward, he might be on his merry way—he the wiser for having explored his feelings for her, she unscarred and able to take up with any other man or go home to Virginia. "Now I see that by breaking old restrictions, and ending old resentments, I have gained far more than I expected."

She was blushing ripe as a strawberry but spoke of business. "I'm glad you like my idea of renting—"

"I like *you.*" He raised his hand, intending to cup her chin, kiss her—and knew instinctively he must not touch her. He had to let her lead them into any physical relationship. He had to woo her with words, logic, integrity. "Let me show you my roses."

Within minutes, Rhys realized that the best painting he could ever have commissioned was the scene of Ann beholding the lush rose bushes that climbed his ancient garden walls. But no one would ever see how she admired them, he vowed. No one would ever know the way her lips parted and her eyes fell over the profusion of white buds and blossoms in his secluded patio. He'd make a point that no other man would ever see her like this, because that fellow would have no compunctions about taking her in his arms and kissing her until she sighed, naked and sated, in his bed. She walked along the garden path, her hand trailing the petals as she bent now and then to inhale the fragrance—and twist his heart with fresh desires.

"They are damask roses from the Levant," he cleared his throat to inform her. "We grow them here, also in Kent at another estate of mine and with some difficulty in the north at High Keep Castle. They grow nowhere so well as here at the main seat of the family." He picked one fat one, pinched off the thorns, and tucked it over her ear. "They suit you. I have never sent them to any other woman."

The way she looked at him with a hint of a tear in her eye devastated his control. She was so utterly lovely, he wanted to show her with a touch and feel her melt with longing at his compliment.

He pictured himself peeling the dress away. She wore so few layers beneath the cloth. The three brief times he'd held her in his grasp, he had perceived that. He yearned to hold her again, to press her rounded shoulder, her pert breasts, her long legs against him. Rock hard and throbbing for her, he chastised himself for his randiness. Wanting her more irrationally, more erotically each time he met her proved that if he didn't hurry to find the reasons his intellect might want her for a mate, his male instinct would seize control. Unleashed, his passion to possess her would put her on her back while he injected himself into her life permanently because he had deflowered her and impregnated her with his child. How, then, would he be able to predict if their marriage could weather the decades? What would the odds become that they would discover bliss?

God knew, he did not want to disillusion her more. Did not want to take her body, teach her how to pleasure him and herself, then by the very claiming cut her off from her own vision of her future. He could not live with himself if he did. Nor did he want a wife whose heart was not his.

He prodded himself to a measured progress with her. Best to let her know all the particulars of his personal and public life. If he were to find her totally enchanting and want to marry her, she would have to deal with the trappings of his status and titles. If he were to marry her, he needed a wife who could not only accept all he was and represent it with a happy heart but also carry out her own duties as his chatelaine. Could Ann Brighton do that? He had to know, and so he found the words to introduce it into this conversation. "I wrote a note to the Queen this morning and told her that I will be calling on you."

"You didn't!" She was outraged and delighted.

"I know she will wish to meet the lady who has caught my eye."

Ann dropped her jaw. "Meet her? Oh, Rhys, I couldn't."

"I am one of merely fifteen dukes of England, second only in precedence to her sons, the three Dukes of the Blood Royal, and her heir, Prince Edward."

"Impressive."

"Fearsome?"

"Formidable. We Americans are not daunted by titles." She laughed at herself. "Or so we say."

"There is more to my explanation."

She smiled. "I should have known. Tell me."

"The first of my titles extends to the Norman period and the first Norman king, William the Conqueror. My ancestor Etienne of the village of Roulard was one of William's stoutest friends and retainers. I still have Etienne's sword hanging on my wall at Roulard Hall in Kent. But for every monarch since William, it is the responsibility of the current Baron Roulard to walk behind the monarch on state occasions and carry that broadsword and leather targe. The Roulards, tradition says, protect the back of the King and Queen of England."

"Like your other ancestor who stepped into the path of an assassin's arrow meant for Henry the Eighth."

"Yes, and also by the third Duke of Carlton who obeyed an order from his friend Charles the First to take the state regalia from the King's Jewel House and hide them from Cromwell's army."

"Did he succeed?"

"Too well. No one has ever found them."

"Your family history is noble, nonetheless."

"I'm delighted you think so." Rhys grinned, feeling very much like a satisfied fox.

"I am delighted you've gone to such trouble for me. Meanwhile, I am certain that with the sale of the painting, your ancestors are rolling in their coffins."

"They are blessing me for my uncommon good sense to sell a painting in order to court a gorgeous woman. If it can make you grin like that, I'll see what else I might find to amuse you." *And keep you.*

She cocked her head, and this time her hat did fall. He lifted it carefully from the tangle of her pins and hair. The feel of dark red satin tresses made him swallow audibly as he placed the straw pillbox on a garden bench.

"Do you have any family skeletons in your cellars?" she asked while his hands circled two finger curls, then settled on her shoulders.

"A few. None who will hurt you."

"Any good wines?"

"Two cases of rare Bordeaux. A lot of ancient trunks filled with old and lovely clothes. Have you ever played charades when you were young? Adam, Bryce, and I used to don doublets, pretend we were cavaliers— What's the matter, darling? What did I say?"

She looked as if she'd cry. "I—we didn't have time to play. The war—"

"Ann, Christ, I'm sorry. I didn't mean to upset you."

She blinked away her sadness. "I know you didn't. What of your treasures? Tell me. I'd like to play dress-up."

You will. With me. He grinned. "Upstairs in the master suite"—his thoughts drifted to the Kendalls' ancestral Tudor fifteen-foot-wide bed—"I have closets full of furs." *Ermine for your skin.* "Caskets of jewelry. Bella's ropes of pearls would look superb on you." *Without another stitch on this lithe body.* "And tiaras." *Diamonds to replace every mundane hat you've ever worn—and lost.*

"Nothing else of high value?" she asked, pink with his proximity.

"That depends on personal taste."

"Really? What is it?"

159

"Me."

"You are the greatest treasure of them all," she said, barely a tone above their heartbeats. "I knew it in Dublin."

She was so near now, he felt her warm breath upon his lips. "Did you?"

"I have never met anyone as tempting as you." She swept one hand into his hair, then snatched it away. She moved backward and could go no farther for the roses embracing her. She had to walk forward again, so close that she stood against him, flush, warm, and trapped.

"Why is that a problem? Don't go," he urged her when she would have sidestepped him. "It is. If I didn't see it when first we met, it was because I had my own conflicts to deal with. But at the ball, you told me you don't want to be ruled by what you feel for a man. Why?"

"That is difficult to discuss," she whispered, looking away. But then she raised her face to him and said, "It is probably just as hard as talking about one's personal income, the sale of family heirlooms and a block of town houses."

"Something tells me it is more difficult."

"Please, Rhys, you're being kind again—"

"Then I'll be kinder. I want you to know that I have been to see the publisher of *The Gazetteer*. Yes." He smiled at her surprise and pleasure. "I have. He will not print anything more about you ever again, nor does he employ the man who wrote those columns about you."

"How did you do that?"

"I had something he valued more than the delight of his readers."

She was laughing. "What?"

"I bought up his mortgage on his printing presses."

"My God." She stood, hands limp at her sides. "When? How?"

"Bryce bought it up for me on a thirty-day note which I paid him for after I sold the first Van Dyck. Friends are very good people to have around when you need them."

She nodded. "How well I know," she murmured. "Is there anything you have not done?"

"Yes." He could not stop the twinkle that shone in his eyes.

"What? *What?*"

"I have not kissed you today, and I need to."

Her throat worked at words.

"But I won't do it."

"No?"

He shook his head.

Why? Her mouth formed the word for which she could not find voice.

She knew, he thought from the blush on her cheeks, what he would say before he did. "Because you must."

"I want to."

He was going to savor her mouth for as long as she'd let him. "Show me."

"You can't imagine how hard you're making this."

"I have a very firm idea, believe me. Do it."

Her gaze caressed his lips. "I have thought about this so often that I wondered if your kisses were just daydreams of you. I tried so hard to remember exactly how you tasted . . ." Her eyes drifted closed.

"Come refresh your memory, sweet lady." *Before I scoop you up like some savage.*

She drew nearer, her hands spanning his shoulders and wending up his throat to his nape. "That first day in Dublin, you protected me. Then you sent me your father's books and offered me something I needed. So few people stop to give what another person needs— only what they want to give. Then, when you saved me from social ridicule, mere words could never thank you. But I didn't see you for so long. I couldn't stop thinking about you. Not during this past month, either, when your roses came, but you didn't." She brushed her mouth on his, she trembled, and when he thought he might have, too, he had to put his hands around her to steady her. "No one has ever shown such dedication to me."

"None of these men who come to call and send you bouquets by the bucketfuls?"

"If they came more than once or twice, I didn't notice. To impress me, they spent little more than their money."

The fires inside him began to burn with torrid flames. "I'd love for you to demonstrate how impressed you are with me, my dear."

She shook back her hair and tossed him a saucy look. "Are there kisses that show that?"

"We won't know until you try." He waited.

She licked her lips with a thoroughness that had him suppressing a groan. "Once I start, I may not stop."

"Fortunate me."

"Well, then. Approval must feel like this." She framed his face and gave him a foursquare kiss. Rolling her tongue around her mouth, she tilted her head. "Want to try out fascination?"

His thick lashes swept up to reveal his hot response.

She nestled nearer, her breasts boring into his waistcoat. She slanted her mouth on his with such swift, sweet force, he dug his fingers into her back. She flung her arms madly around his neck, and she drifted in this new power over him.

This kiss was nothing small or tremulous, but total assurance. He wrapped her to him as if he'd never let her go, knew soon he wouldn't, and clamped chains of decorum on his ravening desires.

"I asked for this," he rasped, and drew away, "and now I'm damned if I can handle it. We are going to go back and . . . Don't look at me like that." He took her in his arms and gave her a kiss that made him wish he were unprincipled and could seduce her without compunction. But he needed more than her in his arms. He wanted her there because she needed to be, because she desired him above all else. "We are going to return to Raine and the others, because if we don't, we will be doing more things we shouldn't." He laughed as he tried to fluff her curls and replace her hat. "I promise you we will find more ways to kiss."

"Soon would be best," she said with coyness while she stabbed a lengthy pin into her hat.

He hooted. Her insatiability was a welcome sign of progress which he wanted to encourage. "I'll rack my brain to find a private place."

"Not much hope there, Your Grace." She flicked a button on his waistcoat. "You could meet me tomorrow in the Row at two."

"With as much privacy as Westminster Abbey." But the nooks and crannies of that church suddenly appealed to him. "Have you seen Shakespeare's monument?"

She shuddered theatrically but caught his drift with a tip of her head and a grin. "I suppose my American education will remain sadly lacking until I do."

"Arrive alone at two at the Bard's statue. I'll teach you a few new lessons."

"Poems?"

"Couplets."

An hour later, as he sat in his chair contemplating the portraits of his parents, Rhys reflected on his afternoon.

His father, who had always distrusted Skip's ruthlessness, would be displeased over Rhys's fear about what was happening to Skip Brighton. Rhys would call on Skip in Watling Street tomorrow at nine and see why Skip went out in rainstorms. Rhys hoped Owen MacIntyre was not the cause. He prayed to God that Ann was not touched by the perversity of Owen's revenge. But the little man in Dublin resurrected like a specter in Rhys's mind. Rhys cursed, deciding to hire his own man to follow Ann night and day henceforth.

Rhys had told Skip he would do all in his power to restore her to society. He'd also protect her, even if Skip's man O'Leary was supposed to be on that job. Rhys would spend every penny he owned to keep Ann safe, too. She was worth everything to him.

That made him smile, too, because both his mother and father, he assumed, were gleefully dancing at this moment in heaven over his choice of a bride. Ann did not yet know he had decided to propose to her, of course. But the inevitability grew as their walk in his garden had progressed—and his desire for her had flowered with the recognition that Ann Brighton would suit him perfectly.

His mother would agree. Ann Brighton had wit, charm, and grace. *His* Grace, he corrected. Rhys would make her that in name and title as she had made herself in his heart.

His father would approve. Ann Brighton brought to the family those qualities a Kendall duchess was expected to possess in abundance. Rare beauty. Courage. Charm.

If she also possessed a dowry, his father would rejoice. But Rhys would reject it. Every penny.

Ann Brighton would come to him only in her skin.

On that arousing thought, Rhys rose to pour himself a draught of brandy.

He wanted her, and he had collected enough evidence today that she cared for him immensely. Oh, yes, he'd court her. But before August first, when he had to return to High Keep Castle for the harvest, he would see their courtship to its conclusion. At worst, he would retire to his country home alone. At best, he'd take her with him to his chapel. There, above the vaults of his ancestors, he'd gladly vow to honor her, keep her, adore her in and out of every bed he owned. Forever.

His challenge remained keeping his hands off her while she worked out her own conflicts about caring for a man.

Because, God knew, he loved her. And he had no idea how he'd cope with his misery if she refused to let herself love him in return.

Chapter 9

"Young ladies must not receive calls from gentlemen alone, unless they have passed the rubicon of thirty summers."

—ANONYMOUS, *The Habits of Good Society*

ANN COULD NOT SAY SHE LOVED HIM.

As the foyer clock chimed the third hour past midnight, she admitted that fact to herself and decided what her approach to Rhys Kendall's advances would be. Enjoyment. She'd never before had a man court her. Not with such romantic sentiments as roses, words, and noble actions. Despite that, she could not bring herself to commit her heart to him. She needed more time to assure herself that her admiration—and her desire—for him were qualities that could endure the test of tribulation.

Straight as an arrow to the mark, Rhys had found the crux of her conflict. When he told her yesterday that he wanted her to confront it, overcome it if she could, she knew she owed it to herself and him to try. She had reaped rewards for her decision, too. His kisses were her prize. She chuckled to herself as she tossed the covers from her bed at dawn and rose. What's more, she'd have fun doing it.

The prospect of taking an emotional risk had her

matching it with the urge to flout her father's rules to take John O'Leary everywhere. She drew on her riding clothes and hurried down the back servants' stairs and out the kitchen door. She headed for the family stable. Not the young groom, the coachman, or even O'Leary came awake to try to waylay her. She felt her heart banging in anticipation of her freedom, even if she did bow to propriety and choose the sidesaddle. Her joy transferred to Raider, who nickered approval of their escapade. She led him down to the Row, and they took the empty lane along the Serpentine until another rider appeared.

Ann turned toward home. She feared it might be Adam Litchfield, and she had no desire to spoil her euphoria with the sour smile of that man.

She entered the square just as the dairyman appeared with his small covered wagon. She slowed Raider to a walk when, within a froth of shrubbery, Ann detected the flower lady. Her floppy hat sat lopsided on her head, and her hunched back was ramrod straight as she seemed to be . . . Ann choked in laughter and then frowned. The woman was urinating into the bushes . . . like a man.

A short, thin man.

He buttoned his flies and let his skirts fall, resuming his bent posture and pushing up his hat on his thick—probably fake horsehair—bun. He turned, pushed aside one tree branch, and looked straight at Ann.

He had a gaunt face, slits for eyes. No mustache. Furthermore, his was the severe face of a man. So similar to . . . the one Ann had seen in Tattersall's stable the morning she had bought Raider and accidentally met Rhys. A short, thin man with dark hair . . . who could have so easily *shaved* his mustache. Who could have followed them from Dublin. Who could have been spying on them all these months. Why?

For the *Gazetteer?* No. That would not make sense. She had been no one of any note until she had snubbed Rhys Kendall in the Row months later. Besides, Rhys had said he influenced the publisher of the tabloid to stop printing articles about her. Therefore, this could not be a reporter. It had to be someone else. Here for another reason than to spy on her. After all, who was she that she should presume everyone was spying on her? She was an American girl who'd entered London society only as father's daughter and . . .

She smiled and waved normally. How many times during the war had she run across shocking sights and not flinched but done what was necessary? Meanwhile, her mind whirled.

Who are you? Why are you disguised? Why do you come at this early hour?

Aunt Peg had praised the woman for frequenting the square as much as she did. Her father had agreed. "Money is tight for the lower classes. The woman's enterprising nature should be encouraged. Buy a few posies from her." He had chuckled. "As if we haven't enough."

Ann decided to tell her father about this person masquerading in the square. After she and Raine had suspected the fat man outside the Rothschilds' house was the *Gazetteer* reporter, her father had made her promise to come tell him if she ever saw that man or any other again. O'Leary had been especially watchful since then, at her father's request. No one appeared to be stalking her. The only surprises she had were when

Adam Litchfield appeared out of nowhere, twice in Rotten Row.

She stabled the horse, handed him over to one of the boys for a rubdown, and took herself up the servants' stairs to her father's bedroom. She knocked. He did not answer. She knocked again.

He was supposed to be resting to recover from his trek into the rain. She'd give him a good tongue lashing if she discovered that he'd gone to work.

She had crossed her arms and was tapping her foot at his door, hoping he was in his dressing room or water closet, when one of the footmen appeared with a bucket of coals for an upstairs fire.

"Marsden, could you please knock and go into my father's room? He's not answering, and I cannot imagine he is still asleep at this hour." Sick or not, Skip Brighton would not sleep this long.

"Oh, no, Miss Brighton, your father left early this morning, 'e did. With his man, O'Leary."

Frustrated that she couldn't tell her father about the flower woman, she became angry at him, too, for going to his office when he was in such poor health. She went down to breakfast to find Colleen, Raine, and Gus alone and once more mulling over the events of yesterday's teatime.

"Good morning, sugar. You're up and out early." Raine noted Ann's attire. "Alone?" The other two, who knew about the man outside the Rothschilds' house, echoed their own concern.

"You need not worry. No one disturbed me." *Until the end.* "Has Aunt Peg eaten?" When they told her that she had, Ann knew they would not be interrupted and asked the footman at the door to have Cook do a soft-boiled egg for her. As he closed the door, Ann turned to the others. "Do all of you have plans for the day?"

"I'm meeting Bryce in the Row to ride with him at two," Colleen informed her. "Raine and your Aunt Peg will take the brougham."

Gus stirred sugar into her tea. "I'm off to my painting class this morning at ten. But you're worried about something. What is it?"

"I need your help. Everyone's."

Gus and Colleen met the challenge with characteristic eagerness, asking questions about what they could do.

Raine waited for details with a tilt of her head.

Ann told them about her discovery that the flower lady was really a man. "We must be careful. If he is a reporter, I don't want him to follow me. Not today."

Colleen, thank the good Lord, caught more mischief than subterfuge in Ann's words. "Anything to do with Rhys?"

Ann told them where and when she was to meet him, "and I don't want to get caught." *Or followed. Not to meet Rhys or to go to Father's office.*

"It's the least we can do," Colleen affirmed.

Raine agreed. "Is this a bolder Ann Brighton?"

"I've been willing to take a risk before," Ann clarified. "Help me so that I can decide if I want to go home to Virginia at all, will you?"

Raine smiled. "Such *progress.* What can we do?"

Ann arrived at the main entrance to the Abbey half an hour earlier than two o'clock. She grinned, proud of herself and her friends for their diversion of the flower "lady." Raine, Colleen, and Ann had dressed in the most similar walking suits they owned, all in shades of almond and cream. Gus, who was so much shorter than the others and wouldn't pass as Ann, helped them coif their hair tightly so that the colors were concealed. They topped off their outfits with the broadest hats they owned. To each monstrosity's inside crown, they basted fine-netted veils with big chenille dots. They giggled as they had when they were younger and nothing more than an afternoon of freedom in Manhattan were the prize.

Today, Ann's reward would be a few minutes alone with Rhys Kendall. The only element marring the excitement was the fact that when she had taken the hired hack from a shop in Bond Street to Watling Street, she had found her father's office closed. A man in a dapper pinstripe suit who had descended the main stairs told her that Mr. Brighton and his secretary had been in at nine but left soon after, locking up their suite. Not knowing enough about her father's daily routine to say if such a quick visit were ordinary, Ann had left. Avoiding the stares of men who thought it odd to see a woman unescorted or chaperoned, Ann brusquely hailed another cab. She vowed to get her father alone before supper to discuss her concerns about the flower lady in the square.

Once inside the gothic cavern of Westminster, she soon forgot her worries. The hushed atmosphere, the awe-inspiring glass and marble had her squinting up through the veil. To see better, she pulled it up over her brim and meandered through the naves and transepts. Crowded into every nook and cranny were the statues of dead heroes, obstructing the passageways to tiny chapels dedicated to kings and queens. It didn't take her long to find the tall monument to William Shakespeare, his wistful pose bringing a smile to her lips the same way the arrival of Rhys's usual white rose did each morning. She drifted toward the tall statue, reading the inscriptions to other men as she passed their memorials.

From the corner of her eye, she saw a tall man approach, and with a smile bursting from her, she prepared to greet Rhys and found instead Adam Litchfield.

Ann girded herself, mentally searching for an escape. Yet the way Adam approached her, he cut off any route out. They were alone in the south transept. *When the odds are against you*—Ann remembered one Yankee captain in Winchester surrounded by Rebs in their barn—*do the expected act with flourish.* The man had surrendered in style, gifting his sword and pistol to his opponent with a smile.

"Hello, Lord Litchfield. How are you today?"

He came too close, towering over her in a move that menaced. He smiled tightly, and she noted that he smelled of cologne, cigars, and a whiff of liquor. "Good afternoon, my dear Miss Brighton. Acquiring a dose of culture or confessing your sins?" His slur on her character made her question his own and the quantity of alcohol he had consumed.

"Both. And you? Do you come here often?" She had to know if he were tracking her. Why was the damn man so many places she was?

"I came in because I saw you enter. Alone. Curious to see you by yourself. I wondered why. But then I deduced you came to meet someone. I thought it should be me, first." He swept her facial features with a greedy glance. "You no longer smell like magnolias. What perfume are you wearing?" He leaned over, his mouth a whisper from her cheek, her distaste becoming bitter as bile. "Hell, roses. Even your hair reeks of them. Well, why wouldn't you smell like Rhys's roses?

I hear you have wrapped ol' Tweedledum around your little finger."

How would he know Rhys had sent her roses? Had Rhys told him? "Excuse me." She had no intentions of listening to his drivel.

"Ah, playing the affronted little American." Adam seized her wrist as she turned toward an opening in the pillars. "Stay and tell me what you find so appealing about him. I want to hear how—"

She tried to tug free. "Do remove your hand from me, Lord Litchfield."

"Yes, Adam," Rhys encouraged in a hot tone. "A good suggestion to keep your hand and your head."

Ann looked over her shoulder to see Rhys approach. She leaned back, her arm brushing his chest, as if by the mere touch of his waistcoat to her sleeve she could absorb solace. She closed her eyes at the security this one man always brought her.

Adam snickered, and Ann glared at him.

"She's yours already," he spat. "Or should I have said always?"

"Listen, Adam—" Rhys took a step closer to him, and Ann could not say if it were in anger or friendship.

Adam warded him off with a raised palm. "I'm leaving." Before he did, he cast such a malicious glance at Ann that she was chilled.

"What did he do to you?" Rhys whispered, his hands on hers and then cupping her face.

"He was forward. He frightens me more each time I see him—and I see him too often. He is persistent and—"

"Much too intense, I know. I'll call on him later and ask him why he acted as he did."

"Odd to see him here . . . when you and I took such precautions to keep our meeting secret." Had Adam followed her? No, her mind was taking the oddest flights of fancy . . .

"Ann, you're shaking. Come with me." He wound her arm in his and led her from the transept toward a set of columns and into a dim, cool chapel where some monarch reclined in eternal peace. Ann found her own in Rhys Kendall's arms.

"He's gone, and you're safe," Rhys murmured against her temple.

She tried to smile but failed. "You constantly say that to me. What would I do," she asked him and herself, "if you weren't around to help me?"

His eyes gave her answers as tender as his words. "What would become of me if I had never found you or protected you? Do you know?"

She shook her head, incapable of an intelligible answer.

"I'd die a lonely man."

"Oh, Rhys—"

Someone cleared his throat.

Rhys groaned and drew back. "I must show you Henry the Fifth's chapel." He led the way around the intruder, his hand on hers as they wandered along, in step, in tune, in one breathless pursuit of some ancient ruler's little room of repose. And when they came upon it, blessedly, no one else viewed the man's effigy. Within the confines, filled with carved angels and swans and bishops looking down on them, Rhys stood against a wall, his eyes on hers, waiting.

She put her hands to his forearms, a revelation to equal his forming in her heart. "I thought of you all through the night."

He took one of her curls and sent it across her mouth. "What did you think?"

"I like your home, your paintings, and your garden." She wound her finger into the chain of his watch, knowing precisely how coquettish she appeared and not caring, but daring to do more. She put the flat of her palm to his chest and felt the steady rhythm of his heartbeat. So safe, so sure, so strong. Her Rhys. Her gaze locked with his, and she took the risk of testing the boundaries of his regard. "But I liked something else more."

"Tell me what it was. I'll make sure you see it again."

"Heaven." When flames of desire sprang to his eyes, she echoed his words of yesterday. "I haven't had a kiss today from you, and I need to."

He flung back his head and laughed. But his joy died like a strike of lightning, and suddenly she found herself against him while he drove one hand into her hair, kissed her until she was gasping, tasting his tongue and lips and teeth in an exotic way. Her hat fell, and she didn't care. His hair got mussed, and he didn't do more than moan his approval. She hooked an arm around his neck and clung to him while she trailed her mouth from his jaw to his ears, his cheeks, and his eyes.

Another person cleared his throat.

Rhys complained about the great number of visitors to national shrines. "Excuse us," he said pointedly as he picked up her hat and led them from the chantry. He frowned as he surveyed the length of the church.

Ann bit her lip but failed to keep her chuckles hidden.

Rhys curved a perplexed brow at her. "At least you are having a laugh over this. That's good to see. Someone should." Humor peeked through his frustration as he tapped his hat on his thigh. "There's no hope for it but to show you the wonders of the English world since the eleventh century."

"I suppose that's fitting, since you've shown me the wonders of the nineteenth . . . in your embrace."

"Darling." He grinned like a wolf. "If you're not careful, you will tempt me beyond my scruples."

"How interesting. What was that we just tested?"

"That was my patience." He led her quickly down an aisle toward a small door. Once inside the dimly lit room, she realized it was the choir's storage for their robes.

Rhys found a bench, took her to it, and sailed her hat across the room followed closely by his. In less time than two breaths, he had her in his arms, her hair flowing into his hands.

"Why—" she asked between ardent kisses, "can't we find comfortable places to do this?" The rough wood gave her a splinter in her derriere. "First pantries and now vestries. I like gardens better."

He chuckled, his mouth against her ear as he whispered, "I know a far better place, but I can't take you there yet."

"Mmm. I have a good idea where that is." The very thought of a bed brought her to her senses. Could she be so enraptured with Rhys Kendall that she could go to a bed with him and make love? Yes, she could, but knew she shouldn't. She needed more time to know him better.

She turned her face away from him and braced her hands against his chest. "No more. I was foolish and forward to encourage you to bring me here."

He stared at her in the mellow glow of light through the windowpanes. He placed a fingertip to her cheek and led her gaze to his. "You wanted to kiss me, and God knows, I wanted to kiss you. Where is the harm if two people want the same things?"

"None." She sat up, and he did not try to stop her. That was one asset of Rhys Kendall. He did not force himself on her, as Adam had. "I don't know yet if we do."

"Then let me tell you what I know." He stood up and brushed his trousers off, then retrieved her hat and his. "No," he said when he tried to put her hat on and she objected. "Let me. I'm good at making bows. And I need to be this close to you to say this." He finished spreading the glossy satin into a huge blossom. "We do want many of the same things. We want a home filled with serenity. With family and friends and children. We want to raise horses and earn a decent living. We don't care if we ever become rich. And Ann, make no mistake about this"—he tipped up her chin—"I want you."

"That's clear, and I am complimented. But I need to be rational. I must not rush into this relationship because I—I made a big mistake in judging a man before. I don't care to do it again."

"What a surprise." Rhys's objective tone showed her how rigidly he was controlling his jealousy and his sorrow. "Tell me about him so I might weigh my liabilities."

"He was someone I'd met when I was six. He'd been a planter. From Jamestown. He rode into my grandfather's yard, a lieutenant in gray and yellow uniform with a dashing hat and feather."

"A hero on a horse." Rhys searched her expression. "Was he so impressive?"

"Oh, yes, but he hated war, and yet he was honored for his actions in many battles, some very big ones at places called Antietam and Gettysburg. He was a colonel by the time the South surrendered."

"He must have been much older than you."

Her lashes lowered. "He was."

"How old?"

"Thirty-four."

"And why did he appeal to you?"

"He was quiet and . . ." She debated if this next were true. "Noble."

"He was also an idiot to let you go," Rhys said hotly, then smiled with a trace of consolation. "What happened to him? Why aren't you married to him?"

"We planned to elope, but he never came to the church. I waited for hours." She still smarted from the shame of having been jilted—and the lack of understanding over why Quinn had rejected her.

Rhys stepped forward. "Why didn't he arrive?"

She raised a shoulder. "I suppose he thought better of the idea. I never knew for certain. I didn't hear from him. Afterward, I agreed to come to Europe with my father for six months and let him show me around. He and I have an agreement that . . . well, has nothing to do with Quinn. But don't you see now why I want to take my time to get to know you better?"

"Yes, but unlike Quinn, I will not spend fourteen years as your friend deciding what our relationship will be."

"I didn't expect you to."

"I realize that you are still chafing from being forsaken." He brought her closer. "But I do need to understand why you liked him."

"Quinn was a farmer, a thinker. A man who never

raised his voice. Never did anything without debating it long and hard. The war was a trial for him because he was not a man of action. He hated killing, wounding, but for him, with his family and his pride pushing him, there was no way out except for him to join the army and fight with his brothers and his friends. He often told me with tears in his eyes how much it hurt him to have no alternatives."

"But he could have declared for the North or become an objector if he didn't approve of killing others."

"He wouldn't have, though. He didn't believe the North was right, and he didn't exactly believe that killing was murder, either. But Quinn thought he was ethical." Ann came to terms with a new realization. "*Was,* I see now, is the appropriate word."

"To have left you, waiting at the church without word of his decision, is not honorable. He is not worthy of you." Rhys pulled her so near their hips pressed. "It means the world to me that you told me this, because now I know what you value."

She laughed, her hands defining his shoulders as she drew back to peer at him. "I think you know already."

"We will not speak his name ever again. And I will work"—he brushed his thumb along the edge of her lower lip—"to make you forget him."

"I didn't love him," she confessed. "I felt more embarrassed than dismayed by his desertion. That shows I couldn't have cared for him very much. If he had come, our marriage would have soon worn thin. When I marry"—she noted the shift in her thinking from whether she would to when she would—"I want to begin with enough love and dedication from each of us to carry us through good and bad."

"Wise beyond your years," he murmured.

And she kissed him. Kissed him first to rejoice that she had told him the most embarrassing fact she could about herself. Kissed him second to thank him for listening so patiently and becoming jealous and possessive over her. Reveled in his own hot response to crush her close and make her breathless in a third kiss. But more than all those other reasons, she kissed him back one last time to show him that she valued him . . . and she wanted him.

"You are going home." He unwound her arms from his neck. "While I am going to go balance my ledgers."

"I doubt I'm complimented if I drive you to mathematics."

"Hmm. It's either that or walk the streets of Belgravia like some besotted swain."

When he grinned, but she didn't, he asked what bothered her. She told him what she'd seen the flower lady or man do this morning, how she'd become concerned and wanted to tell her father. "I didn't want the flower lady to know when I left to meet you, so I asked Raine and the girls to help me. We dressed up and left the house from different doors and in separate carriages. The flower lady, if he's at all interested in following me, will have to track all of us today to find the real Ann Brighton."

Rhys found humor in the subterfuge. "Wonderful job. And what did your father say when you told him?"

"He wasn't in when I went to see him, and I'm worried about him. His health has not been good since we sailed from New York. And since he was out in the rain night before last, his cough has been racking. He is not well at all, and he does not seem to care too much if he recovers. He is working himself to death." The minute she said it, she stopped. "I hope to God I'm wrong."

"Your father is very ill, but he is determined to form this cruise line and to make up to you for years of neglect."

"I am overjoyed to have proof finally that he cares about me so much. But I don't want him to risk his life to do it—and I can't dissuade him. It's as if he is driven—more than he's ever been. Especially since the Rothschilds' ball. That night, something changed. Something happened, and I'm not sure what."

Rhys went very still. "He was blackmailed."

She dropped her jaw. "How do you know?"

"He told me the Monday after the ball. He paid an inordinate amount of money to silence a man who threatened to create a scandal in the newspapers."

She felt weak. "About me?" she whispered.

"No." Rhys embraced her and spoke into her hair. "Something else. It's a story he should be the one to tell, not me. He didn't want it to hurt you or reflect on you, and so he paid the money readily."

"So then this flower lady might be involved in that and following my father."

"That's a possibility." Rhys asked her what the man looked like, and she described him as similar to the fellow in Dublin, in Tattersall's, and in Washington long ago in February.

Rhys narrowed his eyes. "I thought I would always recall that little man's face from Dublin. Perhaps I didn't." He scowled. "Well, I'll make up for any failure now. I won't let you go home alone."

"We can't ride together in broad daylight. It isn't done. Someone will see, and I'll be ruined."

"You went to your father's office alone. This is no more or less an indiscretion. But we'll be very careful." Rhys seized her shoulders. "I will find a cab and bring it around to the back near the Deanery exit. This way." He led her toward the main entrance but off to one side along the south wall. "This opens to a courtyard well shaded by trees and shrubs. I'll come inside for you when I have a hack. Wait here." He settled her into a corner and left. Occasionally, one or two people passed her, and for the next ten minutes or more, Ann stood alone.

Fretting that it was taking Rhys so long, she went to the doors, pushed them open, and emerged into the secluded yard. She had no sooner exited than she heard the heavy doors open again. She thought nothing of it until she felt a hand on her arm. She turned, expecting it to be Rhys, and looked into the face of the fat man who had been on the corner across the street from the Rothschilds' the night of their ball.

"Come with me, Ann," he urged, baring yellowed teeth and tugging her toward the street. "Been looking for you."

His accent was American.

"No." She pulled away, and he yanked her forward. "I know you—"

"Good for you. Come on, girl, move!" He hustled her along, and she cast about for Rhys.

Habit made her think of her pistol. But how to get it with one arm clamped to this man? She stumbled, went down on one knee, her hat dangling, her reticule sprawling before her on the pavement. But he grabbed for her wrist.

She had the advantage of speed and scrambled for the reticule. He kicked it from her grasp. She decided then that the better part of valor was to ram him and reared up, disabling him by hitting him between his legs. As he clutched himself, she rose to her feet and ran from the yard. Out on the street, she saw no cab, no Rhys, and so she ran to the nearest cover she could find—a nook in a gothic building across the street.

Breathless with fear more than exertion, she assessed her chances of hiding from the man. This part of the city was jammed with huge government buildings. Parliament behind Westminster. The Treasury across the street. On a gamble, she ran for the next nook in the building. If she inched along, well covered as she went, maybe she'd escape him.

She heard him, coming for her, scuffling along the sidewalk, panting from running. She heard his footsteps dart the other way, and she took the chance to spring toward the next nook—and stared into the surprised eyes of a bobby on patrol.

"Can I help you, m'lady? You look in a bad way."

She explained that someone had accosted her in the Dean's yard while she was waiting for her husband to hail a cab.

The grizzled man frowned. "We don't usually 'ave problems in this part o' the city, but I'll take you back to meet your husband. Come along. Let me know if you spy the fellow who did this."

She wished she could, but if the man lurked about and saw she had a policeman with her, he had the presence of mind to leave. But Rhys, thank God, had arrived in the meantime.

He stood beside a small black hansom, holding her reticule and madly glancing up and down the street. When he saw her, he paled. She went into his arms without a sound.

"Where did you go?" His eyes swept down her face and dress in horror. "What happened?"

She told him in a flat tone that a man had tried to abduct her. The incident still felt quite unreal.

The bobby looked more concerned. "I wish you'd come around the corner to 'eadquarters and tell my captain about this. If your wife could describe the man—"

"I didn't know him," Ann said, quickly enough to make Rhys question that with a tilt of his head. "I'd rather not go." She pleaded to Rhys with her eyes. "Must I?"

"No. You'll come home. I'll take care of her. Thank you for your help."

The policeman was not happy about them leaving without reporting it, but he helped them into the cab and shut the door with a reminder to come if they thought better of their decision. "I know your class don't like to deal with the police if you don't have to, sir, but we might find him."

"I am certain you are very efficient." Rhys tried to console him. "But you understand I must take my wife home and calm her before we try to get any description of the culprit."

"Now's the best time, sir. She'll remember more."

"Yes, of course, thank you." Rhys bid him good afternoon and gave the order for the cabbie to drive on. He smoothed Ann's hair from her cheeks and examined her head to toe. "Your hands are scraped. Is any other part of you hurt?"

She shook her head and leaned into him, her face against his throat. "I'm . . . terrified. He knew my name, and he spoke to me as if I knew him and—"

"You did." He said it so softly, so serenely as he stroked her hair down her back. "Who was it?"

"He was the man outside the Rothschilds' house."

Rhys brought her closer to him. "MacIntyre."

She repeated the name, recalling what Rhys had told her about him. "He was my father's partner. The one who dealt with you the night of the fire years ago. What would he want with me?"

Rhys continued to soothe her with the touch of his hands, but the rest of his body became taut with concern.

"Tell me what you know," she urged him.

"He is the one who blackmailed your father."

"What could he want with me? I have no money . . . well, not a fortune, anyway. I have the equivalent of almost sixteen thousand dollars with interest, and that's not enough to appeal to a man who would blackmail someone like my father." She pulled back to look into Rhys's worried eyes. "Is it?"

"No," he said emphatically, but tore his gaze away from her to consider his own thoughts.

"What, then?" she asked on a thread of sound, needing to know what hideous possibility Rhys contemplated.

"I fear he may have wanted to abduct you for ransom."

Her breath lodged in her throat. "You mean he's not satisfied by the last payment and he'd decided to ask for more? Why . . . that's . . . so logical." She noted the cab took a direction she had never gone. "We're not going to Belgrave Square but to your town house?"

"Yes. I won't chance it to take you home. MacIntyre might go there to wait for you—or perhaps he's in league with the flower lady. Oh, God, it's such a jumble. I'll try to find your father first so that we can decide what best to do."

"I hope you are luckier than I was this morning."

Rhys knit his brows.

"But something else worries you."

"I don't understand the motivation for these extortion requests. At first, MacIntyre said he wanted money to let the cruise line company proceed . . . and now, to try to abduct you, what would his reason be? What more could he do? The company papers are signed. The construction of the ships is proceeding. To try to stop the business now that there are corporate procedures in effect for the death or resignation of a member of the board is useless."

"My father did something awful, didn't he?" Ann asked with a certainty she felt in her bones. "He created some scandal that MacIntyre is using against him. Oh, God." She put a hand to her mouth. "They're going to kill him. We have got to find him before they do."

Chapter 10

*"There is something about a roused woman;
especially if she adds to all her other strong
passions, the fierce impulses of recklessness and
despair, which few men like to provoke."*

—Charles Dickens

"I can't find your father," Rhys told her hours
later when he returned. "I've been to Belgrave Square
and tried not to alarm your aunt, but I told her you
were here with me. She doesn't like you being here
with me alone, but I insisted there were no alternatives. I went to your father's office, too, but found it
locked just as you had. I did go upstairs to Adam's
office, hoping he might have seen Skip, but Adam
wasn't in—and his assistant didn't expect him, either." Rhys removed his wet coat and struggled to
undo his cravat.

"You're soaked through," Ann scolded. Having
waited for him past teatime and supper, she had
conversed with his housekeeper enough to feel comfortable asking her to refrain from serving the meal
for her until Rhys arrived. "Why were you out in the
rain?"

"No umbrella."

"Where does an Englishman go without his armor?" she muttered, helping him peel off his waist-

187

coat and noting how he dodged giving her a substantive answer. "Change your clothes before you get pneumonia." She nodded in the direction of his dressing room.

When he reappeared in gray trousers, soft white shirt, and wool smoking jacket, he looked more comfortable physically but still mentally preoccupied. "I need a brandy. Would you care for one?"

"After supper. Why not come and eat?" She indicated the silver-domed servers which his housekeeper, Mrs. Pagett, had laid out for them on his small but serviceable Queen Anne table.

"You waited for me," he said as he came to lift one cover, close his eyes, and smell the aromas.

"How could I eat, not knowing where you were or what was happening?"

For the first time since he'd arrived home, he really looked at her. He set his snifter on the table and sighed. "I'm not hungry. You must eat, though."

"Not unless you do. Rhys, did you learn something and you don't wish to tell me?" She hated the possibility that he would prevaricate with her. "I am no schoolgirl who needs protection from truth, you know."

He shook his head sadly and came around the table to take her in his arms. "Oh, Ann," he whispered into her unbound hair. "Some awful scheme is developing here, and I can't discover what it is. I only know Owen MacIntyre intends to hurt you. And since I can't find your father to discuss what is to be done, I must see that MacIntyre fails to put his hands on you again. Let's eat our suppers, shall we? Bryce is coming soon, and we need to have our wits about us when he gets here." He hugged her.

She clung to him. Aware that her body told him she

was afraid, she tried to ignore it by probing for more information. "Why is Bryce involved?"

"I needed help, and that's what friends are for, yes?"

She nodded. "Where is he? What is he doing?"

"Talking to the other directors of the Guardian Shipping Company to see if they know the whereabouts of your father."

"Do you think that Owen MacIntyre has hurt my father? Taken him somewhere? MacIntyre could abduct my father and hold the company ransom—"

"Let's not allow our imaginations to run wild. Come now, we'll eat." He unwrapped her arms from him and held out her chair.

In a silence filled with sad smiles at each other, they tried to choke down the delicious meal of roast sirloin and potatoes, Yorkshire pudding, and wild greens. They were not finished when the knocker banging against the front door had Mrs. Pagett moving along the hall from the servant parlor and down the central stairs.

Both Rhys and Ann rose to greet Bryce from the landing as he handed over his umbrella, hat, inverness coat, and gloves. "Damn messy out tonight," he complained to Rhys with a bravado Ann knew was false.

Rhys put a snifter in his hand with a generous draught of the same brandy he'd been drinking.

"Thank you. Need this," Bryce said, and rubbed a finger under his eye patch. "Cold as January out there."

Rhys indicated they should move to the portion of his large living area which was arranged for discussion. Bryce sank into an overstuffed chair with a sigh of relief, avoided looking at Ann, and shook his head at Rhys. "The most I found out was from Adam."

Rhys skewered Bryce with a tight expression, and Ann wondered if Rhys had told him about her encounter with Adam in the Abbey that afternoon.

Bryce returned Rhys's look of concern. "Adam arrived at the Guardian offices just as I was about to leave Alastair Houghton. Adam was very drunk."

Ann felt no need to speak well of a man who had been so forward with her. "He must have begun early this afternoon."

Rhys told Bryce, "He made advances to Ann which were improper. I haven't seen him so irrational since his first and second wives died. Immediately after Adam left the Abbey, MacIntyre showed up. Odd and frightening." A commotion downstairs caught his attention and made him turn toward the hall door.

Bryce frowned. "It sounds as if your housekeeper is having an argument with someone."

He had barely finished his sentence before Mrs. Pagett was screeching that someone could "not barge in like this!"

Rhys ran to the door with Bryce on his heels.

Ann got to the head of the stairs as Rhys exclaimed his surprise.

"Good God, Skip! What are you doing coming to the back door, and where have you been? We've been looking for you all over the city."

"I hear you've got Ann," her father growled. "What the hell are you thinking of to bring her here?"

Rhys towered over Skip as her father reached the last step up to the first-floor landing. From her vantage point, she could see Rhys grow more fierce than she thought possible for such a mild-mannered man.

"If you had any idea what's happened today, you wouldn't say that."

"I have an idea! That's why I am trying to divert attention from me—and you—and Ann by coming to your service entrance. But I am more concerned about Ann than me right now. I don't want her reputation ruined, Kendall. I told you that a month ago. When my aunt told me she was here, I nearly lost my mind." Skip was jabbing his finger into Rhys's smoking jacket. "If anyone saw you dressed like that and her, here with you—and you, too—" He faced Bryce. "Why, they'll call her—" He spied Ann and snapped his mouth shut.

"Call me what, Father?"

"A woman of shady background. You know these people, Ann. Look what they did with little provocation. Now, to be here in a bachelor's lodgings with not one but two men, Christ, Ann."

Rhys clenched his fists. "It is all I can do, Brighton, not to knock you down the stairs. Tell me what you did today—why we couldn't find you—and then I will show you the way out."

"I won't go without Ann."

"A little late to try to protect her," Rhys charged him. "Owen MacIntyre tried to abduct her this afternoon."

Skip cursed MacIntyre roundly.

"Oh, how I agree," Rhys said as slowly as a rattlesnake before it attacked. "Ann's here and healthy only because of her quick wits and the grace of God."

"And you," she murmured, and walked around Bryce to face her father. "Rhys came with a cab at just the right time."

Her father cursed again. "You rode in public with

him alone in the afternoon? That really seals it. You've got to do the honorable thing here, Rhys. You will marry—"

"Wait," Ann insisted so loudly every man froze. *"Just a minute.* I have something to say about this, and I—"

"You listen to *me,* Ann Brighton." Her father spoke to her in the intimidating tone she imagined he used with adversaries in business. "I have been more than understanding these last few months. You have earned your money, kept our bargain, but this—this breach of etiquette is one I will *not* ignore."

She glared at him. "You will force me to marry a man because I was rescued by him and came to his town house? This is the most absurd thing." She walked around him, heading for the stairs and the front door.

Behind her, Rhys damned her father. "What is wrong with you, Brighton? You're out of your mind, trying to maneuver her into—"

"She cares for you," her father yelled. "What's the problem with *you?"*

"Nothing," Ann told him from the bottom of the stairs. Rhys was sailing down the stairs toward her. "It's your method we object to." She opened the cloak closet door, retrieved her jacket, pulled it on, and grabbed her reticule.

Mrs. Pagett darted forward. "Miss Brighton, you can't go out in the rain—"

Rhys was turning her by the shoulders toward him. "Ann, for pity's sake, you can't leave like this."

"I *will* do as I need to, Rhys. I am sorry." She gazed into his terrified eyes and apologized with her own. "You must see that he's trying to control me again, as he always has—and now he's trying to run your life as well. I won't let him. If you and I were ever to become more than friends, it would never be because he made me or you do it."

Skip rushed down the stairs. "You'll do it, Kendall. I'll see you take her away from here and—"

"You'll see me leave *you.*" Ann dared not even call him Father.

"You can't!" Her father tracked her to the door as she yanked it open.

"Watch me."

"I'll make you."

"Like hell."

"I did it before. I can again. I found a way—"

Anger coiled into rage. "What? How?"

"It doesn't matter," Skip yelled, but the wind was gone from his sails.

Ann detected weakness—and suspected he had used his old method to get his way. "Money," she scoffed.

"It worked with Quinnten Langley."

The rain pelted her as she stepped onto the porch of Rhys's town house. The drops stung her skin as she looked up at this man who had sired her and very slowly asked, *"What* precisely worked with Quinn?"

Skip's realization that his anger had made him imprudent spread shock across his haggard features. He changed the subject. "Ann, come in—don't stand in the doorway so that people can see you."

"I want to know about Quinn," she said, while her hatred went from simmer to boil.

"I knew he was no man for you."

She waited, not even wiping the raindrops from her eyes or cheeks.

"I knew what you planned to do—and I couldn't let you waste yourself on him."

Rhys looked as if he would murder Skip there on the front steps.

Ann felt gutted. "You stopped him from marrying me?"

Skip did not answer.

"How much did you pay him?" she pressed.

"Ten thousand dollars," he said, as if the sum were poison. "I wouldn't allow you to waste yourself on him. He was a mama's boy. Good for nothing . . ."

Ann could find no words heinous enough to fit her father's crime. Instead, she picked up her skirts and ran.

Rhys caught up to her as she climbed into a rickety cab. Pulling on his own inverness over an already soaked smoking jacket, he patted his back pocket to check if he had put his cash in his trousers when he changed clothes a few minutes ago.

Ann looked as if she were about to tell him once more to go home—and he wouldn't let her. "You can't travel anywhere alone, I don't care what you say or do. You won't dissuade me, so don't bother to try." He faced her in the dank confines. "Tell the driver where you wish to go. He's waiting."

She opened the door, and Rhys knew she'd try to escape him, and he clamped her wrist. "Just tell him from here so that you don't get pneumonia."

"Stop this." She shrugged off his hand and plunked herself back in her seat. Rhys wasn't surprised she had told the man to take her to Belgrave Square.

"What will you do?"

"What I should have done long ago. Go home."

His stomach knotted. She meant Virginia. "Because your father pushes you toward me?"

"No." She crossed her arms, the chill of the rain and the wind making her tremble.

He longed to take her in his embrace and warm her, but he knew she wouldn't let him. "Why?" he persisted.

She formed words, but no sound came. "He tricked me."

"Ann—"

"Do not touch me." She was so venomous, he knew he must comply or lose her forever.

"He paid him," she moaned more to herself than to him. "He did that. How could he give him that much money? How could Quinn take it?"

"Ann, darling, listen to me."

"Well, now we know what I'm worth, don't we?" Teardrops cascaded down her cheeks.

Rhys yearned to brush them away. "Don't torture yourself over this."

"He bought him off, and you tell me not to torture myself? Please." She laughed sarcastically. "Why am I surprised?" she asked, face raised to the roof. "Because I thought he'd changed—even a little. I should never have let my guard down. He thinks he can order me around the way he does people who work for him."

Rhys knew now it was best not to try to stop her, even though he felt from Skip's actions and words that some fear had driven him to this outlandish behavior tonight. Rhys concluded this was no time to try to point that out or commend her father to her. Instead, he sat waiting for her to vent her rage.

"I am so ashamed," she whispered to her folded hands.

That she would let Skip's bribery reflect so upon

herself angered Rhys, and even though he predicted what her answer would be, he asked her, "Why?"

"How would you feel if your life were controlled by another person?"

"Anger. Resentment. Hatred. I felt it all. What was worse, I felt it for the man whom once I had loved dearly for all the right reasons. But I grew to hate him because he lost the family fortune in racing bets. Over the years, I also realized that I loved him at the same time. Horrible conflict, I tell you. His actions meant I have spent most of my adult life trying to recoup his losses—and later my own." He considered the landscape outside, and, murky as it was through the old oilcloth window, he saw one thing clearly. "I did resent his weakness, just as you resent your father's strength."

She snorted and faced the window. "I can't let him control me."

At the cost of losing her completely, Rhys asked, "Isn't that what you're doing now?"

"I . . ." She frowned.

The cab had drawn up to the front of Forsythe House. She got out and paid the driver, and Rhys tracked her.

"Go home," she ordered him upon the broad stone steps.

"Not a chance. Whatever you're planning, I will know it—and wherever you go, so will I."

She made for the door.

When she pushed it open without ceremony, Rhys followed her in. Low voices resounded from the dining room. Ann avoided them, realizing probably that she would meet only with more controversy from her friends and relatives. Without removing her coat, she took the stairs, and he was right behind her. She looked over her shoulder once but did not challenge him. Her tears had been stemmed, if not her anger, and she paused only when she opened the door to what he presumed must be her bedroom.

"You shouldn't come in here." She stood at the threshold.

He folded his arms. "I will wait."

An assortment of emotions fled across her face.

Whether amusement or outrage dominated, he didn't analyze. He didn't really care. "I'm not moving."

She shut the door with a huff.

The other members of the household had emerged from the dining room and had begun to climb the stairs. Ann's Aunt Peg led the way with Raine, Gus, and Colleen on her heels.

"Your Grace, I really must ask you to come down to the drawing room." Her aunt faced him with the sweetest smile and firmest tone.

"Thank you, Mrs. Gallagher, but I cannot." He indicated the door with a raised brow. "I can tell you that Ann has seen quite a bit of trouble today, and she insists on acting rashly—"

"I do not!" Ann insisted from the other side of the door. "If he'd just go away, Aunt Peg—"

"Mrs. Gallagher, it is your niece who wishes to go away, I'm afraid. And I cannot let her do it alone."

"You can't come with me," Ann objected.

Rhys could hear her struggling to change her clothes. "Of course, I can." He looked at Peg with a determination he knew was his pose of aristocratic power. "Mrs. Gallagher, it's no use to try to dissuade me."

"Oh, but the scandal—" Peg began.

"I will work to eliminate that, Mrs. Gallagher."

"You can't," Ann insisted. "Remember what happened with the *Gazetteer?* Someone will find out. I'm sure of it."

Raine edged closer to the door. "Ann, you must listen to reason here."

But she didn't. She groaned and walked away. When she pulled open the door a few minutes later, the woman who stood there was dressed in man's attire. Her Bridgeton outfit. Well, why was he surprised?

The women gaped. Objected. Pleaded with her not to go.

Rhys admired her. In the tidy serge suit, Ann's svelte body lent her an aesthetic air. Thanks to her years of riding, her legs were taut and longer than any prize filly he had ever seen. Her breasts, small but perfect, did not obstruct the drape of the jacket. She had added brass cuff links, red silk cravat, and the trim makeshift mustache. She had shoved her hair up into a net and pulled the tophat down. Far down. Not bad, he told himself, rejoicing that she might look like a man from afar and thus help avoid detection.

Rhys took Ann's arm when she'd said her good-byes and made for the main stairs. "No, my dear. The servants' stairs are better. If someone saw you come in, we should not offer them the opportunity to see you go out."

She nodded, disliking his command of the situation but appreciating his logic. "I'm indebted to you," she told him when they entered the stable. "I wouldn't have thought of the diversion of coming out here."

"Exactly. Perhaps you'll agree you need help with a bit more. Now, tell me, have you got money?"

She straightened her spine. "Enough."

He went for the tack room but tugged her with him. "I don't trust you alone. Enough money for what?" He feared she hadn't thought of details beyond leaving the confines of Forsythe House and her father's hegemony.

"I have twenty pounds in cash and my bank book."

He chose the cabriolet for its speed, its inconspicuous looks, and the need for only one horse to draw it. "That might buy you a room and board for two weeks in a dangerous part of town—or a night's lodging at the Grosvenor next to Victoria Station." From the confusion on her face, Rhys could see she had no intention of booking a room anywhere. Just as he suspected, she needed him for more than protection tonight. She needed him for practical reasons. He led out one mare and hitched her to the little carriage.

"I'm not going to stay in London," she informed him.

"What did you have in mind?"

"Portsmouth."

Ah, yes. To sail on the first ship to New York. "It could take days or weeks to book passage on a ship to America."

"Are you here to help me or lecture me?"

He gave her a consoling look which said he had no need to answer that. "Get in." He offered her his hand up into the conveyance when he finished securing the harness to the sturdy mare.

"Where are you going?" she asked minutes later as she realized he was headed toward the Thames.

"Kendall Great House."

"But—"

"If we're to travel, my dear, I'll need more money than I've got with me. We'll stop only briefly."

"You can't come to America with me."

"Who says?"

"You have businesses and responsibilities."

"Yes."

"People count on you."

He nodded but kept his attention on keeping the mare to her duty in the torrents of rain.

Ann mumbled her abject frustration. "Rhys, you can't be serious about leaving England."

He refused to answer her. Her anger mounted so that when he got out to open the tradesmen's gates to the house, Rhys was thankful the rain resembled the force of a hurricane. Ann would never run from him in this. He was inside, opening his wall safe, retrieving one hundred pounds, and out to the drive within minutes. Ann was still in one corner of the little cab and surprised to see a young man right behind Rhys.

"My new coachman, Burnett," he informed Ann as he indicated she should move over enough that the three of them might fit. With another person now in the cab, Ann didn't talk at all, which was a jolly good stroke for Rhys. He was weary of their conflict and yearned for a warm, dry place to battle out her issue—even if it was the confines of a train compartment.

As the gothic entrance of Victoria Station loomed before them, Rhys gave quick instructions to the servant to return to Forsythe House with the cabriolet only in the wee hours of the morning after taking a very circuitous route to Hampstead. He pressed a pound note into his man's hand and told him to buy a pint or two before he reappeared at Kendall Great House, too.

Rhys took Ann's hand to help her out and carried

her little reticule for her. Without a coat or cape, she shivered in the suit. Gusts of wind and rain soaked her and lifted her tophat from her head. She clamped it on, her hair never escaping from its net. The two of them dodged puddles and one skittish draught horse as they ran to the sidewalk and inside the cavernous station.

They strode to the iron caged kiosk, and Rhys purchased two tickets for Portsmouth. Rhys handed over Ann's and, beyond her shoulder, saw Lettie Houghton approach. "Meet me at the train," he urged Ann. "Walk straight past me. Now."

Fright flashed in Ann's eyes, and she darted forward to do as he asked.

"Hello, Rhys, dear." Lettie Houghton was donning her gloves and hefting a tiny valise. She'd been to the country, he supposed, and was just now returning to town. "What a surprise. Traveling?"

"A brief holiday." He smiled.

"Unusual for you, isn't it? But oh so necessary to a hardworking man." Her eyes traveled in the direction of Ann.

"Quite." Before Lettie could ask him where he was going and with whom, he excused himself. Damned if he'd dawdle with Lettie, giving Ann a chance to turn skittish and run from him. He hurried along the concourse. Fortunately, his train left from a quay obscured from Lettie Houghton's view by another train. Ann, he noted with a leaping heart, stood waiting for him, kneading her hands and looking every minute less like a man.

Within minutes, they were rushing toward one of the open doors. When Rhys helped Ann up into the coach, she looked beyond a side corridor to the doors into a cabin. Rhys led her inside, closed the door, and pulled the tidy curtains. Ann sank to the seat with a sigh and great satisfaction.

The steward called out the first stop of the night train along the South Coast Railway route. Rhys knew he had ten short minutes to convince her of the best solution to all their problems.

Chapter 11

"Yet each man kills the thing he loves."
—Oscar Wilde

Ann glanced across the seat at Rhys as he ran fingers through his wet hair and removed his inverness. She couldn't imagine that he truly meant to go with her to Portsmouth, but she was grateful for his protection—and humbled by his desire to do it.

"Ann, we must talk rationally about your plan to go to Virginia."

She noted he hadn't called it home, and she wondered if that was intentional. She wanted to find some secluded place to sit and lick her wounds. "I don't want to talk."

"Then let me. I must say things that I—"

"Good God, Rhys," she shot back, wild to be gone from this agony of his kindness and her humiliation. "Allow me to go with some pride intact."

Rhys caught her chin, and she lifted it higher, defiant. "Ann," he said softly, "I don't want you to leave."

Her throat swelled with sorrow.

"Sweetheart." He came to sit next to her and

wound his arms gently around her. His lips buried in her hair, he whispered, "I know how shocked you are. I am, too. Your father hurt you. I wanted to draw and quarter him as he stood there so smug and hateful."

She caught back a sob.

"Cry, please." Rhys pulled back a little and dashed her tears away with gentle fingertips. "I despise what he tried to do to you tonight and what he did with Langley. But your father is not who is important here. You are."

She tried to stem her tears and failed. "I appreciate you trying to comfort me, and I—"

"This is more than comfort."

"Don't you dare pity me." Her outrage horrified her. She yanked away.

He caught her wrist. "Pity?" he whispered, incredulous. "You think what I feel for you is *pity?*"

"Compassion or whatever it is, I don't—"

He growled and cupped the back of her neck. "To hell with that." He captured her lips with his. He seized her mind, his ardor swiftly declaring who was master of her senses. He broke away. "Tell me what that is."

She stared at him. *Love,* she was dying to say, and would not put words in his mouth and dreams back in her heart. Instead, she said, "Impossible."

"No." He made it sound like a curse. "Not by a damn sight. Listen to me. I can't let you go anywhere alone."

"Rhys, be sensible. You can't come to America with me."

"Of course I can. My businesses and my farms are no longer my first priorities, Ann."

His declaration made her speechless.

"Sweetheart, even if MacInytre were not a threat to your safety, or this flower lady's identity and purpose were not a mystery, I could never let you leave England feeling the way you do. You are too hurt—and much too dear to me. You and I have had so little time together, and I want to see you, Ann, regularly, to learn if we can be more than friends. I cannot allow others to rule out that possibility. I know you want to see me, too. You said so in the Abbey today. Don't you still want that? Even now that your father has been so rash?"

She shook her head, marveling that this man could be so sweet to her, despite her father's actions. "Yes. I would like some time with you, some peace, a respite from his interference—and the mysteries of who has been following me and blackmailing him." She admitted then a truth she had known was necessary to her well-being long before tonight. "I'd like to rid myself of my resentment of my father. My anger does control me more than his actions do. I realize that." *And I owe it to myself to learn if I might care for you deeply. Forever.*

Rhys looked as if she'd given him the sun and the moon. "Then let me offer you a plan not only to keep you safe but to give us a little time to ourselves—far from society, danger, and your father. Come away with me."

"No."

"I'd keep you out of harm's way."

"I'm sure you would."

"I'll give you proper accommodations. You'll stay with me at High Keep. I don't think you should stay at a hotel and attract attention as a woman alone, nor would it be wise for you to be alone. Furthermore, at my house, there is seclusion. I have three servants employed there permanently, and all are devoted to me. I assure you, sweetheart, no one will talk about us, and no one will visit us unless I invite them."

"I don't care what people think of me, Rhys. It's—"

"Yes, you do. You've been insulted by what they've printed."

"I am and will always be just one of those brash American girls. Whatever I do, they'll never change their opinion. It's you I worry about. People would talk about this. *You* would be disgraced."

"I don't give a damn about anyone else but you."

"Your heritage, your title, your integrity are every bit as vital to you as the air you breathe."

"Sometimes one must risk everything one values to save the biggest treasure of all."

His words brought fresh tears to her eyes.

The train's wheels ground down, and the conductor came along the corridor announcing the next town.

Rhys's expression became desperate, and he clutched her shoulders. "When this train stops, we can leave it and catch another to the Dorset countryside. It would be a good diversion, just in case MacIntyre has followed us."

Her eyes widened. "How could he?"

"I have no idea, but I think he is in league with someone else who is very cunning. To escape MacIntyre and whoever else is after you and your father requires an equally crafty plan. To foil them, I want us to catch another run back to London from Dorset—and then the night train to Liverpool."

The destination confounded her. "Why would we go to Liverpool?"

"I want to show you how some people have healed from a catastrophe. They taught me much about survival, anger—and hope. I need you to meet them, see how they have surmounted their troubles—and what it means to me. After that, if you still want to go to America, I'll help you buy passage on the first ship out of Liverpool." He kissed her eyes and whispered, "Or if you'd like to stay and visit with me for a week or more, I'd love to have you all to myself—and my servants, of course—at High Keep Castle. Whatever you want, I'll do my damnedest to give it to you." His eyes gleamed with hope and heartache. "Will you come?"

"Where?"

"Blackburn Farm."

She smiled through her tears and grabbed one lapel of her suit coat. "Mr. Bridgeton has committed so many indiscretions now, what would one more matter?"

Rhys grinned and caught her to him. "You won't be sorry, sir."

"Show me how happy I will be," she pleaded, her arms circling his shoulders.

He stopped breathing. "Ecstatic." He said it like a vow. And then he kissed her. The feel of his lips after the turmoils of the day and evening had her duplicating his fervor in a way she hadn't known she was capable of. She knew only a consuming hunger to have him, savor him, and never let him go. The kisses continued until she couldn't think and couldn't breathe. He pulled away and settled her against him. She shut her eyes, quivering with the recognition that she adored this man as she never before had valued any other.

"You're shivering." Rhys reached to the opposite seat and pulled over the compartment blanket to drape it over her lap. "When will we get you used to English weather?"

She laughed. "Give me time—and lots of blankets."

"Lots of kisses." He gave her one soft, hot one.

"Always those," she whispered, and brought him down to give him more of what she craved for herself. The devotion she tried to express to him flowered in her. With her fingers in the satin glory of his hair, she slanted her mouth eagerly across his. "You are so very handsome. I love your cheeks. And your eyes. But most of all, I love your ears."

He brought her across his lap. "I love your everything, Miss Brighton. Most especially how well you are learning to kiss. But we're going to be together for at least a week or more, my dear, and if you intend to drive me insane, you'll not kiss me first."

She lay back in his embrace, his arms cushioning her from the jostling of the train. "Should I be flattered or insulted at that restraint, Your Grace?"

"Flattered."

"How do I know you'll kiss me at all?"

"Because," he proclaimed, his eyes swirling with wicked promise, "I cannot control my hands when I'm near you."

"Do you kiss with your hands?"

He nestled one palm between her breasts where she knew, beneath her man's shirt and woman's chemise, he felt her heart thumping madly for him. "What do you think?"

"I think I need to learn how to do that. Will you teach me?"

"Gladly." He scooped her closer, demonstrating how many ways their lips could combine until the train rumbled to a halt. Rhys straightened her hairnet and pulled down her hat, then chucked her under the chin. "Let's go, love."

Soon they were headed west on another train in another private compartment. In the station, Rhys had bought bread, cheese, and grapes from hucksters. They settled into the cushions and ate with gusto. The relief to be away from her worries grew by the minute. A thrill traveled her spine at the seclusion she shared here with Rhys.

For long hours, she would avail herself of his companionship, his protection, and she would thoroughly enjoy his company. If she wanted to show him how much she wanted his kisses and caresses, she predicted with her woman's intuition that she could. She also knew that he would not stop her—or not be able to. Because he cared for her.

He had found her so appealing that he had protected her from stalkers, society, reporters, and scandal. He had sold one of his family treasures to afford to call on her. He had rejected any association with her father to court her and probably forfeited a great profit in the process. But what he'd gained—no, preserved—was his honor.

If she made love with Rhys Kendall as she so dearly yearned to do at this moment, she pondered what she might learn. That she liked his hard and handsome body. That she wanted him in a big broad bed with her. That she couldn't do without him. In bed or out.

Did she love him?

She went still as a stone in her seat. She had been wise to come along with him to Liverpool so that she might consider the answer to that question slowly as it deserved.

Quinnten Langley had hurt her. But she'd forgotten the wound of his desertion long before her father revealed his secret bribery tonight. She saw no scars and felt no recurring pain from Quinn's rejection.

Only from her father's interference. She acknowledged that she had recovered months ago from Quinn jilting her. Not because she saw Rhys Kendall as his replacement, either.

It was Rhys Kendall who had no equal. Rhys Kendall whom she desired as she had never desired any man.

She must have been looking at him oddly, because he paused and tilted his head in such a way that she thought he might have read her mind. "It's a long journey. More than an hour here and eight more once we change trains again in London for Liverpool. Don't you want to take off your coat and hat?"

She smiled at him, unable to hide a tremor of anticipation as she made herself more comfortable.

They ate in companionship while the train chugged from the station, and Rhys went on about the weather in Liverpool and how his mills had produced paisley shawls at great profit until the bustle returned to fashion in 'sixty-nine, ruining the demand for shawls. "Even though Adam still tries that market, I got out."

"What do you produce now?" The range of his business interests intrigued her. Textiles, farming, land. How could he meet the challenges of such diversity?

"Men's paisley handkerchiefs. We make a profit, and my employees make a good livelihood, especially for Liverpool."

"Do you have competition?"

"Not in handkerchiefs. I have urged Adam to try it. He still makes a higher-priced shawl, but he has not been so fortunate with his production, and he has numerous labor disputes. To make money, he turns to other industries, like putting his capital in the cruise line. But times are becoming precarious for many of the English." Rhys met her gaze fully. "American wheat and corn come in at a lower cost than we can produce them. It cuts our farmers' incomes."

"I know," she said. "I've read your daily newspapers, and I am familiar with how mine view the issue, too."

Ann knew the outrage the lower-cost American foodstuffs created among British politicians who felt they needed to protect their own farmers by raising tariffs against the imports but dare not deprive their people of inexpensive grain. This brouhaha began a year ago, just at the time when Jennie Jerome had married Randolph Churchill. Rumors flooded New York and Washington not only that the American heiress's dowry had helped to pay Randolph's racing debts and tailors' bills, but that a good portion went to his father, the Duke of Marlborough, to fill the family purse. Since Ann and her entourage had come to Britain, Ann had read about two other American debutantes who had married British noblemen with failing farm estates, and the tabloids gleefully recounted how the young women's money was heralded, gobbled, but nonetheless vastly resented.

Indeed, Ann was certain that had there been no prior conflict between her father and Rhys, and had Rhys been financially secure, this issue of American heiresses' money saving the bankrupt British would still affect them. Many London commentators stated that the least the American heiresses could do for their tiaras was pour their dollars into the British economy to benefit poor British children.

"Despite our common language and heritage," Ann observed, "we don't seem able to solve all our problems."

"Money makes for estrangements between

friends—and for strange bedfellows," he said, she was certain, not without double meaning.

"You and I are friends without benefit of money."

"Thank God."

She smiled at him. He was so proud of his independence, and she prized him for it. Striving to earn his living, Rhys Kendall seemed almost American. A self-made man who had endured hardships and tried to build his businesses despite them. How could she not admire him? For all he had done for her, she would find a way to thank him appropriately. Help him. "Money has never entered into any part of our relationship."

"Priceless and very rare, don't you think?"

"Yes." *Making you more precious to me by the moment.*

His gaze held hers for countless moments. "What are you thinking?"

"I'm very tired."

He gave her a skeptical look. "Why don't you try to take a nap?" he asked at last.

She suddenly needed to be near him. "Could I ask for your assistance?"

He crooked a finger. "Come here, Bridgeton. I've got a shoulder you can lean on."

She grinned, rose, and settled herself against him. "I'm not too heavy?"

"No," he crooned. "Not if I have my own diversions." With one stroke, he had removed the net, and her hair spilled over them both. His fingers trailed through it, massaging her scalp and getting her to close her eyes and moan with the delicious release his ministrations brought.

"Lord," he said against her ear, "I told you I

couldn't keep my hands to myself." One arm brought her up so that their lips molded together, while his other hand wended from her arm to her breast. Beneath the two thin layers of cotton, she felt her nipple harden at the touch of his palm.

"It would be a shame," she murmured against his lips, "to keep them to yourself when I need them so badly."

He groaned, the earthy sound reverberating through her flesh. "You smell like roses, sweetheart."

"Your roses," she clarified.

Crushing her close, he was flicking open the studs of her shirt and baring one shoulder. His lips were moist and trailing fire as they blazed a path from her collarbone to her cleavage and then her bared nipple. "You even look like a rose, darling." His finger traced the circumference of her aureole, and she arched up into his hand and sighed for more. "Do you taste like one, my lovely Grace?"

She shook her head, unsure what he asked, uncaring what the answer might be.

His mouth claimed her, suckled her, shaped her, led her from craving to madness. Then his palm drifted to her ribs and beneath the waistband of her trousers. His fingers splayed into her curls, found her center, and delved into a place no man had ever touched.

She bowed up into his caress as if she'd starve without him. He stopped breathing and kissed her earlobe. "Darling, you even feel like a rose."

She clutched at his shoulders, calling his name.

"A warm, wet rose of many petals—"

She gave herself up to every delight he could elicit. With tender strokes of her hot flesh, he made her feel like a tight bud of desire, bursting open to a new world of sunshine and blinding, pulsing splendor. A world that had her clinging to him, breathless.

He cupped her cheek. "You liked that, I am so pleased to see. That's what happens when you invite me to put my hands on you."

She opened her eyes and licked her lips. "What other kinds of kisses do your hands give?"

"Minx. It's back to your seat for you."

"Exiled," she teased him, rearranging her clothes and plunking into the cushions.

"Be careful what you ask for," he warned her playfully.

"I might get it, eh?"

"More than you bargained."

"I'll take my chances."

"Lucky me." He winked at her. "Try to nap, will you?"

Settling into the little corner of her seat, she could not stop reliving how he had touched her body—and her spirit. As her need for him cooled, something about their conversation began to bother her.

"You're frowning. Why?" he asked.

Roses were what Adam had referred to in Westminster this afternoon. He had smelled her roses . . . just as Rhys had now. She'd given up the magnolia scent when the white roses began to mean more to her. But something else Adam had said about the roses eluded her. "We have not talked about why Adam was at the Abbey today."

"I don't have much to contribute in the way of an explanation. Coincidence seems to be my only answer—and I hate it for its simplicity."

"But he'd been drinking. Are there pubs in the area or his men's club?"

"No. I'm afraid not."

She crossed her arms. "I told no one except the girls that I was to meet you there," she mused.

"Adam drinks too much too often," Rhys reflected, "especially in the last ten years. He has had two great tragedies in his life, both involving his two wives. He can be . . . moody."

"But you don't mind that. You are still friends."

"Yes. The friendship has survived thirty-two years of rivalry in business and in personal conflict. He and I have been honest with each other even in the worst of times."

She didn't ask Rhys to reveal his secrets. But he did.

He frowned out at the quickly passing landscape, amid the grays and blacks of night. "Adam and I have had two differences of opinion over the years of our friendship. Both have been debates about whether he should marry. The first time, he was young, twenty-one. He claimed he was in love and could not deny the lady or himself. He had recently inherited his title and lands, he had no siblings, and he wished for an heir, stability. He thought he had found love and happiness in one woman. He did, for a time, until she died months later in a fall from a parapet in his home in Lancashire. It was during the horrible period after my factory burned down and I was enraged against your father and the need to do for my injured people, but I remember thinking how dearly Adam loved her, and she . . ." Rhys stopped, pursed his lips, and clearly reconsidered what he had been about to say.

"Did his wife love him?"

"I thought so. One never really knows for certain in some marriages."

"How true." Ann thought of her parents. "Love can come in all shapes and sizes, can't it?"

Rhys agreed. "Adam was inconsolable for more than two years after Georgianna died. That's when he and I had our second falling-out. Again, it was over a woman. Or to be precise, over his choice of a bride. But the circumstances were quite different this time, and I . . . I was to blame for some of what occurred. Adam had been in London for the season and I at home in Lancashire. I came down for a party at his request because he wanted me to meet his fiancée. I arrived late at the party. I was tired and irritable. I went in search of a whiskey and instead found a lovely lady crying into her handkerchief. Sooner than I could think, the lady and I traded what I thought were playful kisses. I had no idea who she was, until minutes later, when Adam introduced me to her as his future bride."

Rhys shifted uneasily. "Well, a kiss is only prelude to a rhapsody." He smiled sorrowfully at Ann. "Both must hear the music to become enchanted. I didn't. She did." Rhys's knit his brows. "I never understood how she could have fixed her attentions so much on me, but she did."

"Meaning?"

"Over two or three kisses from a man she barely knew, she tried to break her engagement, but her father would not allow it. She married Adam, and for a while the union seemed a sound one. Months later, she came to me in the midst of night, down the lane from Litchfield Hall. She had in mind a seduction and told me so. I politely refused her. She became furious, and in front of my servants in the forecourt of High Keep, she blurted her feelings."

"What a catastrophe for her and you."

Rhys thanked her with his eyes. "I loved him like a brother, and I would never hurt him. Never."

"Did Adam know she came to you like that?"

"Oh, yes, he had followed her and heard each word. God, I'll never forget how he looked. Crushed and brave. He took her hand, he took her home. I never saw her again."

"What? Why?"

"I came to London soon afterward on business. I thought it best to be away from Lancashire, Adam, and his wife."

"To let distance do what your rejection could not." His mouth curved with pleasure at her perception.

"Did it?"

"Rumors say they were never happy."

"What does Adam say?"

Rhys scowled. "He will not mention her name. Those who came to Litchfield to call say that Mary became despondent, wandering her grounds and house like a sleepwalker. Or a madwoman. She died within months from a horrible fall from her horse."

"Oh, Rhys." She leaned across the seat and took his hands in hers. "You blamed yourself."

"For a time, yes. I was appalled that her feelings had come to such a pass, without encouragement from me. I learned then that one's emotions are not bound by logic," he told her with a wistfulness that had much to do with their current relationship. "I should not have forgotten it."

Ann felt the hair on the back of her neck stand up. "Tragic to have two wives die." *Of accidents.* "Was Adam there the day she fell?"

Rhys looked about the compartment, at last coming back to her. "Yes. In his dressing room when a servant came to tell him. For a while, he became a recluse, as he did after his first wife's death. Now that he has decided to enter London society again, I hope and pray he finds someone he can care for. Someone warm and constant and witty." Rhys squeezed her fingers. "There in the first months you were here, I feared he would make good on his advantage with you. Once I decided to break with your father and court you, I knew I had to get my life in order quickly lest Adam beat me to your doorstep. If he had . . ."

"You would not have pursued me," she said with insight.

"Never." Rhys gave her face a keen survey. "I have never before seen a woman who thrills me or amuses or surprises me as you do. And I can sell paintings and rearrange my investments, but I would not challenge him for you if he objected. I told him so the same day I spoke to your father."

"What did he say?"

"He seemed to accept my interest in you. He didn't seem challenged. I was relieved and yet, oddly, unsettled, because I remember the pain he suffered years ago. You see I would not hurt him, purposely or otherwise, ever again."

Applauding Rhys's honor, Ann fought violently not to take his words as rejection. "What if," she asked with equal mix of trepidation and pride, *"I did not want him?"*

"I could not have let that matter to me."

"You learned that logic cannot control emotions. But your determination can?" she challenged him. "Your Grace, I think you have been misnamed. Instead of the Dour Duke, you should be called the Iron Duke."

At an impasse with anger flowing red as coals between them, his brown eyes swirled in pain. "I have a heart."

She knew he did. He'd shown her repeatedly. To

free him from his past restraints, she had to help him, just as he had her. So she challenged him. "Do you?"

"What else do I have to do to show you?"

"You could tell me that you wouldn't have left me to Adam, not to *any* man."

"Or strangled every man who looked at you, danced with you, sent you flowers? *Yes.*" He seethed as he shook her a little. "I could imagine every time you sighed and smiled that all of it *should* have been for *me.* I would have murdered each man cheerfully. I saw myself as some Othello, wild to possess you, driving myself insane thinking every other man could, would. Only for Adam would I have backed away, but since he isn't here, my independent American, I admit I'll continue to move heaven and earth to have you in my arms. Like this," he said, and lifted her from the cushions to capture her mouth. He pillaged her reason, leaving her stunned when he pulled away and asked, "What more proof would you like?"

"Could you possibly," she said in a steady voice despite the naked embrace she fantasized might be the only way to satisfy her, "just hold me for a little while?"

Chapter 12

"The first and worst of all frauds is to cheat Oneself."

—PHILLIP JAMES BAILEY

THEY CHANGED TRAINS ONCE MORE. THEN, ANN'S BACK to the strong wall of his chest, his arms around her, they settled into the cushions as night deepened into a quiet camaraderie. Closer than friends, cautious at the brink of becoming lovers, they spoke of inconsequential matters. The solitude of their compartment. The coziness of their nest, with the blinds pulled down along the passageway. The landscape, which Ann could tell became more pastoral with the changing umbers of the horizon.

With the rolling rhythm of the wheels over the tracks, a new enchantment suffused Ann. She couldn't sleep and told him so. He agreed, bussed her on the cheek, and told her that with her at last in his embrace, he could never close his eyes "for fear you'd disappear."

She peered over her shoulder at him. "But I'm coming with you to your home."

"You realize I'm going to do my utmost to keep you there."

"Yes," she breathed, and kissed him with a fervor that was wild and sharp as her growing need of him. "I am so fortunate, I can't believe what I'm feeling."

"Believe, darling." He traced her lower lip with a fingertip. "Let yourself feel everything."

"I will," she vowed, and captured his finger in her mouth.

He groaned. "What you make me feel must be illegal." He lifted her chin and puckered her lips to suckle them leisurely, lavishly. "Now, turn around and tell me about your grandparents' farm."

Her first reaction was to refuse. However, modesty combined with reluctance to remember tragedy could not hold sway against her need to please him. Then, too, she knew Rhys sought a picture of what she'd experienced as a child to see how she had become the woman she was.

Ann recounted tales of her youth, the war, experiences she had shut away. The time when a Yankee general, bivouacked in her grandfather's fields, was caught in his nightshirt by a lady who took his dispatches and escaped with the help of her grandfather—and Ann—hiding her in a haystack. Or the night one of Jeb Stuart's scouts slept in their barn and next morning panicked because his irreplaceable black gelding had wandered off. Ann had found the animal grazing behind the smokehouse, and she'd returned him, galloping bareback through Union lines, seven years old. And the worst personal travail, when her brother, Taylor, had been shot by a sharpshooter and, at age nine, she had dug the bullet from his shoulder herself.

"The only doctor in Winchester was working night and day at our town hospital. It was during one of the last raids on the town by a Yankee general who had vowed to burn the Shenandoah valley so barren that even the crows wouldn't stop to pick. If I counted on Doc Anderson leaving his wounded and dying, Taylor would have bled to death. As it was, he just bled on me. So much that I fainted afterward.

"Please don't stare," she begged Rhys when he turned her in his embrace, aghast.

"Where was your mother that day? Why didn't she help your brother?"

"She was down with typhoid. So was my grandfather. Days later, he died of it. My mother recovered, but her consumption set in afterward."

"What happened to Taylor?"

"He survived quite well, I'm pleased to say. I cleaned his wound out with Grandpa Jack's only bottle of bourbon and sewed him up with Mama's last bit of darning thread." She grimaced. "I am a better cook, a good beekeeper—I'm even a superb bookkeeper. But no seamstress. Despite that, Taylor lived."

"Where is he now?"

Her thoughts drifted away just as Taylor had. "He refused to surrender when Lee did. He came to tell us one night when the Yankees flooded into Virginia and the roads crawled with cannon and ambulances and more barefoot men than you can ever imagine. Taylor told us he'd go west with two friends. We haven't heard from him in ten years. My mother thought he was dead. It was one of the miseries that killed her."

She faced Rhys with another truth. "That and her resentment over my father leaving us—leaving *her* and having an affair with another woman. Resentment ruled her, ruined her life, and affected mine and Taylor's . . . and my father's." She ran her eyes over the wonderful man who held her so securely. *I must lose my own resentment to do you justice . . . and myself. And just how do I do that?*

Rhys stroked a hand from her temple into her hair. "Don't worry," he crooned as if he'd read her thoughts. "We'll work this through together." He sampled her lips with swift ardor. "Tell me what your father thinks about Taylor's whereabouts."

"He has never given up hope that Taylor would come back to us. Last summer, a friend of his in California wrote to say he'd heard of a man in the gold fields named Taylor Brighton who had been arrested for murder, tried, and hanged. But my father says that couldn't have been Taylor because he feels in his bones that Taylor's still alive."

"Do you?"

"Yes," she admitted, and then told Rhys what she'd never said to any other person. "But I fear what Taylor has become. My father didn't see how he had changed. He remembers a carefree boy. Before the Southern forces surrendered at Appomattox—that night when Taylor came to say good-bye, I saw a bitter man. The war damaged him—destroyed us all in worse ways than with bullets and cannon."

"The war didn't turn you bitter."

Only against my father. But I'm done with that now. "I think its horrors made me much too serious. Raine's like that, too."

"Raine," Rhys stated firmly, "is a cynic. She finds the sharper edge. You find some humor in everything and survive by other means."

"Doing the necessary things."

"Mmm," he agreed. "Forgetting to have fun."

"Or not knowing how."

"You could learn." He grinned. "I'd like to suggest you do it with someone who needs to remember that himself."

The thoughts that danced in his eyes had her chuckling out loud. "I shouldn't ask what mischief you're planning."

"I can't help but think of the old clothes and other relics I've stored in the Kendall Great House vaults." He winked and trailed a finger along her jaw.

She melted against him. "I want to play charades with you."

"My wish exactly. Who would you like to be?"

Your lover. The thought careened through her like a bullet, stopping her heart dead.

His gaze seared her. "You can tell me anything."

She moistened her lower lip with her tongue. The joy—the rightness of wanting Rhys Kendall—rushed through her bloodstream. "I'd like to be abandoned, free." *Yours.*

He swallowed audibly. "I can arrange that."

It was her turn to gulp.

He arched a brow. "When we go up to High Keep, I'll show you what I've got there. Compared to the London stash, it's not much . . . not much at all," he said, his eyes dropping to her breasts and lap. "But, oh God, you'd look good in what I have in mind."

"You must wear something equally wonderful." She chastised herself for being so devilish, wanting to play love games with him.

The fires in his eyes told her he more than understood, he matched her desires. "Dear heart, my ambition is to make you feel so secure that you'll tell me whatever you want of me."

Love me. The idea shocked and delighted her. *Tell me you love me.* "Kiss me," she urged him instead.

"Ah, my." He rolled his eyes but brought her close to do her will. "If my friends could only see me now, they'd marvel that I'm getting so used to kissing a man with a stubbly mustache!"

Their laughter filled the compartment and dwindled to a lovely peace. The black cocoon of night enveloped them. As the clime became cooler, Rhys wrapped the blanket closer about them both, and they dozed. Finally, the swaying of the train fell to a *clomp-clippety-clomp* that jostled them awake as dawn outlined the stark silhouette of Liverpool.

"It's almost seven o'clock," Rhys told her as he closed his watch and the train pulled into the small station. "I'll buy us some breakfast from the nearby inn, and then I'll hire a wagon from a stable, and we'll be off to Blackburn—and High Keep Castle."

Ann quickly roused as the brisk sea air swept away the serenity of sleep and companionship. Their ride to the docks took no more than five minutes. She alighted to stand before a one-story row house, which back in Alexandria a dockworker might own. In a neighborhood where all the other houses looked exactly like it, save for the color of the door or the design of the brass knocker, Rhys's town house was another indication of how modestly he lived. At this hour of the morning, few people walked the street, most of them already at their jobs. Rhys took a key ring from his pocket, opened the door, and held it for her.

While he turned up the gas, filled the grate with coal to start a fire, and went to the community well to pump water for them, she removed her coat and hat and noted the presence of a long wooden settle, an overstuffed chair, and one narrow bed. She investigated the contents of his tiny kitchen with its cast-iron range and small larder. His cupboard, as she expected, had a few staples in tins. But flour, salt, and baking soda could not a meal make, and they were both so hungry now their stomachs gurgled.

"You can wash up while I walk over to the corner for our breakfast," Rhys told her when he returned, carrying a full bucket of water. "The convenience is out back. I'm afraid I'm not fancy here."

"I'm all right, Rhys," she told him. "You have seen me in so much finery in London that it might be difficult to realize that these surroundings are more like what I'm used to. I grew up on a farm, and I assure you I can make bread, skin a snake, and fire a derringer."

His grin grew easy. "In five minutes total, I bet."

"I can demonstrate."

"I'll give you the opportunity."

"At Blackburn?"

"Anywhere on earth."

She put her hands on her hips and inclined her head toward the door. "Then you'd better get a move on there, Your Grace. I have a need to prove myself."

He gave her a cavalier's bow.

She was chuckling as he left. She then set to work to change her clothes from the man's suit to the only other attire she'd shoved into her reticule. A serviceable day dress in an inconspicuous pearl gray cotton would be more likely to endear her to a group of farmers. And endeared to any and all of Rhys's people was what she longed to be.

Rhys swung the rickety buckboard he'd rented from the stable along a street past his cotton factory, pointed out Adam's along the opposite wharf, then headed east into the dawning sun. She did not speak, nor did he. The journey was rouged with an aura of promise. Rhys took on an expectancy, as if coming home had a deeper meaning than mere familiarity. As if it were the sustenance of his soul.

Ann tried to see what he saw in the green countryside, so similar to what she'd known and loved as a child long ago and thousands of miles away.

When they came to a fork in the road, Rhys said, "These people are very friendly, and I think you'll like them."

The right road rounded a crest and curled into a long drive up to the biggest farmhouse she had ever seen.

Two stories in the shape of a U, the building was of white stone with a gray slate roof and chimneys at every corner and in between. Its broad face blushed a rosy gold in the first light of day, its large black windows creating a warm expression that Ann could have sworn smiled up at her. To the back of the building, a long barn spread out on one side to a pigpen. To the other side were a stable block, a paddock, and smaller sheds, where two men climbed over a plow and another tinkered with a huge thresher. To the right, behind rough-hewn fences, stood trellises and poles in anticipation of the sprouting of seedlings Ann could barely see from so far but which dotted the freshly turned soil. To the left, within another fence and a wire rim, chickens pecked at the earth. A litter of puppies scampered among them, yelping and tumbling over each other and two young children.

Rhys pulled the wagon to a halt in front of the main block and climbed down. Coming around to her side, he offered Ann his hand. From the top of a knoll, a dog appeared, barking and scrambling down the slope, tail wagging furiously in greeting.

"Zeus!" Rhys yelled to the huge sheepdog and patted his thigh. "Come here, boy!" The shaggy

Jo-Ann Power

animal took Rhys at a run, and the two of them embraced and talked to each other the way friends of long standing communicate after being too long apart. The dog then took time to sniff and circle Ann. Petting the dog's head, she was reminded of her grandfather's hounds, one of whom had been hers until he took to tracking rabbits in Union camp one night and caught a bullet in his fun.

"Zeus loves company," Rhys explained, and lifted her chin to examine her eyes. "I didn't bring you here to shed more tears, sweetheart. We're done with that. Let's go in, shall we?"

Rhys examined the house with pride, wound her arm over his, and told her, "Blackburn Farm is a virtually self-sufficient community ten years in the making, run by thirty-two adults with the help of their fourteen children. Those two in the yard are three-year-old twins and the newest members of our group."

Ann's heart swelled with melancholy that this was the farm for which Rhys had wanted to buy the Irish draught horse. For which he had wanted the proceeds of the sale of his stallion, Raider, so that he could buy them another mare. These people were those who had suffered when Rhys's mill burned and they had been caught in its blaze.

Ann turned to him, awed but saddened. Why had he brought her here? To witness the other destruction her father had wrought? She did not know if she had the strength to endure more, and she raised her hand to his jaw to make him look at her. A man and a woman hailed him and rushed out the front door, cutting Ann off from asking more than, "Why did you bring me here?"

228

"Yer Grace." The man who bustled toward them wore a wreath of a grin across his ravaged face.

"Hello, Bill," Rhys called, hand out to shake his with gusto.

Before the man took it, he pulled his forelock in deference. " 'Tis wonderful ta see you, it is. We're not expecting you. But you know we will always set a place." He looked at Ann through lashless eyes. "We'll be happy to set another, too."

Ann summoned every bit of graciousness she'd ever been taught and did not stare, but smiled and extended her hand as Rhys introduced her to Bill Hignell and his frail wife, Ivy.

Ivy sank into a small curtsy, overjoyed to greet Rhys but leery of Ann. Covering one scarred cheek with an equally disfigured hand, Ivy gravitated toward the men. Her heart-shaped face was more severely injured than her husband's, with white lacy scars that gave her skin the appearance of warped parchment. What was worse, her lips had been seared so badly that she had difficulty forming words. She tried, though, her eagerness to greet Rhys overcoming her impediment. Her eyes, small slits of desolation, took in Ann's hair and clothes, then darted back to Rhys as her husband and Rhys rattled on. Ivy knit her ragged brows and sneaked a peek at Ann again, her uneasiness a tale of looks lost, life endured, and embarrassment abated—except when a stranger came to call.

Bill Hignell hooked his arm in his wife's and walked a pace behind Rhys and Ann as they headed for the house. The sounds of their voices on the morning air had others pouring from the building and poking their heads out of the barns and stables. Three others were marred as badly as Ivy Hignell; most bore marks like Bill, distinguishable but, Ann thought, forgettable. With time.

Then, as she and Rhys sat down at the long oak trestle table to share a small meal of leftovers from the early morning, Ann felt Rhys's fingers reach for hers. The men and women around her seemed not to notice, but she knew they did. Had he ever brought another woman here? Why would he? And why, she pondered again as she picked up her fork, had he brought her?

She did not believe Rhys wished to show her people's woes compounded by her father's actions. Rhys was not a mean or vengeful man. She had no other possible answers and could seek none until their meal drew to an end and, with it, the conviviality of their hosts.

"We've much to do," Bill Hignell told Rhys, but he glanced at the others who had gathered for a spot of tea to greet the lord of the manor and his guest. "If there is anything ye need, Yer Grace?"

"Thank you, Bill. I want to show Miss Brighton around. After that, I would like to borrow two horses, if you don't mind, to escort her up to High Keep Castle. I'll return your horses before noon."

"Take 'em, Yer Grace. As long as ye like, ye know that." He pulled his forelock in deference and indicated with a lift of his chin that the others should leave the Duke and the lady alone. They shuffled out.

Rhys rose. "Will you walk with me?"

She went willingly to view things that recalled her years on her grandparents' farm. Not all of those memories, she discovered, were sad ones. Blackburn's dairy consisted of a small shed with numerous cream-settling pans and giant skimmers. Outside, two huge vats for making cheese and barrel butterchurns stood side by side. The ciderhouse contained presses wider than she'd ever seen in Winchester, where apples and peaches were regular summer and fall crops. The smokehouse was big, too, but today contained only two whole hams, which she supposed was the remainder of last autumn's curing. At length, Rhys took her to the top of a little knoll from which they could view the panorama of the farm's prosperity.

Within a little copse of budding trees, a wooden settee nestled. He asked her if she'd care to sit, and when she did, he faced the sight of people going about their daily rounds. "I could have told you about these people and the success they have made of this venture. But I thought the sight of it—and the remnants of their hardship—might draw a stronger illustration than my words could convey."

He turned to scan her expression. What he found there, she knew, was agreement with his premise, and so he inhaled some measure of serenity and turned away. In profile, one hand to the branch of a tree, his silken hair ruffling in the breeze, he looked young but far from carefree. "I also hoped they would make a stronger argument than I could."

That puzzled her.

He saw it and explained. "I wanted you to see what had been nurtured and blossomed out of tragedy. I needed you to see how hurt these people were from a catastrophe for which so many of us blame your father."

She clasped her hands together, cold perspiration making her skin slick. "Some are severely maimed," she admitted with a clench of her stomach.

"Outwardly, yes. But even those like Ivy, who will not venture beyond the fences, live with friends in laughter and love." He came to stand over her. "You can, too, if you allow yourself."

He sounded so desolate, she looked up. His hand wended through her hair. Wound back into a loose chignon since she'd changed her clothes, it gave up its pins easily to tumble down her shoulders.

"I brought you here to show you that many people, most people, survive the worst tragedies. They marry and build homes and have children. They go to church and school and enjoy their friends. They live with scars, big and small, inside and out, finding a measure of joy to lighten their burdens on their way toward tomorrow. When we started this farm, the land had been fallow for years. The forest had encroached, and weeds grew like a jungle. The house did not exist. I brought in the stones and wood and mortar. We built it together and then started on the outbuildings. I waived the rent. They voted to overrule me and send it up to High Keep anyway. With their money, I buy them more seed."

"Or mares."

"Whatever they need."

"They are fortunate to know you, and they do right to show you how highly they value you." She turned her face into his hand and kissed his palm.

He sank to his haunches and looked up at her. "Ann, when I went to see your father weeks ago and tell him that I wanted to call on you, I had lived with these people and their sorrows for ten years. I knew their pain, their lost joys. Women who could not bear to look in their mirrors again, afraid they might never attract a husband or soothe a child. Men who felt crippled by their inability to work as they once had and provide for their families."

He ran a gentle finger over her cheek. "But after a

decade of hating your father, I suddenly realized I needed to cast it off. My resentment of him bound me up, and until I saw you—and wanted you—I never knew it. Never saw how it crippled me. Held me back from taking from life as much as I could give back. Then I learned that to be with you, I had to surrender the hatred and the pain. Never had anything been so easy. Never have I been happier." He took both her hands in his and squeezed them tightly. "I want to make you happy, too."

"You are an amazing man."

"If you choose to see it that way, I won't argue against my own cause." He smiled briefly. "But I want more than your admiration."

Her heart beat a frantic tattoo, thinking what more might mean. But oh, she knew. In measured steps, Rhys Kendall was asking her to marry him.

He stood and held out his hand. "Let's go up to High Keep."

They took two horses from the stable and traveled a well-used lane past dense forest north. Above the treetops in the distance, a tower and a spire drew Ann's eye. The closer they came, she saw these were only the largest of numerous others. Suddenly, the view opened to a circular drive to a three-story house—rather a mansion—of three main parts.

"The main block of the house was begun by the third Duke of Carlton to compete with his best friend, the first Earl Litchfield."

"An ancestor of Adam's?"

"Yes, neighbors as the Kendalls and the Litchfields have been for centuries, I am afraid to say we've been enemies more often than friends. These two had a bet going over who could build the biggest and most ornate house to replace the castles each had inhabited since the thirteenth century. It seems Kendall had more available cash than his friend Litchfield, plus Litchfield chose not to tear down his castle—as my forebear did—but to add on to his abode. The result is that this structure is still called High Keep Castle, as the original one was, but in design it is a Restoration country house."

"It looks like pictures Raine has of Italian palaces." The dun-colored stone plus the Ionic columns and carved angels holding arrows and roses along the gables created a mammoth impression of neoclassical beauty.

"Yes. Meanwhile, the east and west blocks were additions in the last century. The east for the servants, the west is a nursery." Rhys's eyes twinkled. "My grandfather had great ambitions, but he and his wife could not fulfill them. I must tell you that for the past two generations, we Kendalls haven't sired but one child."

"Ah, but quality is preferable to quantity."

He shot a startled look at her and burst out laughing. "Thank you. The compliment is returned."

She inclined her head, then grinned. "If I wanted to see each room, how long would it take us?"

"Hours. Not counting the servants' quarters or the sixteen rooms of the nursery wing, we have here twenty-six public rooms, plus a double-sized conservatory, two-story library, and formal state dining room along a balcony with a view of the formal gardens. To top it off, we have forty-six bedrooms for guests."

She widened her eyes. "Your family likes to give very large parties."

"When the monarchs traveled, we often supplied

lodging and entertainment for them and their courtiers."

"And lately?"

Rhys lifted a shoulder. "This Queen prefers Balmoral in Scotland and a little house in the south on the Isle of Wight to traipsing about the countryside. This has been all well and good for us Kendalls, as well as other noblemen, who haven't the money any longer to subsidize entertainment of a whole court."

"Oh, but surely the kings and queens did not come to visit and expect their hosts to pay for everything?"

"Of course they did. It was the polite way they could inspect the nether reaches of their realm and not pay a penny for the opportunity. Even today, the Prince of Wales enjoys the practice. One of his friends has been driven to bankruptcy because he supplied Bertie with his every whim."

"All because no guest ever reimburses his hosts for their hospitality," she concluded.

"Absolutely."

"How have any of you prospered to this point?"

Rhys dismounted, looped his reins around a post, and walked toward her. "A question I answer with hard work and frugality, I am afraid."

He helped her down from her horse, and they strode along the neatly trimmed forecourt walk, up the broad steps, and under the portico. He lifted the huge brass knocker and rapped it against the thick oak. No one answered, so he took Ann along a pebbled path around to the kitchen entrance. "Don't want to frighten them by just walking in. My housekeeper here, Mrs. Connelly, is a bit of a stickler for form and will be surprised—and somewhat disoriented and angry at me for coming unannounced. My butler, Fitzallen, is aging, deaf, but a dear man who has a frail heart."

"I will do my utmost not to ruffle their feathers."

"I know they'll love you instantly."

Fitzallen, the butler—from what he could see of Ann through his thick spectacles and watery little eyes—liked her well enough. But Mrs. Connelly had that strained prune look of a woman whose authority was about to be challenged—and usurped.

She played up to Rhys while clearly trying to judge if Ann were her equal. "If I'd known," coupled with "I'm not prepared, you realize," sprinkled her conversation as she showed them to his morning room, removed the dust covers from all the furniture in a tizzy, then asked if they'd care for luncheon.

"What do you say, sweetheart? Hungry yet?"

If there'd been any doubt in Mrs. Connelly's mind about Ann's purpose for being there unescorted in midday, Rhys's endearment deleted it. The woman virtually donned armor before Ann's eyes—and Ann decided to try to divest her of it with a bit of kindness.

"Perhaps in an hour or so." Ann thought that might make her seem less intrusive.

"As you wish, Miss Brighton." The woman backed herself out the door as if Ann were already her duchess.

Rhys sat down behind his desk chair and watched Ann. "Don't frown. She's harmless. Bark is worse than her bite type of housekeeper. She's wonderful, really. Very skilled. Good cook. Efficient. Brisk but usually polite."

Brusque.

"She grows her own garden vegetables, saving greengrocer charges for me. She even balances my books for the estate."

"She is valuable," Ann conceded.

"But you still don't like her."

"Rhys, I am sure she has proven her worth to you, and I am the invader." The barrier to Ann and Mrs. Connelly getting along had been erected by the housekeeper. "How long has she been with you?"

"Four years."

"There you have it, then. I do not know her as well as you." *Nor have I any reason to question her abilities.*

He lifted a shoulder. "I hardly know her personally. One doesn't necessarily become friends with one's servants here. We are interested in performance only. Besides, she was referred to me by Adam when my previous housekeeper wished to retire and go live with her daughter Ivy, down at Blackburn Farm."

"Well, I am no one to judge her, Rhys. Especially not on ten minutes' worth of discussion." She trailed a hand along a sapphire japanned escritoire and admired a floor-length gold mirror. "I would like it if you'd tell me about the furnishings and the house. It is far and away the loveliest place I've ever seen."

"So you shall see it. Come along. We'll start just here with my library." He swung open the ivory and gilt-edged doors and opened up a whole new world for her. A land of park-sized rooms with floor-to-ceiling fireplaces and, shrouded though they were in white sheeting, numerous settees and fine old chairs. A state dining room which she was certain could hold more than the famous four hundred which Mrs. Astor could fit into her ballroom at 34th Street and Fifth Avenue. Finally, on the second and third floors, he showed her around to three of the various guest bedrooms and the master suite set aside for the dukes and duchesses of the house of Kendall.

"This suite," Rhys informed her, "consists of a mirror-image set of bedroom, robe room, water closet and sitting room, which runs along the full south side of the house. They are connected by an interesting set of two more rooms."

Ann was taken by the ceilings. Trompe l'oeil paintings of a cerulean sky filled with angels similar to those who sat on the rafters outside. Each angel held a white rose, the family emblem.

"Roses in the sky." Ann craned her neck to note that each flower was different from the next. "Beautiful."

"You like them. I'm glad. Some people think it an affectation. I was inclined to agree with them when I was younger."

"And now?"

"I realize why the Duke commissioned the painting."

"Oh? Why was that?"

"Family lore says that he did it to please his wife. She adored alba roses, and she wished to see them"— Rhys grinned—"even when she was lying down."

Ann felt her cheeks flame. "In every room of the suite, how novel." She chuckled, and Rhys joined her. "Any other oddities here?"

"Two."

"Will you show me?"

"You might blush more."

"And laugh?"

"I hope so," he said with fervor.

"If you do it with me, then I want to see."

He took her through his suite, where the biggest bed she'd ever seen stood facing the south bay window and a door to the balcony. The view of his grounds spread over endless forest. He took her inside and showed her a large black and white tiled water closet and lion-footed tub big enough for two. Then he swung open another door for her, which connected the suites of the Duke and Duchess. "A joint private dressing room."

This resembled no such room Ann had ever heard of, much less seen. This was a room of mirrors. Against the four walls, antique plates of finest silvered glass captured the figures of Rhys and herself. She stood amazed at the brilliance created by the numerous candelabra sconces hung on the walls, the thick Persian cartouche carpet of white and red—and the one piece of furniture that commanded the middle of the floor.

Rhys walked over and flung away its cover. A plush red satin couch with two gently scrolled ends and no back, supported by four plump golden angels, was wide enough for two reclining but entwined people. Ann did not have to ask what the couch was used for. "Are my cheeks on fire?" She faced him.

"Beautifully so," he got out amid his chuckles.

"Surely you must have some family tidbit to tell me about this room."

His own cheeks grew pink. "The room was fashioned after the reception room at Versailles in France, where the Kendalls lived for a few years with Charles Stuart when he was in exile. The mating couch was one the tenth Duke found on a visit to Italy. He brought it here and used it to seduce the woman he loved."

"Was he successful?"

"Terribly so. She was a baroness, and her parents thought the Duke too worldly and his title too lofty for their darling daughter. Evidently, my ancestor would not take no for an answer. The baroness not only ran away with him to marry him in Gretna Green, but she became pregnant, so the legend goes, with each of their six children on this piece of furniture. The couch seems to have had special powers which have dwindled over the years."

"Perhaps it hasn't been used often enough." Ann's words were out before she thought of their suggestiveness.

Rhys roared in laughter and hugged her close. "Before I am tempted to use it myself, let me show you the last private wonder of the house." He took her beyond his suite through a private little door.

Similar to his public gallery in his London home, this one had walls backed in red silk and dotted with a collection of portraits. In the subjects' faces and demeanors, Ann could see the family resemblance to the current lord and master of High Keep Castle.

"Why do you keep these portraits here and not show them?"

"They are unique portraits of the family, and we do not wish to share them. My father told me they are here assembled to allow each new duke and duchess to contemplate their actions in light of their past."

"A practice from which many might find benefits." She strolled along the corridor, occasionally sitting on a bench to admire a piece at length. "So many handsome people. Most of them are funny, too." She indicated one man in hunting pinks who held a spaniel. The dog faced the viewer and was gritting his teeth.

"The ninth Duke," Rhys supplied to her questioning glance at him. "His major sport was quail hunting. However, none of his dogs ever could track well for him. Hence, the frustrated hound with his equally stymied master." Rhys went to stand before another

man. "Each duke and duchess of the line is repre-
sented here in an informal way. Usually a formal
portrait of the newest duke is commissioned by him
as soon as he inherits. That one is meant to hang in
Kendall Great House. When he marries, his wife has
her portrait done. Then the two of them begin to
think what aspect of their natures should be shown
here in the High Keep gallery."

"You have no portrait of yourself in Kendall Great
House, do you?" When he shook his head, she asked,
"Why not?"

"I told myself I didn't sit for a painting because I
hated to spend any money on something frivolous,
but I also needed to put the family's finances in the
black again before I proclaimed to the world that I
was the worthy heir."

"But you are so worthy of the glory, Rhys. You
must have it done and very soon."

He took Ann's hands and placed a tender kiss on
each palm. "God, you are so very sweet."

"Promise me you will do it."

"I will. I hope I might add something else to the
commission."

"What?" she asked, and dared to hope she knew
where his thoughts led.

"I never thought there would be a duchess to paint.
Until recently."

She could not move but reveled in the moment.

"Ann, I have wanted you to see my factory, Blackburn Farm, and High Keep before I said this. I wanted
you to see what I was, where I came from, and why I
am the man I am. Beyond my feud with your father,
my own decision never to want a wife, and even far
beyond your own determination to remain independent, I want you."

He smiled slowly, as full of conviction as trepidation. "I don't want your money. I certainly don't want your father's or even his connections. I just want you. As you are. Heaven help me, I'll take you naked. In fact, I'd like to insist on it. Ann," he beseeched her when all she could manage was to stare at him, "I am asking you to marry me. I am asking you to stay here in England with me. Have children with me. Raise wheat and chickens and——"

"Churn butter and bake bread," she told him, shocked by her own inanity at this joyous turning point in her life.

With a groan, he wrapped his arms around her. "If that's what you want. Ann, marry me, be *my* Grace. My saving Grace. I need you badly to add laughter to my days. What's more, I yearn to make you happy, and I think I can. I think *only* I can. I might never be rich, but you don't want that in any case, do you?"

She shook her head. "No, I don't care about the state of your bank account. But there are other things that disturb me."

Fear that she was rejecting him swam in his eyes. "What?"

She sniffed back tears and hated herself for what she was about to say. It was a portion of a larger truth that concerned her and made her ache. "I hate the English weather. I'm forever cold."

Tears lined his own dark lashes as he swept hers from her cheeks. "I'll keep you warm. I'll build more fireplaces, and I'll plug any drafts here or at Kendall Great House. Hell, I'll go into wool instead of cotton——"

She put two fingers to his lips. "Oh, don't change your whole life for me."

"I am asking you to change yours for me. What else?"

She bit her lip to keep it from trembling. "I wanted to have a farm. My own land—"

"Have mine, then. All of mine! Christ, darling, I have fourteen farms from High Keep down to Kent. Two aren't even worked. Pick one—or both. I'll make them yours. Plow and plant, I don't care. Just come home to me."

"I want to," she whispered, hating to list her objections but needing to be honest with him. "But I'm torn between wanting to be with you and wanting my own landscape, my own familiar country."

"Can you love one piece of land so much?"

"Don't you?" she asked pointedly.

He gazed over her shoulder as if he surveyed his domains. "I do, but I regard it in a different way since I have met you." She swallowed the lump in her throat. "I saw this as my ancestral home. A place my family had lived, worked, flourished in for six hundred years. I loved it because it was where my past was. But it now takes on new meaning as the place where my future with you could be. A future made brighter by the knowledge that I could create a happy family here with you."

She looked away, and she remembered the shape of his Lancastrian hills. It was a landscape so similar to western Virginia. "I always thought if I went back to Winchester someday, my brother would come home."

"We could hire detectives to search for him."

Joy that Rhys would even think of this shot through her like strong medicine, but the reality of the situation killed it. "I wouldn't know where to begin."

"It doesn't matter. Detectives get paid to do that."

Hope nibbled at the edges of her despair. "What do you suppose a good detective costs?"

"I have no idea, but some things are worth whatever the price."

"Yes, and this is one of them." *More important than raising walking horses—or buying land which could never be worthy of the word* home. *Not without you.*

Rhys nodded. "And when they send us evidence of Taylor's whereabouts, we'll travel to America together."

She couldn't control the tears that slid down her cheeks like a silent waterfall. "You would come with me, wouldn't you?"

"Locating your brother is only one piece missing from your broken heart."

"You have found so many of them," she told him with conviction.

"I'd like to find more. Give me the chance."

Rhys Kendall was everything she ever desired in a man. A husband. But the one thing missing from his proposal was the one declaration she needed more than all the others. She needed to hear him say he loved her.

"Ann?"

Chapter 13

". . . there can be no doubt that, of all the factors that have contributed to the social revolution of London, there are few more important and none more delightful than the American Invasion."

—OSCAR WILDE

PERHAPS IT WAS FOOLISH OF HER TO WANT THE WORDS. HE had, after all, proved to her time and again that he valued her, wished to protect her from all sorts of hurts and slights. Now he wanted to bestow on her the highest honor he had to give. So she understood with an assurance down to the marrow of her bones that Rhys Kendall could never marry her for less than love.

Of course, he had not spoken those three words because he wondered if she could hold that fine emotion for him. She had led him to believe that she would have married Quinn because she was afraid to love. Her mother's resentment had helped to ruin that lady's own marriage and affected her two children adversely. Her attitude had already claimed too many casualties. But no longer.

To free herself of resentment, Ann needed not time or space, only resolution. So in one decisive moment, she tore down the only remaining obstacle to their happiness. With her words.

"Since I've come abroad, I have discovered so much more than I expected. I've learned new facets of myself, my friends . . . even my father." She scanned the mirrors and the many ways she could now see herself. "I was shortsighted, limiting my perception of home to a childhood that really held as much horror as delight. Because I am tied to my past by memories does not mean the landscape of my future must be bound by that. My heart can seek wider horizons."

He fisted his hand into her hair. "What do you see there?"

"I am raising walking horses."

"We could raise them together."

"I want to raise children."

"Can I persuade you to raise *our* children?"

"How soon?"

He crushed her close. "We could start whenever you like."

"That would scandalize all of England."

"Then you'd better become my duchess quickly, darling."

"What would you say"—she stood on her toes to touch his lips with hers—"to now?"

He kissed her swiftly. "We have no licence, no vicar. The banns must be posted for three Sundays—"

She laughed. "Are you misinterpreting my words on purpose, Your Grace?"

He pressed his hands to her back and slid them down to her derriere. He lifted her against him. She almost swooned at the hard, long declaration of his body's intent. "I'm testing you because I must be sure you want this—and me. I want you, Ann, for all the right reasons, in all the ways I can get you. On that couch. On the carpet. In my bed. *All* my beds." He was adamant as he peered into her eyes. "But I could not bear to have you once or twice—and not for the rest of my life. So if you want to share that couch, dear heart, I tell you I won't let you leave me afterward."

She leaned back, admired him, and told him with every ounce of her desire for him shining in her eyes, "I love you, Rhys. I love you more than I thought it possible or even wise."

His fingers bit into her. "Say you will marry me. At High Keep in the Kendall family chapel."

"Four Sundays from this one," she answered, thrilled that their wedding would be an intimate ceremony and not the circus so many London events were. She began to undo his waistcoat buttons as she walked backward toward the mirrored room and his alluring couch.

His eyes darkened with hope. "You are serious that you want to do this before we're married."

She paused at the threshold. "Aren't you?"

"God, yes. I love you."

His words were the only encouragement she needed to unbutton her bodice. Smiling as the soft gray material gaped to reveal the pearl lace of her chemise, she grew suddenly shy and turned. But the woman she faced in the mirror knew there was no need to feel anything other than joy.

He stepped into the mirrored room, closed the door, and locked it. She stood there, tall and serene, little goosebumps of delight prickling her skin as Rhys approached. In the endless reflections, she saw him from so many angles coming toward her, his eyes intensely burning, his hands reaching for her hooks, brushing aside her hair, and placing his mouth beneath her ear. "I love you," he murmured, and planted little kisses down her throat. "I love you."

His hands cupped her breasts and traced her nipples. She caught her breath and swayed back against him. Forcing herself to witness this first claiming of her body and her soul, she saw a woman she barely knew. She looked the same, as long and lean, but her demeanor was languorous, her head lolling to her lover's shoulder as he turned her in his embrace and pushed aside her bodice and her chemise to draw in his breath and say, "My God, you are incomparable. Ivory skin and pale pink nipples. A special rose of my own. Look and see if it isn't so."

She opened her eyes. Sultry and dark, they stared at this woman who was bare to her waist. Her breasts felt heavy, ripe to bursting with want as his fingers circled her nipples.

"They are long," he said admiringly, shaping one and then the other to tender peaks.

"Is that good?" she asked with someone else's deep and needy voice.

"Oh, yes." He arched her over his arm and leaned toward her. "For babies to nurse—but just as much for me to make into little buds of need. Tell me if you like this."

She reeled when he sucked her into his mouth. "You—you're making me tingle." *Gush, crave.*

"Before the hour is up, sweetheart, you'll do more than that." He picked her up and carried her to the edge of the couch. "Let's get these off you."

His words may have been urgent, but his hands were deliberate as he peeled away the tapes to her skirt, petticoat, and drawers. In a moment, she stood, amazingly unashamed in only her black garters and lisle hose. He pushed her to sit as he went to one knee before her, rolled down her stockings, and cast them away. His hands skimmed her calves and drifted up to her parted thighs to massage her woman's flesh with leisure. Her cheeks burned in embarrassment, but not as much as the rest of her body.

"From the minute I saw you in Dublin, I wanted you like this. Free. Abandoned with me." He caressed her breast, her waist, and the curve of one hip before he inserted one finger to separate her folds and trace them. "You are softer than a flower. All wet with dew for me." His words and actions had her clutching him closer and moaning. "You are so giving. I could do this all night."

"All day." She undulated to his rhythmic touch.

"I have a house in Ireland where we could go—"

"Oh, very soon." She was beyond following his logic when the only pleasure she sought was in his hands. "Hurry." She beseeched him to remove his own clothes by working at his shirt studs.

"This is best done slowly. Say you trust me."

"Only you," she insisted, plucking at his shirt.

"Then lie back and let me do what I want." His breathing grew thick as he led her down so that she had her legs open to him, shamelessly wide at the edge of the couch.

"What do you—?" she asked on a thread of sound.

"This." He dipped his head, and she felt his hot breath against her as he rolled her apart, petted her, and put his gentle tongue to the neediest portion of her body. "To savor you." She bucked. He bathed her with kisses and crooned how she must remain still for the best part. He lavished her with an homage that had her melting.

"I can't wait anymore," she moaned, and he relented by looming above her. The glorious completion she had felt in his arms last night on the train paled in comparison to the pounding ecstasy he brought her to with tender flicks of his tongue and fingers. She was panting, quaking in his embrace when he covered her with his body. "I need you inside me."

He smiled wickedly as he draped her along the length of the couch. "I know you do, love. I need to be there, too." He illustrated with a gentle kiss, the essence of her on his lips an exotic fragrance to spike her desire for him. But when he levered himself away, she gasped and whimpered to have him back. He removed his clothes with efficiency. His perfection took her breath.

She marveled at the sight of his broad shoulders, lean waist, long thighs, and an erection she wondered if she might be able to absorb. But she knew from years of watching farm animals couple that no matter the male's daunting size, his mate always accommodated him. Ann had plans to do more than that for Rhys. She wanted to give him pleasure, all that he could hold. He'd had so very little in his life until now. And he had given her so much, so generously.

She trailed a hand up his corded leg. He waited, his lids heavy with desire, his head falling backward, his jaw flexing.

"I love your hands on me," he ground out as she ran her palm along his hip and threaded her fingers into his crisp hair, then defined him from hilt to point. "I never thought I could have you, and now that you're here, I must go slowly."

"You are so tender, Rhys. You couldn't hurt me." She beckoned him with open arms, drew him down, and put her mouth on him everywhere she wanted. His furry chest. His throat. His mouth. "I love you," she told him. "I have for so long, I think, and couldn't bring myself to say it. I was so afraid—"

He silenced her with a commanding kiss. "No more about the past. Not now." His hands flowed over her like liquid flames. "I need to show you what the future holds." He settled between her legs and curled them around his waist, running his penis along the core of her and making her writhe against him. "You're so instinctive—"

"So empty—" She arched against him, tired of delay.

His breath flared his nostrils as he swallowed and curved two of his fingers into the part of her that needed him so desperately. "Once we start, you must tell me if you can't take me, sweetheart." He placed himself at her entrance. "We can wait—" She moaned as he slid inside, stretched her over his impressive girth, and paused.

"I can't wait," she objected, and tossed her head on the cushion.

He was still as stone and just as hard. "Be sure. Be very sure. No, no, don't move for a minute, please." He placed a hand to her belly and caressed her. "There," he crooned, and drove in a little farther.

His extra length had her hips rising off the couch. "More," she insisted.

"Your wish," he rasped, "is mine." He complied, completing his journey with a small rending inside her—and a stab of discomfort. He put his hands in her hair, on her breasts, his mouth imparting words of praise. The girth of him was stunning. His length mind-shattering. The heat he created in her was a cauldron. He stoked the fires higher with a smooth and constant rhythm that she learned easily and welcomed. Her flesh encompassed him, blossomed to take him and make him her own. So it was with great surprise that she felt a driving urge to have something more of him. Duty, resentment, grief had all been elements of her experience with love. But never before had she known this mad delight.

She gripped his forearms. "This is delicious, but—"

One corner of his mouth hitched up. He hovered above her. "Is this?" He withdrew, and she gasped, thinking he'd go away, but just as quickly he glided deep inside her. The friction singed every nerve. His repetition brought every cell in her body to pulsing life. His sweet assault had her moving with him in a reach that blinded her to time or place. In a bright flame, she rose and burst with a white-hot pulse of love.

She burned back slowly, smoldering to embers. He combed her curls from her cheeks and buried his lips in the crown of her hair. She bit her lip, and he kissed her, soothing her with little words and gentle hands.

So when she drifted to her senses, she found herself entwined with him, naked and sated. Warm and cared for as she had not felt ever before in her life. His eyes were closed, his breathing erratic, his arm flung over her hip. Suddenly, she longed to see him in other ways and rose on her elbow to view him and herself reflected in the mirrors.

It was not so much a shock to stare at herself clothed only in her skin as to see her reclining next to this superbly muscled man. Who smiled at her in the mirror and kissed her shoulder. Who cupped her breast and pulled her back against him. Whose hand sank from her breast to the nest between her thighs and in a few slick moves had her calling his name and turning in his arms.

This second time Rhys made love to her was

neither slow nor sweet. But torrid, sharp, and earthy. Amid her cries to have him deeper, faster, harder inside her, she heard his own desires harshly whispered in her ear. "All of you. I want all of you."

She gleefully obliged him.

She had no idea how long it took her to recover from their rapture. She knew only the brush of his mouth over hers and the promise to have his footman draw a bath for her. "Don't move."

She couldn't.

He returned with a robe, dressed in another. She felt boneless in his arms as he held it for her, and she wrapped its velvet warmth around her. "Can't have you catch cold, can I?"

He left again. Long minutes later, when he returned, he scooped her up and carried her into his bathroom. Standing her near the tub, he tested the water temperature with his foot. "You'll like this," he smiled, and slid the robe away.

"Only if you come with me," she urged against his mouth.

"It's not big enough."

Her hands ran down his torso to his body's renewing interest in her own. "Give me a minute, I'm certain it will be."

He choked on laughter. "You're becoming more adventurous."

"Let's be, together."

He climbed in, sank down, held out his hand, and she stepped in and straddled him.

He sucked in his breath. He positioned her over his rigid length, and she took him inside her with a sigh of satisfaction from them both.

"I can see," she told him much later as her head

rested against his shoulder, "that there are a few skills I need to perfect in my English riding technique."

"For a novice in this sport, darling, you show great promise. Do come to me for any lessons you think you need."

"Are you always available?" She skimmed his hip with her nails. "You never know when the urge can strike."

"Night or day, I'm yours. What I want to teach you is not written anywhere"—he nuzzled her ear—"but in my heart."

"Ah, me." She traced the whorls of his chest hair. "The never-ending smugness of the English."

They ate in Rhys's sitting room as the sun sank. The meal was a cold concoction of roast chicken, bread, and greens, because of the lack of notice Mrs. Connelly had of their arrival. Though the lady had not let Rhys know her displeasure with that, she did cast Ann a few surreptitious looks as she laid the table. Clearly, the woman censured Ann for her hours of seclusion here with Rhys today.

"Don't let Mrs. Connelly's attitude bother you," Rhys instructed as they ended their supper. "She has been here in charge for so long, she forgets her place. I won't allow her to judge you—or mar the beauty of what has begun here between us. I will speak to her."

Ann shook her head. She would be mistress here, and not in name only. "No. I will."

He met her gaze levelly. "The best solution, yes."

"I don't wish to rile her. She knows High Keep and how to run it efficiently. I need to learn much from her if I'm to be a credit to you."

He picked up her hand and kissed it. "You are, without lifting a finger."

"I will be your wife." She sat back, stunned with the statement, and the reality of it spread through her in an objective way it hadn't before. She found herself well pleased with her future. "I want to be your helper, too." She pondered what skills she had that she might use on his behalf, and aside from her knowledge of farm management, she had one other. "I'm very good at mathematics. Is Mrs. Connelly? She does your books for the estate, didn't you say?"

"It was a duty I willingly delegated to her when she said she could add and subtract. Take it over, if you like. I suspect she'd like fewer responsibilities. Most servants do."

"I kept books for my father at Forsythe House and in Alexandria. I like to feel useful."

"Then start tomorrow."

She grinned. "You are very indulgent with me."

"I will be more so, too. Tell me what you'd like for this wedding in four weeks."

"No overpriced florist."

His eyes glittered. "A bouquet of alba roses?"

"From your garden here. If there are enough. It's June, but I do see it is a bit colder up here and—"

"You shall have them. What else is on your list?"

"Is there any tradition that the dukes of Carlton and Dundalk have invited their staff and tenants?"

"Yes, a long-standing one, honored more often in the breach these past two hundred years."

"Then we shall honor them in the observance. Unless there are too many and it would cost too much to—"

"No. It's what pleases you. Money well spent from all viewpoints."

"We'll give them a feast they'll tell their children

about long after you and I are gone." The thought of all her tomorrows among people she did not know turned her attentions to her friends, her cousin, and Aunt Peg.

"We'll invite them," Rhys told her, and lifted her chin to peer into her eyes. "Raine and Colleen and Gussie. And your aunt. We'll find a way to keep you safe here and yet have them come north."

She hung her head, reminded again of her father's demands.

"Don't dare to think of him. You leave him to me."

"You'll see him?"

"I must, sweetheart. Some things are very wrong with him—and I must not only know what they are but help if I can to find Owen MacIntyre. Only then will you be safe. And in the meantime, I must notify your father that you are safe. I dare not send a telegram or trust anyone with news of your whereabouts. I also must appear in London soon so that no one suspects you have come here with me. I want no one to wonder if you and I have absconded for a clandestine reason. And where better to come looking for you than at my home? No, I must take them off the scent and at the same time calm your father's fears for your safety."

"He'll gloat when he hears that you and I will be married."

"Let him. He'll do it sitting alone."

"People—your people here—will talk if he is excluded from the ceremony. They'll criticize you for being rude. They won't know what he did. Oh, Rhys, I don't care about him, but this kind of tarnish rubs off, and you will suffer."

"No, I won't. Neither will you. Skip bears the brunt

of his own misdeeds. He can't hurt you any longer. You belong to me now."

"And you to me."

"Yes, from the first time you tossed your hat away, you seized my heart." He picked up a curl from her shoulder and wound it around his finger. His expression tantalized her for its sexual perusal. "Finished with your supper?"

She nodded.

"Well, then." He smiled secretly and crooked a finger. "I'd like to show you a portrait of the fourth Duchess of Carlton and Dundalk. She's rather toothy, but some say one of the Kendall raving beauties nonetheless. See what you think."

"The woman's naked!" Ann was choking with laughter at the sight of the sensual duchess reclining upon a malachite carved couch, a rope of diamonds the only decoration upon her flawless dusky skin.

"But an inspiration to succeeding dukes to find a comparable woman, wouldn't you say? Aside from her buck teeth, I mean." Rhys tried desperately not to chuckle.

"No wonder you put her along the back wall here. She'd catch her death of cold anywhere else."

Hands on her hips, Ann approached the ten-foot portrait of the raven-haired duchess and tried to read the illegible artist's mark in the left corner. "Who painted this?"

"We are not certain, though my father did spend some time and money attempting to discover its providence. With inconclusive evidence, he and my mother decided they couldn't continue to care. The infamous Constance would remain upon this wall, admired by the family only, as you might agree is appropriate for her state of deshabille."

"Your Grace." Mrs. Connelly waddled into the gallery. "I have the adjoining suite ready now as you ordered."

"Thank you, Mrs. Connelly, we'll be along."

The woman mumbled to herself. "Your tea and brandy are ready, too." Then she scuffled off below-stairs.

"Is she always this happy?" Ann stared after the woman, who had glanced at Ann with as much relish as if Ann were a muddy pair of Wellingtons one had to clean.

"She suffers from lumbago. She becomes more chipper as the summer wears on," Rhys explained as he took Ann's arm and led her back through the impressive house. So big was High Keep Castle that the mere idea of dusting the place was daunting.

So was the matching suite for the Kendall duchesses.

Like the rest of the castle, this room showed its modernity only on its surface. The walls were of large, rough-cut stone, covered here in this bedroom with plaster but in many original portions of the house, such as the grand ballroom, exposing the dun-colored blocks. The walls were alabaster, richly stamped and gilded. The ceiling bore the same celestial painting and embossing, edged in a shell pink and cerulean blue crown molding. The bed—immense, bolstered, canopied, and surely ancient—was adorned with a pink silk coverlet shot with golden thread. The matching drapes at three casement windows stood atop two underlayers of sheerest voile and delicate lace. The chimneypiece bore veins of gold through its glistening marble, and Ann knew that a blaze set within its cavern could warm a platoon of soldiers from across the thirty-foot expanse of the room.

"It's this," Rhys said, "which I wanted you to see at your leisure. Ann?"

"It's beautiful." She faced him. "But I could never sleep here. Not alone. Not after what we've shared."

"My thought exactly. Unless, of course . . ."

She crossed her arms. "What?"

"You snore."

She narrowed her eyes. "I have better ways to keep you awake."

He swung her up and around. "What did I do for laughter before I found you?"

For an answer, she kissed him.

"Seriously, darling, you must sleep somewhere—and I really think we must give a show that you do it here."

"Then I had better 'sleep' down the hall and far away from any connecting doors. Mrs. Connelly does not appear to be deaf, dumb, or blind."

"I'll give her to understand she must take on the discreet attitude of my footmen and butler. I will emphasize how important secrecy is to your safety, too."

Ann shrugged a shoulder, unsure a simple warning would suffice to silence the woman and thus cover her whereabouts. "People gossip."

"And for that they can also be sacked. I've known Connelly to act rashly in only one case. There have not been many rumors to take from this house."

"No?" Ann threw him a winsome smile.

"I detect you are asking if other ladies have come here?"

"Or been brought here."

"None," he confirmed, but a shadow of doubt crossed his eyes and had him frowning at the door.

"What bothers you?"

"The one time I have known Mrs. Connelly to engage in rumors was after Adam's second wife came here that night and made such a scene in the court-yard. I reprimanded Connelly for talking with Adam's coachman about it. She was new in my employ then. Only a week or two . . ."

"How did you know she spoke about this?"

"I overheard her tell it. At Mary's wake, no less. I walked in on her after the servants' viewing one afternoon."

"What did she say?"

"I can't remember her words. It was her tone that I objected to. She sniffed at Mary's indelicate choice to run to High Keep and proclaim her feelings to the rooftops." He banished the worrisome thought and kissed Ann's nose. "You will be a good taskmaster for Mrs. Connelly."

"You approve?"

"Of you? Yes. Of you taking over the house now? The sooner the better. Have at her, with my blessings, sweetheart."

"What if I stayed at Blackburn instead?"

He pursed his lips. "You would prefer it there, wouldn't you?"

She let her expression tell him just how much.

"It's as good as done, then. A very wise idea, too, for you to stay with all those people. High Keep is big and old, but no fun for you."

"No cows to milk?"

"No snakes to skin."

She chuckled. "There is room at the farmhouse, I

hope. I do not want to put anyone out of their lodgings."

"Two spare rooms for you to choose from," he assured her. "And now you must sit here." He led her to a huge Tudor chair with plump vermilion cushions. "Promise me you will not move, just close your eyes."

"What are you doing?" she asked as she heard his footsteps waft across the carpet.

His voice came to her from his bedroom. "Observing tradition."

She folded her hands and smacked her lips. "We Americans like to make our own—and quickly, too," she called after him.

"As good as done," he said as he returned. He warned, "No, you can't open your eyes yet." He was making a bit of noise with boxes and clasps. "I have presents for you."

"How many?"

He chuckled. "One, for now. A family heirloom. A wonderful adornment for your body. I plan to spoil you by giving you everything I can."

"What you give me is priceless." She licked her lips in anticipation. "When can I see? You're fiddling a lot there." He didn't answer, intent on his task. "My birthday comes soon, too."

"Really? When?"

"The end of June. The thirtieth."

"I know just the gift for that event."

She ground her teeth. "Tell me what you brought, Your Grace."

He laid a long case in her lap and dragged a chair closer. "You may look now."

A jewelry case of heavy mahogany, long as her forearm, sat before her.

His eyes danced as brightly as if he were Santa Claus on Christmas morn. "It is given to every prospective Kendall duchess at her betrothal. Open it."

Her hands, hesitant at first, calmed, and her nail flicked the tiny brass hook up and away. She lifted the lid to sit starstruck.

Tiny diamonds winked at her from a bed of aged azure satin. An incredible three-foot-long chain of them. The same one the sensual Constance wore.

Ann touched a fingertip to one stone. "How old?"

"The family Bible downstairs in the chapel records that the fourth Duke in his rakehell youth argued with his father and sailed away with a dastardly pirate across to the Dry Tortugas and back to the Cameroons. When his father died, the heir, we think, brought these diamonds home to add to the family cache. He also brought with him Constance, whom he claimed was an English lady, an orphan, and soon to become his duchess. Constance, many thought, was as skilled a pirate as her husband had been. Charles the Second was said to be horrified publicly, but he privately admired the lady's beauty, and subsequent to his proclamation of it, he was forced to admire her abilities with a sword."

"Setting a noble precedent for the rest of us."

"She is not half as impressive as you." Rhys trailed a hand down her arm. "I must see you in those diamonds." He rose and began to kiss her as he undressed her. "But you must wear nothing else."

She became caught in his spell, fantasizing about the spectacle a naked woman swathed in such a rope of diamonds would make. Decadent was surely the way she felt as Rhys swept aside her hair, secured the clasp of the cool chain on the back of her neck, and arranged its drape between her breasts to hang past her navel into her other curls.

"My love," he rasped as he rubbed the hard little gems against the larger one of her desire, "you outshine them," and then he took her down to his carpet. So from that vantage, Ann came to understand completely one duchess's appreciation of angels and roses in the sky.

Chapter 14

". . . My Transatlantic friends . . . have what I call the three f's: figures, francs and faith!"

—Charles Worth

Two mornings later, Rhys kissed Ann good-bye in the kitchen at Blackburn Farm. He promised to return in "three days, maybe two, if I accomplish all my goals. Why not begin work on High Keep's accounts?"

Uneasy as he felt to leave her alone, he consoled himself to think of her huddled over his ledgers, supervising his household as if she were his consort already. God knew, in his heart she was. He needed only church blessing and state license to proclaim it official. To those ends, he had applied for a marriage license—and had asked the Blackburn village vicar to read the banns privately. Rhys knew the request was extraordinary, but the cleric understood Rhys's reason to protect Ann from public censure and any harm. Meanwhile, Rhys had charged Bill Hignell and his wife, Ivy, with the duty of requiring everyone at Blackburn Farm to keep secret the news of a new resident.

Rhys left her reluctantly, but his urgency to see Skip

Brighton ate at him like acid. He needed to go to London and learn why Skip had acted oddly the other night and come to the back entrance of Rhys's town house. What had frightened Skip so? Enough to make him demand that Ann marry him? Enough to weaken him into revealing the most awful crime he had committed against her, buying off Quinnten Langley?

Rhys had told Ann of his intentions to pursue those issues with Skip. He had not mentioned to her his request to Bill Hignell and his two best friends to patrol the roads between Blackburn and High Keep vigilantly to see that no strangers traveled there and to see that Ann remained well and happy.

Rhys boarded the train southeast for London two hours later.

By eight o'clock, Ann was on the road north to High Keep. During the past two days, she and Mrs. Connelly had come to a working relationship in which each smiled, conversed about cleaning preparations for opening new rooms in the mansion, then parted. Ever since Rhys and she had called the housekeeper before them the morning after they'd arrived and Rhys informed her that Ann was soon to be his bride, Mrs. Connelly had trained her waxen face into a smile.

"As future chatelaine here, Miss Brighton wishes to understand the dynamics of running the estate. You will be happy to hear that she will relieve you of the task of keeping the household accounts. This frees you to concentrate on opening the other wing of the castle in anticipation of our wedding."

Mrs. Connelly had stood motionless during Rhys's

monologue, eyes straight ahead, their small glassy depths revealing no emotion whatsoever. "As you wish, Your Grace. When is the happy event to occur?"

"In four weeks. We expect guests for at least the week before the ceremony. Miss Brighton will notify you of the number and their arrival dates as we learn them. In the meantime, we wish no one to know that Miss Brighton has been here, nor that she will be staying at Blackburn Farm." Both Ann and Rhys had caught the woman's telltale flicker of disapproval. "It is an important matter, Mrs. Connelly. A matter of life and death, in fact, so it is not an order of which I will brook any disobedience."

"Yes, Your Grace." She sniffed, insulted that he had implied she might defy him.

Rhys turned away. The woman took it as her dismissal.

Some aspect of her umbrage did not sit right with Ann and she told Rhys so. He reassured her that he expected the woman to come around with a proper attitude quite quickly.

Reveling in Rhys's company—and not wishing to antagonize Mrs. Connelly unduly—Ann had waited until Rhys's departure for London before she asked the woman to produce the household ledger for her perusal. Once ensconced in the duchesses'—soon to be her *own*—sitting room, however, Ann took less than an hour to come to the shocking conclusion that she should have demanded to see the record when she had first thought of assuming the function the afternoon she and Rhys had arrived.

Ann tapped her pen into the inkwell and once more added the figures. No. She had made no mistake in the addition of the monthly bills. Nor had Mrs.

Connelly. Their totals were not only similar but correct.

They were also exorbitant. Each item, no matter what it was—flour, sugar, thread—cost Rhys close to its London price per unit. Ann knew it to be so, because she remembered the amounts she had paid to milkmen, hucksters, fishmongers, and butchers for supplies at Forsythe House. There, she knew her father paid to run a household that served him, Aunt Peg, and four young women, supported by a staff of fourteen. Here at High Keep, only Rhys resided intermittently throughout the year, served by Mrs. Connelly, the aging butler, and one young footman. What mattered was not the number of people who resided in the house but the fact that this was Lancashire, where items should cost less than they would in metropolitan London.

The housekeeper had been skimming a tidy amount of profit from her employer each month for God knew how long. Since she had begun work at High Keep? Certainly, Rhys would have questioned the suddenly greater expense to run the house. So Mrs. Connelly's activities must have evolved over time, given Rhys's growing trust in her services and his attentions going to his farms and the mills. Since, too, the housekeeper would have come to Rhys just after his father's death and before the traumatic one of his friend Adam's wife, Rhys would have been preoccupied with grief.

Ann was filled with rage at the thought that this woman had stolen from him. She longed to call her on the carpet and dismiss her. But she waited for Rhys.

She was not yet the Duchess of Carlton and Dundalk. She had limited powers.

Other than to demand to see the previous years' books.

Rhys arrived in London's Euston Station after ten o'clock at night but went straight to 15 Belgrave Square no matter the late hour. Ann's Aunt Peg swept down the main stairs at his insistence to the butler that he see Skip.

"Thank God, it's you, Your Grace." She met him in her dressing gown, her mouth thin with worry, her eyes brimming with tears.

Rhys took her hands. "Ann is safe, has been with me these past few days. We're to be married in a month."

Peg cried at the good news. Raine, Gus, and Colleen appeared one by one and hurried to greet him and listen to his description of what had happened.

"But before we are married, I must solve this mystery of who and what threatens Ann's safety." Because he could not be certain what the four women knew of events leading to Ann's anger the night she had left, Rhys summarized as best he could Owen MacIntyre's attempted abduction of her at Westminster and Skip's reaction later that evening.

"Skip has been a wild man since that day," Peg confessed once they were all seated in the morning room, the doors closed against the servants. "He has spoken with Scotland Yard. They're trying to find MacIntyre. That is where they are tonight. Someone broke into the Guardian Shipping offices tonight after closing and stole numerous papers. Skip, Bryce, and Adam are incensed at the crime. The three of them went to the Yard to complain that the police seem incapable of finding MacIntyre."

Colleen glanced at Rhys. "Bryce has been a big help to Mr. Brighton these past few days."

Raine wrung her hands, the only sign of fear Rhys had ever seen in her. "Uncle Skip is not well."

"Skip is more ill than he has told us, Raine. He's hiding it to form this company and make a significant amount of money quickly."

"As if he needs more," she complained, swallowing her own tendency to cry.

"We must convince him his wealth consists of other kinds of valuables." Rhys squeezed her hand. He looked at Colleen. "I'm glad Bryce has been of assistance." But the specter of Adam rose to torment Rhys. Adam as he had been in Westminster Abbey. Angry. Drunk. The way he had seen Adam only twice before in his life when . . .

Peg's mouth quivered. "Did you know"—she tried to stop a sob—"that MacIntyre has been blackmailing Skip?"

"Yes." Rhys put an arm around the lady's shoulders and let her weep until she recovered herself.

"Continually. It's awful." Peg waved a hand and fumbled for a handkerchief from her pocket.

Rhys produced his own for her. "Forgive me. I must go to the Yard, too."

"But they promised to return here and tell us everything," Peg pleaded. "Stay and tell us more about Ann."

"No one will hurt her again, that I promise you. I have friends keeping guard over her, too. So don't worry. She is utterly secure." He bussed Peg on her forehead.

He left them and told his driver to take him around to the Yard. But as he alighted from his cab, Bryce was emerging from the main door.

"Rhys." Bryce's face was haggard. "This must be fate for you to arrive just as the worst is over." He clamped a hand on Rhys's shoulder. "Let's find ourselves a pint, shall we?"

"No pubs, Bryce. I must know what's happened."

"They've got MacIntyre." He nodded toward the stoic building. "Brought him in an hour ago. We saw him, and he confessed to blackmailing Skip and stealing some records from the Guardian office tonight."

"Where is Skip? And Adam?" The last question eroded any joy Rhys felt in MacIntyre's capture, though Rhys could not find a logical reason why that was.

"Adam took Skip home. The man is very sick. He must go south now that this mystery is over, assuming, of course, you can assure him you have Ann tucked away."

"Snug as a bug."

"Good. That will encourage Skip to leave England. Adam and I said we would take over for him. Run the board of directors. Just until he recovers."

Rhys gave Bryce a halfhearted smile. "Is that legal?"

"Adam prepared a document to make it so. Skip will sign it, I assure you, especially now that we know Ann is well and with you." Bryce settled back into the squabs and crossed his arms. "What bothers you, old man?"

"So many things," Rhys said after long consideration. "Too many questions remain unanswered."

"Such as?"

"Have you got a few hours?"

"All night. Your house or mine?"

"Mine, if you don't mind. I'd like to make certain my housekeeper isn't frightened to death by me arriving in the middle of the night after I've been gone a few days."

So it was they roused the lady and sat in Rhys's little drawing room sipping anisette before a small but serviceable fire. There, Rhys recounted the horrors Ann had lived through these past few months since she'd arrived in Dublin. "The arrest of Owen MacIntyre puts a man behind bars who blackmailed Skip and who attempted to abduct Ann."

"And who stole papers from the office tonight," Bryce added.

"But who hired the little man who trailed Ann in Dublin?"

"Owen, probably."

"Where did he get the money to pay him? Such surveillance must cost a hefty amount, and Owen was never rich. What about the flower lady who stood watch over Belgrave Square? Who hired her—or him, I should say? And why? Why?"

"Ann certainly has had her share of problems out of this old rivalry between Owen and Skip. She's even endured the blasting by the newspapers."

Rhys licked his lips. "Yes." He had forgotten that. Thought he had ended that problem. Thought it unconnected, but what if it had been an attempt by Owen to ruin her? Had Owen paid the reporter of the *Gazetteer?* Hell, those stories had been an attack on him as well. And Skip.

Fresh fear made his gut clench. "I've got to talk with Skip now regardless of the hour."

"I don't know, Rhys. Skip looks like the very devil. I tell you, he must leave immediately for some sun, or the man will be dead in a fortnight. Adam thinks so, too. You can't imagine what these past few days have done to Skip. He's gone gray."

Rhys stood. "It's past midnight, but if I don't see him now . . ." He let the implication hang between them that Skip might fall too sick to converse with Rhys. But Rhys let Bryce think that, rather than describe the growing horror Rhys felt that all their troubles were not over. Owen MacIntyre's incarceration did not end the mysteries. It solved only two of them.

"I'll come with you."

Adam was bidding the women good night in the foyer as Rhys and Bryce arrived. Bryce greeted Adam with a nonchalance that Rhys tried hard to emulate and wondered if he succeeded. Rhys could not erase the memory of Adam acting so badly toward Ann, yet he asked Adam how Skip was now.

"Resting," Adam told him, as if he were a doctor. "He's had two brandies, and I think that should put him to sleep. He needs it very badly, Rhys."

Rhys turned to Peg. "Do you mind if I see him? I know it is irregular. But these are extraordinary circumstances."

When Bryce offered to accompany him, Rhys refused.

Peg rang for a footman to direct him to Skip's suite.

Rhys closed the door gently and walked through Skip's sitting room into his bedroom. Skip sat up in the bed, his expression going from exhaustion to satisfaction as he saw Rhys approach. Bryce's description of Skip had been mild, to say the least. Skip had aged a decade or more in three short days.

"I marvel that you are still talking to me," Skip rasped, and coughed.

"So do I," Rhys offered, and dragged a chair close to Skip's bedside. In a quiet voice, he told the man what he would need to know about the safety of his daughter—and then her future. "She's going to marry me."

Skip offered silent words of thanks. "When?"

Rhys told him the details. "If we can send you south for a few weeks to the French Mediterranean, you might recover enough to be able to attend the wedding."

Skip shot him a wary look. "Ann won't have me. I don't blame her."

"Bribing Quinnten Langley was despicable."

Skip bent double with a spasm of coughs. "Langley was a milquetoast. Wanted her for her money. When I offered him more, he jumped at it. I was torn in that moment between paying him or strangling him. That left her available for you, though, didn't it?"

"You couldn't predict that she and I would like each other or even meet."

"I could and did predict you'd be the kind of man she would value—so noble, if you'll pardon the pun here, Your Grace—that she couldn't help but fall for you."

"I attended the Dublin horse trials as a last-minute decision."

"You're right. I didn't know you'd be there. But I did know you'd come to London for the organizational meetings of the company."

"You invited me into the company so that I would meet her?"

"As much that as to pay you back for whatever hardships I had caused you when I made you pay me for that cotton back in 'sixty-four. I know what a financial mess you'd been through after the fire trying to get your mills going up to capacity and helping those people at Blackburn Farm." He took a long sip of his drink. "I profited despite those catastrophes. I wanted to help you." A smile drifted across his face. "If I could also show you my most precious possession and hope that both she and you could find happiness together, well, then, I could die happy."

"Skip, you are not going to die. You're too tough—"

"I am not, Rhys. This business with Owen has taken the starch out of me. I see the truth of how bad I look reflected in your eyes, so don't give me bullshit, Kendall."

"Then don't give me any, either. Did you see MacIntyre tonight?"

"Yes."

"What did he say?"

"Admitted to blackmail, attempted abduction, and theft."

"Just like that?"

"Had him by the short ones, so he had to admit it."

Rhys shook his head. "I understand the blackmail and Ann's abduction because MacIntyre wanted money. But why steal papers from the office? What were they?"

Skip smiled. "Designs for the ships. They'll be the fastest, sleekest steamers to cross the Atlantic."

"Years of running a blockade lend a certain expertise in how to fly with the wind," Rhys conceded. But the theft was so different a crime from the other two. Had MacIntyre hoped to sell the plans? To whom? "Did MacIntyre volunteer any other information?"

Skip frowned. "For example?"

"Did he hire a man to follow Ann in Dublin?" When Skip shook his head, Rhys asked, "Or hire a man to pretend to be a flower lady and watch Forsythe

House? No. Very well. What about giving information to the *Gazetteer* reporter?"

"I thought you were going to take care of that matter. Didn't you? The stories stopped."

"Yes. But . . . yes, they did," Rhys said, unable to explain the desperation he felt at not knowing all the answers to this riddle. He needed time to figure this out.

"Frankly," Skip was reflecting, "I never thought to see him again. He ruined me, or tried to. I always thought he set that fire, knowing I needed to collect the money on that shipment. His actions destroyed your friendship and mine. Only MacIntyre knew why. I treated him well, paid him well, too. Clever bastard. Even O'Leary couldn't protect us from him. The odds were too great."

Rhys shoved a hand through his hair. "Don't you think the odds were against you because Owen was not alone?"

"I've asked myself that. But who would do this? Hurt Ann and me—and you, for that matter?"

"To destroy the shipping company? Perhaps there are more than we bargained for, Skip."

"There are no competitors. Not yet. To build cruise ships is too costly. No one has the funds. I have researched it, and I tell you, Rhys, there are none in America or Britain who wish to try. Only three men in Bremen who consider opening a New York to Southampton run."

"Germany? The Rothschilds could be backing such a company, Skip."

"No. I asked Lionel the night of the masquerade ball. He is not."

"What about his cousins who run the German branch of the bank?"

"Alastair Houghton found that out for me. He had his people in the British Embassy in Berlin inquire on that possibility."

"Inquire?" Rhys asked with an arched brow.

"Spy, then." Skip chuckled and ended up coughing worse. "No. The German Rothschilds are not the investment bankers for the Bremen group."

Rhys watched Skip wrack himself in his malady. "I'll leave you to sleep. Do it, too. Tomorrow, go to the south of France, will you, and return mid-July."

"You have great faith I'll live."

"To see your daughter married? You'd walk on water to do it, Brighton. Good night."

Rhys prayed to God it was a good night for Skip. For himself, he doubted he could rest until he found more missing pieces to his puzzle. If he concentrated on motive, he thought he might discover them.

Six days later, Rhys arrived in Liverpool. The previous day, he had shipped two heavily wrapped bolts of cream merveilleux satin and five French cards of handmade Valenciennes lace. These purchases went via a circuitous route to a friend in York, who would then send them on to Rhys at High Keep. With them were three new steamer trunks Rhys had bought to contain Ann's clothes, lovingly packed by a tearful Aunt Peg.

His own luggage bulged with wedding attire for himself and three of the family jewel cases, including the emerald and diamond tiara with matching necklace and earbobs which every Duchess of Carlton and Dundalk had worn to her nuptials since fifteen sixty-two. He crossed over the cobbles and walked toward King Street to the livery stable he had used last week when he had brought Ann to Blackburn.

"Ah, Yer Grace, yer back agin, ye are." The bald owner of the Three Coaches grinned.

"I trust no one knows that but you and me, Harry."

The toothless man leaned across a saddle he soaped. "Why, I haven't seen ye in so long, Yer Grace. It's my hair, ye know, hangs in my eyes." He winked with an open mouth. "Come home early for the Solstice at High Keep, I'd wager."

"Right you are, Harry." The fewer people who knew that Ann lodged at Blackburn Farm, the better, and he had asked Harry not to divulge his visit last week. His visits with Bryce and an old friend in the Foreign Office had been unenlightening and therefore unsettling. His friend in the Foreign Office had offered the best advice, which was to trust no one completely. "I'm in a hurry, too. That's why I'd like your fastest horse, Harry."

Before the next hour was up, Rhys rounded the ridge where he had stood with Ann and told her about his resentment of her father and the building of Blackburn Farm. He had caught an early-morning train from Euston Station, and as he pulled up on the reins of the gelding and viewed the U-shaped farmhouse below, the sun had sunk to the horizon level of the oaks, filtering the orange and red rays of day through their lacy leaves. Two men climbed down from a plow in the west field. Three women noted Rhys's figure and stood up one at a time from their weeding in the vegetable garden to peer at him and wave. Rhys waved back. A gentle breeze ruffled his hair and lifted his coat, wrapping him in the warmth of a homecoming made all the more enchanting by the sound of a woman's laughter floating up to him.

From the stable block, a horse emerged with a slender rider whose body moved forward and head came down as she urged him from a trot to a canter and a full gallop through the paddock gates and out along the lane toward High Keep. She wore pants. Rhys chuckled. He'd know her anywhere in the trousers, her long hair flowing out behind her like a pennant burnished in the sun.

He spurred his mount toward the other side of the ridge and a shortcut to the lane Ann took. His gelding was no race horse, but he gave a good performance despite the distance they'd traveled from Liverpool. So that when Ann charged around a bend through a copse of oaks, Rhys was calmly sitting, waiting for her as if he'd been there all day.

As she cleared the overhanging branches, the sun was in her face. When she noticed him, she squinted, startled, and veered her horse to the right, the only way she could find sure footing on the lane at such a clip. But as her animal slowed his pace and she flung a hand up to shield her gaze, she grinned at Rhys, spoke his name in silent wonder, and kicked her mount forward to meet him.

The beam of welcome on her face could have lit the halls of Kendall Great House for a year. He drew his horse alongside and grabbed her around the waist, lifting her to him for a scalding kiss that had their horses dancing.

"Where have you been so long?" she chastised him as her lips sought his more than an answer.

"Getting a license and clearing the way to marry you." He hooked his hand over one of her trim thighs. "Come here."

She kicked free of her stirrups and swung a leg over his lap so that she wound herself around him with a purr of joy. Her hands dived into his hair, and her breasts pressed against her rough linen shirt to remind him of what a treasure she was to hold. "I missed you."

"Let me see how much." His hands gripped her knees, and, anticipating what he wanted, she circled her legs around his hips. Sitting on his thighs, she dropped her derriere to his saddle and inched toward him away from the pommel. The move brought her feminine core against his instantly hard erection.

She sucked in her breath, the sound erotic music to his straining and starved body. "Enough?" she whispered on a husky voice.

"Not nearly." He captured a handful of her curls and indulged in the slippery feel of wild silk through his fingers.

One of her hands slid to his chest and began to flip open the buttons of his coat, vest, and shirt. Cool air rushed over his skin, but her lips followed the column of his throat downward with kisses of sweet joy. "Close enough?"

He broke into a sweat. "I'm going to go away often, just so I can come home to this."

"You can't leave. Not without me, not ever again."

Fear and the need to keep her close had him tipping up her face and claiming her mouth with his own. He took her with command and sought her surrender with a hunger that rekindled the rapture they had shared.

Her hands kneaded the muscles of his chest, and he chafed with the urge to strip her of her shirt and pants so that he could feel the tensile strength and beauty of her. "You get yourself in trouble, darling, doing this."

"I'll be good, then." She pushed the fabric aside and slid her palms beneath his shirt. "And do this."

She caressed him in sworls as her mouth kept his busy—and her woman's cleft fit so neatly around the bulge of his shaft that he sent a hand between them. He had meant to stop her, but the plushness his fingers skimmed lured him, and he couldn't stop himself.

His fingers grew greedy. Her work pants were of tough cotton twill, which someone here at the farm must have loaned her. She wore no suspenders or belt, and the garment had no fly buttons. Just a drawstring, which he pulled free so that the material sagged down her hips to open to his quest. He groaned when his fingers met no more fabric, no drawers, not man's or woman's, but only luscious skin. He could not believe this good fortune he held in his arms, a lover and friend—and soon to be his wife. She sighed at his perusal, giving herself up to him without hesitation. Time spun out, stood still as he caressed her. How utterly sinuous she was, the arc of her hip, the curve of her belly, and the plump lips of her woman's core, so sweetly flowing for him. "God, sweetheart, how long have you been like this?"

For all her sauciness, she pressed her face to his shoulder in embarrassment as she admitted, "Since you left." She flung her head back, her hair a cascade of dark red waters, her eyes keen with her ardor. "You don't think I'm bold, do you?"

He stroked one of her creamy folds with a gentle fingertip, and she gasped, only to receive one of his fingers and arch into his hand. "That's what marriage is for, to make two people bold together." He continued to circle her succulent flesh as he held her closer to him and whispered what other delicacies he'd show her soon.

The breeze carried echoes of other voices toward

them. "They're looking for us," he said with regret, and eased his hand away.

She whimpered with his denial and placed a tender kiss to his throat. "We have worried about you." She straightened, her lips full from hard kisses, her eyes gold with gaiety and a glaze of passion interrupted. "They'll want to know where you were. What kept you?" she asked for herself.

"A bridegroom needs time to prepare for his wedding."

"Hmmm. So does a bride."

He touched the tip of her nose. "I have provided for you, too." He patted the pouch of his saddle.

"Interesting. Is that *all* of my trousseau in there?"

He chortled and kissed her forehead. Throughout all the trials and tribulations that had befallen her, she had not lost her sense of humor. "Lucky me, if this is all you'll wear."

More voices from the valley drifted upward. "Supper," she informed him. "We must go." She poked a fingernail into his chest. "But afterward, I want a full accounting of what you've done."

"And I want to give you what I've brought."

Her smile spiked his need to dispense with food and nibble on her lips. So he did, then tore away lest he feast on her. "I have a feeling this will be the longest meal I've ever eaten."

"Or the shortest," she teased as she righted her clothes and mounted her horse. "I made the stew and the bread. Ivy was responsible for the pudding, though. You might want to stick with that."

Rhys enjoyed the entire meal. The fare was a spicy vegetable stew with a bit of mutton, and even the most regular critics among the Blackburn group hailed Ann as a cook of rare talent, especially with tough meat. The conviviality was a tonic to Rhys, as it had always been a reprieve from the city and the cynics there who prevailed too often for Rhys's taste. But what he learned in the hour after supper as they sat before their hearth with full bellies, gleeful hearts, and a few cigars and pipes made him glance at Ann with a sounder conviction that this woman would make a significant contribution in her role as Duchess, not because she would be regal but because she would be respected.

She could cook. She could milk. She could and did hoe and weed, without invitation or urging.

"She volunteered to help me balance my monthly bills for me, Yer Grace," Bill Hignell told Rhys with a twinkle in his eyes. "Quick as a wink, she found four pound six hiding in that reckoning of mine. I wonder, Yer Grace, if she might be available to do it again, as I have no head for it like she does."

"That's up to her, Bill," Rhys told him, but sent Ann the question in his look.

"I'd be delighted to help you again, Mr. Hignell."

Rhys wondered how she'd gotten on with Mrs. Connelly, and so he rose, eager to be alone with her. He doused his pipe, tapped its contents into the spittoon near the fire, and extended a hand to Ann. "Would you like to walk with me?"

Wordlessly, she nodded and slipped her hand in his as they went through the back door. The moon hung low on the eastern horizon yet, and stars shone like little pinpricks in the stunning cobalt canvas.

"Are you warm enough?" he asked when she crossed her arms against the night air.

"I'll accept your coat," she told him with a smile. When they had gone past the barn and neared the copse, she inhaled with closed eyes and began to talk. "In late June in Virginia, the temperature can be like this, hot in the day, the earth not warm enough yet to hold its heat. The scent of honeysuckle is so sweet, the air gets so thick you wonder if you can breathe it in."

Her reverie cut him to the bone. He paused along the path, trying to contain his fear. What had happened while he was gone? "Have you thought more about my proposal?"

"Oh, yes," she told him, and he cursed the wavering trees which obscured her expression.

"Is there," *God help me,* "something else you want to tell me?"

"Yes, there is. A lot." She turned her profile to him, and though the moonglow limned her features in silver, he could predict nothing about what she thought. "Can we ride? Do you mind saddling up the horses again?"

"No, of course not, if that's what you'd like."

"I would."

He let her lead. He thought it best they have some distance in case she meant to tell him she had reconsidered her acceptance of his proposal and she meant to leave him. He told himself that he could understand, if that was her decision. But he knew he wouldn't understand at all. Her greeting this afternoon had been too full of love and laughter for her to tell him now she could not marry him. As for himself, he had come too far. He loved her too much, too dearly to see her walk away from him easily. He'd put up one hell of a fight. He had to make her care for him more than her own country . . . because it seemed the landscape of Virginia was what he fought tonight in this battle for her affection.

To his surprise, she led him along the lane toward High Keep. She was more quiet and pensive than he had ever seen her. Finally, they stood in sight of his sprawling home, and he waited for her to speak. When she did, her voice was soft, muted by a brimming emotion he could not name. "Bill and his two friends whom you set upon me would not let me ride far alone," she was telling him as the wind rustled the oaks and pines to make his heart colder than he'd known it could be.

"I only meant to protect you. I would never restrict you."

"I didn't think you would." She cast a glance at him, and he felt her scrutiny. "Are you angry with me about something?"

"No." He was not lying, he told himself.

She tilted her head, the rippling shadows of the trees providing enough cover for his prevarication. "Oh, good. I thought from your attitude that you might know, then. That Bill or one of the others had told you."

"Told me what?" he asked too sharply.

"They did, didn't they?" She pushed her dangling curls back from her cheeks. "That I came out to race so often that they couldn't get their work done for following me." She let that sink in a minute, and when she got no more than his sheer surprise, she mistook it for silent reprimand. "Well, I needed to ride. I couldn't be cooped up any longer, so I took the one horse in the High Keep stable, but he was so old and lame that I had to get another. I had to ride fast. I know how you value the Blackburn farmers, and I didn't want to be a burden, but I had to see where I'd live, your estate, all of it. So if you're angry—"

He hauled her against him so quickly, he felt the air whoosh from her lungs. "Don't do it again." He kissed her, a crushing claim to her lips that had her clutching at his shirt and their poor horses jostling each other once more.

He set her back on her saddle and peered down at her. "That's not all you wanted to tell me, though."

"No, you're right. I . . ." She looked younger than ever before, wistful. "I wanted to say more than that."

"The night is yours, and so am I."

"I know," she whispered, awed. "I've been trying to believe that, and since you left, it's been very difficult. We've known each other such a short time. Being able to live down here at Blackburn has helped me, though. I am so used to farm life, the routine and the functions seem the same no matter where you live. But then, too, the little differences add to the sense of fantasy of Sleeping Beauty and her Prince." She laughed a little at the appropriateness of the costumes they had worn to the Rothschild ball. "The image is not far off the mark. But if I stay here, no fantasy would make our marriage work. I wanted to make certain when I married you, I did it with a rein on reality. I wanted to ride over Kendall land because I wanted to understand what you are, what you do, what you mean to so very many people. I had to know you better, see where you had grown up and what you love and why."

He traced her jaw with his fingers and sent them spiking up into her heavy hair. "You are who I love."

"I am," she declared reverently, her lithe body quivering in the breeze, the look in her eyes warming him to his toes, "and I can barely believe my good fortune. But in this last week since you've been gone, I begin to."

He could not bear to breathe, her sentiment filling his heart to bursting.

"Oh, Rhys." She turned her lovely face up to him, her golden eyes twinkling with stars, her hair sheened by the moon, her lips parted. If he had never seen her before this moment, he would have loved her instantly. But as it was, he now adored her as she circled her arms around him. "I want to help you preserve your family's past and build its future. I want to help you help others make a living for today and all their tomorrows. I see that this is not Virginia. But home is not a location on a map." She indicated the valley spread before her with an inclination of her head. "It is a place people create with love. I can be very happy here. With you."

Once more, he scooped her from her saddle and claimed her with lips and arms and hope. His fear, too new that she might reject him, and the other fear, too great that someone might harm her and take her from him, combined to create a tidal wave of emotion in him. He growled as he kissed her and caressed her. She met him, moan for delight, until he realized he had undressed her to her waist, and those firm breasts he loved to taste were now in his palms, and she looked like a sylvan nymph, disheveled, straddling him, and as needy as he.

Heedful of her modesty and comfort, he tried but could not halt his fingers from stroking her breasts to turgid points. "We should stop. You'll catch your death of cold and—"

"I found a place where we could do this—and both of us would be lots warmer." She undulated in sensuous invitation. "Tell me, Your Grace, would you like to come?"

It was probably not the first time he had chuckled *and* groaned as he kissed her. But his brain had gone blank, and his body took control as he asked, "Where?"

Chapter 15

"A girl shouldn't run after money, but plenty is a great comfort in this world, when it can be had without blushing for."

—ANTHONY TROLLOPE

HE MARVELED AT HER UNCANNY ABILITY TO PLEASE HIM. His favorite place to think on a summer's afternoon, a resort from his worries of his people on this farm, this was his nook in the rafter of the old dovecote. No one had used it for decades except as a storage shed.

Tonight, his hidey-hole was going to add a new function to his trove. Courtesy of the breathless woman who led him up the ladder into fresh hay, coverlet, and blanket.

"When did you think of this?" he asked, not caring, eager only to watch Ann in the moonlight which streamed in the little window of the loft.

"Yesterday," she crooned, and discarded his coat and began to work on the buttons of her linen shirt once more. She stood back, and, quicker than his mind could grasp, she pulled off her shirt, took the chemise over her head, and stepped out of her work pants. She stood there, lithe and lean, a fluid arc of femininity.

"Darling, you are quite . . . incomparable."

"I'll do?" she asked in a tight little voice.

"Do?" He heard himself, and thought he was sounding rather senile in his older age. "My love, come here and *do* anything you like."

A ripple of pleasure seemed to rise from her knees. "Anything?" she asked, tremulous and seeking his acceptance of her as a woman, an assertive woman.

"In our intimacy and in all other matters." He crooked a finger at her. "I'll let you see and feel the proof." His eyes heaped praise on her nude splendor.

"Will you want me if I'm brazen?"

"I'll encourage you until you are intrepid."

"I could become a nagging wife," she warned, strolling toward him and putting her arms around his waist.

"Not you." He drugged himself and her with little kisses while one hand caressed her breast and shaped her nipple to a diamond.

"Oh, but I don't think I'll ever have enough of you like this." She arched up against him, offering him more of her.

"Then don't." He took her tight little gem in his mouth. Gossamer could not compare. He had to have the other and slid his tongue over to lave her. Her knees went lax.

He sank to his own. His hands braced her hips. He whorled his tongue inside her navel and then drifted down her belly to her humid curls. With one hand, he parted her heavy lips and found the sweetness of her. He bent and sipped at the musky evidence that she cared for him.

She groaned so loudly her ardor pierced his passion. She was sagging, and he caught her, laid her down in the fragrant hay and the soft counterpane she had acquired from the house. He ran his hands up her thighs and spread her legs apart.

He drew her hard nubbin into his mouth, feasting steadily until she lolled her head and clutched handfuls of his clothes. "I want to feel you."

He let her work at his shirt. His suspenders and flies fell at her urging. He stood and discarded every stitch he wore. But when he sank to her, she paused and rolled away, laughing. "My turn," she insisted, pushing him to his back.

Her eyes traveling over him like a golden flame that licked and sparked. "You're very impressive." Her hand sought him out, and his mind went dark while she learned his length and moaned at what she felt. "You are soft and hard. How can that be?" she asked in wonder.

"The same as you," he proclaimed, grinding his teeth at her languorous touch.

"And how do you taste?" she whispered, and bent to find the answer.

As her lips surrounded him, he had no words to give her. Only his fingers clutching her hair and urging her on. Only his hips rising to her tentative rhythm.

When he knew he'd soon roar and wake every person in the farmhouse, he set her away and levered himself over her. In a fluid move, he tucked her beneath him, settled between her thighs, and joined her to him.

"I wanted you so," she declared, eyes clamped closed, nails digging into his back.

"If—my wife—cannot make requests of me," he asserted with vital reassurances of his body, "how can I go to her?"

She gave a cry of joy as the first tremor of her

climax shook her. "I'm not too rash to be your wife? Wearing trousers and no corsets? Riding astride—"

"As long as you wear nothing when you ride astride me, my love." He kissed her lips and slid deeply into her as their mutual laughter shook them. "I'll be a happy man," he whispered to her ear when their passion had died enough for him to talk.

He drew the edges of the counterpane over them, while the moon glided across the heavens and she curled against him.

He combed her curls from from her cheeks. "I brought presents for you up from London."

"How many this time?" She licked her lips, feigning greediness.

"These might suffice for a birthday present—and a wedding gift."

"Now is the perfect time to give them to me."

"You must promise not to move and especially not to dress while I'm gone."

"An easy vow to make. Go."

He was up, dressed, gone, and back before she had much more cause to miss him than suffer a few shivers of remembered delight. When he reappeared, he came laden with a wine jug, two mugs, and two jewelry cases, larger than the one that held Constance's rope of diamonds.

He sat cross-legged before her. "Open them."

To do so, she could no longer hold up the blanket for modesty's sake. She let it fall.

"Truly," he whispered when she wore the wealth of the brides of Carlton and Dundalk, "you were meant to be a duchess," and then he took her into his care and proved it with his love.

Later, they sat on the hay in the shaft of moonlight.

With his arms about her, his voice toneless, Rhys related the results of his rounds in London. First thing, Rhys had gone to Forsythe House.

"Your Aunt Peg was beside herself with worry over you. So were the girls. They were thrilled to see me even though I arrived at a late hour."

"Where was my father?"

"With Bryce and Adam at Scotland Yard. Owen MacIntyre had been arrested." Rhys summarized Owen's capture and confession of blackmail and attempted abduction. "MacIntyre will stand trial here in England even though he is an American citizen. And that brings something else to mind which we must discuss."

Rhys had gone to see his lawyer in Savile Row three days ago. "I made all the legal arrangements for our marriage. I applied for the license and learned that under British law, once you wed me, darling, you become a British subject. I don't like it, and, predicting you wouldn't, either, I asked my solicitor to appeal the matter. We won't know what the courts say about it until months from now when the case is heard. I am sorry, Ann. I wish I'd known this before. If you wish to wait to see what they say, I won't argue. We'll wait for this wedding, even though we have rushed its benefits a bit. Provided we can wait—and nothing has come of our hours together. Because if you do carry our child—"

"Yes." She agreed with his implication that he wished to make their children legitimate. But this news was a shock. She never thought of herself as anything other than American. "Do I lose my citizenship according to American law?"

"I am not certain. I asked my solicitor to investigate that, too."

"I feel like an American. I always will. We Americans hold different views from you about government and society. But my nationality doesn't change how I love you," she assured him, "and whatever happens with the legalities of my citizenship in America, it won't induce me to change our wedding date."

"I am relieved as hell," he confessed, and kissed her. "Especially since I also saw the Queen, and she expects us to marry soon."

"Does she approve of one of her premier noblemen marrying an American?" Ann had heard the woman did not care for the American invasion, which was what so many pundits called the advent of American heiresses to English soil and English aristocracy.

"She gave me her blessing to marry, though I will be honest and tell you that she frowns on 'these American alliances,' as she calls them."

"What does she object to about us?"

"She thinks too many girls come over with too many dollars and no sense, looking for a man and a castle. I assured her that you had wanted neither. I also told her I had rejected your money and that you and I would marry with me paying for the wedding and all after it, too."

"Did that change her opinion?"

"She will invite you to one of her 'afternoons' after our wedding trip and season of retirement."

"Retirement?"

"All newly wedded couples retire to the country for at least three months before opening their homes in London. It is considered a weathering, if you will."

Ann chuckled. "Time for the novelty to wear off."

"To make them more presentable in public, I suppose."

When he went quite still, she asked, "What's wrong?"

"After those three months, it is normal practice for the couple to accept separate invitations for social events. I cannot see myself ecstatic to have you go to dinner parties and the theater without me. The men will flirt with you and want to take you away from me." His brown eyes grew fierce with dark possession. "I fear I'm going to be as unconventional a husband as I was a bachelor."

She wound her arms around him. "I don't care to be conventional, either. We don't have to live like the rest, do we? I wanted, *hoped,* we could live in the country. Anywhere, High Keep or Kent or anywhere else you name. I don't want to be with any of them if they're going to try to tear us apart."

"Darling Ann, I intend to be such a loving husband that no one will ever take you from me."

The idea chilled her and motivated her to marry him soon. "But people will soon learn I'm here. We can't keep the marriage a secret, and I don't want to. Not now that MacIntyre is in jail."

"Your father and aunt have come up with a story to cover your disappearance from London. They say that Skip hired a chaperone for you so that you might visit an American school friend who begins her grand tour in Paris this month."

"Darcy Warfield." Ann recalled the petite blond heiress to the Washington dry goods fortune. When her parents had learned Ann and her contingent were to go to Europe, they announced plans to take Darcy, too. "So he has preserved my reputation."

"And your safety. Your father has given it out that you have gone to Paris to think over my proposal."

She ran her fingers over his lips. "How convenient that we already know the answer to that."

"The tale will also progress when your Aunt Peg and you come to Lancashire to take up residence in the guest wing at High Keep."

"Soon?"

"Does day after tomorrow suit you?"

"How is this to be done? Must I go south?"

"Your aunt and you will board a train, and no one will be the wiser. You will be heavily veiled, as I understand it."

"Ah." Ann saw the ruse. "One of the others—"

"Colleen volunteered readily. She will dress in your clothes, go to the station with your aunt, and . . . return to Forsythe House."

"But if she returns without Aunt Peg, who will chaperone them?"

"Your aunt hired a duenna days ago. She told your father some time ago that she cannot keep up with all of you adequately."

"Events have taken a toll on her." Ann regretted the turmoil she'd caused Aunt Peg. "Do Colleen, Gus, and Raine know that my father bribed Quinn not to elope with me?"

Rhys squeezed her hand in compassion. "Yes. He confided in them the night you and I left. He really is a changed man."

"Not that night at your house, he wasn't. But I realize that he was so afraid that he reverted to his old self." She fought tears. "He had tried for so many months to be a true father to me, and he had succeeded in so many ways. I wanted to forgive him for those things I criticized him for these past ten years. I had, but had not yet told him. I now know that where love is concerned"—she admired the man before her—"resentment is a foolish waste of time."

Rhys kissed her hand. "Your father is terribly ill."

Rhys's grimness made her breath catch. "Worse than he was?"

"He is weak, thin, worn out from the fear inspired by MacIntyre. But now that the man is behind bars, Skip will go to the Mediterranean to recoup some of his strength. He leaves in a few days."

Ann dared not ask if her father's health could be remedied by mere sunlight. "Perhaps Aunt Peg should go with him."

"Skip demands some time to himself, no matter his physical state. That decided, Skip and your aunt have agreed she must come north for you. Besides, there is another reason Peg will remain in England. It seems your Aunt Peg has herself a beau. Shocked? So am I. So are Skip and Raine, but it seems your aunt has known the gentleman for decades and—"

"Good heavens, who is it?"

"She's going to marry Gordon Worminster. Seems she knew him years ago when she first came to Europe, and his mother would not approve of him marrying an untitled American, rich though she was. As a result, your aunt married a man she says she respected but never adored. She is very happy that our relationship will overcome the obstacles she encountered of country, class, and money."

"Uncle Timothy." Ann recalled Aunt Peg's husband, a gentleman twenty years Peg's senior, gouty and grumpy in his later years. "I like Gordon much better for her."

"My other news is not as wonderful. Colleen has been behaving rather scandalously lately. She had an argument with Bryce, and on two occasions she has been seen alone with Jason Rutledge in his carriage."

"Colleen loves her fun. She was very strictly supervised as a child. Her mother has some definite ideas about how a lady must act, and Colleen never took to restrictions well."

"Perhaps that's made Colleen too headstrong."

"Have the newspapers gotten wind of it?"

"I'm afraid so. As with us, they allude to her vaguely, but people know who it is. Bryce is very angry that they would hurt her—and that she'd act this way with Rutledge."

"You spoke with Bryce about this?"

"It came up, but he is uncomfortable about what to say to me, I suppose, because you and Colleen are so close. Colleen means much to him, but he is frightened by what he calls her intensity."

"I see. What a shame."

"Try not to worry too much about Colleen."

"She can be foolhardy." Ann voiced her concern about his own reckless friend. "You saw Adam, I gathered, but did you have a chance to talk to him?"

"If you mean about his actions toward you in the Abbey, no, I did not. I tried to speak with him privately, but neither he nor I could agree on a time. He was a great help to your father the night MacIntyre was arrested. He also helped to take over the interim operations of the company since your father is so sick."

Ann examined Rhys's befuddled face. "Confused by his actions, aren't you?"

"One minute, he's rational, the next, not."

"Does he know I am here at Blackburn?"

"I didn't tell him. The others didn't, either. We

have agreed no one is to be let in on the secret. To preserve your reputation, we'll all declare you came to High Keep with your Aunt Peg." The concern in his eyes told her he still feared for her safety.

"Adam wouldn't come here and act as he did in the Abbey."

"Of course not," Rhys said, but doubt was in his voice.

"What bothers you?"

"I'd like him to come to our wedding, but I must talk with him before I invite him. I must be certain he will not drink and act abominably." He smiled wanly, but she knew there were more things that disturbed him. "What have you done while I've been gone?"

She summarized her days of helping on the farm but then told him what she had found in High Keep's ledgers. "Mrs. Connelly has been siphoning off money from the accounts almost since she came into your employ. The prices for everything inched up, a few cents here and there every month, discreetly so that you'd never question."

Rhys was shocked, then angry. "Did you confront her with it?"

"No. I am not yet your duchess, Rhys. I couldn't."

"We shall turn her out tomorrow."

"Where will she go?"

"With my money from four years of skimming in her pocket? I don't know. I can't care."

Ann didn't, either. When she saw how dispassionately the woman reacted the next morning to Rhys's dismissal, Ann quelled her own anger, then said a silent good riddance. The question that remained unanswered was why the housekeeper had taken the money. Financial gain was the primary reason, but Mrs. Connelly's attitude—her dislike of Rhys—was an extraordinary one. How many people did Ann know who disliked Rhys?

The day after, Ann and Rhys met the London train and escorted an effervescent Aunt Peg up to High Keep. Ann had employed Ivy Hignell and two of her friends to come up to the castle and take over the housekeeping until Ann could begin to interview applicants from a notice she had posted in Liverpool with a servants' employment agency. The eager way the three woman accepted the project of taking over for Mrs. Connelly, whom they had never befriended, and spearheading work for the wedding calmed Ann's indefinable sense of unease.

She chose not to say anything to Rhys about her worries. She sensed he had his own. In fact, she often caught him brooding, a condition he had previously claimed her presence in his life had destroyed.

To add more tension to their hectic days, they found themselves engulfed in prenuptial preparations and surrounded by well-wishers. Rhys decided to stay down at Blackburn until their wedding, for propriety's sake. Chances to escape to the hayloft were nonexistent.

Nearly a week after Aunt Peg arrived, Rhys came up to High Keep early one morning after breakfast. He had in tow large packages which he had his footman carry directly up to the duchesses' suite. Then he grasped her hand and led her up to the rooms.

He had his footman deposit there two large packages wrapped in shipping paper. From the shape of one, Ann could tell it was a bolt of cloth. She had no idea what the square one could be.

"I hope you approve," Rhys said, his expression reminding her of a young boy giving a gift that meant the world to him. As she opened them, he explained,

"They come from two mills outside Paris. Madame Fladry in the rue Richer makes the most coveted bridal gowns these days, and I wished I could have imported her for you, too, but with short notice it is not possible. Ivy Hignell is an accomplished seamstress who—"

Ann rushed into his arms, eager to hold him when she had gone too long without his intimate embrace.

"Darling," Rhys told her, pulling her away. "If you don't like my choices, I won't be offended. I don't have much experience with what you'd prefer. I tried to choose beautiful fabrics."

"It's not the fabrics. They're lovely. More than I expected."

Rhys traced the backs of his fingers along her jaw. "Then tell me what's wrong." When she studied the pearl buttons of his waistcoat, he worried. "If it's not to your taste, we can change it. You needn't wear them if you don't want to." When her eyes scanned the room, he went on, "Or is it the room's decor you don't like? If it is, you must say so. I have money. In fact, I have more money—a regular income—because of you."

Confused by his rush from one subject to the next, Ann frowned. "What are you talking about?"

"I got a letter from my solicitor yesterday, and your idea to rent my town house in Marylebone instead of selling it to the hospital has taken root. They agree to a lease in perpetuity with rate of rental to be renegotiated every five years. So you see, if you wish new drapes and counterpane, if you want a new coach and livery, we can afford it and have money to spare. Ann?" He tipped up her chin.

She flung her arms around him. "No. I don't want

new livery." She was laughing when she kissed him. "And I don't need a new coach. We'll invest the profit in . . ." She flourished a hand. "Whatever pleases you."

He got a winsome look on his face. "My prudent duchess. Well, I tell you I'd love to put some cash into Gordon Worminster's designs for a new omnibus."

"We'll do it, then." She hugged him.

"But that still doesn't help me understand what eats at you these past days."

She was so new to the physical demands of her love for him that she blushed as she whispered, "I miss you."

He groaned as he wrapped her close. "I need you, too."

"Why are we forever surrounded by people?"

A person cleared his throat.

Rhys rolled his eyes and drew back. "Yes?" he asked, facing his footman.

"Will that be all, Your Grace?"

Rhys dismissed him, but Ann was walking off, embarrassed to the roots of her hair.

Rhys was hooting like she'd never seen him. "Go ahead," she called over her shoulder as she headed for the hall, "double over. This is not funny." She was struggling with a grin of her own, but she spun away and took the oak-lined staircase in successive rounds. Rhys was right behind her but unable to catch her until she hit the first landing, where he picked her up like a sack of flour to haul her inside a shadowy room and lock the door behind him.

"What? Not a pantry?" she accused him. "Or a dressing room?"

"Anywhere—" He pressed her to the wall, his

fingers encircling her wrists. He began to undo the buttons of her bodice, and his knee spread her legs open. "With you."

"We can't. Not here." She pushed at him with her shoulders and succeeded in tormenting herself with the rub of her breasts to his chest. "What are you doing?"

"I think," he said quite calmly as his fingers lifted her skirts and found the slit in her drawers to probe her sensitive but oh-so-willing flesh, "I'm making a point."

"Your eloquence leaves me—" She gulped, digging her nails into his serge frockcoat and sighing as he inserted two tender fingers into her.

"Not cold, my love. Definitely not that," he told her, and, in his impatience, ripped the seam wider. "Thank God we have only two more weeks before we're married, since I can't seem to keep my hands off you." To illustrate, he massaged her to high keen.

Wild and wanting everything he provided here in this room, whatever the hell it was, she moved with his smooth cadence and melted in his hands. She groaned and asked for more.

"My thought exactly," he replied. He picked her up and spread her on some flat and chilly surface. Flipping up her dimity and petticoats, he pulled her to the edge where her legs enfolded him. In her tilted world, she grabbed a thick flat cord above her head and held on as he undid his flies and thrust inside her, smooth, hard, and hers. He arched, eyes closed, head back.

She felt him sink deeper, recounted the rooms she had explored in this colossal house, while her reality slipped another notch. "Where are we?"

"Doesn't matter . . . we don't need a bed for this."

"Or a hayloft."

He pulled out of her so fast, she thought he took her very breath with him. But the removal of his penis gave way to the insertion of his tongue. And she writhed in ecstasy as he murmured, "Tell me what to do to make you happy," which of course he knew by the way he tended her so artfully, "and I will."

"I want you—" She practically shouted in her delirium.

"Anytime." He crooned and with gentle fingers parted her pulsing lips to insert himself once more, but this time with a stunning and satisfying ram. "Especially on impulse."

He leaned over her to kiss her lips and share her fragrance with his touch. "Can't you see that is the benefit of trust and commitment?"

She was splintering, shattering, but so focused on her own goal that she clamped one hand around the base of his sex. "I'll make a rule, then."

"Sweet woman"—he froze in place—"you'd better make it quickly, then, before the butler comes."

"The . . . the *butler?*"

"Mmm. That bellrope you're pulling, my dear, rings in the servants' hall. Fitzallen will hear there's a need in the servants' cloak room and come running as fast as his frail legs can carry him. I really don't think the fellow would like to see his future mistress in a pose that rivals the fourth Duchess for her, shall we say, exotic nature."

"You are awful."

"Yes." Rhys grinned, more wolfishly than she'd ever seen him. "So drop that cord, and I'll oblige us both quickly. Fitzallen is eighty-two, darling, and he wouldn't survive another heart attack."

* * *

The following evening, Raine, Colleen, and Gus arrived with their new duenna, Mrs. Newton, in attendance. A worldly woman who seemed congenial and at the same time hawkish, Mrs. Newton had been governess in the Earl of Fingall's household.

Ann thought Mrs. Newton a raving beauty with her strawberry blond hair and eloquence. What made her more appealing to Ann was the fact that she obviously loved working for the exciting Americans. "You are the rage in London, I tell you."

Ann demurred. "As in absence makes the heart grow fonder?"

"Absolutely," Ellen Newton replied. "Two smart stationery shops in Bond Street have an entire window of goods which they devote to the American Beauties. They are capitalizing on the truth of your loveliness by reproducing your photographs."

"No." Ann wondered, "Where did they get them?"

Raine looked aghast. "No one knows."

"But this shop sells them, and they now grace drawing rooms across the city." Ellen Newton looked well pleased with her news. "The effect has been to popularize you, Ann, and your friends and cohorts, even more. A man can do himself proud to court an American 'gel' these days."

"Mrs. Newton seems very agreeable," Ann concluded after the woman had excused herself to go to bed early, "and rather young for her position."

"Thirty-two and a widow, but very cosmopolitan and very well informed," Raine praised her. "Having been employed in the Earl's household, she has met Thackeray and Disraeli and Prince Bertie. She also understands British politics."

"I like her very much," Gus piped in. "She's got a

sense of humor, as well as intriguing little stories to tell about famous people."

"Colleen?" Ann pressed her when Colleen had remained sullen in her chair.

"She's fine, I suppose."

Raine and Gus gave Ann a deadpan look which was a plea for help.

"But you don't like her," Ann determined.

"On the contrary!" Colleen snapped, and vaulted from her chair to pace the drawing room. "I enjoy her company. She's funny and wise, but she was employed for one reason." She faced the three of them. "To tie me down."

"Do you need restraining?" Ann asked, knowing how blatant the question was, even for a friend of such long standing. Ann also knew Colleen was in such a fit that she would not respond to diplomacy.

"So. Someone told you about my days out in a carriage alone with Jason Rutledge. Well, nothing happened. I was only enjoying myself."

Raine inhaled and glared at the ceiling. "Coll, you must stop this. Ann, she thinks she must secure a man before the season is out."

Gus shook her head and stared at Ann. "Mama has heard that you are to be married, and to a duke, no less. She has written that she expects Colleen to do her part, and soon."

"Aunt Peg insisted," Raine went on, "that if any of us is to hold our head up in society, we must act the part of respectable young ladies."

"What precisely," Colleen was raving now, "have I done that was any worse than what Ann did?"

Gus gasped.

Raine sighed. "Coll, this attitude is not worthy of you."

"I don't care!" Colleen spun away. "I apologize, Ann. I do feel sorry for what you endured, but Rhys obviously loved you from the start and tried to save you from yourself. Bryce, on the other hand, needs a little encouragement."

Gus's mouth dropped open. "Are you saying you went out in Jason Rutledge's carriage alone to . . . to make Bryce jealous?"

"Oh, come on, Gussie." Her sister spun on her. "Grow up. Bryce is the man I want. I'm just making certain he comes to me."

Ann sat, silently stewing about what to say. She knew from what Rhys had told her that Bryce did care for Colleen. But having come to know English sensibilities firsthand as she did, Ann also would wager that too many escapades could make Colleen less of a cherished prize and more of a liability to Bryce or any other man, noble or not. "Why not let the courtship progress in its own time and manner, Colleen?"

Colleen turned around slowly and crossed her arms. "I am amazed you of all people would say that."

Ann felt the insult but would not rise to it. Clearly, Colleen was too determined to have Bryce in any way she could, even at the expense of Ann's friendship or her own integrity. "There are benefits to going slowly. How do you know you could live with Bryce? Actually, what do you know about him after seeing him at public functions?"

Colleen only glowered at Ann.

"I see." Ann relented. "You consider me a poor source of advice. I can understand that. Perhaps, then, I will say no more on this matter." She made her excuses to go to bed.

"Look, Ann." Colleen followed her to the drawing

room door. "I didn't mean to make you angry at me. You and Rhys had an odd courtship and a quick one. I understand why and how it happened, and I would like to think the same could happen to me. It must, you see." She reached for Ann's hands.

"Your mother can ruin your life, Colleen. Stop letting her rule you."

Colleen's eyes filled with tears. "The way you ended your father's influence?" When Ann nodded, she whispered, "It's not easy."

"I know. But you will never be able to claim happiness until you do." With that, Ann left her and went up to her bedroom to sleep the soundless rest of one who has conquered her greatest challenge.

Ann's days became merry-go-rounds, filled with fittings of the merveilleux and lavish lace, races and rendezvous with Rhys, and plans for a small but traditional wedding for the sixteenth Duke of Carlton and Dundalk to his American fiancée.

Aunt Peg and the girls added to the festive air. At Blackburn and High Keep, preparations for the annual festival of Solstice began, keeping all of them abustle with cooking and cleaning tasks—and laughter. When Bryce Falconer arrived for the wedding and took up residence in a guest suite in High Keep, even Colleen lit up.

Ann and Rhys's official betrothal four days later in the Kendall family chapel added to the gaiety. Rhys bestowed upon her another of his gifts. This time, it was the family engagement ring. An elaborate band of gold up to her knuckle, encrusted with tiny rubies. Astounded and eager to give him something as wonderful, Ann racked her brain for a suitable wedding gift and wondered what to give a man who wished for nothing but her love.

As the day of her wedding approached, she pondered the issue with her aunt and cousin and two friends. Riding five days before the wedding with Rhys, she realized she had two gifts she might give him—and never find their equal elsewhere. She sent a message to the Forsythe housekeeper to assist her, and she waited for the stallion and the mare which she had taken from her mate when long ago she had intended to go to America and raise horses alone.

Three days later, she rode down to Liverpool, not stopping at Blackburn at the early hour before breakfast. She had arranged with Harry at the livery to take the two horses off the London train the night before and stable them for her. She intended to take the animals up to High Keep and give them to Rhys that afternoon.

She was struck with sheer surprise, then, to round the corner of King Street and see Rhys standing outside with Harry.

Harry pulled his forelock in deference. "Miss Brighton, yer here as promised!" His eyes were apologizing.

"Am I here in time?" she asked him with a grin.

"Before 'is Grace got inside, yes, ma'am, ye are."

"What's this?" Rhys asked. "Conspiracy?"

"Can I lure ye inside, Yer Grace?"

The three of them ducked their heads to enter the low door. Rhys halted at the sight of the Irish mare and Raider. When he turned to her, his eyes glistened with delight.

"They belong here," she affirmed, going into his open arms.

"As you do," he whispered.

Minutes later, she left Rhys to see to the two horses while she walked over to the telegraph office. She had

two errands to do that morning. One was to send a
note to Edward Whittier, Rhys's solicitor, to have him
invest her savings in Gordon Worminster's omnibus
designs. The other note concerned the issue that
remained unresolved before her wedding—her relationship with her father.

She had tormented herself over it for weeks. But
yesterday, she put pen to paper. Of reconciliation or
forgiveness, she wrote nothing. Her simple words
were only an invitation to come, and she knew he
could. Bryce had said Skip had returned from Nice
via ship a few days ago. He was, Ann was thankful to
hear, much recovered in health. And so, if he wished,
she would like to have him with her on this momen-
tous day in her life.

But when she walked into the telegraph office, Mrs.
Connelly was just leaving.

Shocked to see the woman in Liverpool, Ann sent
her telegram to her father and tried not to stare at her.

"It's a free country, Duchess," she seethed at Ann
as she passed her.

Anger for having her fired did not surprise Ann. It
was Connelly's vehemence that stunned Ann.

She followed the woman out, intent on asking her
why she hated Rhys and her so. Much to her amazement, the woman climbed into a coach whose seal
declared it to belong to Earl Litchfield. Ann blinked in
disbelief but hailed her.

"Wait a minute, Mrs. Connelly. I want to know
what your problem is with the Duke of Carlton."

A hand on her elbow had her turning. "Adam!"
Ann was not surprised but terrified. Inexplicably
terrified.

"Well, well. I do find you at a choice time. Days
before the wedding, and he lets you run wild, does

he?" Adam was grinning in a sardonic manner that made Ann's skin crawl. He leaned closer and sniffed her hair. "You still smell like his damn roses." His eyes raked her. "Does he put them in his bed for you?"

Ann wrenched away. "Go to hell." She meant to tell Rhys how hideous Adam had been. To be so insulting as to speak of Rhys's roses again. Again . . . as he had the day he accosted her. Her mind whirred, and she spun on him. "How do you know about the roses?" He'd known at Westminster. "How did you learn?" No one outside Forsythe House had been told; she and her father had made that stipulation to the household staff, especially her maid. Her maid. Nora knew. Did Nora tell Adam? Was she his paid informer? "Nora—"

Adam's face was thinning into a predator's. "Convenient and inexpensive to pay a little maid. To send one rose a day was a sweet touch, wasn't it? I know Rhys Kendall. He would send any woman roses. White ones, so fitting for the family legend."

"He's never sent any woman roses, except me."

Adam lifted a brow in reproof. "So he would tell you. He loves many women . . . uses them, has them in his bed, too."

"That's not true, either."

"My lord?" This was Mrs. Connelly, appealing to Adam from the inside of his coach.

"What is she to you?" Ann pressed him. "Why is she with you?"

"She is in my employ."

"God, who is not?" Ann scoffed, and when Adam looked smug, she was repulsed. "How do you know her?" Ann was wild to know the truth now. All of it. From the satisfied look on his face, Adam had pieces of it she had never heard. Nor had Rhys. "Have you two cooperated to hurt Rhys?"

"For seducing my wife? Why, how astute of you, dear."

Ann gathered her dignity like a tornado. "I warn you—"

"Bah!" Adam sneered. "Another virago in love with Rhys Kendall. What a waste. But it is I who will set you straight. And why not now, today?" He reflected a moment. *"Before* the wedding is such a perfect time. Get in, damn you." Adam pushed her inside his coach and yelled at his coachman to drive on. "We will do this now. Why should I wait to have my justice?"

Chapter 16

"It's a complex fate, being an American, and one of the responsibilities it entails is fighting against a superstitious valuation of Europe."

—HENRY JAMES

THEY COVERED THE MILES FROM LIVERPOOL TO LITCH-field Hall in a red haze of Ann's fear. She knew the terrain, remembered the hall was but four miles from High Keep, yet on her rides out, she'd never jour-neyed there. She should have. If she had, she'd have some familiar landscape to fill her heart with hope. As it was, the man and woman before her took what hope she had and cast it away with their hatred.

Connelly had reason, she claimed, to spite Rhys Kendall. "He seduced my lamb. My baby." She leaned forward, and Ann could smell her fetid breath, rife with a taste for revenge. "He took my Mary and turned her head."

Mary. Adam's second wife. The one Rhys had never encouraged. The one who had died . . . in an accident.

Ann glared at Adam. "How did Mary fall from her horse?"

"Alas." He sighed theatrically. "She was clumsy."

"Or you pushed her."

"Actually, it was the girth strap on her saddle which was extremely worn."

Connelly turned huge eyes to her employer. "You wouldn't have hurt her . . ."

"Really, Connelly. Not I."

The woman scowled, and Ann swallowed in disgust at the woman's manipulation by Adam. "You killed her, Adam."

"You have no proof."

"How convenient for you," Ann taunted.

"My lord, did you kill my Mary?" Connelly had tears in her eyes.

"Shut up, Connelly." Adam grinned at Ann. "A real man makes his opportunities. As I did with you."

Maybe it was foolhardy to prod him, but she had to know his methods. All of them. "And you were so successful, too," she said sarcastically.

"You never knew you were being followed. Neither did your father." Adam was gloating. "The man in Dublin? I see you do remember him. And the flower lady? Such excellent men at their nefarious trades, don't you agree?"

"You paid them."

"Money speaks so strongly," he agreed.

"My God, how you hated us all."

"Not you, sweet Grace. You, I wanted to marry. Not just to have your body at my disposal but to know that you were Skip Brighton's and I could hurt him every time I made you cry in pain or anger. But you favored Rhys, and the idea of taking you from him delighted me. When you wouldn't come to me, I had to find ways to torment all of you—and now that it's come to you marrying him, I must take some compensation for my loss. I think it very fair."

Ann stared out the window and hated to think of the types of compensation Adam required.

He reached over and jerked her head around. "Look at me when I'm talking to you!"

"This gets you nowhere," Ann told him, more coolly than she thought possible. Her hands convulsed on her purse . . . and the feel of her little derringer brought her a tangible comfort.

"No? That's for me to say, eh? I knew the day would come when I could take you for myself. My revenge. Sweet." His eyes raked her. "I didn't think that it would come so soon."

"Rhys will come looking for you. The man at the telegraph office will tell him."

"I'm certain of it."

"Whatever you plan"—*please, not an accident for me*—"Rhys will never allow you to do it."

"Rhys. Rhys. Rhys. I am sick to death of Tweedledum." Adam put out a hand, and Ann yanked away, thinking he meant to hit her, when in fact he ran his palm across her mouth. "I plan to make it so you will be sick at the sight of him, too."

"That will never happen."

"Oh, do trust my judgment, pretty one. What I have in mind for you will make it a joy if you never see him again."

"None of us will live that long," Ann taunted him.

"I pray God *your* life will be long, so that you see my words come true."

She told herself not to let her courage die, but she had to know his intentions. "What do you mean to do?"

"Wait and see."

They fell silent as the coach rounded a bend similar

to the one at Blackburn and High Keep. Adam took his watch fob, removed it from his waistcoat, wound it around one of Ann's wrists, and pulled her from the coach. In their walk, she made certain to keep her grip on her purse.

Mrs. Connelly began to badger him about the details of Mary's death. "I can't let you hurt this child, if you are responsible for Mary and the other one."

Adam said not a word but swung around with such force that he punched the old woman in the face and sent her sprawling against the stone wall. Her head cracked with a sickening *thunk*.

"Adam, you can't leave her!" Ann pleaded with him but knew it was useless.

He cursed her and dragged her through his medieval hall and up a circular staircase, his gold chain biting into her flesh. Up to a tiny room he took her, shoved her inside, and followed her.

"Now, my dear, we'll make this fast."

"Why are you doing this? You and Rhys are friends."

"He destroyed that friendship long ago when he seduced my second wife." Adam uncoiled his stock and sauntered near. He scanned her body as if she were scraps for a flock of buzzards. "So, since I can't seem to ruin his businesses, I'll take great pleasure—great pleasure—to ruin what he values just as much. *You.*"

"You hired Connelly to rob him of his money and—"

"Much worse than that, too."

"What?"

"I planted those stories in the newspapers about

him. And you, of course. I had to when you preferred
him over me. Sad choice, sad." He got a wild look in
his eyes. "Take off your dress."

She stiffened. "I will not."

He flared his nostrils. "I like a spirited woman.
Good. Unfortunately, the women I have liked, others
have, too. You are my succulent reward for taking
Rhys's and your father's leavings." He advanced,
stalking her one slow step at a time, so that when he
reached her, she still had not moved from the shock.
Only when his big hands snaked out to hold her to
him did she try to step around him and fail.

"My father?" What did he mean? Mary had been
romantically interested in her father as well as Rhys?
Then she remembered her father had had affairs . . .
and Adam had a first wife . . .

"Yes, the man was a devil. Take off your clothes. I
will see what the great Rhys Kendall has acquired this
time."

She shuddered as he grabbed for her, and she jerked
away.

"Elegant as a reed. He never did relish the Ruben-
esque type. Too bawdy for the refined Kendalls."

"You cannot maul me, Adam."

He clamped her against him. "Do not fight, my
dear. I will be kinder, make this heaven for you if you
comply."

"I won't let you kill me." She shook her head and
strained away.

"Kill you?" He sank a hand into her hair, then
twisted so her head arched back. "I could break your
lovely neck in one snap." He ran one hand over her
throat. "But I won't. I want you alive and screaming
my name when I do this."

She willed herself not to tremble. "What?"

He ripped her bodice in one deft tear. "Rape you."

"Rhys will kill you."

Adam chuckled as he nuzzled her throat. "He will want to. But he is too rational."

"He'll see you in jail."

"No. He'd never let the world know a Litchfield had enjoyed his darling wife. Oh, make no mistake, Rhys will marry you, because I have seen how deeply he loves you. And every night, every day, when he takes you to his noble bed, he'll know that I had you. Your father will know it, too."

He crushed her against him, and before his mouth laid claim to hers, she turned her face away, straining to get away from him, wondering why he kept bringing up her father. "My father and you were friends. He made you one of the directors."

Adam's blue eyes glowed with rage. "To end his guilt! I couldn't bear it. That's why I hired MacIntyre to blackmail him."

"You did that? Why?"

"Your father owed me that."

"How?"

"To compensate me for taking my first wife."

Ann froze. "My father had a relationship with your first wife?"

He blew a gust of air in disgust. "An affair, dear girl. He carried on with her and destroyed what we had together."

"When?" she asked, but knew the answer.

"More than ten years ago."

"The fire." She recalled the timing. "You have harbored this resentment for a decade." *As my mother had.* "Oh, Adam, don't do this."

"I liked you better when you had starch, Duchess. What's the grief for? How would you feel if you thought Rhys preferred another woman to you, especially"—he nuzzled her mean and hard—"after he had examined every inch of you in his bed?"

She knew. Her mother's hollow look of remorse and shame rose before her mind's eye. Her own love for Rhys—her trust, too—told her she would die if he ever did that. "I'd feel betrayed."

Adam pushed her away. "Well, that, pretty lady, has happened to me *twice*. With your husband and your father."

"But Adam, enough people have suffered for that transgression." *My mother, my brother, me . . . my father.* "You especially."

"And Georgianna. Let us not forget her."

"Yes . . . not . . . her."

Adam's face contorted and became a caricature of itself. Eyes bulging, mouth lax as he repeated his first wife's name like a curse. What was wrong with him? He looked, dear God, quite mad.

"You loved her, didn't you?" Ann asked with a compassion she had never thought she could feel for Adam.

He swallowed, his eyes glazed in memory. "She was my angel. Beautiful."

"I am certain she loved you."

"She did. I know she did in the beginning. She must have. No woman makes love like that, wanton and urgent, if she doesn't care for a man." He caught back a sob.

Ann felt his body weaken. She put her hand to his cheek. Tears welled in his eyes.

Ann thought of her gun and hoped she wouldn't need it.

Below in this ancient castle, shouts and objections

rang up the ancient stairwell. Rhys had come. He was angry. Furious—and there was no way out except through the door she had come in with Adam.

"Love is so rare," Ann murmured. "So unique to two people. Georgianna must have loved you dearly."

"She said so, just before I pushed her over the parapet."

Oh, Adam, you murdered her. God help me here.

"You see, then, she admitted she cared."

"Do you suppose she still does?"

Ann had no reply at first. "Oh, yes," she finally managed. "I am cert—"

"I talk to her every night, and she says she does. I can hear her voice, but I can't see her. She won't come out from behind the walls because she's angry at me for marrying again. Georgianna says when I got a whore like Mary, I deserved her because I betrayed her. Georgianna laughs at me, and I don't like that."

"No one should laugh at you. You have loved Georgianna and—"

His eyes darkened. "Mary didn't love me. The *fool!*" He reached for Ann and shook her as if she were Mary and deserved the punishment.

"Adam! Adam." Ann tried more calmly. "Georgianna must know if Mary really loved you, don't you think?"

He scowled. "I'm not—I can't think." He grimaced, shoved Ann away, and began to prowl the perimeter of the room.

Footsteps were running toward them. Arguments among those out in the staircase raged. Ann backed toward the door. She suddenly found a serenity she had not experienced since her youth. And war. When Taylor had asked her to take from his shoulder a bullet to save his life. "I think we should talk about this more, don't you, Adam? We could, you know. If you were rested."

He cast her a sharp look. "No, no—you can't!"

But she had spun for the door and swung it open. Rhys halted in his tracks, stunned to face her. "Ann!"

Like a wounded animal, Adam ran for Rhys. Tackled him. With the disadvantage of surprise, Rhys went down backward, hit his head against the stones, and his eyes rolled up white. Adam went for his throat and began beating Rhys's head against the wall.

How Ann got the derringer out she did not know. But soon she pressed it to Adam's back. *"Stop it.* Stop it, Adam, or I'll kill you."

He turned on her, teeth clenched and hands out. She cocked the hammer and was ready to fire when Harry thrust Adam to the ground. Trussed him on his stomach.

Rhys sat up and back, dazed. His wobbling gaze found Ann, and he stumbled up.

She was shaking when Rhys got to her. His face white as a dead man's, he cradled her gently and reassured her that she was going to be fine, just fine.

She ran her fingers over his face and shoulders. Well, unhurt, she told herself, and at that reaffirmation, she did something she had not done in years. She fainted.

She and Rhys slept the day and night away, recuperating from their trauma, each in her and his own bedroom. At suppertime the next day, Rhys knocked on her door, and she drew him inside.

"You feel better?" she asked, and each of them made the other sit down. "No headache?"

Rhys shook his head. "And you? Not lightheaded?"

"No. Just . . . sad. For Adam. You. My father. Adam's wives. My God, Rhys. Who would have thought he killed them?" Even Mrs. Connelly had left that morning for London, recovered from her stunning blow to the head but appalled at her own misjudgment of Adam Litchfield's perversity.

"I know, sweetheart. But he's ill. They will take good care of him up at Northam." The institution was a private one for those with mental illnesses. Rhys had telegrammed the director to come see Adam and take him for treatment. The man had complied immediately. Rhys would see to the disposition of Adam's financial affairs until Adam's solicitor could come up from London.

"You have been such a good friend to him. But he hated you and my father so much that he became demented. He committed such awful crimes."

"Arson, blackmail, theft, murder. The list ended when he tried to hurt you, thank God." Rhys and she held each other for long minutes. "Are you up for this wedding tomorrow, do you think?"

"I've come all this way, Your Grace," *from resentment to freedom,* "from America to Lancashire to marry you, and I think the ceremony must be tomorrow."

It would be more complete if she could tell her father that she had forgiven him, but she hadn't heard from him. She thought she might. At least an answering telegram from him to say no, thank you. But there was nothing, and her heart grew sore. If he meant to be here for her wedding, he would have had to arrive on this evening's train up from London.

She went down to dinner and threw herself into the

gaiety which she knew would have been more so had Skip Brighton shared it with her. She did not want him to die alone or think she didn't value him at all.

She did.

The next morning at ten o'clock, she left her suite, the thirty-two-foot train of her wedding gown gliding behind her, a gigantic spray of alba roses in her hands, and concentrated on balancing the heavy diamond and emerald tiara that crowned her tulle and Valenciennes lace veil. Head up, gloriously happy, she vowed she would not let her father's absence mar the ecstasy of becoming the wife of Rhys Kendall.

She had often come to the Kendall family chapel in the past few weeks. She came to sit and marvel that she was there. Or she came to open the giant illuminated relic which was the family Bible to the right of the altar upon a blue marble pedestal. In the book, notations of births and deaths, events in the lives of men and women gone to their rest, gave her a sense of her new family's history and embroidered a new sense of family pride.

Today, she absorbed the warmth within the chapel's walls. Its four-century-old stained-glass windows threw a kaleidoscope of rich and welcome sheens across the eager faces of more than two hundred guests from Blackburn, High Keep, and London. Ann paused at the threshold to feel her heart pick up a beat at the sight of her future husband.

Rhys wore a morning tuxedo of black swallowtail coat and dove-gray trousers. His shirt was snowy white, and in his matching cravat he wore a stickpin in the shape of the family seal of arrows and rose.

But nothing equalled his eyes. They flowed over her like a dark waterfall, a sweet and rushing declaration of possession and delight. Her heart paused, and at

Raine's exclamation behind her, Ann knew she must go forward.

No organ graced the confines of the chapel. But Rhys had arranged to have a duo of violinists play as the guests assembled and now for her. The aisle was short, Ann's gratitude immense that it was. She had waited for eternities, it seemed, to be united to this man, and her traverse of the aisle was too long for her patience.

The vicar was a short, bald man. His kindly eyes were skipping with glee to be able to officiate for his lord, the Duke of Carlton. His voice was soft, a baritone that glided over Ann's nerves as she gave her hand to this man whom she adored and whose wedding ring she now accepted.

The Anglican Church's ceremony held a few different words from the Episcopalian service she was used to in Virginia. But what the words meant was no less satisfying, and when their vows were exchanged, Ann rejoiced that it was done. And then, instead of walking down the aisle, her husband whisked her through the nave's side door to lift the veil and take her in his arms.

"My Grace," he rejoiced. "At last." And he sealed their promises with a kiss. His claiming was no peck. His timing was not quick. The kisses multiplied, as did their passion, and the results had them both gasping and laughing . . . and grabbing for her falling tiara.

Rhys chuckled as he tried to reset it into her curls.

"I can do it." She took it from him but couldn't secure it with her pins.

"Leave it." He put it atop a vestry box and put one arm around her waist.

"Oh, but don't you want me to wear it?"

"I *want* to get this wedding breakfast over and done so that we can send these people *home.*" He arched two wicked brows. "You can wear it later for me."

"Just this."

"Promise me."

The irony made Ann chuckle that once she would have married a man who demanded she wear hats and skirts, and now she was wedded to one who didn't care if she wore the family coronet as long as she wore nothing else. She threw her arms around his neck and kissed him madly. "Let's go, then."

Only her father stood in the chapel.

His hazel eyes locked with hers. He appeared tired, sallow, a little hunched. His hands twirled his tophat by the brim. But he stopped, cleared his throat, and glanced at Rhys before he spoke to her. "I received your invitation."

She might have sent it to him, but he would have to do more than appear here to begin to heal the breach he had carved between them.

He licked his lips. "I was happy to accept. *Thrilled* is really the word. I wanted this . . . wanted you two to meet because I always thought you were cut from the same cloth. And I couldn't see you wasted on anyone, Ann, who wasn't as noble as you are, sweetheart."

She swallowed.

"I did terrible things to get you to come to England. I never meant for you to know about me bribing Quinn, but then I couldn't bear not to be honest with you, either. I wanted you to be happy and, if I knew that when I . . . was no longer around, you'd be happy with a man worthy of you, I thought it'd make a wash of all the awful things I did." He cleared his throat again. "But I misjudged myself. In the past weeks, I will tell you that I missed you, honey. And it eats me alive to think that you'd hate me."

Ann controlled the urge to sob. Rhys squeezed her hand in understanding.

"I don't hate you," she acknowledged. "I once thought I did, but that was because, underneath, I loved you so."

Tears made Skip squint. "Can we enjoy what little time we've got?"

She had not hugged her father in more than ten years, but it felt like ten lifetimes she'd been lost when she went to his arms and found their love renewed. "Yes," she assured him. "And we're going to start now."

Epilogue

"American girls are pretty and charming . . . in a vast desert of practical common sense."

—OSCAR WILDE

London, England
November 1875

ANN EXITED THE GREEN DRAWING ROOM AND SQUIRMED in her corset.

The ten powdered, bewigged footmen who lined the reception hall did not blink but stared straight ahead. Ann offered silent thanks that they didn't seem to notice how the sixteenth Duchess of Carlton and Dundalk put her hand to her bosom and wondered if they knew she wished to writhe in her layers of finery.

She headed down the red-carpeted hallway, waiting until the circular stairs to pick up her skirts and run. At the landing, she throttled her speed, demurred by the sight of another set of liveried servants posted like wooden soldiers. The head steward approached with her cape and her walking stick, bidding her good afternoon without looking her in the eye. Head high, hands itching to yank off her slipping hat, she took the wide marble steps down into the portico of Buckingham Palace's Royal Mews. The Queen's ebony and gilt brougham idled there, awaiting the end of Ann's audience of precisely thirty minutes. Despite the date, autumn sunshine fell upon her face. Ann wondered if her husband might have ordered the radiance especially for her.

She grinned, which the Queen's coachman took for her readiness to depart. She hoped the man would fly.

A testament to his years of service to an elderly woman whose job it was to impress any whom she passed, the driver fairly crawled to the Embankment. So that when he turned into the circular drive at Kendall Great House, the Duchess of Carlton and Dundalk had removed not just her hat and its pins but her gloves, earbobs, and shoes.

She gave great thanks to her footman, who then thanked the coachman, who doffed his hat and rumbled away. Ann passed Mrs. Pagett with a few words of reassurance all had gone well and handed over to the woman her numerous gewgaws. In soundless glee, she hoisted her skirts and ran up the grand staircase to where her husband said he would await her.

She burst inside the master's suite. She did not need to call his name. Beyond the sitting room, inside their bedroom, she could see—and feel—how the fire blazed in welcome. She unbuttoned her Spencer jacket, dropped it to a chair. The door closed quietly behind her, the lock clinking in the latch. Rhys's arms around her told her she was where she belonged. His lips blessed her temple and slid along her throat. His fingers undid hooks and tapes, divested her of gown, petticoats, bustle, liner, and then worked upon the laces of the corset.

He peeled away the garment and dropped it to the floor. He turned her in his arms and drew the chemise up over her head. "Oh, my," he crooned, each hand lifting one breast, enlarging in preparation for their heir, "I think we've got it now."

"What's that?" she managed to ask above the rush of heat his hands created in her body and her mind.

"Another reason not to let you wear this again." He pulled away, his brows furrowed, his index finger tracing a red groove along a swell where a bone had marred her flesh. "We'll have to fix that."

She licked her lips. "Oh, yes." She was anticipating the delicious fix he was about to put her in. "And do, let's hurry."

He scooped her up, his laughter bright, and plunked her down on their wide Tudor bed. "Would you like juice or—"

"Something stronger, sweeter—you—instead."

He obliged her deftly, swiftly. He had not touched her since the dawn, and appetites, especially in her condition, needed to be assuaged.

At long last replete, reclining along his sinuous length, she recounted her "afternoon." "I enjoyed her company," Ann told him about Victoria. "She's kind but forthright. She told me she's pleased about our happiness and has heard I make you smile. 'No longer the Dour Duke,'" Ann imitated the little lady's tiny voice, "'and you have made him so. We are pleased.' But she says one good marriage in the lot doesn't change her opinion of these American alliances, as she calls them. Too many differences. She mentioned Gordon and Aunt Peg. The problems that drove them apart thirty years ago still exist. Prejudices against money and class on both sides, and she's right. But she especially dislikes Anglo-American alliances if they occur more quickly than reason will allow."

Ann referred to the hasty wedding of Colleen

VanderHorn and Bryce Falconer. The ceremony was a perfunctory if exquisite one in the American Embassy last week, with the elder VanderHorns over from New York to join Skip, Raine, Gus, Peg, her new husband Gordon, and the Kendalls. The London newspapers, atwitter with the slur that the marriage was occasioned by the imminent arrival of an heir to the twelfth Earl of Aldersworth, were—for once—not wrong. Few knew the truth.

Colleen had cautioned her sister, Skip, and Raine, plus the Worminsters and the Kendalls, not to tell her parents about the baby for fear of a tirade by her mother. They had complied, agreeing to make the best of the situation and pave the way for Gus to remain abroad as she so dearly wanted to do in order to study fencing and painting further.

"I tried to tell the Queen that Bryce and Colleen loved each other," Ann explained, her fingers combing back the curls from her husband's brow. "They do, don't you think?"

"I am an expert on only my love for you."

Ann knew Rhys well enough by now to know this was his English diplomacy speaking. "Colleen has wanted him since the moment she saw him. But that's no indication that the union will work."

Rhys's fingers traced her mouth. "It's a good beginning."

"But leaves much to solve."

"For them." He rose, his muscles rippling in fluid grace. She admired the elegance of her mate. He matched her in so many ways. Desires, energies. And since they married, laughter and hope. "We've begun our journey."

Together in the past four months, they had solved many of their challenges, big and small.

Her dislike of the weather was pervasive, but he had made every one of his three homes secure from drafts and built huge fires in every room they regularly inhabited. At Dundalk, that had not been difficult. The house was two floors in lush meadows which in August smelled of sun and rain—and love upon their sheets. Their wedding trip there was a fond remembrance of hers.

Returning to High Keep Castle, they had not had to do many renovations to make his bedroom suite secure and cozy. Thicker drapes upon the panes, new caulking, more blankets did the job for Ann. Meanwhile, she and Rhys had given depositions against Adam for his attempted abduction of her, and the local magistrate had bound him over for trial on theft and blackmail charges. All of the criminal charges had been dropped in light of his permanent commitment to Northam Home for the Insane. Rhys had turned the running of Adam's estate over to Adam's solicitor as soon as he could in August. Rhys did what he could out of friendship, but he was glad to relinquish the duties.

This trip to London was their first since their wedding trip to Dundalk, and they agreed they were quite ready to go home to Lancashire, especially now that the weddings of the Worminsters and the Falconers and Ann's private audience were done. Tomorrow, they would close up this house, take Mrs. Pagett with them as well as the four other Great House servants, and go north for the winter. There they would await the birth of the heir—or heiress—to the Duchy of Carlton and Dundalk.

Rhys leaned over her and whispered in her ear. "Enough of serious matters. Want to come play with me, Duchess?"

"Didn't we just?" She teased him with a lifting brow.

His eyes narrowed. "Sinfully, is what I have in mind."

"Really?" She undulated in anticipation. "What have you dug out of your treasure trove this time?"

"I won't spoil it by words, madam. This you must see. Or rather, I have a fancy that I must."

The gown he'd put out in their dressing room for her today lay atop an ancient trunk which he'd had carted up from the vaults. Yesterday, she'd worn a costume that some Kendall lad must have used to meet King Henry or his children. The tights had sparked her husband's pleasure, but not so much as when she slowly removed them for their mutual delight. But this dress today was a confection of blush satin and once-ivory lace, now yellowed. Ann knew it had once belonged to a very daring woman.

The bodice told the tale more than the wide skirt meant for panniers. But even if the bone forms had survived, Ann would not have donned them. Her game and Rhys's only allowed one garment at a time, all the better to be discarded. Ann picked up the gown to let the skirts fall as they may to create a swirl of cloth about her. But as she tried to fasten the hooks and laces of the bib, she eyed Rhys. He sat, mouth firm, hands steepled, examining her every move from his armchair.

She tried to secure the laces but quickly realized she couldn't. "I'd say this gown belonged to Constance." He grinned, and she wondered if he knew it before he exhumed it.

"Turn around." When she swirled, she dropped her hands, and his eyes noted what she meant. "Come here and let me see." She walked toward him, the ends of her laces in each hand. He took them from her and tugged her closer, to stand snug between his legs. "Perhaps," he conjectured, "if we tie them like this."

She bit her lip to keep from chuckling as he tied the front so loosely she could have gotten pneumonia in the draft. "My lord Duke, you cannot dress a woman."

"My lady Duchess"—he brushed his hands across the swell of her breasts—"you are not dressed at all. Your nipples, madam, rise above the lace."

Her gaze traveled down to where, in his skintight hose, his erection showed her how pleased he was at that.

"Where do you suppose her husband let her go in this?"

"To see Charles, I'm sure."

She gasped, less from shock at such royal debauchery than at the marital joys her husband brought her. One long finger to her laces, he pulled them out, then slid his big warm hands inside her bodice, pushing aside the fabric to claim her breasts with fingertips and lips.

"I have a present for you," he said against her skin.

The wealth of family heirlooms had quite amazed her but never exhausted her appreciation. "What is the occasion?"

"Unique news." He urged her to sit atop him, pushing up her skirts as she straddled him. "We are, I think, very well off, for once. And maybe for a long time."

With his fingers making little sworls upon her inner thighs, Ann found it difficult to think of priorities. "Money is not something I want to talk about now."

"Nor I. But you need to know this." His fingers parted her and began to stroke her. "I went to see my solicitor."

"Mmm," she purred. "Money and law. I'm excited."

He slipped a finger inside her, said, "So I see," and she knew she could become enamored with any topic he discussed like this. "He tells me that you are still a citizen of America, according to their law. I knew," he whispered in her ear, "that would make you happy."

"Delighted." She arched as he massaged her and positioned her much closer to his body.

"But in England, it seems everything you have is mine."

"Yes," she rasped. "I understand this so well." She pushed at his hose and reached for him. "Everything you have must also be mine."

"Of that there is no doubt."

She took his erection into her hand, and she admired how very much of him was hers. She rubbed herself against him, but he refrained. "Why not now, my husband?" He always took as much time with her as she could endure.

"It seems you have spent some money on a venture whose profits will come to us both, though they will appear—according to English law—in my name."

She frowned. "I haven't spent any money. You know I haven't. I keep all the ledgers, and I'm frugal with the household expenses."

"I told Edward that he must be mistaken, but it seems you haven't told me everything I should know."

She paused, heartbroken that Rhys would question her, when she noted his smile was not bland or intolerant but filled with a mirth that she loved.

"You invested in Gordon's designs for the omnibus line for Liverpool."

"Good God."

"That's what I said."

"But I forgot about it completely."

"Well, my love, the group did not forget you. Investing with Edward Whittier saved you for this while. He honored your request not to tell me."

"I planned it to be a wedding gift for you. But then I forgot!"

"Edward had to tell me this morning who the last few investors were because we are capitalized so well now, we can begin the legal paperwork. I think by the summer we should be able to commission the manufacture of the buses. Already we have prospective buyers in Liverpool and Leeds."

"You're not angry."

He filled her to her sighing satisfaction. "Do I seem angry?"

"No, no." She rose with him, moved with him, her hands caressing his bare shoulders, his jaw, his lips. "But it's the old conflict of money, again."

"You keep my books, you run my house, you carry my child, and you hold my heart in your hands. What value is money to all that?"

She didn't have to answer. And for long and luscious minutes, she couldn't. But when their breathing returned to normal and she realized how far they'd come together to a daily bliss, Ann kissed her husband and urged him to their packing.

"I am eager," she told him, "to go home."

AUTHOR'S NOTES

The marriage of American debutantes to European noblemen became the rage more than one hundred and twenty-five years ago, as numerous American millionaires bestowed their wealth on their heirs—and heiresses. The precedent, once set, sparked the desires of many adventurous young women to become titled. They crossed the Atlantic, jubilant at their prospects and eager for the glamour of the Old World—and love.

Some discovered happiness with their mates. Many had to work at it. A few endured tragically bad marriages, paying for their new-minted nobility in more than money. Many wed their "princes" only to find themselves ridiculed by their in-laws, snubbed by society, and bored with their lonely lot. Many found themselves much the poorer for their lofty experiences because they could not condone their husbands' penchants for men's clubs, mistresses, gambling, and fiscal irresponsibility. Many American Beauties often saw not only their dowries but also their hopes and naïveté squandered. By the time the First World War began, examples like the famous Jennie Jerome Churchill and Consuelo Vanderbilt served to stem the tide of transatlantic alliances.

However, Ann and Rhys Kendall seem well on their way to surmounting any barriers to their mutual happiness. Colleen and Bryce Falconer have married and must discover their own means to make a bright future for themselves. Gussie, who loves them both dearly, follows her mother's orders to prepare herself for a noble alliance as brilliant as Ann's and Colleen's. Meanwhile, Raine has ambitions of her own, and none of them includes marriage.

Join me for the second book in the American Beauties series, *Never Again,* when Raine vows to make amends to a prominent politician whose career she ruined. As Raine learns who really destroyed Gavin Sutherland's name and reputation, she falls deeply in love with him and must reveal her own treachery to restore him to his seat in Parliament, his estranged family—and his former fiancée.

I heartily enjoy receiving your letters. Please write and include a self-addressed stamped envelope to:

Jo-Ann Power
4319 Medical Drive, #131–298
San Antonio, Texas 78229–3325

If you enjoy cyberspace, I also invite you to contact me via E-mail at jpoweron@aol.com or my Web page at http://www.tlt.com/authors/jpower.htm, where you can read excerpts from all my Pocket Books releases.

ARNETTE LAMB

"Arnette Lamb ignites readers' imaginations with her unforgettable love stories."

— *Romantic Times*

Pocket Books
Proudly Presents

NEVER AGAIN
by
Jo-Ann Power

Coming from Pocket Books
Winter 1998

The following is an excerpt
of *Never Again*. . . .

June 1877
Norfolk, England

For a man whose career she had helped to destroy, Gavin Sutherland looked remarkably recovered from his public assassination at her hand.

"Come in, Mrs. Jennings."

Raine would even conclude he was serene.

"Sit here." He indicated the chair before his colossal desk. His gaze sluiced her body like icy spray from the North Atlantic, then darted up to hers with the prick of curiosity. He turned his back on her to his window overlooking the sea, thank God. His swift inspection of her plain plum walking suit made her heart thump. His scrutiny of her eyes made her palms sweat.

Does he know who I am?

No. He couldn't.

Only her publisher knew her identity and what she did for a living. Raine had never told anyone the truth.

Her Uncle Skip had seen her leave their fashionable Belgravia home each morning for a year and a half to go to work at *The London Times-Daily*. Although she'd been hired to draw advertisements, within six months her publisher had asked her to substitute for the newspaper's ailing political cartoonist. Secrecy, said her publisher, Matthew Healy, was useful for collecting information and protecting herself from harassment. Raine had followed his order and not even confided in her cousin and best friend, Ann Kendall. It had been easy to avoid discussion of her job with Ann, who lived far north of London in Lancashire with her husband, the Duke of Carlton and Dundalk, and their small son. Ann, like her father, thought Raine worked at the same kind of job she'd had at *The Washington Star* before the three of them had come abroad two years ago with their Aunt Peg and two friends.

Only Healy knew that last June, Raine Montand had been transformed into Raynard the Fox, the political cartoonist for the city's largest paper. She prayed now that Gavin Sutherland didn't know it, either. Her success here depended on it.

She strode across the length of his library and forced herself to look comfortably seated in the old ruby leather chair that faced the barricade of his desk. Its mahogany expanse gleamed with refracted rays of morning sunlight, causing her to squint as she noted his neatness. He had put one stack of notebooks in the middle, another of correspondence to its side. Between them lay one fountain pen. Raine was not surprised. Many attributed Lord Sutherland's rise to fame in four short years to his passion for order and his dispassion for patience.

"Thank you for responding so quickly to my application, my lord." She had walked her letter across the cove from her cottage to his house yesterday after breakfast, and within the hour, he had sent his summons to an interview via his housekeeper.

When he remained silent, Raine resisted the urge to arrange her skirts and instead worked at removing her gloves, finger by finger. "My letter was only one page, I realize, but demonstrated my abilities to write well."

He could have been deaf or dead, for all the movements he made. He wished to test her nervousness, did he?

"Even without references, I hope my letter might demonstrate that I am qualified to become your secretary."

"I could say it is my pleasure to see you so quickly, Mrs. Jennings." He did not face her, yet she could feel his low bass voice sink into her skin. Whenever she had heard him from the visitors' gallery in the House of Commons, the resonance of his tones had always stirred her blood as much as the spare beauty of his rhetoric soothed her soul. "It is necessity."

"I understand. I know you wish to write your second novel quickly." He needed the money because his family had cut him off not only from their affections but also from their funds. Since his resignation from his seat in Parliament last September, he had written one novel which still sold well after four months in bookstores. Rumor mills had it he wished to follow that success with another.

"How convenient you know so much about me." He jammed his hands into his trouser pockets.

The move tautened the navy wool across his hips, and Raine frowned at the fact that she had noticed once again how appealing his huge male body was to her. She didn't usually think of men in any physical way. She was drawn to their mental agilities first and last.

"I do hate idle talk, Mrs. Jennings, but in interviewing applicants for this position, I must make an exception. I am bone tired of those who have come to twitter at my door, hoping to fly away with a worm to feed to some tabloid."

Raine's stomach lurched. She shut her eyes. No, she had not moved here to this little fishing village four weeks ago to draw him and destroy him further. She had done her damage. Her depiction of him exactly as she had seen him, arguing with another member of Parliament in Hyde Park one hour before that man and his paramour were murdered, had led the Metropolitan Police to question Lord Sutherland about the crime. It made him the prime suspect in the still unsolved case. Later, politicians and pundits alike cited her cartoon as evidence that the usually rational Lord Sutherland could be unpredictable and therefore did not deserve to sit in a deliberative body like Parliament. They had led the fight in the public outcry for his resignation.

The clamor had taught Raine the power of her pen. She had learned at his expense that she must not use her art to expose people to criticism—or to ruin them. She had rented the cottage in the cove so that she might meet him, help him, compensate him in some small way for the damage she had wrought. What better way than to apply for the position which after two months was still vacant?

"So you will understand, then, Mrs. Jennings, how I must hear what you know about me and my unfortunate past."

"I have heard in the village that you wish to hire an assistant to help you write your next book. You have searched for two months now with no success." She paused, seeking the diplomacy she required to continue and the bare facts he would welcome. In truth, few wanted the position of secretary to this outcast. Her publisher had told her that fewer still had applied in response to Sutherland's ad in the *Times-Daily*. Who wished to work for a man so notorious that no advancement in prestige or salary would ever come their way? "I am here out of necessity, my lord."

"Financial?"

"Yes."

"Political?"

She gave a short laugh. She'd been prepared for his suspicion that she wished to work for him so that she could spy on him. "If you mean to ask if I am collecting information for the opposition party, then I must say no. I agree with many of your own views, actually."

"Really? Which ones?"

"Your attempts to improve public transportation and better lighting and sewage are ones I applaud."

"Ah, you believe that government can be a force for change."

She nodded. "When it is quiet and deliberative. Not when it engages in war."

"You declare it with such passion that I gather you have suffered from war in your own country?"

"My parents and three brothers died in our War between the States. Our home was burned, our farm destroyed."

"And yet after such loss, you trust that government can serve constructive ends?"

"Yes."

"Can it serve justice?"

"Government must try. I believe that justice must prevail. That criminals should be punished."

His big hands coiled into fists. The move did not

frighten her. At twenty-five, Raine had recovered from her childhood wartime horror, witnessing men becoming savages. Besides, she had often seen Gavin Sutherland show his frustration with this curl of his hands. He was reputed never to have hit anyone, except with the force of his words. That was one reason Raine doubted he had committed murder. One reason she had summoned the courage to come here and try to discover more facts about the crime for which no one had been charged.

"I applaud your beliefs," he told her, though he did not turn. "I share them. I have worked to make them a reality in government, but I don't seem to have benefited from them. I wrestle with my newfound cynicism and my daily proof that life is not fair." He inhaled, the breath expanding his broad shoulders with a magnificent ripple of muscle. "Forgive me if I belabor a point, but tell me more about why an attractive widow applies for a position as secretary to a disgraced politician."

Raine couldn't stop the smile that curved her lips. He was doing with her exactly what he did with his peers in politics. Shocking his opponents first, demanding honesty, lulling them with kindness, finessing them to his cause. That way he gained the advantage, controlled the action—and won. This morning, Raine would not let him dominate their meeting. She had a duty to herself to discover if he was guilty of the deed many suspected he had committed. She had tried for six months to find evidence of that and failed. Stymied in solving the crime, she was determined to help Gavin Sutherland build a new career.

"I wish to work, Lord Sutherland." That was the truth. "You have interviewed a few applicants. Three, the villagers tell me, each of whom you have rejected. Yes, I would predict that anyone who came in response to your advertisement would have curiosity for the details of the crime for which there seems to be no motive and no perpetrator. But I will speculate that whether the applicants sought titillating information or not, you rejected them because they were unqualified in more important ways. Yes, you value people with ambition. But you revel in intellectual companionship. Even if you could suffer an ordinary mortal day in and out, you work best with those who are articulate, witty, and bold. While I can only demonstrate those qualities daily, I can say I had an excellent education. I write and read English and French. I have traveled in America, Ireland, and here. Last year, I visited the Continent briefly to study painting. I am intelligent, healthy, and eager to help you. To finish your novel quickly"—she spoke the words she prayed would not be a lie—"I offer you hope."

He swung around, and she felt as if she should recede into the leather. She didn't. She knew how to hold her ground with strong men.

This one was the opposite of most others she had known.

He was hurt. The agony pooled in his cool gray eyes. She had helped to put it there.

He was impressive. His impossibly broad chest, his towering height as he came around the desk, illustrated graphically why the visitors' gallery in the House bulged with women when word went out that the striking bachelor would speak. He had been powerful, charismatic, revered. She had helped to bring him down.

"Hope?" He snorted. "Hope," he repeated with sad

consideration. He sank against his desk, his trousers conforming to thickly muscled legs, his eyes boring into hers. The ivory linen shirt he wore shifted over the contours of his chest as he crossed his arms. In the village, they said the Sutherlands descended from Viking raiders. Gavin looked it, every inch. Raine could render him that way with ink in hard lines, long arcs, not one an exaggeration. Even his straight bronzed hair, slicked back in a blunt cut across his nape, added to the image of might. He needed nothing more—except perhaps the removal of the boyish dimple from his left cheek.

He now used that very asset which had sent women into rhapsodies over him when he had been the talk of the town and unscarred by scandal. "Mrs. Jennings, you are very young and recently bereaved." His gaze dropped to the hair brooch at her throat and then the dark purple of her skirt, those indications she had worn to signal her half-mourning for a husband who had never existed. "How can you talk of hope?" His return journey to her eyes seared her with a languid heat Raine could describe only as hot ice.

"I am old enough, Lord Sutherland, to know that I must look for it each day. I find it when I feel useful. When I work."

"Why work for me?"

"Your situation attracts me. Saddens me. Angers me. My situation compels me to apply to you. I want to be helpful. I can be to you. You need not educate me about English society. I am American, but I have lived in England for two years, and I enjoy the people and their politics. I am energetic, awake with the sun. You need not inspire me to long hours with high pay, because I want to work for you. I understand your need to make a success of your writing career by following your first mystery novel with another—and soon. Furthermore, I live close to you, less than a two-minute walk across the beach. I fill my days with activity, but I can amuse myself with reading books and writing letters and cooking for myself for only so long. Then solitude loses its appeal. In assisting you, I would do more than exercise my brain. I would become useful."

He rolled his tongue around his mouth. "You *are* bold."

She suppressed the urge to laugh. "You will not hire me if I am otherwise."

He toyed with his own grin. "True. But we have another problem."

"You cannot pay much, that I know. I have heard from the villagers that you are willing to spend ten pounds a week. That sum will do nicely for me."

"It's less than many a London maid receives."

She nodded. "Yes, but I will not be working as a maid, or in London."

"I wished to supplement the low wages with room and board. My home is large." He made a sweeping gesture to indicate the twenty-two-room mansion which hovered over the rocks and sands. "Too big for me alone. I wished to offer the secretary a suite in the north wing."

Raine shivered at the thought. "I like the sea but prefer a southern exposure. I'll stay where I am in my cottage, thank you. If you'll hire me, that is."

"You're awfully accommodating." His relief battled wariness. "But the problem I wished to discuss is not money."

She cocked her head. "What then?"

"You are a woman."

This time, when she smiled, she did it so broadly

that he arched both brows in his own mirth. "You cannot refuse me on that count, can you, my lord? Not when you have given such great voice to the movement for a woman's right to vote. Equal to a man there, so am I everywhere. So must I be here in your presence. Deny me nothing on grounds of my gender, sir."

"You do not fear scandal?"

"I will not live here in your house but work in it. You employ a housekeeper and a maid, both in residence. Neither of whom has ever been linked to you romantically by the local residents or the London papers. You also retain a gardener. To hear Ben Watkins talk, Lord Gavin Sutherland may as well multiply loaves and fishes. He doesn't engage in many excesses. Certainly not wine or women."

"Only work."

"A great deal of that." She smoothed her gloves across her lap. "I think these people are suitable chaperones."

"Rumor has little regard for facts, Mrs. Jennings. Opportunity need only present itself."

"I am aware of this." Raine knew it too well. Her cousin, Ann Kendall, had suffered a lambasting in the gossip sheets when first she and Raine and their two friends had arrived in England more than two years ago. Ann, who had done nothing worthy of censure, found herself discussed and unfairly characterized in the papers. Only her future husband, the Duke of Carlton and Dundalk, had saved her from more ridicule.

"If you hire me, Lord Sutherland, I take that risk of ridicule by a gossip-hungry society. But no one knows me, values me, depends on me. I have no family and no friends to dissuade me from any course I set for myself." That was half a lie, for her cousin Ann had probed Raine for the reason she wished to retire to this fishing village for the summer. She had told Ann she needed a vacation by the sea to ponder whether she would return to her job at the newspaper. Raine already knew she would never again draw cartoons for the fun of it.

"My lord, I wish to work for you more than I fear criticism. But your perspective is different, I realize. If you hire me, you risk public censure. However, you are in need of help to meet your deadline for publication, and no male has shown up on your doorstep who fulfills your requirements. Besides, who is to say that employing a man would ensure your integrity? Lord Chuttlesly did not find it so." Raine referred to a Conservative MP who only last month was caught by his wife with his pants down in his bedroom with his assistant—another man.

"You have thought of all the issues, Mrs. Jennings." His observation held a hint of compliment.

"You're certain?" She couldn't help but tease him.

He chuckled. His head thrown back, he afforded her a view of his strong profile in the sun. He looked so jovial, Raine dug her nails into her palms to quell the urge to grab up his pen and sketch him that way. Where had her resolution fled never to draw again? Especially not Gavin Sutherland? Because she saw that he could still laugh despite what she had done to him?

His mirth drained from his face, and when he turned to her, his eyes looked empty. "Now I am intrigued. I think I am even flattered."

Can I make you smile again? "Enough to hire me?"

"Enough to marvel at my good fortune."

His words sounded accepting, but she feared he

would soon want to know more and there would be questions she could not avoid. "What else can I tell you about myself?"

"How quickly do you take notes? How good is your memory? Do you tire of reading easily?"

"Let me see. In order, I would say I am speedy, but I can only improve with practice. I have a steel trap of a mind, recalling conversations verbatim, which can save time and breath." She did not add that she also possessed a vivid memory of scenes, an invaluable aid when she wished to re-create a sight on paper. "I never tire of reading. Fiction is my favorite, followed closely by politics."

"I must count myself fortunate you and I share the same interests. To what do you owe the development of these twin passions for prose and politics?"

"My mother demanded that her four children read the classics. We discussed them in the schoolroom on our plantation with the teachers whom she hired but usually dismissed for their lack of erudition. My father served for two terms as a congressman in the United States House of Representatives before our state seceded from the Union. Politics were discussed at suppertime, and my brothers and I were expected to participate."

Gavin stilled. "How extraordinary. Here it is not so. A child does not eat with his parents, and when he—or she—becomes an adult, politics never appears on the menu in finer dining rooms."

"Regrettable, isn't it?"

"Deplorable. Did your husband share your enthusiasm for politics?"

"No," Raine replied truthfully. Winston Jennings had been a nice young man, with a passion for his career. She had met him when he was the military attaché to the British Embassy in Washington four years ago. He had called on her twice, taking her rejection of his attentions very hard. When she had accidentally seen him last year on a street corner near Whitehall, he looked ashen. He'd taken her to a tea room, where he had told her he was diagnosed with tuberculosis and that the disease was incurable. He had died in March. When she considered coming to Norfolk to meet Lord Sutherland and apply as his secretary, she felt she needed a false name—and a good reason for an American woman to be in England. Whose name better to take than a man she had known and a rationale she found plausible?

"I read a lot of British newspapers. At home in America, I did, too. When I moved to London, I began to read and learned quite a bit about British politics." She paused and considered her fingers, idle now but once so deft at cutting anyone down to size. She had not lied to this man yet about her motives. She would not do so now. "I understand your predicament in its complexities. Doesn't that make me more qualified than the next applicant?"

His dimple appeared in a wry expression. "You mean, of course, if there were another applicant."

She stared into his eyes. "You do not trust me."

"Whom would you trust, if you were I?"

"No one," she whispered. Aching for him, she felt her hope absorbed like sand into the tide. In this attempt to help him, she had failed. She would need to find another way to live with the cruelty of what she had done to him. Another way to salve her conscience.

He whirled away, to his window toward the sea and the sun.

She rose, drained, one hand gripping the leather

armrest. How would she right this wrong she had done him if she could not work for him?

She had reached his open door and would have bid him good-bye when he called her name and she paused on the threshold.

"Return tomorrow morning at six, Mrs. Jennings."

Look for *Never Again*
Winter 1998
Wherever Paperback Books
Are Sold